THE BONE MINE

Chris R. Parris

First Edition.

Edited by:

Tony Douglas-Beveridge.

An

"Archie Leggitt"

Murder mystery.

With

Detective Inspector, **"Tony Church".**

The characters and situations in this book are entirely imaginary and bear no relation to any real person or actual happenings.

THE BONE MINE.
By
Chris R. Parris

First published in Great Britain in 2014 by Chris Parris
23, Lurkins Rise, Goudhurst, Cranbrook, Kent. TN17 1EE

ISBN 978-0-9555233-3-5

A CIP catalogue entry for this book is available from the British Library.

Edited by: A. J. Douglas-Beveridge

Printed and bound in Great Britain by:
Berforts Group. Stevenage, Herts. SG1 2BH

ACKNOWLEDGEMENTS.

Thanks are due to my good friends, Joan and Eric Skinner for their help in proof reading my original copy.

For their input and suggestions at the proof reading stage of this work, I am again indebted to my sister and brother in law,
Lyn and Tony Douglas-Beveridge
and
To Tony Douglas-Beveridge for editing my manuscript.

Once again I thank Mr. Dale Burgess, of
Berforts Group,
for his continued assistance in the production of this book.
Dale, whilst with his former company, was instrumental in the successful production of my first, 'Archie Leggitt' novel,
"Arch", in 2007.
Since his move to Berforts, his continued co-operation enabled me to produce my first sequel to 'Arch', another murder mystery,
'The Watermill', in 2012.

This, the third novel in the 'Archie Leggitt' series, completes the 'trilogy'.
'The Bone Mine'. (2014)

Set in 1996, in the village of, 'Wigglesworth', in West Sussex, it includes many of the original characters, plus a few new ones.

Chris R. Parris.

FOREWORD.

A note to our 'Colonial' friends.

There is no such thing as a furry, housetrained alligator!
They simply do not exist.
Likewise, there is no such thing as, 'American English'.

I try to write English as I was taught many years ago. It will therefore, not be acceptable to the Microsoft spell checker. I realise (not 'realize') that this may not sit well with our Colonial brothers, who fail to recognise (not 'recognize') that we, the English, have a superior grasp of our own language! 'Faux' is not acceptable as a substitute for 'fake, it is taken from the French, 'faux-pas' which is defined in Roget's thesaurus as, 'blunder'. This adequately describes those persons who persist in using it as a description for nylon fur and fake tanning products!
I nail my colours (not 'colors') firmly to my mast, on this issue.
Similarly, throughout the dialogue in this book, a lift will not become an 'elevator', pavements are not, 'sidewalks' and a desk has a drawer, not a 'draw'. We will continue to dismantle equipment, not 'disassemble' it. Our cars will not be described as 'automobiles' and they will have bonnets and boots, not 'hoods and trunks'. They will have front and rear bumpers, not 'fenders'. Sentences will be terminated with full stops, not 'periods'.
By now, I hope that you will have got (not 'gotten') the gist of what I am attempting to illustrate.
Perhaps one day, Bill Gates will accumulate sufficient wealth to enable him to provide us with a Microsoft, 'English English' spell checker.
I am aware that this is pure wishful thinking on my part, for it would entail our American friends, accepting that we, the English invented our language, not them!
(They merely 'burglarized' it!)

Chris P.

4

PREFACE.

The Sussex Flint Mines.

Beneath the Sussex Downlands green,
Some seven thousand years ago.
In galleries both dark and mean
Flint miners toiled far down below.

With tools of antler, wood and bone
Then flint on flint, with skilful hands.
Formed knives and axes from the stone,
To fell the trees and tame their lands.

Unseen, their spirits round us fly,
Whilst 'neath the verdant grass we walk,
The bones of ancient miners lie,
Entombed in vaults of flint and chalk.

CHAPTER 1.

October 7th. 1996. Flat 3, 259, The Rides, Lincoln.

Douglas Fielding, A.M.I. Mech. Eng. and tutor at the Kesteven Technical Institute, was in his lounge, marking his students' test papers. It was officially his day off, but he always found it easier to concentrate on the papers, in the comfort of his flat. Doug had made himself a cafetiere of fresh coffee and opened a pack of digestive biscuits. Dressed in jeans, a blue polo shirt and wearing his hand made moccasin slippers, he began to mark his students' work.

He was disturbed by someone thumping impatiently on his front door.

'Why can't people use the bloody bell?' he thought to himself as he got up from his desk. He opened the door to find a rather agitated man of around thirty years, who attempted to push his way into Doug's home.

'Whoa!' Doug shouted. 'Where d'you think you're going?' He grabbed the man by the shoulders and spun him round, firmly pushing him back out of his front door. Turning to face him, once again, the man said,

'I want to speak to Hilda, I know she's here, I've come straight from the hospital. They told me she's just finished her night duty.'

Doug knew that his neighbour, Hilda Jempson and her twin sister, Hannah, were both S.R.N's who worked at the local hospital. Hilda had been living alone in the flat for the past four years, since leaving her father's home in Wigglesworth, West Sussex. Her sister came to join her around four or five months ago, but Doug could not recall having seen her for several weeks. He had been introduced to Hannah and she told him that she had left her husband of five years, due to his unreasonable behaviour. Jeff Davies was apparently a bully and a jealous control freak. He had somehow managed to keep the dark side of his character concealed from others for several years, but not, of course from his wife. She had endured his unreasonable rants during which he would become destructive, smashing his fist into doors and throwing household items to the floor. One evening in a fit of uncontrolled temper, he had assaulted Hannah and she had fled to the comparative safety of her sister's home, in Lincoln.
Now he was one very angry man.

'So, just tell her I'm here and I'm not going until I've seen her.' He shouted at Doug, who stood in his doorway, regarding him with a mixture of amusement and contempt.

'I don't know who you are and I don't very much care,' Doug said, 'but I'll give you some advice before you continue with your quest. To begin with, this is not the home of Hilda Jempson. Secondly, you have disturbed me in my home, whilst I was engaged in important work and finally, both your attitude and your manners are in serious need of moderation. For your information, Miss Jempson lives opposite in Flat number 4. Now calm down and try to behave yourself, because if I am disturbed by you again, I will not be happy. I bid you, "good-day" sir, now just go.'
Giving the man no opportunity to respond, Doug returned inside and quietly but firmly closed the door.

'Idiot,' he muttered to himself as he turned the central heating down and poured himself another coffee. Before he could resume his task, he heard the man thumping on the door of the flat opposite.

'He hasn't taken the advice I offered,' Doug thought to himself. He wasn't exactly eavesdropping, but he stood and listened, more out of concern for the nurse, who had finished her night duty only an hour or two earlier. He heard the man begin shouting at her.

'Open this door, Hilda. I know you're there and I demand that you let me get to Hannah!'

Doug heard the door open and then Hilda's voice saying,

'Jeff, calm down and stop shouting. You'll be in more trouble if you carry on like this. Hannah's not here. She heard you were looking for her and she left last Friday week.'

'She's made me look stupid at the hospital,' he shouted at her. 'She's even packed her job in. She's told them that I was violent and that she was afraid of me.'

'That's because she is afraid of you, Jeff. You probably made yourself look stupid, if this is how you carried on at the hospital. You're a controlling bully. She wanted to get as far from you as she could, but you stole her passport, didn't you?'

'Just tell me where she is, now!'

Doug heard him shout. Then he heard the nurse shrieking,

'Jeff, stop, you're hurting me. I don't know where she's gone, but if this is what she had to put up with, I don't blame her. She's my sister and I won't give her up to you.'

Doug silently crossed the room and released his door catch, opening the door slightly so that he could hear. The shouting continued,

'Tell me where she is now, or I'll cut you!'

'No! No! No!' Hilda screamed in panic. 'You'll go to prison for this, Jeff. Stop it now!'

Doug had heard enough. He silently opened his door wide and took in the scene. The woman was dressed in slippers and a blue dressing gown. The colour had drained from her face and she was obviously traumatised. The man had hold of a bunch of her dark brown hair and was waving what appeared to be a knife in her face.

Without a sound, Doug crossed the landing from behind him. He quickly reached over his shoulder and took a firm grip of the man's windpipe between the fingers and thumb of his left hand. At the same time, he grasped the man's forehead with his right. His index finger found the eye socket and he began to apply pressure.

'Drop the knife now, or lose an eye! It's your choice!'
He shouted.

With a loud cry, the man let go of her hair. As he dropped the Stanley knife which he had been holding, Hilda brought her knee up into his testicles. He went down with a groan and lay on the floorboards.

'Thank you,' Hilda said, tearfully. 'I'm sorry about the disturbance. His name is Jeff Davies. He's my twin sister's husband and he needs her to get money for him.'

'I strongly suggest that you telephone for the police, Miss Jempson. That's the best way to put a stop to this sort of thing. I'm not normally a violent man, but I won't tolerate bullying, especially against a lady.'

Hilda nodded in agreement and pulled her mobile phone from the pocket in her dressing gown and keyed 999.

'Will you wait with me until they get here, please?'
Doug nodded in the affirmative, saying,

'I'm not going anywhere and neither is he,' he pointed at Davies, who was attempting to sit up on the floor.

'Just stay where you are for now, or I may lose my temper and do something which we'll both regret.' Doug bent his right knee and pushed Davies back down with his foot.

'Don't touch that knife, Miss,' Doug advised Hilda. 'Just kick it into your flat, so it's out of his reach. The police will get his fingerprints from it.'

Hilda was speaking with the controller and explaining what had happened.

'Yes, we will. Thank you very much.' Doug heard her say. She looked at Davies and then at Doug,

'They say they will be here in five or six minutes,' she told them both. 'They have a car in the area.'

'Can someone get me a drink of water, please?' Davies asked, looking at Hilda.

'You'll get all the water you need at the police station,' Doug advised him. 'Just sit there for a few more minutes.'

There was a clatter as the front door to the block opened and a deep voice called out, 'Miss Jempson?'

'Up here,' Doug called down the stairs to them.
A very large police Sergeant, wearing a flat hat, appeared on the stairs. He was followed by a very slightly built woman police officer, who immediately went to Hilda's side.

'I'm Sergeant Hill,' he said.

'WPC Thornton,' said the lady officer as she turned to face Hilda.

'Has this man assaulted you, Miss Jempson?' She asked.

'Yes,' said Hilda 'he pulled my hair and threatened me with that knife.' Hilda pointed at the Stanley knife where it lay on the floor.

'You haven't touched it at all, have you?' The Sergeant asked her as he held Davies at his feet.
Hilda shook her head.

'Good, well done,' he said. 'Is this gentleman a friend of yours?' he asked facing Douglas Fielding.
Hilda smiled and replied,

'No, officer, Mr. Fielding is my neighbour. He lives at the flat opposite. I believe he has been a good friend to me this morning, I dread to think what could have happened had he not intervened when he did.'

'I heard the disturbance and came to investigate,' Doug explained.

The woman PC pulled on a latex glove and picked up the Stanley knife.

'There's no blade in it.' Davies shouted from the floor.

'Just remain seated for the time being,' said Sergeant Hill.

'It's just a handle,' Davies protested. 'I wouldn't have cut her. I just needed to scare her into telling me where my wife is.'

'He's right, Sarge,' PC Thornton confirmed. 'There is no blade, just the handle.' She held up the polythene bag which now contained the item, for him to check.

'He assaulted me!' Davies shouted, pointing at Doug.

'I wonder whatever could have prompted him to do that!' The Sergeant said, sarcastically, as he bent towards Davies and grasped the shoulder of his jacket with one hand.

'You can stand up now, sir,' he said as he lifted him to his feet. 'I'm advising you that you are now under arrest for assault. You can think yourself very fortunate that there was no blade, or the charge would have been, 'assault with a deadly weapon.' You'd be looking at six months holiday at one of our guest hostels for that'

He produced a set of handcuffs and fitted them onto Davies' wrists. He continued to address him in the same bass monotone.

'You have the right to remain silent but anything you do say may be used in evidence. I have to advise you that you may harm your defense if you fail to mention, when questioned, something which you later rely on in court. Understand?'

Davies nodded.

The Sergeant then addressed Hilda and Doug,

'We will need statements from you two, please. We can do them now, or, if you prefer we can come back later.'

Doug spoke next. He looked at Hilda and said,

'Well, Sergeant, I don't mind getting it done now, but this lady is a nurse and she has just finished night duty. I'll leave her to decide.'

'I think I'd prefer to do it now,' Hilda said. It will be easier to be accurate whilst it's still fresh in my mind. What about Mr. Davies? Won't you need to take him to the police station soon?' The Sergeant looked at PC. Thornton and said,

'We'll put him in the 'paddy wagon'. He can cool off in there whilst we get these statements. It shouldn't take long. Would you like to help Miss Jempson with hers?'

The PC nodded her agreement and turned to Hilda, saying,

'I think you could use a cup of tea, you've had a nasty shock, haven't you?'

'Yes, thank you,' Hilda replied. 'Shall we go into my kitchen, its warmer in there?'

The two ladies went into the flat and Sergeant Hill, his hand on Davies' shoulder, walked him towards the top of the stairs.

'I'll be back in a few minutes, sir,' he called to Doug. 'Flat number three, wasn't it?'

'Yes, thank you Sergeant, I'll make some fresh coffee,' Doug said.

The Sergeant followed Davies down the stairs to the van.

'You can wait for me in the van,' he told him. 'Back in a minute or two,' he called to Doug as he went.

Hilda and WPC Thornton went into her flat and as the door closed, Doug heard the policewoman ask Hilda where the tea and sugar were kept. He went into his kitchen and emptied the cafetiere, recharged it with coffee and switched the kettle on. Sergeant Hill tapped on the door a few moments later.

'Come in, Sergeant,' he called out. 'It's open, I'm in the kitchen.'

The big policeman wiped his boots on the coir mat outside Doug's door, before setting foot on the deep pile beige carpet.

'This is a very nice place you have here,' he said to Doug. 'Have you lived here for very long?'

Doug had set another cup and saucer on the small table and returned with the coffee, milk and sugar on an ornate galleried tray. He poured two cups of coffee, placing one in front of Sergeant Hill's chair.

'I've lived here for almost seven years now,' he told the policeman. 'Please help yourself to milk and sugar,' he added.

'Thank you, sir,' said the big policeman, 'We'll keep this short and sweet, I don't want to keep you from whatever you were busy with.' He nodded his thanks as he took the cup from Doug, added a spoonful of sugar and a splash of milk. He produced a biro, a notebook and some statement forms from his breast pocket, set them on the table and stirred his coffee. Doug began his statement by explaining the way Davies had tried to burst into his home. With some guidance from Sergeant Hill, he had completed his statement in about a quarter of an hour. The two were chatting whilst they drank a second cup of coffee, when the doorbell rang. Doug answered it.

PC Thornton, accompanied by Hilda Jempson, now dressed in slacks and a jumper had completed their statement.

Doug invited them in and they waited a few minutes until Doug's statement was checked.

'Right,' said Sergeant Hill. 'Let's just read through them out loud, in case we might have missed a detail or two, and then we'll be out of your way.'

There were no discrepancies with the statements and a couple of minor details were added. They each signed their statements which were witnessed by the police officers.

'Thank you both very much for your hospitality and co-operation,' said Sergeant Hill. 'Sorry if we have deprived you of your rest, Miss Jempson. Now we'll book our friend into his temporary lodgings and, as the saying goes, 'we'll be in touch' when we have any more to tell.'

Hilda thanked Doug again for his timely intervention into what could have been a nasty incident. She declined his offer of coffee, but asked him to call on her on Sunday morning, after ten. She said that she would enjoy a better chat when she wasn't so tired.

13

CHAPTER 2.

Thursday November 9th. 1996.
The old watermill, Wigglesworth, W. Sussex.

November can be a funny old month, strange and sometimes eerie shades of daylight, fogs, frosts, even snow on occasions. Today, Thursday the ninth, it was raining. Archie Leggitt was busy making a guard rail in the old watermill.

'Seventy four and a half,' Archie said to himself as he allowed the tape measure to retract into its casing. 'Now where did I put that pencil?'

This was the second pencil he had mislaid in the past ten minutes, whilst cutting the handrails for the safety barrier on the milling floor. Health and Safety inspectors had recommended some additional barriers between any visitors and the unguarded moving parts involved in the milling operation. Wigglesworth Mill, fully restored last year, had become a popular tourist attraction in the West Sussex village.

'Ah! There it is,' Archie retrieved the pencil from where it had fallen onto the floor, next to his workmate bench. As he retrieved it, he noticed a large spider's web at the base of the stone. It had collected an assortment of fine particles, some flour, some chaff and now some sawdust. The spider must have been a bit confused, as it kept examining the web to discover what it had caught. Archie watched it for a few seconds before returning to the task in hand. He scratched his head and continued talking to himself.

'Now, was that seven feet four and a half or seventy four and a half inches? They say 'measure twice, cut once', I'll measure it again.'

Bang! Bang! Bang!
A fresh supply of debris fell from the hopper with the vibration. Some grain and flour and a considerable helping of dust, bounced across the floor, adding to the spider's anxiety.

Bang! Bang! Bang! There it was again.
Someone was banging on the big oak front doors. Archie could hear someone shouting.

'Archie, Archie, are you in there? It's me, Bill Pickering.'

'Alright, hang on a minute, I'm upstairs.' Archie hollered back. He dropped the pencil back onto the workmate and heard it roll off and hit the floor as he descended the stairs. He unbolted the door and opened it just wide enough to let the village policeman in.

'It's bloody horrible out there, Arch,' Bill said as he shook the rain from the sleeves of his coat. 'Elsie tried to call you on your new mobile phone, but then we heard it ringing in your jacket pocket, hanging in the hall. She said you'd probably be either here or up at the timber yard.'

'What's up then, Bill?' Archie enquired. 'Is it urgent? Has something happened to Elsie?'
Bill Pickering smiled.

'No, it's nothing that urgent and Elsie's fine, Arch. Old Joe Skrobe is the one with the problem. His bungalow is sinking into the ground at the kitchen end. It looks like some of the brick piers are subsiding. He wondered if you could come and have a look at it, see what you think is causing it.'
Archie, a retired builder, had spent most of last year helping with the restoration of the old watermill. It had been open to the public

15

at week-ends, throughout the year and Archie was now preparing for next year's visitors.

'I wouldn't have thought it was a police matter, Bill.' Archie said. 'I'll have a look at it and see what I can do to help the old boy. It's not a good day for outside building work so I don't s'pose I can do much until the rain stops. How am I goin' to get there?'

Bill laughed and explained,

'You're right, it's not a police matter Arch, although there are one or two things up there which may eventually turn out to be. Joe's had several items go missing from his garden. It's my day off, as it happens, I'm in 'mufti' under this police raincoat. I just saw Joe at the shop, and he told me about it. He's been having a few problems with the people who are building that new spa hotel next door to him. The old boy looked really worried about his home. He thinks that the excavations and blasting at the building site next door are probably to blame. I'll run you up there, if you like and bring you back when you've had a look. I think he just wants your opinion as a builder, before he takes it any further.'

Archie and Bill had been friends ever since the P.C. had been installed as Wigglesworth's village 'bobby'.

'OK,' said Archie, as he brushed some sawdust from his old blue pullover, picked up his Barbour coat and put it on. 'I'd better tell Else where I am and I'll collect my mobile phone whilst I'm there. Will that be alright with you?'

'Yes, mate,' Bill replied. 'Are you going to lock up here, before we go?'

Archie nodded and went back up the stairs to get his tobacco and the mill keys. He picked up the pencil which was on the floor and adjusted the collar of his coat. Another pencil, which had been behind his ear, fell onto the floor.

'Ah!' he said out loud, 'that's the one I spent ten minutes looking for.'

He put it on the workmate and went back downstairs. As he locked the door, he saw that Bill was sitting in his car in the

16

driveway. He leaned over and opened the passenger door as Archie approached.

'Old Joe's not English, is he Arch?' Bill enquired. 'His name sounds a bit foreign, but there's no trace of an accent.'

'He's a Polish refugee,' Archie told him. 'He's the only one of his family to survive the holocaust. He's been here since he was a small boy, so he's about as Anglicised as any of us now. He's a nice old boy, always keeps himself to himself. His wife died of cancer some years ago. His daughter, Lakshmi, is married to a solicitor, they live at Petworth.'

Archie went indoors to tell Elsie where he was going, he collected his mobile phone from his jacket and picked up a notepad from the telephone table.

'It's not much good having a mobile phone if you leave it at home all the time, is it?' she scolded. 'Will you be back for your lunch or do you want me to make you a sandwich now?'

'No, Else, I'll get something to eat in the village. That will see me through until dinner tonight. I was goin' to wear that jacket, but then I thought it looked like rain, so I took the Barbour instead. I've got the phone now, so I'll call you if there are any problems.'

'That's what you had the phone for, to keep in touch when you weren't here,' she repeated. 'It won't be much use if it's hanging up in your jacket, whilst you're somewhere else, will it?'

'O.K. point taken,' Archie said. 'Bill's waiting, so I'll see you later.' He patted the pocket of his Barbour coat and left through the back door.

'I just got a bollocking for leavin' the mobile behind,' he giggled as he got into Bill's car. 'I s'pose it'll be best to go up Grumbles Hill, won't it?'

'Yes, Arch, it's only a couple of hundred yards along from the junction to Joe's place. I see he's still got that old A35 van, I think he must have had it from new.'

17

'He has, I don't remember him buying it,' said Archie, 'but he told me once that it was now worth more than twice what it cost him new. I think it's only done about forty thousand miles in forty years.'

'What age is he, Arch?' Bill asked. 'It's not easy to guess. He looks about sixty to me.'

'I think he's about a year older than me, so that would put him at about sixty seven. He had the bungalow built when Lakshmi was still a baby. He bought the plot and the farm shop shed from old Bob Jempson and that's when I first met him. He told me then that Lakshmi was a late thirtieth birthday present for him. That was in 1960 or '61, so he must be about the same age as me. His wife, Helena, died in 1971. She was a very kind lady. It was very sad. Lakshmi was only just starting secondary school. It must have been tough on them both.'

Bill nodded as he began to find out more of Joe's history.

'Didn't he have any problems getting planning permission, Arch? They don't usually like allowing private homes to be built on agricultural land.'

Archie thought for a moment before replying.

'I 'spect it would have been allowed because it was built on the site of a former farm cottage. Mr. and Mrs. Jempson had bought it from the Eldridge family, who'd had the farm for donkey's years. When old Harry Eldridge died, the farm was split into two halves. The level land at the top of the slope was sold to an aggregate firm. It's now the fishing lakes. His wife, Ruth, used the money to emigrate to Canada, where her younger sister lived. This end, about a hundred acres, was left to his daughter, Mary, but she unfortunately married a nasty piece of work by the name of, 'Jason Davies'. He's known locally as, 'Diddler Davies'. He used to act as if he was, 'Lord of the Manor' but it was her father's money, not his. He used to be a real mean man and greedy as they come. It came out that he used to beat her. He finished up in court a couple of times. She finally got sensible and left him. She even left her six year old son with him, which some folks didn't understand.'

'I suppose if she was desperate enough, it might have been her only hope of survival?' Bill suggested. 'So what happened to the cottage?'

Bill braked suddenly, catching Archie unawares. There appeared to be a burst water main at the bottom of the hill. The water board workmen were busy digging and there was a pump discharging water from the hole, into the stream.

'It's about time they renewed this bit of water main,' Bill said. 'This must be at least six times in the past couple of years that its burst. Poor old Mrs. Davidson must be getting fed up with them tracking through her garden with all their kit.'

The workman controlling the traffic, with the 'Stop-Go' sign on a pole approached the car. Bill wound the window down so that he could he could hear him above the noise of the compressor and drill.

'Sorry about this, guvnor,' he said. 'Only be a few more minutes and we'll get a plate down, so you can drive over the trench.'

Bill nodded and wound the window back up.

'Where were we?' Archie asked him.

'You were going to tell me what happened to the cottage,' Bill said. 'I always learn something from you, Arch. Today it's a local history lesson!' Bill chuckled. 'So now tell me about it'

Archie laughed,

'Oh, so you think I'm a schoolteacher now, do you? History lesson, I'm not that old, it's more sort of, 'stale news' than history!' He paused while he regained his thoughts.

'Anyway to finish the story, it caught fire and burned to the ground. That would have been around 1958 or '59, in the early hours of one September night. It was completely gutted, Bob managed to rescue the twins, but his wife, Sally, became trapped whilst collecting some possessions. The Fire engine arrived at the same time as the roof collapsed and Bob's wife was killed.'

19

'So the poor sod was left with no wife, no home and two young daughters to bring up?' Bill said.

'That's right, Bill,' Archie continued. 'Hannah and Hilda were about four or five years old. Bob had a sister who lived in Slindon, her husband was shot down over France, in the war. She had a big house and took all three of them in, until Bob could make other arrangements.'

'So did he still carry on with the smallholding and the farm shop?' Bill asked.

'Yes, he still had the farm shop for a while, but it took ages for the insurance claim to be settled,' Archie told him. 'Once he got the insurance money, he bought a smallholding a bit closer to Slindon, and sold the plot to Joe a year or so later. The police suspected arson, but after extensive investigation there was insufficient evidence to bring a prosecution.'

'What made the police suspect arson? Or don't you know?' Bill asked Archie.

'I've got a couple of ideas about that,' Archie said. He scratched his head as he tried to think back to that time. 'They said that an accelerant was used at the back of the house. It was paraffin, I think and they found a half burnt leather glove, which wasn't Bob's. As I recall, Bob Jempson had the cottage, the farm shop and his smallholding with a couple of greenhouses. All his land was beside the road, 'Diddler Davies' wanted that as well. I s'pose he'd have a job selling his bit to a developer if there was no access to it.

Bob told me that Davies offered him more than it was worth, but he didn't want to sell, especially to Davies. Bob just took a dislike to him. He did allow a shared access over his frontage, but that was all. Davies' reputation as a nasty man had spread far and wide. Bob once said to me, that for someone who wanted a favour, his manners were sadly lacking. Anyway, back to Davies, after Mary left him, there was a problem over the ownership of the land. It was in Mary's name y'see? I think he eventually

20

managed to get it registered in joint names, probably by some devious route.

The police suspected foul play, but it seemed that she'd taken her jewellery and a couple of suitcases of her clothes. They found the taxi driver who'd picked her up and he said he'd dropped her at Pulborough station. The ticket clerk remembered her buying a single ticket to Victoria. That was the last anyone saw of her. There were extensive enquiries to find her, but without success. It was as though she'd just vanished.'

'I suppose if she didn't want him to find her, she could have changed her name or just kept low,' Bill said. 'Maybe she thought losing her land was a small price to pay for a bit of peace and quiet.'

'It's possible,' Archie replied, 'there was a rumour that she'd gone to Canada to find her mother. The police even contacted her mother, but she said that she hadn't heard from her.

The strangest thing was leaving the boy, although he was at boarding school in Hassocks, so he wasn't told immediately

It just seemed strange that nobody ever heard from her again.'

CHAPTER 3.

The road eventually became passable and they continued their journey. As they approached the junction with the main road, at the top of Grumbles Hill, they heard the siren from an emergency services vehicle. A police car sped along the main road towards where Joe lived, blue lights and sirens going. They were about to pull out across the road, when an ambulance appeared from their right, going towards the village. It was travelling slowly, but still had the blue lights flashing.

'Looks like there's been an accident,' Bill said. 'When they go as slowly as that, it usually means somebody's in a bad way.'

'We'll find out soon enough,' Archie said as Bill pulled across the junction. 'I hope it's nothing to do with Joe.'

As they rounded the left hand bend on the Arundel Road, it all became clear. A large tipper lorry was blocking the road and there were three police cars in attendance. The one which had passed them whilst they waited at the top of Grumbles Hill had stopped outside Joe's front garden. On the Arundel side of the obstruction, they could see two more police cars, a large police van, a single decker bus and several other vehicles, waiting for the road to clear. One of the policemen, who had been controlling the scene, approached them as they slowed in readiness to pull into Joe's driveway. Bill lowered the driver's door window.

'I'm sorry sir, the road will be blocked for at least another fifteen minutes, while we take measurements and get some witness details.'

Bill smiled at him, saying,

'It's alright, Peter, we're only going here. We'll pull into the driveway and I'll come and have a chat with Sergeant Dean.'

The officer bent down to look into the car,

'Sorry, Bill, I didn't realise it was you. You picked a good day off, what with this drizzle and everything. Not much you can do outside on a day like this. They reckon it'll clear up a bit later on though. I don't know much about this situation yet, but it'll all become clear eventually I suppose. A young moped rider has been taken to hospital, from what I've been told, he was in a pretty bad way.'

Bill walked over to where the police were standing and nodded to Sergeant 'Dixie' Dean.

'Bit of a nasty one, Bill,' he told him. 'The lorry driver says he didn't see him, but there's something very strange about his driving. We've got several witnesses who say that he drove straight across the road and then deliberately reversed into that fence. He then seemed to panic and tried to drive away before anyone could stop him.'

'So he's in more trouble than he bargained for?' Bill suggested. 'I wonder whether someone told him to hit the fence, or whether he has a personal grudge against old Joe.'

'Do you know the man who lives in that bungalow, Bill?' Sergeant Dean asked.

Bill smiled and told him,

'Yes, its Joe Skrobe's bungalow. I've got Archie Leggitt with me. He's come to have a look at his brick piers. Joe thinks they're subsiding because of the excavations and blasting, next door. What are they building there, anyway? It looks pretty big to me.'

'I think it's going to be one of those spa hotels. You know, pay a thousand pounds to let them starve you for a week and kid yourself you feel healthier! You'd better tell your friend to come and look at his fence, I suppose. Someone will have to put that right, whatever the cost.'

Bill winked at Sergeant Dean and said,

'You don't look as though you'd want to starve for a week, Sarge, let alone pay for the privilege.'

Sergeant Dean laughed and patted his ample waistband,

'I'll stick with the meat puddings, Bill, especially at this time of year.'

They both laughed and then Bill walked back to the bungalow. He saw Archie and Joe in the garden, towards the back of the bungalow. They were examining the brick pier at the corner, which looked as though it was sinking and leaning at a slight angle. Both men looked up as Bill approached,

'You'd better leave that for a minute and come and have a look at your fence, Joe,' Bill said.

The three men walked down to the front corner of Joe's garden. Sergeant Dean stood in the road on the other side of the broken fence, waiting to speak with Joe.

'Good morning Archie, and Mr. Skrobe,' he began.

'I'm afraid that your fence has been wrecked. We are holding the driver of the lorry, and now we have to wait for the firm to provide a relief driver, before we move it.'

'Good morning Sergeant, do you know how it happened?' Joe asked.

'Oh yes, we have several witnesses, half a busload to be precise,' Sergeant Dean explained. 'It appears to have been a deliberate act of criminal damage to your property, in the first instance. The driver was so anxious to flee the scene that he drove straight into the path of the moped and knocked him and his machine into the ditch opposite. The bus driver and several passengers witnessed the whole thing, so your fence will be repaired by the owners of the tipper fleet. I'll give you their

24

details presently. Don't let them pass the buck, it's definitely their responsibility. I expect their insurers will have to pay for it in the end. They'll need to rectify it to the original standard. It looks as though it was a professional job, so don't let 'em off the hook.'
Joe nodded and said,

'Thank you Sergeant, I'll get onto it as soon as you let me have the details. How badly was the young man hurt?'

'It didn't look pretty, gentlemen,' said the Sergeant. They were still working on him as the left for the hospital. I just hope they can keep him alive until they get there. He's only a young lad, he wasn't doing anything wrong, but he didn't stand much of a chance against a ten ton tipper lorry.'
Joe walked along the fence line to inspect the damage. The corner post and two sections of feather board fence, complete with arris rails, lay on the ground, smashed to matchwood. He looked across the road to where two policemen had pulled the moped from the ditch. It was completely wrecked. They had to carry it into the police van. A man, whom Joe took to be the lorry driver, was seated in the rear of a police car, behind the van.
Archie stood beside Joe and said,

'I bet the passengers on that bus are getting fed up with the delay, don't you?'

'They just ought to be thankful that the lorry didn't hit their bus instead,' Bill interjected. 'There would have been a few serious injuries if that had happened. I think the delay might be preferable to a trip to A and E in an ambulance, don't you?'
Another police officer came towards them. He had a camera and a pad on which he had drawn a sketch of the scene.

'Almost done now, gentlemen, we're just waiting for another driver to move the tipper lorry. Our road safety people will need to check it out before it goes back into service. I just keep thinking about the lad.'

'I take it his injuries were severe?' Bill asked him.
The officer frowned as he replied.

'I suspect he will be on the critical list for a while. The ambulance crew managed to stabilise him, but he still looked pretty poorly to me. Moped riders are among the most vulnerable on our roads. They are lightweight machines and not particularly stable in adverse weather. That tipper lorry hit him broadside at full force. The driver says he didn't see him, but there's more to this than just an accident. Anyway, sir, if you'll excuse us, we need to make sure we get all the details before we re-open the road.'

'I understand officer,' Joe said. 'We'll let you get on with your work. Thank you for talking with us. I expect the full details will come to light eventually.'

Archie and Joe resumed their examination of the brick piers which supported the bungalow. Archie took a builders line from his pocket and cut off a length of about three feet. He attached a plumb bob to the short length and then walked to the front of the bungalow. He turned to Joe and said,

'If you hold this end against the front pier on the top course of bricks, we'll see how far out of alignment they are. I'll use the plumb line on any that don't line up, so we can see how much they've moved, O.K.?'

Joe understood the principle of what Archie was doing.

'That will tell us which ones we have to investigate, won't it?' There were two more piers which were out of alignment. One had sunk a good two inches into the ground.

'It's definitely subsidence,' Archie said. 'I think you can say with some certainty that it is connected with the excavations next door. Look at those cracks in the ground. They all come from your fence line, where the earth has been removed.'

'So will the house fall down, Archie? What can we do about it?'

Archie began to explain,

'When compacted earth is disturbed, the edges of the hole have to be left at an angle, not vertical. Structural engineers understand this and check the site before they begin to excavate.

26

The correct term for it is, 'the angle of repose', which would be around sixty degrees. The way they have left this so steep, is pure negligence. A solicitor would obtain the accurate information before making a claim, but there is a claim for damage here, Joe.'

'I think I'd better get my son-in-law involved, Arch. Stephen is a solicitor, you know, Lakshmi's husband. He has a practice in Petworth. I'll phone him tonight. Thanks for your help and thanks for the knowledge you've provided. I feel a bit better now.'

At that moment, Bill returned, he had been chatting to the officers in the road. Joe looked up at him and said,

'Arch reckons it's definitely subsidence and all because of the excavations leaving the sides too steep.' Joe saw the expression on Bill's face and asked,

'Have you got any more details from your colleagues?'
Bill nodded,

'Yes, the lad was from Storrington,' Bill replied. 'On his way to college in Arundel, poor chap. He didn't stand a chance by all accounts. The lorry just lurched into him and took him across the road straight into the ditch. He's got a broken arm and leg and probably a few cracked ribs. He was concussed when he left in the ambulance. Good job he was wearing a helmet, or we'd be talking about a fatality, for sure.'

'You were saying that you thought it was possibly deliberate damage to my fence, Mr. Pickering,' Joe prompted.

'Don't keep calling me 'Mr. Pickering',' Bill said. 'We're all friends here, so whilst I'm off duty, it's 'Bill'.'

'What, just, 'Bill'?' Joe asked with a grin, 'Not 'old Bill''
Bill laughed loudly,

'No, I think that's for when I'm on duty, isn't it Arch? To answer your question, Joe, that's the general consensus of opinion. It would be better not to mention it when you claim for your fence.' He handed Joe a slip from a notepad, 'Here's the details of the tipper firm, any trouble, just refer them to us. We'll soon put 'em straight about whose responsibility it is.

27

The bus driver and three of his passengers saw it all. The lorry pulled out of the site access road, straight across Arundel Road and then reversed at full force into your corner post. We think it was then that he saw the bus and decided to make off with all speed. Unfortunately, in his agitated state, he failed to see the moped rider approaching from his right, with disastrous consequences.'

Bill paused to gauge their reaction.

'Has the driver been arrested?' Archie asked.

'He has,' Bill assured him, 'and the charge is 'dangerous driving,' not the lesser charge of careless driving. He'll likely lose his license and his job. In my opinion there's a bit more to this than we know at present. Have you been threatened in any way, Joe?'

'I wouldn't say, threatened', Joe replied, 'but they wanted me to sell my house and land to them. They made me an offer, but I don't want to sell. The site manager told me that I wouldn't have a choice if it went to a compulsory purchase order.'

'That's an implied threat,' Bill told him. 'They wouldn't get a compulsory purchase order for your property for a private development. You would be well advised to get a solicitor onto them. Their actions won't sit well with the planning department of the council. They don't like adverse publicity of this sort.'

'Thud!'

A muffled explosion caused the ground to shake. They heard a large dog barking, inside the house

'What was that?' Bill asked, wide eyed.

'Happens once or twice a week,' Joe told him. 'They're blasting at the flint in the slope at the back of the site. The diggers can't always break it up, so they use a small charge to loosen the ground. A licensed bloke comes and sets it off, I've seen his van. I think we'd better go and pacify old Thunder, he doesn't mind general noise, but these explosions upset him.'

28

'But it shook your ground, Joe,' Archie said. 'That could cause the subsidence which is disturbing the foundations.' There was a hush as the men looked at each other's expressions.

'I think Archie has a good point there, Joe,' Bill advised. 'If there has been any movement of your foundations because of their activity next door, they are liable for any rectification work that may be needed. Your solicitor will know a surveyor who can provide a comprehensive report. That should be enough for any court to act on. I think that's your best advice, Joe'

'I'll put the kettle on,' Joe said. 'I think it's time we all had a cup of tea. Arch, could you let old Thunder out the back for me. He knows you, so he'll calm down when he sees you.'
As he opened his front door the dog stopped barking. Archie opened the kitchen door and a very large German Shepherd bounded to greet them in the hallway.

'He's a gentle giant,' Archie said to Bill, who stood transfixed by the sheer size of the dog.

'Come on Thunder, old boy,' Archie called to him as he opened the back door. The dog turned towards Archie, his tail wagging frantically. Standing up on his hind legs, his front paws on Archie's chest, he began licking his face and rubbing his head against Archie's.
The telephone began to ring. Joe answered it. He covered the mouthpiece with his hand and told them,

'It's the Transport Manager of Tickner's Transport, the tipper lorry company.'

CHAPTER 4.

Bill sat and listened to Joe's side of the conversation. It seemed to be amicable enough, but Joe's facial expression told him that he was not comfortable with the discourse.

'Yes,' he said at one point, 'you can come to inspect the damage, but I need to make my garden secure today. I have a dog and he needs to be allowed out.'

There was a pause.

'I just told you, I need my garden to be secure today, not next week.'

Another pause.

'Well, Mr. Grover, I can assure you that whatever you've been told, the damage is serious and it needs to be repaired now. The police are still here with me, would you like to speak with them, to verify the situation?'

Joe's frown turned into a smile.

'So you'll be here within half an hour, then. Thank you Mr. Grover, I look forward to meeting with you.'

He replaced the phone on its rest and looked up at Bill.

'Sorry to take your name in vain, I know you're off duty, but he needed a bit of a prod. He said that he was told that a lorry had 'brushed' against my fence and it would need a few nails to repair

it. He would send a man out next week! He was on the point of arguing with me. As soon as I mentioned that the police were still here. He said he will be here to inspect it within half an hour.'
Archie returned to the living room with a tray and three mugs of tea.

'Is Thunder still outside?' Joe asked him.

'No, he's in the kitchen.' Archie told him. 'I filled his water bowl and gave him a few biscuits. I expect he'll be here in a minute. I closed the back door. I didn't want him to go round to the front until the fence is repaired'
Bill looked at his watch.

'Its half past eleven now chaps,' he said. 'I'd better get going. Will you wait, Arch? I can come back for you in an hour or so, if you like. Just phone me when you're ready.'
A short discussion ensued; Archie said he would wait with Joe for the arrival of Mr.'Grovel', as Archie so eloquently put it!
Bill took his empty mug out to the kitchen, made a fuss of Thunder, and then bade them all 'Goodbye'.

'If you have any difficulties with the tipper magnate, Joe, you can call me at home. I'll be there for the next few hours. I can be back here within a few minutes. I expect Archie will provide his usual degree of support.'
Joe and Archie were in the front garden inspecting the remains of the fence, when a dark green Vauxhall estate car stopped in the road outside. A dapper little man got out and retrieved a notepad from the rear seat.

'Mr. Skober?' He enquired.

'No.' said Joe. 'Its little wonder you get wrong information about the damage to my fence. You can't even get my name right. It's 'S,K,R,O,B,E', pronounced as 'Skrober'. I take it that you are Mr. Grover, of 'Tickner's Transport'?'
The man appeared flustered. He looked at the smashed fence sections.

'Just the two panels, is it?' he asked over the wreckage.
Archie decided it was time to intervene,

'Are you trying to be dismissive about this incident, or don't you really know anything about fences?' He asked.

Grover looked as indignant as five foot six of cheap suit can manage.

'I don't know who you are, but I don't like your tone and I'll thank you not to interfere. I'm discussing this with the house owner, not one of his 'lackeys'.'

'This is my good friend, Archie Leggitt,' said Joe. 'He's not a 'lackey'. He's here to ensure that the fence repairs are carried out to my satisfaction and as quickly as possible.'

Joe was beginning to dislike this man. He continued,

'Now, to answer your somewhat vague question, this is a close boarded fence, not 'panels'. It has oak posts at six foot intervals, the feather edge boards are supported on horizontal arris rails, mortised into the oak posts. The corner posts are six inches square and the intermediate posts are four inches square. The repair will not be a cheap fix, but will be carried out to the same professional standards as the original, by a qualified tradesman.'

Grover appeared a little subdued, but still attempted to command the situation.

'I can send a man round with a couple of fence panels, this afternoon. That will make a temporary repair. It won't have to last long, anyway. Mr. Bettis tells me that the developers are buying your property, so you won't have to worry about it matching the rest of the fence.'

Archie was getting angry, very angry.

'Who is 'Mr. Bettis'? Are you one of his 'lackeys'?' He responded, with some venom.

The man obviously realised that he had already said too much.

'W..well, I heard that it was part of their original plan,' he stammered. 'Perhaps it has been revised.'

32

'This house, this land, is mine. It is not for sale and never has been,' Joe stated emphatically. 'Any notion that you or your, Mr. Bettis, may have had on that issue is entirely erroneous.'
Joe walked over to within a foot or two of the man.

'Now, Mr. Grover, are you going to pay for the proper restitution of my fence, or not?' He asked.

'I will have to put it to our insurers, and await their decision, before I can answer that.' Grover replied.

'I will not accept your delaying tactics, Mr. Grover,' Joe told him. 'The police and several witnesses have confirmed that this was deliberate damage to my property. Now I will tell you what is going to happen.'
Then turning to Archie he said, in a loud and confident voice,

'Archie, I would be grateful if you can please arrange for Mr. Clarke to carry out the repairs as quickly as possible. I will then present the bill to Mr. Grover. He will arrange prompt payment by his company or his insurers. In the circumstances, since it appears to have been a deliberate criminal act, I doubt his insurers will accept liability. His company would be foolish in the extreme to dispute the bill. In the meantime, I will contact my solicitor and notify them of the damage and of the developers stated intention to purchase my property, with or without my consent.'
Joe quickly turned to face Grover again, saying,

'I must thank you for your disclosure, though it was, in fact, further confirmation of what I had suspected. I have noted the various annoyances from your, Mr. Bettis. I have listed all of the details, with dates and approximate times. If, perchance, this was another of his ideas to persuade me to sell, it has gone disastrously wrong.'
Grover opened his mouth to speak, but Joe ignored him and continued. He was going to make his point, regardless of Grover's attempts to stop him. Joe continued apace,

'An innocent young man is in a critical condition in Chichelster Hospital. Your driver is currently under arrest at Chichelster police station. I am informed that he is to be charged with dangerous driving, a most serious offence, which could result in a custodial sentence and almost certainly the loss of his driving license for twelve months. My fence is a minor inconvenience when compared to the poor lad whose life may have been destroyed. You or your insurers will pay for the restitution of my fence. There will, I suspect, also be substantial costs involved with regard to the injury to the moped rider. I suggest that you notify your insurers at your earliest opportunity.' Grover again made as if to say something, but Joe continued his tirade.

'Mr. Grover, you have taken ambivalence to a new level. I believe that this concludes our meeting for today, you may now return to your office. I bid you, 'Good-day'.'

Grover stood like a reprimanded schoolboy, his mouth open, seemingly lost for words.

Joe turned away and together, he and Archie walked briskly back to the house. Once inside, Archie gave a roar of laughter and patted Joe's back so hard it almost took his breath away. Thunder seemed to realise that it was a happy occasion and bounced toward them both with his tail wagging furiously.

'You should have been a politician, Joe,' Archie told him. 'That was the best 'put down', since Winston's stated opinion of Hugh Gaitskell, when he described him as, 'A modest man, with much to be modest about.' I don't believe Grover could think as fast as you could talk. When you told him that your meeting was finished and he could go back to his office, He just stood there with his mouth open.'

'He was just trying to make himself feel important, Arch,' said Joe. 'We'd better phone Andy and ask him to come and fix the fence. Will he have all the materials we need?'
Archie nodded, he was still savouring the moment.

'He'll soon cut some more boards.' He told Joe. 'He's got oak posts in several sizes, so that won't be a problem. Would you like me to talk to him?'

'Yes please, Arch. You're more familiar with the timber business. We'll be in with a better chance of getting it right first time.'

Archie phoned the yard and gave Andy Clarke the short version of the events leading to the destruction of Joe's fence. He gave him the dimensions of the damaged section and an idea of what tools to bring. Andy said that they would be there within the hour'

Joe went into the kitchen to rinse the mugs and make another pot of tea. He returned to the living room, where Archie sat with the dog.

'I'll phone Stephen later,' he said. 'Maybe get him to write a letter to Grover, so that he knows we mean business.'

'You said you'd had stuff pinched from your garden, Joe.' Archie reminded him.

'Yes, that's right,' Joe replied. 'An old petrol strimmer, some edging shears, one of those heavy duty pruners and a few other bits and pieces. I think I saw one of the men put the strimmer in my farm shop shed and lock it up.'

Archie was surprised,

'You said, 'your' farm shop shed! Is it yours, or theirs?'

Joe sat down,

'It's still mine. The strip alongside the road is still mine, Arch. The old smallholding still belongs to me, but they've taken over most of it with their equipment. That's why their security fence is behind my shed, not in front of it. Come into the kitchen and I'll show you, you can see it all from there.'

They stood at the window and Joe began to point out the scene.

'The front, where they come in and out, is the old pull in for the farm shop, that's why it's so wide. They could get tractors and trailers in and still have room to turn round in the car park. That big greenhouse is mine. They've smashed most of the glass, just for fun I expect. If you look along the road line to where that electricity box is on that pole, you can see another gate.'

'Yes,' Archie said, 'I can see it.'

Joe continued,

'That's where my bit finishes, but it goes back from there as far as the hedge, which you can just see the end of, past that digger.'

'Blimey!' Archie said. 'So they really are trying to force you out, Joe. I think you need to tell your solicitor son in law all about this, as well. Just tell me something, Joe. It's your land, your entrance and your shed. Why don't you just go and get your stuff back?'

Joe looked embarrassed,

'The trouble is, they've changed the lock on my shed, the old farm hut. If I tried to go in there, there would be two or three of them blocking my way and they would stop me. I suppose if I'm honest, I just got fed up with trying to fight for my rights. All the time they leave me alone, I tend not to bother about them. It's the line of least resistance, I suppose, but I just want a bit of peace and quiet.'

Archie looked at his friend and saw that the situation had worn him down. The fight had gone out of him and at this rate they would soon have him out of his mind, let alone out of his home. Archie had made a decision.

'I'll go and get your stuff back, Joe,' he said. 'You watch me from this window, and phone Bill Pickering if it looks as though things are getting rough. But first, we'll have that cup of tea, be a shame to waste it.'

Archie smiled at Joe as he poured the tea and they went into the living room to sit and drink it.

'I don't know how you'll get into the shed, Arch,' Joe told him. 'They've put their own lock on it and I don't have a key.'

Archie smiled and said,

'It's made of wood, isn't it? It's your wood, so if it gets damaged by you, there's nothing they can do about it. I only need a big screwdriver to lever the hasp and staple off the door. Have you got one I could borrow?'

'Yes, Arch,' Joe replied. 'The problem is that once you've gone home they'll come after me, won't they?'

'If they do, they're really going to feel some heat,' Archie told him. 'It's your shed, with your stuff in it and it's standing on your land. They've got enough to worry about with the police probing their activities over this morning's problem. You just get your son in law to get that letter written and copy it to the police and to Arun District Council's Planning Department. That will give 'em plenty to do, without pestering you.'

Joe looked up at Archie. It seemed that a weight had been lifted from him.

'You're a good man, Archie Leggitt, I'm glad I listened to Mr. Pickering's advice when he said to ask you about the subsidence.'

Archie handed Joe a card with his mobile phone number on it.

'You'd better keep that handy,' he told him. 'It could be useful at some stage in this fiasco!'

Joe took the mugs back into the kitchen whilst Archie began putting his coat on. A few seconds passed and then Archie heard him call out in an urgent tone,

'Archie! Come out here, quick! There's another police car going into the site next door. I wonder why they need two cars, something must be up!'

CHAPTER 5.

Archie went into the kitchen, where Joe was watching the site through the window over the sink. Yes, there were two police cars there, outside the portacabin site office. A wooden shed stood next to it, the door partially open.

There seemed to be no other activity going on at all. The two men contracted for the blasting operation, were sitting in their van which was parked, facing Joe's home. After a few minutes, they heard Andy Clarke give a toot on his horn and Joe went out to greet him. The drizzle had stopped and the sky was brightening.

'Come in, Andy,' Joe said, 'we're in the kitchen, watching the action next door. I've just made another pot of tea.'

'Thanks Joe,' Andy said as he followed him in. 'I've left young Chris to lock up the yard. He'll be along presently, on his bike, I'll take Arch back when I drop him off. Can you hear me Arch? I thought it might get the job done a bit quicker, with three of us on it. What's happening next door then?' Andy asked, as he entered the kitchen.

'We don't know yet,' Joe told him. 'We've got to keep watching, or we may miss something.'

Archie had been watching intently. He turned to look at Andy and in mock indignation, said,

'What d'ya mean with three of us on it? I'm a supervisor, not a 'lackey', ain't that right, Joe?'

'We'll tell you all about it presently, Andy,' Joe promised. He winked as he noticed the puzzled look on Andy's face.

'Hold up a minute!' Archie called from his observation post. 'One of the policemen has just come out of the cabin, with a workman. He's put him in the police car and gone back in.'

'What happened to the fence? Did a tank hit it?' Andy asked. Archie took 'centre stage' and gave him verse and chapter, beginning with Bill coming to find him at the mill. He explained about the young lad being hurt and the way that the police had thought the damage to Joe's fence was deliberate.

'Are they trying to get you to sell up and move?' Andy asked Joe. 'You could get them stopped, y'know. Come to that, you could probably make 'em stop work on their project, if it's causing damage to your property.'

'Yes,' Joe said. 'I'll be speaking to my solicitor later and giving him all the details.'

Archie began telling Andy about Grover. He gave a detailed account of how he had been put in his place by Joe.

'You would have been proud of him, Andy,' he chuckled. 'He delivered a real knockout punch from the other side of the fence.'

Andy Clarke was obviously amused by it all.

'So you dismissed the poor chap, without letting him say anything else? Did he just go away, or did he try to follow you indoors?' He asked Joe.

'I believe he just went,' Joe said. 'I wasn't going to put up with any more of his condescending claptrap. My solicitor son-in-law will deal with him. The next step will be to find out who this Bettis chap is and exactly what he's up to. Now we've got the police involved we can probably put a spoke in his wheel.'

'They're bringing another one out of the site hut, Joe.' Archie called out excitedly from his observation post in the kitchen. The other two rushed to the window to get a better look.

'Is that one Bettis?' Archie asked Joe.

'No, I don't think so. I believe he's just the office chap. I think he only works part time.'

'They're putting him in the other police car,' Joe said.

'Must have been some sort of a problem between them, or they'd both be in the same car.'

Archie looked from the window. One of the police cars was just leaving.

'It won't be any good trying to find out what's going on today,' he said. 'Bill won't know any more until he's been to Chichelster tomorrow. I s'pose we'll just have to wait and see.'

'I don't want to disturb you two mind readers, but hadn't we better make a start on this fence?' Andy suggested. 'It'll be dark by about five and we've got to dig some holes for the posts yet. I thought Chris would have been here by now.'

They quickly drank their tea and went outside to Andy's pick up. The first job was to extract the old stump of the corner post. Andy began digging close to the post. The idea was to be able to lean it sideways, to lift it clear. The new post would then be placed into the hole and the void filled with concrete. Two bags of ready mixed concrete were on the pick-up and these would be tipped into the hole dry. Water would then be added slowly, whilst the mixture was being agitated with a steel pole, to eliminate air pockets. Chris arrived as they were finishing the corner post.

'Hello, Arch,' he called, as he leaned his bike against the garage door. 'Elsie phoned the yard about half an hour ago, I told her what was happening. She said she would expect you when she sees you.'

'Thanks, Chris,' Archie replied. 'She could have tried my mobile first. She ticked me off this morning for leaving it at home.'

'She said she'd tried that, but it was switched off.' Chris told him.

Archie pulled it from his coat pocket and inspected it.

'I must have switched it off when I took it from my jacket pocket,' he said, sheepishly. 'That'll be another bollocking, I 'spect!'

'Best get the arris rails in while we've still got a bit of flexibility on the posts,' Andy told him. 'Once the concrete has set, we won't be able to move 'em to slot the rails in. You may need to trim the ends to fit, Chris. I wasn't sure of the exact length, so I made 'em all a few inches longer than standard.' Chris nodded to show that he had understood.

Whilst they were working, another two cars arrived and drove up to the site. Archie thought he recognised the second one, a dark blue Volvo. He tried to take a look at the driver, but it went by too quickly and he was on the wrong side of the car to see properly. He thought for a moment and then realised that it was probably, DS. Brian Pace, the forensics officer who had come out when he had found the boot last year on the mill footpath. He decided not to say anything to the others just yet. Perhaps Bill would shed more light on the subject, next time he saw him.

As they completed the fence repairs, the second police car left the site, followed closely by a dark green Range Rover.

'I think that's Bettis,' Joe told them, 'in that Range Rover. Note the number plate, that's pure ego, isn't it?'

Andy called out the number on the back of the vehicle,

'BET715, pity he couldn't get a longer number plate. He could have had his address and phone number on it as well!'

'The man they took away in the police car was definitely his office assistant,' Joe explained. 'I've seen him several times.' Archie tried to get low enough to get a look at him, but his face was obscured by the car roof.

'There's another two cars coming in now,' Archie called from his corner post vantage point. 'There seems to be a lot of vehicular activity just now, but not much in the way of work going on. Did you see who was driving that first car that just went in?' He asked Joe, who was fitting the top arris rail.

41

'Nobody I can remember seeing before,' Joe replied.

'Well, I can tell you now, it was young Jeffery Davies, Diddler's son.' Archie told him. 'When I saw that the developers were, 'J. Davies Associates', I thought it would probably be 'Diddler', but perhaps it's his son and not him. I recognised him from his wedding photo in the paper a few years back. I remember being surprised that he had married young Hannah Jempson. I can't see that sitting well with her dad. He always suspected that 'Diddler' had some connection to the fire that killed his wife. Who's this 'Martin Bettis' character, anyway? What's his involvement in this set-up?'

'I think he's probably the site manager,' Joe suggested. 'He's the only one who's here every day.'

Archie looked at Joe,

'You remember when you bought this plot and the smallholding from Bob Jempson? Well, he bought it from the old farmer, Harry Eldridge. Well, when Harry died, the northern half of the land was bought up by that aggregate company. Harry's wife had the proceeds from the sale and went to live with her mother in Canada. The other half was left to his daughter, Mary, who married old 'Diddler' Davies. That's how he got his hands on some of it. After she went missing, it was re- registered as equal share, joint ownership in both their names. He probably greased a few palms to get planning permission for this project. The rest of the land has been rented to Peter Bailley, for the past ten or twelve years.'

Joe had been listening intently,

'I thought Mr. Bailley owned it, but now what you just said makes sense. He just uses it for silage, there's never any stock up here. The only other time I see him is when he's spreading fertiliser, in the spring.'

They tidied up a bit, and began taking the bits of broken fence out to Joe's back garden.

'Just throw them up there past my workshop, Arch,' Joe called out from a few paces behind him. 'There's a square bonfire bin on the left, leave them next to that, please.'
Archie followed the brick path up towards Joe's workshop. He turned left onto some rough grass and stopped.

'I can't see a bonfire bin, Joe, but there's a bloody big hole in the ground,' he shouted.
He dropped the bits of fence and looked around.

'There's soil and bits of turf all over the place, even on the roof of your workshop, Joe.'
Joe caught up with Archie and looked at the hole. It was about four or five feet across. The edges were irregular and did not look very safe.

'There's a crack in the ground, looks like it goes under my workshop. I bet that was a result of that explosion we heard,' Joe said, as he walked along the fissure.
Archie had been studying the hole and surrounding area, now he called Joe over to where he stood.

'I've got a theory, Joe.'
Andy shouted to him from the side of the bungalow.

'Come on, Arch, if you want a lift home, you'd better get a move on. We're all ready to leave. Chris's bike is on the pick up. We're just waiting for you.'

'Come and have a look at this, Andy,' Archie hollered.
The other two came around the side of the house, towards the workshop.

'What's up Arch?' Andy called out. 'Is Joe alright?'
They approached the hole in the ground.

'Blimey!' Andy and Chris exclaimed, almost in unison.

'What's your theory, Arch?' Joe reminded him.
Archie looked at his friend's faces. They seemed to be expecting a grand revelation.

'Well, it's just a theory,' he began, 'but in the Neolithic times, this area was riddled with flint mines. No records of where they were. No markers or anything to stop people falling down them.

Most are only about thirty feet deep, but then radiate out from the vertical shaft. They discovered some more, near to Cissbury, only a few years ago. My theory is that the ground beneath us could be concealing some of the galleries. That explosion we heard could have caused some to cave in. This hole could have been one of the old shafts, which burst open with the air pressure from the charge. That crack, which goes underneath your workshop, Joe, is headed in the general direction of the blast we heard. It's probably directly over one of the galleries.'

They agreed that this seemed to be an entirely likely explanation to them. It coincided with the blast which they had heard and felt earlier. It also added credibility to the suggestion that Joe should consult with a surveyor, to ensure that his home was not being damaged by the activities of the developers.

'I'll certainly take some advice from a surveyor,' Joe said. 'My solicitor will need to be involved in this latest damage claim. I can't have them destroying my property without paying for the repairs. My workshop will have to be moved, I can't risk it becoming damaged by erosion or explosion. I'll get onto him as soon as I go indoors.'
Joe continued as they walked back towards the house.

'Thanks to all of you, my friends, for your help. Andy, make sure you present me with a nice fat bill, for Mr. Grover! I suggest you work out what the actual cost is, then add a twenty five per cent surcharge for his bad attitude.'

'Whatever you wish, Joe,' said Andy, grinning. 'Now perhaps we'd better leave Joe to sort his problems with his solicitor, and go home for something to eat.'
Joe came down to the front of his home to wave them off. Thunder was allowed into the garden again, now that the fence was secure. Joe turned to Archie and said,

'May I come down to see your mill tomorrow, please, Arch? I've heard all about it, but I'd really like a guided tour, if you can spare the time. I've always had an interest in mills, both wind and water.'

'Of course you can, Joe,' Archie replied. 'Any time after about ten in the morning is OK. Perhaps if you go to my house first, then if I'm not there, Elsie will tell you where to find me.' On the way home, Archie and Andy arranged to meet at the Old Bell for a couple of beers, later. Archie was dropped of at his home, where he found Elsie on the telephone to her sister, Joan. She paused, briefly to ask him,

'Did you get everything sorted out at Joe's?'

'Yes, well, we fixed his fence, but he's coming to see me tomorrow. I'll take Jimbo for a walk later. I'm meeting Andy for a beer. What's for dinner?'

'Men!' she exclaimed to Joan. 'All they're interested in is beer and food.' Elsie turned back to Archie.

'I saw Jenny whilst I was out with Jimbo. I told her that you had been delayed. She said she would tell Reg. Did you get the stuff you wanted from Jimmy's?'
Archie stood there grinning at her.

'I didn't, get to Jimmy's' he told her, 'Bill called before I'd finished the handrails. Andy said he's got what I need at his yard. He'll drop it down in the morning, so I won't have to go to Jimmy's now.'

'And why was your mobile phone turned off when I tried to call you?' She asked him.

'I can't hear you Else,' he shouted from the bathroom. 'I'm just washing my hands ready for dinner.'

'Never mind,' she thought to herself.

CHAPTER 6.

Archie showered and changed and came downstairs to find Elsie in the kitchen.

'Its salmon steaks with boiled potatoes and broccoli,' she told him. 'There's a fresh pot of tea, you can pour mine as well, please. Your dinner will be about another five minutes.'

'Thanks, Else,' he said as he poured the tea. 'Poor old Joe's got a few problems with the developers on that site next door to him. It seems that they're trying to drive him out, so they can buy his place to add to their spa facility.'

'What happened to that young lad, Arch?' she asked. 'It was on the local news, at lunchtime. They say he's critical, but stable, whatever you want to read into that.'

'It was a bit of a mess, Else,' Archie began telling her. 'The police have several witnesses who say that it looked as though he was deliberately trying to damage the fence. In his haste to flee the scene, he failed to spot the young lad on his moped and hit him full force. As the policeman I spoke with told me, 'a moped is no match for a loaded ten ton tipper lorry'. The lad was lucky to survive, by all accounts.'

'The road was blocked for more than an hour, it said on the news. So the accident was right outside Joe's bungalow?' Archie began to give her more details.

'Yes, Else and there was no reason for the lorry to hit Joe's fence. The police measured the access road and he said it was twenty two feet wide. That's why they think it was a deliberate act. They will be charging the driver with criminal damage and dangerous driving. I don't envy his situation, but I also don't have much sympathy for him.'

'Will Joe be able to get an injunction to stop any more harassment?' Elsie asked.

'I think he'll be alright, Else. He's nobody's fool and his son in law, Lakshmi's husband, is a solicitor. He was going to call him after we left. He wants to look over the mill tomorrow, so I'll probably know a bit more when he gets here,' he told her.

They chatted as they ate their meal, Jimbo sat in anticipation of a small left over, from Archie's plate. His patience was rewarded with a small portion of salmon and a dog biscuit.
At around eight o'clock, Archie put his Barbour coat on and picked up Jimbo's lead.

'Coming for a pint, Jimbo?' Archie asked him.
The affirmative reply was too obvious to need the spoken word!
As Archie and Jimbo turned the corner into Forge Lane, Andy's pick up passed them. Instead of pulling in to the pub car park, he continued up the lane.

'I wonder where he's off to,' Archie thought to himself.
Jimbo gave a soft bark, and then another.
Archie heard the clang of Bert Brooks' front gate closing. Was he going home or coming out? Archie wondered. Jimbo gave a tug on the lead and another soft bark.

'Is that you, young Arch?' Bert's voice boomed out of the darkness.

'Guilty as charged,' Archie called back. 'Go steady though, Bert, I've got my guard dog with me. If you call him, I'll let go of the lead.'

'Jimbo, Jimbo, come on old boy,' Bert hollered.

An enthusiastic Jimbo raced up the lane towards the sound of Bert's voice.

'I've got 'im, Arch' Bert called out. 'We'll go on ahead and get you one in.'

Archie just caught sight of them against the pub lights as they were crossing the road. A couple of minutes later he joined them in the bar. Bert took his usual bar stool and Archie and his dog sat at one of the tables by the window. Jimbo opened his bag of crisps and was just beginning to enjoy them, when Andy Clarke walked in.

'I've just been up to the yard and collected your bits and pieces. I'd cut your wood before I came up to Joe's, so I've put it all in the pick up. I thought it might save me a double trip in the morning.'

'Thanks Andy, I wondered where you were going when you passed us in the lane. I'll get you a pint for that, mate.'

'You're too slow, Arch,' Bert chimed in. 'It's already here on the bar.'

'Cheers, Bert,' said Andy as he collected his pint. 'I need to come and find you, tomorrow, mate. I need some iron hinges, to match a pair on an old oak door. I'll take one off and bring it as a pattern.'

'Righto, Andy,' Bert said. 'I shall be presiding over the establishment all the mornin', so just pop down when you're ready. D'you know what 'appened along the Arundel Road this mornin'?'

'It was a bad one, Bert,' Archie told him. 'A tipper lorry from the site where they're building that new spa hotel, hit a young lad on a moped.'

'I heard it on the local news at lunchtime,' Bert said. 'They said he was stable, but remains on the critical list. Does anyone know who he is? Was he a local lad?'

'Comes from Storrington, he was on his way to college. They're charging the lorry driver with dangerous driving, so he'll be lucky if he stays out of prison. He's sure to lose his license, so that means he won't have a job either,' Archie explained.

'Poor little sod,' said Bert. 'He didn't deserve that. Let's just 'ope he makes a full recovery. I bet his parents are a bit anxious, I know I would be. I'd want to get my 'ands on that driver. I know that wouldn't put the clock back, but there'd be two on the critical list, by the time I'd finished with 'im.'

The conversation turned to Joe's problem and how the developers were trying to force him to sell. Archie told them about the succession of police cars and the way the police had taken two of the workers away. He told them about the hole in Joe's garden, after the explosion.

Andy confirmed what Archie had described.

'There was soil and bits of flint and turf all over the place. Even on the roof of old Joe's workshop, it was quite a blast.'

After a couple of beers, Andy said that he was going home. Archie drank the rest of his pint and stood up to go.

'Come on, Jimbo, we've got a ride home in a nice warm pick up,' he told him.

They said 'goodnight' to the company and left the pub. A few minutes later Archie, complete with dog, timber and a bag of 'bits' from Jimmy's, was dropped off at his home.

Elsie was watching the television as he entered the lounge. Jimbo greeted her enthusiastically, washing her spectacles with 'cheese and onion crisp flavoured kisses'!

'D'you want a 'cuppa', Else?' Archie enquired.

'Yes please, Arch. I'll have a cup of tea if you're making one. Detective Sergeant Ian Stuart, phoned just after you left. He wanted a 'quiet word' with you. I told him you were out with Jimbo, probably in the pub by now. His phone number is on the pad by the hall phone. He said if you were back by ten, would you please phone him?'

Archie checked his watch, it was nine-forty.

'I wonder what he wants,' he said to himself.

49

CHAPTER 7.

Archie poured the tea and took Elsie's through to her. He took his mug to the hall table and then dialled the number which Elsie had written on the pad.

'Ian Stuart,' said a familiar voice.

'Good evening, DS. Stuart,' Archie began. 'Its Archie Leggitt here, Elsie said you wanted a word with me.'

'Archie,' he responded enthusiastically. 'Thanks for calling back. It's 'Ian', by the way, this is completely off the record, so the 'DS' prefix is unnecessary.'

'Congratulations on your promotion, Ian,' said Archie. 'I know it was considerably overdue, but your patience has now been rewarded.'

'Thanks, Archie, I wondered whether you had any more details of the accident in the village earlier this morning?' Ian asked. 'Brian Pace attended, but found nothing worth investigating, but he mentioned that he saw you in the garden of the house next door.'

'Yes,' Archie replied. 'I was there to check on the damage to the fence, for my friend, Joe Skrobe. I thought it was Brian Pace's car, but I didn't get a good look at the driver. One of the policemen told me that it looked like a deliberate act of criminal damage. Have you heard how the young lad is doing? He was in a bad way, from all accounts.'

'He still hasn't come round yet, Archie. They've sedated him to keep him stable, so we may know more tomorrow. Can I come out and have a chat with you in the morning? We believe there's something a bit 'fishy' going on at the site. We've interviewed several people, but had to let them all go because there is nothing in the way of concrete evidence. I'm sure at least one of them knows more than he's telling us.'

'Yes, Ian, you can come over in the morning, about what time were you thinking?'

'Sometime after about ten, would suit me very well. Is that OK with you?'

'I'll tell you what,' Archie suggested, 'make it half past and I'll be over at the mill. Joe's coming to look at the mill later in the morning. You could have a chat with him about it, as well, if you want to.'

'Can we rely on his discretion, Archie?' Ian asked.

'I think so, Ian,' Archie told him. 'Joe keeps himself very much to himself. I've known him for nearly forty years and never heard anything in the way of gossip from him. He'll probably be able to give you more information about the site and the developers, than I can.'

'Right, that's settled then,' Ian said. 'I'll see you at around ten-thirty at the mill. Thanks Archie, sorry to disturb your evening, I'll let you go back to whatever you were doing, bye for now.'

'Goodnight, Ian, no apology is necessary.' Archie said as he replaced the receiver.

'What was that about, Arch?' Elsie asked as he returned to the lounge.

'He wanted to know about the accident this morning. He's not happy that everything is as it seems. Brian Pace, the forensics man, had seen me in Joe's garden. He suggested to Ian that I may have some more information, which might be helpful. He's coming to see me over at the mill, tomorrow,' Archie told her.

51

'But you didn't see the accident, did you?' She queried.

'No, but I think he's more interested in the background information. Like the way they're trying to get Joe to sell to them. It sounded as though there's something a bit devious going on with the site manager and one or two of the other workers. Anyway, I won't find out what he's thinking, until I've spoken with him, will I?' Archie asked her.

'No, I suppose not, did you ask how the young lad was doing?'

'Of course I did, Else. Apparently he's still out of it, under sedation, to help with his pain. The police are hoping to talk with him when he wakes up.'

They sat watching the local evening news, the accident was mentioned, but with no fine detail. The weather for tomorrow was good, sunny spells and still quite warm for November. At five past eleven, Elsie went to bed, whilst Archie let Jimbo out into the garden for a last pee, before settling down for the night.

CHAPTER 8.

Friday was a better day. The sun was shining, the birds were
singing, not coughing like yesterday!
Archie finished his breakfast and put his plate and mug on the
draining board. Elsie was washing up, so he picked up the tea
towel and began putting things away.

'Are you going over the mill just to meet your policeman
friend, or have you got work to do over there?' she asked him.

'I've got a job to do, Else. Andy collected the stuff from his
yard, last night. It's in the garage, so I'll take Jimbo for a walk
first. Then collect my bits of wood and screws, to take to the mill.
I'm fitting a safety rail up on the milling floor, so that visitors
don't get too close to the moving parts. Jimbo can come with me,
but I'll need to make two trips. I'll take the wood over first, and
then pick him up when I come back for the small stuff.'

'What time will Joe be coming?' Elsie enquired.

'I don't really know,' Archie said. 'He'll come here first, so
you can tell him I'm over the mill. Ask him to hoot when he gets
there, it'll take me a couple of minutes to get down from the top
floor.'
Archie picked Jimbo's lead from its hook and stood by the back
door. Jimbo's hearing was such that he heard the slight scrape of
the clip as it was taken from the hook. He was at Archie's feet in

less than a second, head erect, eyes focussed on Archie's face and his tail wagging furiously.

'We'll go and have a look at the weir first, Else. See what the water levels are like and adjust as necessary.'

'One man and his dog', left the kitchen and strolled down Slindon Road, towards the footpath leading to the mill. The grass was still wet from yesterday's drizzle. Archie was pleased that he had put his gum boots on. He was surprise how much it had grown after Peter Bailley had 'topped it' in late September. Jimbo was getting a lower half wash, as he ran back and forth in front of him. The weir looked fine and didn't need any attention, so they strolled back along the bank of the mill pond. Reg Tobin, the mill owner, was standing by the mill bridge.

'Good morning, Arch,' he called out as they approached. Jimbo saw him and bounded enthusiastically along the bank towards him.

'Hello Jimbo, old boy, you look a bit on the wet side, have you been in the pond?'

'Morning Reg,' Archie replied, 'No, it's just the wet grass, he's rolled in it as well. Stay down, Jimbo,' he called out. 'Sorry about yesterday, Reg. I expect you heard about the bad accident on Arundel Road. I was with old Joe Skrobe, that's why I got held up. It was at his place that it all happened.'

'Yes, Arch, Jenny saw Elsie, and told her about it. Are you here today?'

'In a little while, Reg, I've got to collect the stuff from home, so it will be about half an hour before I'm back.'
Reg nodded that he understood.

'I'm just off to work, so I'll see you later Arch and thanks for your help, Jenny will make you a cuppa, just tap on the door when you're ready.'
He got into the big Peugeot and drove slowly down the lane towards the main road. Archie took the grass footpath to the corner of Slindon Road, where he clipped the lead back onto Jimbo's collar. He took his boots off in the passageway between

the garage and the kitchen door and called out to Elsie for a towel for Jimbo.

'Has he been in the pond?' She asked as she handed Archie the old towel.

'No, Else, the grass is very wet, that's all. I'll have a quick cup of tea before I go to the mill. Give him a chance to dry out a bit before I come back for him.' Archie dried the dog as much as he could, with the old towel. Jimbo gave a huge shake, shedding more water and spraying Archie's trousers.

'D'you want your tea out there, or are you coming in for a few minutes? She asked him.

'I'm coming in, Else,' he said, 'I need my shoes. I'll walk back along the road, to save getting soaked on the footpath.' Ten minutes later, suitably refreshed, Archie gathered the timber from the garage and set off for the mill.

'I'll be back in about twenty minutes, Else,' he told her. 'I won't bother with a flask today, Jenny's home, so I'll get a drink from her.'

He took the bundle of timber, hoisted it onto his shoulder and walked over to the mill. Jeff Harden, the milkman was waiting for the road to clear at the end of Copton Row.

'I might as well wait for you an' all, Arch,' he called out from his milk float.

'Thanks, Jeff,' Archie responded. 'This is just beginning to get a bit heavy. I might have to change shoulders before I get to the mill.'

'Stick it on 'ere, Arch, I'll take you over there. I got to deliver the milk to Mill House and the cottages.'

Archie did as suggested and climbed in next to Jeff. The traffic cleared and the next stop was Mill house, where Jenny was closing the garage door.

'Morning Jeff, oh, morning, Archie,' she said, sounding surprised.

'Mornin' Mrs. Tobin,' Jeff replied. 'Total service this mornin', I'm deliverin' milk, wood and workmen, all at once.'

Jenny smiled and took the milk from him as Archie retrieved his bundle of timber from the top of the milk crates.

'Thanks, Jeff,' he said as he leaned the bundle against the garage door. 'I'll take this lot up first,' he told Jenny. 'I've got to go back for the small stuff and I'll bring Jimbo back with me.'

'OK Archie,' she said. 'I thought I'd better close the garage door, the weather forecast wasn't very good. They said that a band of rain would be with us by lunchtime.'

'Let's hope it's only a band, not a complete bloomin' orchestra, like last week!' Archie returned, with a grin.
Jeff departed and Archie carried his timber over to the mill and up to the top floor. He looked at his watch. It was twenty minutes to ten.

'Plenty of time before Ian Stuart gets here,' he thought to himself.
He closed the mill door on his way out, but didn't lock it. He would be back in less than twenty minutes. There would probably be time to make a start before Ian arrived.

CHAPTER 9.

Archie was just screwing the last of the corner post brackets to the floor, when Jimbo barked loudly. Archie crossed to the small window and looked down. DS.Ian Stuart was just parking his car, so he went down the stairs to greet him, Jimbo at his heels.
He opened the mill door as Ian began walking towards the sleeper bridge.

'Good morning Archie, thanks for letting me come to see you.' Ian said, as he offered his hand. 'As you may have guessed, it was Tony's idea. He sends his Best Wishes, by the way.'

Archie shook his hand, saying,

'Come inside and have a seat, it's a bit breezy out here.'

Archie closed the door behind them and offered Ian a seat on the wooden bench. Ian was looking all around the mill. He appeared to be fascinated by his surroundings.

'I'm impressed with this old building,' he told Archie.
'I understand that it is now a working flour mill, mainly due to your efforts. I'd really like to have a proper look when we've had our chat.'

'Yes, Ian, I will give you the full guided tour.' Archie promised. 'In fact Joe is coming later and he wants to see it. I might even get the wheel turning, so you can see all the gear working, but let's find out what I can do to help you, first.'

Ian began to explain,

'Well, the main purpose of my visit was to find out whether you could add anything to what we already know about the accident yesterday.'

Archie nodded, as Ian continued,

'But before we go there, I have a question for you. Does the name, 'Robertson', mean anything to you, Archie?'

Archie thought for a few moments before replying.

'Golly,' he said, with a mischievous grin.

Ian looked puzzled,

'Golly' he repeated. 'What does that mean?'

Archie began to laugh,

'Robertson's marmalade and jams all had a golly as a sort of trade mark. I s'pose they had to stop using it because it wouldn't be considered politically correct these days.'

Ian pulled a slip of paper from his pocket and read from it.

'We had a call from this gentleman a couple of days ago. He said that he was an old friend of yours and asked if we could give him your address and phone number. You understand that we have to be careful what information we divulge to people who are not known to us, so we told him we would look into it and call him back. Tony said that we should check with you first.'

Archie thought for a few moments, and then asked,

'Is that all the details he gave you, just, 'Robertson'?'

Ian referred to his slip of paper again.

'His full name, he said, is Robertson Stanley Jempson. Does that help?'

A knowing look appeared on Archie's face,

'Bob Jempson,' he said, 'Yes he's an old friend. I didn't know his name was Robertson, I thought it was just 'Robert'. We used to refer to him as, 'R.S.J.' when he had the farm shop on Arundel Road.'

'So you don't mind him having your details, Arch?' Ian asked.. 'Perhaps it would be better if I gave you his telephone number, so you could contact him?' He offered the slip of paper to Archie, who took it, saying,

'I'll give him a call later, thanks, Ian. I hope that's cleared up any mystery.'

Ian Stuart smiled,

'You understand our need for caution over such as this, Archie, don't you? He asked. 'Now perhaps we can get down to the real reason for my visit. As you already know, a young lad was badly injured in the accident yesterday. We've questioned the driver and we believe him when he says that he didn't see the moped. As far as we are concerned that part will be logged as an accident. The reason why he didn't see him seems to be that he was hell bent on getting away from the scene. That still justifies the charge of 'dangerous driving' which he currently faces.'
Ian looked up from his notes,

'You understand that this is confidential information, so we don't want it made public just yet?'
Archie nodded,

'You know it won't go any further from me.'

'Yes, Arch, that's why Tony Church suggested that I give you a call,' Ian continued. 'The part which we are not at all comfortable with is how he came to be in that situation in the first place. I can tell you, in confidence, that the other witnesses are saying that reversing at full tilt into the corner post of the fence, appeared to be a deliberate act. He is denying this, so far, but when Tony suggested that if it had been accidental, his competence and underlying health conditions would be called in to question. He began to waver a little, searching for alternative reasons for his actions. He seems to have been intimidated, but he won't admit it, of course.
We measured the width of the site access from the main road, at between twenty two and twenty four feet, so plenty of room to

enter and exit the site to turn left, without crossing the centre line of the main road.'

Archie was listening intently and so far, could only concur with what Ian was describing.

'So, what other details are you not happy with, Ian?' He asked.

Ian continued,

'Well, our officers went into the site, in the first instance, to notify the site manager of the incident. Mr. Bettis seemed more concerned with what the driver had told us about the fence, than the injury to the moped rider. This struck the officer as somewhat suspicious. Whilst he was there, one of the other workers came into the office and began to berate Bettis for his apparent casual attitude to the poor victim. The other office worker then began to shout abuse at the workman, telling him to mind his own business and have some respect for Bettis, who was the site manager. The workman then said words to the effect that Bettis was a callous bully, who didn't care about anyone else, so long as he got his way. The other office person then began threatening the workman with physical violence, so the officer decided to place him in the police car. This calmed the situation somewhat, but Bettis then said he would fire the workman. At this, the other office chap said, 'perhaps you'd better think about that, it could come back to bite you!' Bettis then told him to mind his manners, or he might be next.'

'He sounds a nasty bit of work, this 'Bettis' chap, Ian.' Archie observed. 'Perhaps now would be a good time for me to tell you something about the exchange of words between my friend, Joe Skrobe and a certain 'Mr. Grover' of Tickners Transport.'

'Oh, so you've met him as well, have you?' Ian replied. 'Yes, Arch, please go on.'

Archie explained the telephone call from Grover, followed by details of the rather unsatisfactory meeting at Joe's front fence.

'He began by talking to us as though we were a couple of peasants and he was the 'Lord of the Manor'. Archie explained.

'He said he'd send a man round with some posts and a couple of panels. That would do as a temporary repair and then he said 'Bettis' had told him that the developers were buying Joe's property, so he wouldn't need to worry about it for much longer.'

'Oh, did he now?' Ian said with some astonishment. 'Is your friend planning to sell up, Arch?'

Archie shook his head and placed a finger alongside his nose.

'No, he isn't and this isn't the first attempt at damaging his property. The developers threatened him with a compulsory purchase order, if he didn't sell to them.' Archie continued, explaining to the detective, 'Old Joe is nobody's fool, he knows that just wouldn't happen for a private development. Anyway to get back to the little man from Tickners Transport, Joe soon had the upper hand. He told him that from the information he had been given, it was a deliberate act of criminal damage. He went on to say that whatever the cause, he would be billing for a complete repair, not a couple of cheap panels. The bill would be paid by either Tickners Transport, or by their insurers. Then he said to Grover, 'I think that is the end of our meeting, you may now return to your office.' Joe just turned his back on Grover and we both went indoors, leaving Grover standing in the road with his mouth open!'

Ian was laughing.

'Don't you just love it when these little 'Hitlers' come unstuck?' He said. 'I'm looking forward to meeting this friend of yours, Archie. Now, in the light of what you've just told me, I'm wondering whether Bettis had offered some incentive to Tickners lorry drivers, to cause your friend to change his mind about selling. That would certainly explain the driver's sudden doubt over whether it was actually an accident, or something else. Maybe that was what the other workman was holding over Bettis. It would perhaps explain why the other office type reminded him to think about it, before dismissing him.'

Ian paused and looked at Archie, who said,

'Would that be enough to stop him sacking the workman?'
Ian stroked his chin and replied,

'Possibly not, Archie, but there's something else, we're not too sure of.'

There was a loud knock at the door.

'Perhaps that's your friend, Mr. Skrobe?' Ian suggested.

Archie opened the door to find Jenny Tobin waiting with a tray of tea, milk and sugar and two mugs.

'I'm sorry Archie, I thought perhaps your friend Mr. Skrobe was here. Shall I fetch another mug for him? I expect he'll be here soon, won't he?'

Archie introduced Ian to her, he explained that Ian was one of the detectives involved in the boot mystery and had just dropped in for a chat and a look at the mill.

'Thanks, Jenny,' he said. 'I expect old Joe will be here soon, but don't worry about bringing another mug, I'll come down and get one when he arrives.'

Jenny turned to Ian and asked,

'How is the young lad doing? Is there any news of him? I hope he makes a full recovery. What a terrible thing to happen to him, on his way to college.'

Ian nodded, saying,

'I understand that they will probably allow him to wake up today, Mrs. Tobin. He's been heavily sedated to help with his pain, whilst they dealt with his injuries. We won't know much more until he's awake and hopefully, able to talk with us.'

'Yes, that would be good news,' Jenny replied. 'I'll leave you two to get on with your chat. See you later, Archie, nice to have met you, Detective.' She shook hands with Ian and left.

'Where did we get to?' Archie asked, smiling.

'Oh, yes,' Ian continued. 'I was about to tell you what we had been told by the workman. He said that they had found some

bones, but Bettis told them they were probably from a Neolithic flint miner. He said he wasn't about to put the entire project on hold for some three or four thousand year old bits of skeleton.'
Archie broke in to explain.

'The land around here is riddled with old flint mines.'
Ian continued,

'The workman said that they should be reported, but Bettis told them to bag them up and throw them into the crumbling tunnel where they had been found. He then arranged for the blasting team to place a charge in the hole, thereby destroying any evidence. That was why we asked Brian Pace to attend, but he, of course, found nothing left to examine.'
Archie had been listening intently, now he began to tell Ian about the explosion.

'There was a particularly strong blast whilst we were all at Joe's, before Grover's phone call. Even Bill Pickering said it would be worth checking that the foundations had not moved. It shook the whole place. Later, when we'd mended the fence and were clearing the old debris to the back garden, we discovered a big hole. It was about four feet across and there was soil and bits of turf all around, even on top of Joe's workshop roof. There was a big crack in the ground, which ran right under his workshop. After we left, Joe was going to phone his son-in-law, who is a solicitor in Petworth. We'll maybe find out what he said if Joe turns up before you have to go.'

'That could be interesting, Archie,' Ian said. 'Shall we have a look at your mill, while we wait for him?'

Archie was pleased to show him round, and described the process whereby the power was transferred from the water wheel to the mill stone. They had just reached the milling floor, where Archie had been working, when they heard a car horn.

'That's probably Joe, now.' Archie said. 'I'll go down and let him in. We'll have that cup of tea now, shall we?'

63

Ian followed Archie down the stairs and went to the open doorway. Jenny had heard Joe hoot and had come out to give Archie another mug. The men then walked the short distance back to the mill, where Archie introduced Joe to the detective.

'Right,' Archie announced, 'we'll have this cup of tea now, and then we can catch up on the news.'

'I've just heard a bit of good news on local radio,' Joe told them. 'The lad who was knocked off his bike has woken up. His parents are at his bedside and the report said his condition is improving. He is still slightly sedated, but able to converse with his parents. The police are hoping to be able to ask him some questions later today.'

'That is good news,' the others agreed.

'Let's hope he continues on the road to recovery.' Ian said. 'The police won't want to cause him any more stress, but it is important to try to get his take on what he remembers of the accident as soon as possible. I think we're all hoping he can remember a few details, but time alone will tell.'

Joe began telling them what he had been up to, whilst they were drinking their tea.

'I phoned Stephen after you left, Archie. I got a telling off from Lakshmi, for not saying something about it sooner, but Stephen was more practical. He told me to get the bill from Andy, and make it as hefty as possible within the bounds of reality. He came down this morning to collect it and to have a look at the hole in the garden. He's going to copy the bill with a claim for damages, to Tickners Transport. He thought it must have been a deliberate act, possibly instigated by the developers or their site manager, but that is just his opinion. The access road is plenty wide enough, so there was no need for him to have crossed the centre line on Arundel Road and therefore, no need for the destructive reversing manoeuvre.'

Ian had been listening to Joe, and told him,

'That's exactly what we believe. The access road is between twenty two and twenty four feet wide. I can tell you, in

64

confidence that the driver's story is decidedly 'wobbly' and he may yet come across with the true version. I'd just like to ask you about this explosion, Joe. Did you find anything besides soil and turf, ejected from the hole?'

Joe thought for a moment, before replying.

'We, that is, Stephen and I, examined the hole and the debris, this morning. Incidentally, Arch, we found my burning bin in the field behind the workshop, so it must have been 'airborne' for quite a distance. To answer your question, Mr. Stuart, it was mainly turf, soil and bits of chalk and flint, but there were small bits of what looked like animal bones. Another odd thing we found was a bit of old deer antler, but whether that came from the explosion or was there already, we can't be sure.
Joe paused briefly before continuing,

'The main thing is that Stephen has now obtained a curtailment order on any further blasting, until the extent of the ground erosion and subsidence has been assessed by a qualified surveyor. Archie, I also mentioned your bit about the 'angle of repose' on the excavation next to my fence. Stephen will take it up with the surveyor, but he agrees with your opinion.'

'So you will have a qualified assessment of any further damage, Joe?' Ian asked.

'That was the idea, yes. I'm very pleased that I involved Stephen on this, because one of the surveyors with whom I would have consulted, also happens to be in the employ of Davies, the developers. I'm not saying that he would have misrepresented the issue of subsidence, but as Stephen put it, there would have been a 'conflict of interests'.' He turned to Ian and asked,

'Mr. Stuart, why did you ask about what other materials we may have found ejected from the hole?'

Ian smiled,

'I wondered whether you might pick up on that, Joe. May I call you, 'Joe'? I'm Ian, by the way, whilst we're chatting informally. None of this conversation will be repeated without your prior consent, I'm just grateful to be able to get an inside view on the situation.'

Joe nodded and smiled, as Ian continued.

'But to answer your question, as I was just telling Archie, one of the workers had mentioned finding some old bones. Bettis told him to put them in a sack and place them back in the old tunnel where they had been found. That's when he arranged for the blasting crew to blow them up. I'm sure he didn't anticipate the destruction of your garden, as a result.'

Joe smiled as he spoke,

'I think he'll find there will be a lot of problems coming his way, which he won't have anticipated.'

CHAPTER 10.

Ian glanced at Archie, who was smiling to himself as he asked,

'You know more than you've told us, don't you, Joe? Are you going to spill the beans, for us?'

'I'll tell you what I've heard, but you'd be well advised to let it happen first. Nobody's going to get hurt, not physically anyhow,' he said to Ian, 'All the information which I have been given will be classified as, 'hearsay'. I think if you give me a little more time, you will eventually have a stronger case. If you begin asking questions at the site now, they will just deny any knowledge and you'll be back to square one.'

Ian nodded as though he understood. He said to Joe,

'I am a man of my word, Joe. Anything I may hear from you or Archie will not be acted upon without your say so. I accept that any information you have, has been given to you in confidence and I would not ask or expect you to betray that confidence. You have said that nobody will be physically hurt, that's good enough for me.

I just hope that the source of your information will not become a victim of his own honesty.'

'I rather think he has already resigned himself to that fact, Ian,' Joe said, smiling. 'The only reason that he still has a job is because Bettis believes that he knows something incriminating about him. My contact also knows that once this information becomes public knowledge, then Bettis will take pleasure in firing him.'

'I'm guessing that this is something to do with either the accident, or the prehistoric bones. Am I somewhere close to the truth?' Ian asked.

'Let's just say that the bones were not disposed of in strict accordance with Bettis' instructions,' Joe continued. 'The main problem is that unless this situation is allowed to unfold in the correct sequence, there is a real danger that the perpetrators will walk free, whilst an innocent man is forced to take the blame.'

Archie had been listening most attentively and now it was his turn to add something to the discussion.

'There are a couple of things which we need to find out, before coming to any conclusions. We need to find out if it's the same lorry driver who damaged the fence the first time? They may all have been told to cause problems. The second question is how many other people know about the attempts to force Joe out of his home?'

Joe responded,

'Well, on the second point, it's fairly obvious that both Bettis and Grover are party to the same scheme. We know that much from Grover's comments to me, when he came to inspect the damage. After Stephen left, Bettis sent one of his men round to tell me that he's coming to inspect the hole in the garden himself, this afternoon. I suppose he'll try to say that it's due to 'natural subsidence', but we know differently, don't we? Anyway, I told him that this afternoon was not convenient, as I need to go to Petworth to see my son-in-law.'

'What did he say to that?' Archie asked.

'The cheeky sod said that if Bettis was coming to look at it, it wouldn't matter whether I was here or not.'

Ian raised an eyebrow, as he responded,

'He's out of order there, Joe. You need to be there when he visits and if he comes against your instructions, then that will constitute trespass.'

'I've got an idea, Joe,' Archie said. 'How about if I come back with you and stay there whilst you go to Petworth. I'll keep low, so he'll think you've gone off in your van and then if he comes round, I'll tell him to go away.'

'Be careful, Archie,' said Ian. 'He'll probably have someone with him. I don't want you to risk getting hurt if there's an altercation.'

'Oh, don't you worry about that, Ian,' Archie quickly replied. 'I'll have old Thunder with me. They won't want to chance an altercation with a big German Shepherd. I'll just tell 'em to go away and come back when they've made proper arrangements.'

'That sounds like a good idea, Arch,' Joe said, smiling. 'Are you sure you can spare the time to do that for me? I'll probably be gone for an hour or two, maybe a bit longer.'

Ian sat looking at these two old boys and then he said,

'You seem to have it all worked out, if I was a somewhat dubious character like Bettis, I don't think I'd want to tangle with you two. You think it all through in advance, so you don't have to ask for outside help. You seem more than capable of managing your own problems, so I'll leave you to get organised. Please let me know the outcome, Archie. If you need any assistance, you've got my mobile number, haven't you?'

'Yes, thanks, Ian,' Archie replied. 'Don't worry. I'll keep you in the loop. I hope you'll let us know of any other significant developments.'

Ian agreed, they all shook hands and Ian went on his way back to Chichelster. Joe had a quick look at the milling floor, where Archie explained what he had been doing. He promised Joe the full guided tour next time he came.

'I'll just take these cups and things back to Jen,' Archie said. 'I s'pose I'd better pop in to tell Else where I'll be. I can take Jimbo for a walk again when I get home.'

He handed the key to Joe and picked up the tray.

'If you wouldn't mind locking up for me Joe, I'll only be a minute.' He said.

Joe pushed the heavy door open for Archie, who carried the tray. A gust of wind caught the door as he passed. It struck his elbow causing him to tilt the tray. One of the mugs bounced gently off the sleeper bridge and landed with a 'plop' in the water.

'Man overboard!' He called to Joe, who had witnessed the mishap. 'Better go and confess to Jenny. I'll be back by the time you've turned your van round.'

Jenny saw him pass the kitchen window and opened the back door for him.

'I've just had a mishap, Jen,' he told her. 'The door blew shut on me as I came out of the mill and one of your mugs slid off the tray. It didn't look as though it had suicidal tendencies, but you can never tell with mugs!'

Jenny was smiling as she took the tray from him.

'It bounced off the bridge and landed in the water.' Archie explained.

'Did it break when it hit the bridge?' She asked.

'No, it survived the impact, but it splashed down into the water and sank without trace. It went down with all hands and colours flying, I'm afraid.'

Archie said this, head bowed and his hand on his heart.

Jenny laughed,

'Never mind, Archie,' she said. 'You can't beat bad luck and if that's the worst thing that happens today, we'll count ourselves most fortunate. Have you finished in the mill?'

Archie smiled, saying,

'Not so much finished as just, 'left off' for a while. Old Joe's got a problem, so I'll be at his place for an hour or two. I'm just going to let Elsie know where I am and then we're off. Joe's

70

waiting for me, so I won't keep him. Sorry about the mug, Jen, tell Reg to deduct it from my salary!'

Jenny waved to him as he passed by the kitchen window.

'I hope she didn't mind you losing her mug,' Joe asked as Archie got in the van.

'No,' Archie replied with a wink, 'They're both very nice people. Jenny wouldn't get upset if I'd dropped all the mugs in the stream. Archie went indoors to let Elsie know what was happening and picked up his camera on his way back out.

CHAPTER 11.

Joe turned the van around whilst he waited for Archie and then they drove up to the village.

'I thought we'd get a couple of pasties or something for a snack, before I go off to Petworth.' Joe explained. 'There's plenty of tea, coffee and milk at home, so you can help yourself whilst I'm out. Old Thunder will be pleased to have some company. He seems to have taken a real shine to you, Arch.'
Archie looked at Joe.

'Truth be told, Joe, he's just a big old softie. He'd be happy to have anyone make a fuss of him, wouldn't he?'
Joe nodded, saying,

'He is a gentle dog, Arch, but he's also very loyal. If anyone looks or sounds threatening, his hackles go up pretty quick. I think he'd have a go if anyone tried to attack whoever was with him.'

As they approached the bungalow, they saw two police cars parked outside. Two big tipper lorries were parked side by side, completely blocking the entrance to the site. Grover, of 'Tickners Transport', was standing in Joe's garden, shouting and waving at the driver of the lorry nearest to him.

'What's he doing?' Joe asked a surprised Archie.

'Can't be all that sure, Joe,' Archie replied, grinning. 'It looks like something between a fandango and a heart attack to me!'
Joe turned into his driveway and the two friends got out of the van. A policeman came towards them, he was smiling.

'Good afternoon, gentlemen,' he called. 'Would you like me to caution him for trespass, or just evict him from your property?'

'I think, just evict him, please.' Joe said, smiling.
Archie was beginning to enjoy the charade.

'What's going on, officer?' He asked.
The police constable came closer, to avoid having to shout.

'He's an irritating little man, isn't he?' He said to Joe.

'From what I can gather, he's upset his entire workforce and they've decided to stage a bit of a demonstration. Mr. Bettis can't get out in his car, so he telephoned this Grover chap. He turned up and began threatening the lorry drivers with the sack. That just made the situation worse. Now they're saying they'll lock their vehicles up and leave 'em there all the week-end, unless he apologises. Mr. Bettis called us, saying that he wants them prosecuted for obstruction. We explained to him that if we did as he asked, we would need to arrest them. He thought about it for a few seconds and I think he realised that would mean an even longer delay, so he changed his mind!'
Archie was laughing so much that it brought tears to his eyes.

'He called me a 'lackey', last time we met', he told the constable. 'Blessed if he don't look a bit of a sketch now and it's his bosom pal, Bettis, who's stuck behind the road block! Where is your colleague?'

'The officer who came with me is with Mr. Bettis, in his office,' he explained. 'He's trying to calm him down. He was almost as animated as this one, when we got here. I think I'd better tell him to leave your garden, now. We wouldn't want him having a heart attack on your property, would we?'

'I don't think we're especially bothered where he has it, to be honest. Whose is the other police car?' Archie asked.

'Oh, that's your local man, Bill Pickering. His panda car is in the garage, so he's got one of our spare patrol cars for a few days. He's chatting with the other driver in that lorry on the other side of the access road. I think Bill Pickering's probably our best chance of resolving this situation.'

The officer walked up behind the animated Grover and tapped him on the shoulder.

'I think you'd better leave this gentleman's property now sir,' he told him. 'You don't seem to be making much progress in calming this situation and this gentleman doesn't want you on his property.'

Grover turned to face the officer and began shouting at him,

'Get these bloody lorries moved. Use your authority, man. Don't just stand there chatting with the idle spectators!'

Joe was laughing now.

'We're not 'idle spectators, officer. We're legitimate spectators.' Joe called out. 'The lorries are of no concern to me. They're not on my property, but he is. I'd like you to tell him to leave immediately, please,' he asked the officer. 'He's not welcome here under any circumstances. He's a nasty, bad mannered little man.'

'Yes, I think it would be best if you leave now sir, before I have to arrest you,' the policeman told Grover.

'What could you arrest me for?' Grover asked, indignantly. 'What could you possibly charge me with?'

The officer turned to Archie and Joe, saying,

'He's not very happy with us, either. We issued him with a 'producer' on the way here. He had only one brake light. When we stopped him and did a quick check, we found that one of his headlamps wasn't working either and there's a split in one of his front tyres. He's got to get them all fixed and report to a police station within seven days!'

The officer walked across to where Grover was becoming even more excited. Archie heard him say,

'Right, that's quite enough, Mr. Grover. I've asked you once to leave this gentleman's property. Now I'm instructing you to leave this man's garden immediately.'

'And if I refuse, then what?' Grover shouted at him.

'That would not be in your best interests, sir. I would first have to arrest you and then you would be handcuffed and taken back to Chichelster Police station to be charged.'

'Oh, am I not the victim, here?' Grover protested loudly.

'Victim of your own arrogance and stupidity,' the lorry driver shouted. 'You're a devious and vindictive little man. All you care about is getting your own way, no matter who gets hurt in the process.'

'Right! That's enough,' said the officer. He took Grover's arm and began leading him away. 'You're not helping yourself by being abusive. Stop now or you'll both be arrested.' He roughly marched Grover back out onto the roadway.

'Now, I suggest you sit quietly in your car, sir, whilst we try to ease this situation. If you persist in your attempts to cause a breach of the peace, I will, make no mistake, arrest you.' Grover did as instructed, but not without further protest.

'I've got your number, officer. I'll be reporting this to the Watch Committee.'

'That is your prerogative, sir,' the PC. told him. 'Just leave us to try to resolve the situation. You have an industrial dispute on your hands, conversation, not confrontation is the best way forward.' He left Grover, sitting in his car and walked back to speak with Bill Pickering and the other lorry driver.

After a few more minutes, the driver with whom Bill had been speaking, drove his vehicle out of the access road and parked in the lay-by, just along the main road. He conversed briefly with the constable who had been with Grover and then spoke with his colleague on the radio. Archie heard him say,

'The access road is now clear. I suggest that anyone wishing to leave with a vehicle should do so now. I cannot guarantee that it will remain open indefinitely. There is an unresolved dispute between the drivers and the management of Tickners Transport. I strongly advise that the staff should take advantage of this brief concession and get their personal vehicles out, whilst they still can.'

The lorry driver got out of his vehicle and walked back from the lay by, to converse with his colleague. Grover attempted to intercept him as he walked past his car, but the constable closed his car door and held it firmly. In a loud voice, Joe and Archie heard him say,

'This is the last time I will warn you, Mr. Grover. If you so much as touch your driver's arm, it will constitute an assault and I will arrest you. Do you understand?'
Grover lowered his drivers window and asked,

'If you're now in control of the dispute, there's no point in my being here. I may as well go back to my office.'

'Yes sir, our officer appears to have calmed the situation. I think that would be a wise thing to do. Drive carefully sir.'

With a 'scrunch' of tyres, on the loose mud and gravel, Grover tore off down the road. The two lorry drivers began to laugh. The one closest to Archie and Joe, called out to them,

'Sorry about the upset gents, but he's a nasty little sod.'

The two friends moved closer to the lorry, so that he didn't need to shout. The driver continued,

'We just got fed up with the way he's treated our mate. The poor bugger's almost suicidal over hurting that lad, but Grover couldn't care less. He don't care about anyone else, just as long as he gets what he wants. It don't seem to matter to him that some poor lad could have been killed. All he's interested in is money and keepin' in with Bettis. He thinks they're mates, but Bettis is another one out of the same mould. He'll drop Grover whenever it suits him, they're both arseholes!'
Archie grinned mischievously,

'I think your blockade has closed the site for the rest of today. What made you decide to relent?'

76

'Well,' the driver said, 'we decided that it wasn't right to trap all the other workers on the site. We only wanted to get the message across to the managers, not punish the entire workforce.'

Joe and Archie went into the bungalow where Thunder gave Archie as big a welcome as Joe.

'I'll have a quick cuppa before I go,' Joe said. 'I'll eat my pastie on the way. I don't want to keep Stephen waiting. You can smoke in the kitchen Arch. You'll be able to watch the site better from there, anyway.'

'Don't worry about time, Joe,' Archie told him. 'Do you want me to feed Thunder whilst you're out?'

'You can give him a few of those shapes biscuits, if you like. He'll have his proper meal when I get back. Now, you know where everything is, don't you?' Joe asked. 'That's Stephen's number, just in case you need to contact me.'
He pointed to the notepad on the worktop above the fridge.
'I'd best be on my way now, thanks for this, Arch. I'll have to come again to get my tour of the mill, once this episode is done with.'

Joe left through the kitchen door. Archie saw him go past the window and heard the van start up. He poured himself another cup of tea and stood watching through the window. They had seen Bettis and a couple of others leave the site and watched as the last one secured the entrance gate. It was a tubular steel frame with a weldmesh screen, secured with a chain and a large padlock. The two lorries were still parked in the old lay-by. Archie opened the kitchen door and walked with Thunder, around to the front of the bungalow. They went over to the new section of fence, which looked good, but needed a coat of preservative. Archie saw the lorry driver with whom they had been chatting, walk back towards the gate. He noticed Archie, who was looking over the fence.

'They think that's it, but they're mistaken again,' he called to Archie. He produced a large padlock and proceeded to double lock the chain securing the gates.

'Just another little message for 'em,' he said. 'It'll take 'em a while to get the gates open on Monday. I've got the only key to that one and it's a Chubb. They'll have to cut their chain!'

Archie could not help laughing. He had taken an instant dislike to Grover and could imagine that he was not a nice man to work for.

'He'll maybe think twice before he starts threatening people again.' Archie observed. 'The way he was going on, I thought he was going to have a heart attack!'

'Couldn't be a more deserving case!' the driver retorted, with a twinkle in his eye. With a wave, he turned and walked back to his cab. Archie watched as both vehicles drove away and then he and Thunder returned to the kitchen. He poured himself another cup of tea and opened the kitchen door so that he could enjoy a smoke. Archie thought that he might have another look at the hole in the garden, so he lit his cigarette and strolled up towards Joe's workshop. He could see the whole of the site next door, over the fence. He stood watching for a few minutes until a movement caught his eye. There was still somebody there. They must be locked in, or perhaps they had left and then returned by another route. As he watched he saw a man come out of the little generator shed. He was carrying something which looked heavy. It was a large hessian sack. The man closed the shed door and looked around furtively. He picked up the sack and swung it over his shoulder. Archie let him get about half way across the open space of the site and then he called out.

'Excuse me!'

The man looked all around but failed to spot Archie, standing some twenty feet or so above him, in Joe's garden.

CHAPTER 12.

'Up here, in the garden.' Archie called to him.

'Oh, Mr. Skrobe,' the man called back to him. 'I was hoping to find you in but your van was gone. I need to leave these somewhere safe.' He indicated his sack, which he had now placed on the ground.

'I'm not Joe Skrobe, I'm Archie Leggitt,' Archie called back to him. 'Why don't you come down towards the front gates? The ground's more level there and the fence is lower.'

'Are you the police?'

'No, did you want the police?'

'No, no, I'll come down to the gates and explain, don't call the police. Is the dog safe or shall I wait until you shut him in?' Archie assured him that Thunder was safely in the house, he went on to say,

'I've got a cup of tea going cold in the kitchen, I'll drink that first and then we can talk.'

The man nodded and picked up the sack again.

'I'll wait for you, Mr. Leggitt, is Mr. Skrobe coming back later?'

'Yes,' said Archie. Give me a couple of minutes and I'll be down at the front.'

Archie was a bit puzzled by the man's willingness to show Archie and Joe, what the sack contained, but did not want the police to be told. He drank his tea, gave Thunder a pat and a couple of biscuits and then went down to the front corner of the garden. The man stood on the other side of the new fence, waiting for him. The ground here was only slightly lower than Joe's front garden.

'I'm Don Palmer,' he said, holding his hand up to the fence for Archie to shake. 'I'm pleased to meet you, Mr. Leggitt. I take it that you are a friend of Mr. Skrobe?'

'That's correct,' Archie told him as he reached over the fence to shake his hand. 'What's in the sack, Don?'

'Bones, Mr. Leggitt,' he said. 'I had to wait until everyone had left, before I could get them. I started to explain to Mr. Skrobe, but Bettis was watching me, so I had to stop. Did he mention anything to you about it?'
Archie thought for a moment, and then replied,

'Yes, I think he did, I believe he told me that you were supposed to put them back in the tunnel, and Bettis arranged an explosion to destroy them. Is that what happened?'

'It's what Bettis thinks happened,' said Don Palmer. 'He fired me today, so I shouldn't have been on the site just now. I'd hidden the sack of bones in the generator shed, so I had to get them out before Bettis found them. He said they were ancient, but some don't look ancient to me. I expect I'll be in trouble with the police for trespassing as well as withholding evidence, if that's what they turn out to be.'
Archie nodded that he understood.

'Why did he fire you, Don?' he asked him.

'He has written, 'insubordination' on the dismissal letter. He's a nasty bit of work and so's his boss, Davies, but he hasn't been around much just lately. There are things I could tell you that you'd find hard to believe and I'd have a hell of a job to prove. Steve Foggarty would probably bear me out, but I haven't seen him since he had his accident. I expect he's too scared to say anything now, in case he makes things worse for himself.'

Don Palmer appeared resigned to the fact that things could only get worse.

Archie thought for a moment and then he said,

'I've got an idea, which may help you to deal with this problem. Just listen for a minute or two, to what I'm proposing, before you make up your mind about it.'

Don Palmer looked him in the eye, saying,

'I'll listen to anyone who's willing to help me. I've lost my job all I've got is a bag of bones and some information which I'm frightened to use, in case it's refuted by the other victims.'

'Why don't you pass that sack up over the fence to me and then come round here and have a cup of tea, whilst we have a chat about it?' Archie suggested.

Don hoisted the sack up to the top of the fence, so that Archie could grab it. As he lifted it over the fence, he noted that it was not as heavy as he had thought. He took it with both hands and placed it gently on the grass.

'It'll be OK there for now, how will you get out of the site, Don?' He asked.

'I'll have to climb up the back, into the field and then walk round the road. It'll take me about five minutes,' He said.

Archie nodded his acceptance, and said,

'OK. I'll go and put the kettle on. Come round the back and tap on the kitchen door when you get here. Thunder will bark, but he'll be OK once he sees you're a friend. He's really a gentle old boy, but he barks loud enough to scare any intruders.' Archie assured him.

He went back into the house, filled the kettle and switched it on. As a precaution, he closed the door between the kitchen and the hallway, so that Don Palmer could get into the kitchen before the dog met him. He stood at the window, thinking about the best course of action. He saw Don as he reached the top of the slope and began walking along the field. A few minutes later he saw him pass the kitchen window and opened the back door for him.

'Come on in, Don, would you prefer tea or coffee?' he asked.

'I don't mind, a cup of coffee would be nice, thank you, milk and one sugar, please.' Don answered.

Archie made the drinks and then let Thunder into the kitchen to meet his guest. The dog sniffed Don, thoroughly and then stood with his tail wagging, waiting for a pat.

'He's a lovely old dog, isn't he?' Don remarked as he rubbed Thunder's head. 'Now, Mr. Leggitt, what do you suggest I should do?'

'Let's assess the situation,' Archie said. 'First, you can call me, 'Archie', not 'Mr. Leggitt'. Now, tell me more about these bones you found.'

Don began, slowly to explain the circumstances of the find.

'Well, the digger broke into a tunnel from the top and a large chunk of soil, chalk and mud fell down. As it hit the ground, it broke up a bit and I saw some bones mixed in with it. I stopped the digger driver and went to take a closer look. I had my rigger gloves on, so I started pulling the bigger bones out first. As I disturbed the lump of soil, I saw a skull and then some smaller bones and a jawbone. I went into the office and told Bettis what we had found and he came out and had a look. I said that we should phone the police, but he refused. He said that they were ancient bones from a Neolithic flint mine. He told me to put them in a sack and replace them in the tunnel which the digger had exposed. He told the blasting people to set a charge against the tunnel, and then clear the spoil. His words were, 'I'm not holding this job up for a few old bones'. I threw some rocks and a bit of soil into another sack and placed that in the hole. I hid the bones in the generator shed. Nobody else goes in there, except me. I have to keep it topped up with fuel every couple of days.'

Archie had been listening intently and now he asked,

'What's this information which you're afraid to use, Don?'

'Oh, that,' Don began, 'Firstly, Bettis has moved the whole footings four metres further back than the approved plans. This means that he has pinched about three metres of the field behind.'
Archie nodded, saying,

'That's easily checked, Don. I can arrange for a visit by the planning officer and the borough surveyor. You know who the land belongs to, don't you?'
Don knew the answer to that question,

'Its part of Houghton Farm, which is owned by Davies' father, but the field is let to a farmer named, Peter Bailey. I just kept all this to myself, because I didn't want to lose my job, but now that's happened, I suppose it doesn't matter. The only things that are worrying me are whether the police will take action against me and whether I may make Steve's situation worse. I know he's worried sick about that poor lad he injured. His mate told me that he's feeling so guilty about that, even more than about your friend's fence.'

'So that was a deliberate act, was it?' Archie asked.

'Whatever he says about that, we know that he was set up by Bettis and that evil little 'Hitler', Grover.' Don confirmed. 'They told the drivers that there was fifty pounds in it, if they caused enough damage to make Mr. Skrobe decide to sell up and go. Of course, when the police got involved, they denied all that. It all got worse when your friend got the court order today, to stop any further blasting. Bettis was worried in case the hole in the garden had thrown up some of the bones he thought he'd destroyed. That's why he wanted to inspect the damage, not to make any recompense for his actions, just to cover his arse!.'

'Is that why the drivers set up their blockade today?' Archie asked. 'Was it in support of their colleague? Perhaps they'll give evidence about the cash incentive to destroy Joe's property. That would make one less problem for you, Don, wouldn't it?'
Don nodded his agreement, but asked,

'How can I find out if they'll go that far? They may feel that it would cause a greater problem for Steve.'

'Hmm, I see what you mean,' Archie sympathised. 'I've got some friends in the police force, one is a detective Sergeant, would you mind if I had a word with him, to see what he thinks we should do?

'Well,' Don replied, 'I can't keep allowing it to drift on, like this, can I? Something's got to be done, even if I do get into more trouble for keeping quiet about the bones, when that forensics man asked me.'

'That was, 'Brian Pace', he's another member of the Chichelster force,' Archie told him. 'I don't think you'll be in too much trouble, if any at all. It depends on the age of the bones, I suppose. They may be ancient bones, but until they are examined by a forensic scientist, we won't know for sure, will we?'
Don Palmer looked thoughtful,

'I suppose you're right,' he agreed. 'So will you telephone your policeman friend and explain the circumstances?'

'I think that would be best,' Archie said. 'It would be best to do it now, so that they can get here in the daylight. Joe will probably be back soon, he's gone to Petworth to see his solicitor son-in-law.'

Archie made the call to Ian Stuart's mobile number. He had decided that this would save the possibility of being quizzed by the switchboard officer. Ian answered almost at once and listened whilst Archie briefed him. When he had heard Archie's latest information, he responded.

'Thanks, Archie, I'll find Brian Pace and we'll get to you as quickly as we can. Tell your, Mr. Palmer not to worry. We won't be taking any action against him. I can't say the same for his boss, but that will depend upon our findings. We'll be with you very soon, thanks for your help.' As an afterthought, Ian added, 'Good job you didn't leave it any longer, tomorrow's Saturday, Brian's day off.'
Archie replaced the phone and addressed Don Palmer.

'He said to tell you that they won't be taking any action against you, Don.' Archie explained. 'It will depend on their findings whether they will be questioning Bettis. Whatever the outcome regarding the age of the bones, they are classified as, 'human skeletal remains', which should have been reported to the police, not placed into a hole and blown to smithereens!'

Archie, still chuckling, returned his attention to his companion.

'Drink your coffee Don, before it goes cold. I just heard a car door slam, it's a bit too soon to be the police, I expect it will be Joe.'

Archie went to the front door and opened it. Joe was smiling as he came across the lawn to meet Archie.

'That all went very well, Arch,' he said. 'None of the people from the site are allowed to inspect the damage, until it has been checked and documented by a qualified surveyor.'

Archie nodded his approval,

'Well, we've got one of the former employees here already,' he said. 'His name's Don Palmer and Bettis sacked him today. He's brought the bones they found. They're in that sack by the fence.' Archie pointed towards the corner by the new section of fence. 'I've phoned Ian Stuart, he's coming over with a forensics officer presently. The kettle's just boiled, come in and I'll make you a cuppa, then you can fill me in on your progress with Stephen.'

Joe went into the lounge, where Don Palmer sat with his coffee. He stood up to greet Joe, holding out his right hand.

'Sorry about this, Mr. Skrobe,' he said. 'I'd already confided in you, but things sort of came to a head today and I didn't know what I should do. I didn't want Bettis to find the bones which I'd hidden, so after they'd all left, I got back into the site and retrieved them. I'm not sure what I was going to do with them, but your friend saw me and suggested that I brought them here. I hope you don't mind?'

Joe nodded to show that he understood.

'Archie usually gives good advice, Don,' he told him. 'I did half mention what you told me, to the detective and to Archie, this morning. I didn't mention your name, in case it got back to Bettis or Grover, but that's a bit of an academic detail now, I suppose. Let me get my cup of tea, Archie's poured it by now. I'm as dry as dust. All that talking without a drink can't be good for one.'

They went over the details again whilst they waited for the detectives to arrive. Joe explained that everything should be left exactly as it was, until the surveyor had completed his inspection and presented his report to Joe's solicitor. He was not all that surprised to hear that Bettis had extended the site beyond the boundary on the approved plans.

'That's a job for the planning officer and the borough surveyor,' he told them. 'We probably won't be able to get them here until Monday. These public officers don't like work, let alone week-end work!'

'I've refilled the kettle,' Archie said. 'I expect the policemen will be glad of a drink. We'll know a bit more, once they've had a look at the bones.'

'Will they be OK out there on the lawn?' Joe asked.
Archie's face creased into a smile as he replied,

'They've been buried in a load of soil, chalk and flint for several years, Joe. I don't s'pose a bit of damp grass is going to hurt 'em. In fact, it's probably the best they've been treated since they were found. What did you want to do with 'em? Bring 'em in and make 'em comfortable? P'raps they'd like a lie down on the settee!'

They were still laughing at the thought, when there was a knock at the door. Joe went to answer it and saw that it was Ian Stuart and another man, carrying a doctor's bag.

'Come in, gentlemen,' Joe said, smiling at Ian. 'Would you like a cup of tea or coffee, before you begin?'

'Thank you, but no,' Ian replied. 'I think we should take a look at the specimens first, or the light will be gone. Could you oblige us with a bucket of clean water? We'll need to get some of the dirt and soil off, before we can check them for age.'

The introductions completed, the whole group accompanied DS Brian Pace, to where the sack of bones had been left, by the front fence.

CHAPTER 13.

The Detectives began by collecting some equipment and evidence bags from the big Volvo estate, which was parked in Joe's driveway. A large canvas sheet was placed on the grass, close to where the sack lay.

'I must ask you gentlemen not to stand on the sheet, please.' Brian said to them all. 'The first thing will be to try to establish whether there are any more recent bones here, or whether, as our Mr. Bettis unilaterally decided, they are all ancient flint miners' remains.'

He carefully began to empty the sack, onto the sheet. The first object which emerged was a skull, minus the jaw bone. This almost rolled onto the sheet, it still contained some soil and flint fragments. Brian carefully picked it up in his gloved hand and using a new paintbrush, began to gently clean a small area.

'The jawbone is in there, as well,' Don volunteered.

'Yes, thank you,' said DS Pace. 'We'll get to it all in due course, but I need to establish which of these skeletal remains, if any, are more recent.'

Small particles of soil, chalk and flint were falling from the skull, as the DS gently cleaned it with water and the soft brush.

'What's that?' Archie asked, pointing at a small, rounder piece of debris.

The DS looked up at Archie.

'What are you pointing at?' He asked him.

Archie leaned forward to point more precisely.

'That bit, there,' he said. 'It doesn't look the same as the other bits of soil.'

The DS carefully picked it up. He drew in a sharp breath, through his teeth and announced,

'It looks remarkably like a bullet, a point 22 rifle bullet, to be precise. Did it fall out of the skull, Archie?'

'Yes, I saw it bounce off that piece of flint,' Archie confirmed.

'Thank you,' said DS Pace, 'now for the moment of truth.'

He took a small battery powered torch from his bag.

'This, is an ultra-violet wand,' he explained. 'Bones aged up to about forty years old, will glow in ultra- violet light. The newer the bones, the brighter the glow will be. It's not as accurate as the lab tests, but it is a good basic indicator for this sort of thing.'

He shone the light onto the small area which he had cleaned.

'There,' he said to the spectators, 'can you see that?'

There was a reflective glow from the skull. He looked directly at Don Palmer and asked.

'Were there any other witnesses to your find, Mr. Palmer?'

'Yes,' Don replied. 'Mike Maylam, the digger driver and one of the lorry drivers. I think it was the one who had the accident.'

'Well,' said DS Pace, looking at Ian Stuart. 'We'd better see if we can get a couple of statements from them. It's now pretty obvious to me, that Mr. Bettis is not the expert he believes himself to be. I'd say that this particular sample has been dead and buried for approximately twenty five to thirty years. It also seems likely that whoever it was has been shot by somebody who owned or had access to a point 22 rifle. At best it could be an accident, or at worst, possibly even a murder.'

He tilted the skull to look at the teeth. Another small bullet fell onto the canvas sheet. They all saw it this time and looked enquiringly at the DS.

'One bullet may have been an accident, two bullets in the same skull, must have been deliberate. I'll have an evidence bag, please, Ian. The skull and all the various debris which fell from it will be 'material evidence number one'. There are some labels in my bag, have you got a biro?'

'Yes,' Ian told him, grinning, 'I never go anywhere without one'

Next out of the sack were a couple of longer bones. These were cleaned by the same method. Just a small area, but enough to check with the UV torch, DS Pace looked up at the row of expectant faces.

'No need for the light on this one,' he said. ''It is so badly pitted and soft, that I can immediately classify it as 'ancient'. The local archaeological group may be interested, but not the police.'

'Should Bettis have notified the police?' Don asked.

'The short answer is 'yes',' Ian replied. 'Don't worry we'll be having a word with Mr. Bettis. The site will be closed until we've carried out a full and thorough examination. It is now technically a 'crime scene', so he will have no powers to go against that decision.'

Archie looked at Ian Stuart and asked,

'I suppose we'll have to treat this as confidential?

Brian Pace looked at his colleague and said,

'I don't think there's any need for secrecy now. Do you, Ian? The site is now officially a crime scene. It will be cordoned off with police Crime Scene tape and we'll have to have a uniform here to keep people out. I'm sure one of the local 'hacks' will soon pick up on it. It will probably be in the local news later tonight, or tomorrow. All I would suggest to you all is that you don't volunteer any information to the media. They can be very good at putting words into your mouth, when they can't get a

straight answer. We will put out a statement indicating that excavations at the site of a local development have revealed some human remains. I think we'll probably state that forensic evidence indicates that the victim was murdered.'
Brian looked to his colleague for confirmation.

'I think it'll go something like that, Brian,' Ian agreed.
He turned to Archie, Joe and Don, saying,

'Just make sure you're not quoted as having said anything speculative. I'm sure we'll have enough of that from Bettis and his cronies, but we'll be having them in very soon, as the saying goes, 'helping us with our enquiries'!'

'I'm not going to say a word,' Don stated emphatically.
'I really think I'd like to remain anonymous, if you don't mind.'
Ian smiled at him,

'Don't worry, Don, you won't be mentioned in any of our output to the media. We're just grateful to you for reporting your find and preserving the evidence.'

CHAPTER 14.

It was a little after four when Archie arrived home. He began to tell Elsie about his day. He put his hand into his jacket pocket and felt the slip of paper which Ian Stuart had given him this morning.

'Perhaps I should try to telephone old Bob,' he thought. 'I expect he'll be surprised to hear my voice after all this time.'
He told Elsie what Ian had said this morning.

'Well, Arch, he obviously wanted to get in touch with you, so why not phone him now?'
Archie went out into the hall and picked up the phone, there was a clean sheet on the telephone pad and the biro lay on top. He dialed the number, a female voice answered.

'Greenbanks Nursing Home, can I help you?'
Archie thought perhaps he was disturbing a routine, he said,

'I'm sorry to trouble you, but I have been asked to contact Mr. Bob Jempson. I'll understand if it's not convenient just now.'

'Are you a relative of Mr. Jempson?' She asked.

'No, just an old friend, my name is, Archie Leggitt, would you like me to spell it for you?'
The lady asked him to repeat his name, which he did.

'Just a moment please, Mr. Leggitt, I'll see if Mr. Jempson wishes to speak with you. Can you hold the line for me?'

'Yes, thank you, I'll wait,' Archie replied.

A couple of minutes passed and he heard Bob's voice,

'Hello, Arch, I'm so grateful that you phoned me, I've been waiting to hear from the police at Chichelster for several days.' Archie noticed that Bob's voice sounded tired and he seemed a little breathless. Archie asked him,

'How are you, old Bob? You sound a bit tired, would you prefer if I phoned tomorrow?'

'No, no,' Bob said emphatically. 'I need your help, Arch. Can you come to see me tomorrow? It's all a bit difficult over the phone. I really need to talk with you in complete confidence.'

'Yes, I expect I can do that,' Archie told him. 'But you'll need to give me the full address, where is the nursing home, Chichelster?'

'Lord, no,' Bob said. 'It's in Salvington, just this side of Worthing. Do you know it?'

'I know of it, Bob,' Archie said. 'Give me the address and tell me what time I should get there. Is there a private room which we could use?'

Bob gave him the full address and some rough directions to find the home. When Archie had read it all back to him, Bob said,

'There is a private room here, but I was hoping perhaps we could find a pub somewhere. Maybe we could have a spot of lunch, my treat. The best time to get here would be after about ten thirty, can you manage that alright?'

Elsie had heard bits of the conversation and came out to where Archie was standing. She looked at what he'd written on the pad, and tapped him on the arm. He looked round at her as she nodded her approval of his visit.

'Elsie's here now, Bob, so the answer to your question is, 'yes'. I'll see you between ten thirty and eleven, tomorrow. Take care, Bob.'

'Thanks Arch,' he said. 'You've taken a load off my mind already. Bye for now, old friend.' He hung up.

'Had you got any plans for tomorrow?' Archie asked Elsie, when he had finished his phone call.

'Why? I hadn't planned anything, but you don't need me to come with you, do you?' She asked him. 'I don't really know Bob, only from years back when I used to buy a few bits from the farm shop. The twins both trained at Chichelster General. Hannah actually worked on my ward, when I was the Senior Sister there. They both moved on after they qualified with their S.R.N's.'
Archie thought for a minute or two before replying.

'No, I don't mind if you wanted to come,' he said. 'I'll leave here at about ten. That should give me time to find the place and park somewhere close to it.'

'I expect there's a car park at the home, Arch.' Elsie said. 'They wouldn't expect their patients to walk to the nearest car park. Most of them will be either sick or frail.'

'Yes, Else, you're right, of course,' he said, adding in an undertone, 'as usual!'.
The pair of them went back into the lounge. Archie found a street map of Salvington and Elsie switched on the television.

CHAPTER 15.

Houghton Farmhouse, Houghton Lane,
Wigglesworth W. Sussex.

At nine fifteen on Saturday morning, Jason Davies poured
himself a cup of coffee and sat down in his favourite armchair.
He had celebrated his seventy-eighth birthday the previous
evening and was feeling slightly overhung. He had heard the
front door bell as he sat down, but decided that whoever it was
would soon go away if he left it unanswered.
A few minutes later, he thought he saw a shadow pass his front
window.

'I thought they'd give up if there was no answer,' he said to
himself.
He pressed the remote control for the television thinking that he
would catch the Southern TV headlines at nine-thirty. It had been
good to see a few old friends last night. His son, Jeffery had been
there, but as usual, he wanted help with a problem. His mistake
was always that he didn't think before he acted. It seemed to
Jason that he was following in his father's footsteps. He had the
same illogical approach when he was younger and each time he
lost his temper, he found himself in more trouble than he could
handle.

'I suppose he'll learn, one of these days,' Jason thought. 'I don't believe he went all the way up to Lincoln, to get arrested for assault.'

He sipped his coffee, decided that he'd like another and took his cup through to the kitchen. On the way, he noticed an envelope stuck in the letterbox on the front door. He put his cup on the hall table and went to the door to collect the envelope. He opened the front door to look out at the weather. He looked at the doorstep and froze!

It was one of Mary's.

His cleaner would be here soon, she mustn't see it. He grabbed the suitcase and pulled it into the house. Jason looked left and right outside for any sign of movement. There was nothing!

'Don't panic!' he told himself. 'It can't stay here, but where?' Jason looked at the envelope he had pulled from the letterbox. The postmark was 'Brighton and Hove' but the date stamp was, 22nd September 1966!

A shiver ran down his spine.

'It wasn't delivered by the postman,' he thought. 'He won't be here until lunchtime on a Saturday.'

Jason stood in the hallway and heard the television sound the gongs for the TVS news update.

'West Sussex police have confirmed reports that human remains have been uncovered during excavations for a spa hotel, near Wigglesworth. The spokesperson has indicated that initial forensic tests indicate that the victim was murdered. A number of people are assisting the police with their enquiries.'

Davies felt very unwell. He poured a brandy to calm himself down.

'That bastard, Gorse' Jason said aloud. He looked at Mary's suitcase on the hall floor. Cathy, his cleaner would be here soon. Jason picked it up and hurried through the back door with it.

'The log store,' he decided. 'Nobody ever goes there.'

He tripped on the back steps and let go of the handle. The case bounced end over end down the six steps to the yard. The stitching along one edge had split and several garments were visible through the gap. Jason pushed them back and picked up the case. It was heavier than he remembered, or was he not feeling so fit as when he and Gorse had packed it. The yard was muddy. He slipped a couple of times and almost fell down. Jason reached the log store and began to move some of the logs, to make a space at the back. He was sweating profusely as he worked, the pile of logs built up behind him. He had reached the back wall at the top of the store. The five foot length of six inch diameter black plastic soil pipe was visible. It was fastened horizontally to the back wall. This is where he had hidden his rifle when Gorse had left.

'Damn you, Gorse' he said aloud, looking at the suitcase. 'I'll get some gloves before I get the rifle,' he thought. 'It must still have his prints on it.'

Jason walked back towards the house. Cathy was standing at the bottom of the steps, holding the letter which he had dropped on the hall floor.

'Good morning Mr. Davies,' she called. 'I just found this on the - my goodness, are you alright? You look terrible. Have you had an accident?'

She came towards him, her arms outstretched to help.

'I think you'd better come inside and sit down for a while, look how you're sweating. Perhaps you have the flu. I'll make you a fresh coffee and then I think we'd better call the doctor.'

'No, no, doctor, I'm fine, Cathy. I've been moving some wood, that's all. I just came in to wash my hands and get an old pair of gloves.'

'You have a sit down for a few minutes,' she insisted. 'I'll come and help you with the wood. We don't want you having a heart attack, do we?' Cathy gripped his elbow and almost pushed him up the steps to the back door.

'Just look at those muddy boots,' she admonished. 'Sit on that kitchen chair and I'll take them off. The place will be in a state if you walk through the house with them on.'

Jason could feel his anxiety rising. Damn this woman, why was she always so concerned for him? Why couldn't she just leave him alone and mind her own business?

'I'm fine, Cathy, really,' he said. 'Now where's that letter you found?'

She put her hand into the pocket of her cardigan,

'Here it is,' she handed it to him. 'You can sit and read it while I make you some fresh coffee.' Cathy turned her back on him and busied herself on the worktop.

Jason opened the letter. A single sheet of paper with today's date and a typed note,

£10K BY MONDAY 12TH.
SECOND CASE AND KEY TO DEPOSIT BOX.
I WILL CALL AT 12.00 L.G.

Jason's face went white. He folded the sheet and replaced it in the envelope. His hands were shaking, he felt sick.

'Here you are, Mr. Davies,' Cathy handed him the cup and saucer. His hands shook so much he could scarcely hold it.

'Thanks Cathy,' he mumbled. 'I'm feeling better now. I was a bit puffed when I came in. Don't let me stop you with your work. I'll just sit and drink this and then go back to my wood. I'll work a bit slower now you're here. I was trying to get it done before you arrived.'

'O.K. Mr. Davies, if you're sure you're going to be alright. I'll do upstairs first and then sort the washing for the machine.'

For the first time since he opened his front door, Davies felt a little relief. He still had to hide the case and get the rifle. He thought to himself as he reflected on the note.

'Who does he think he is? 'I'll call at noon', indeed!

Be like bloody 'high noon', Mister clever, Gorse. You'll be surprised what an old man can still do.'

He heard Cathy moving about upstairs, so decided to finish hiding his wife's suitcase. He put his boots back on, picked up a pair of gloves and went back out to the log store. He decided to hide the case first, so pulled more logs out until he had enough room at ground level. When he had hidden the suitcase under he logs, he reached around and put his gloved hand into the end of the pipe. It must have been put in from the other end, he couldn't feel it. Jason moved along to reach the other end of the pipe and put his hand in to feel for the weapon.

It had gone!

'Damn that man!' he said out loud. 'Gorse must have taken it. This is not good. Now, he probably thinks he's got the upper hand again.'

Jason 'Diddler' Davies was not having a good day. He tidied the logs as best he could and went back into the house. He took his boots off at the back door, leaving them on the step. The television was still on. The eleven o'clock news update again mentioned the lad who had been knocked over on Thursday. The police report was repeated, verbatim, but nothing further.

Cathy came back downstairs with a bundle of clothes for the washing machine.

'Are you feeling better now, Mr. Davies?' she asked.

'Much better, thank you, Cathy, I think I was just trying to be too quick.'

'Shall I make another coffee?' she asked. 'Whilst you were outside, your son phoned. He's at the police station and wanted to ask you something. I said you were busy, and he asked if you would phone him on his mobile. The number is on the pad, by the phone.'

Jason's blood pressure was at maximum, now it seemed he had more trouble to deal with.

'I'll phone him when I've had my coffee.' He told her 'Thank you for your concern earlier Cathy, but I feel much better now. I don't like to bother the doctor with trivialities, especially on a Saturday.'

CHAPTER 16.

It was a pleasant morning for a drive. Archie took his time but still arrived at the nursing home twenty minutes early. He locked the car, rolled himself a cigarette and went for a short stroll. It was a very nice area. Some of the larger houses were most impressive with sweeping drives and well kept gardens. He returned to Greenbanks Nursing home at a little after ten-thirty A smartly dressed young lady met him in the hallway.

'Excuse me,' she said. 'Are you by any chance, Mr. Leggitt?'

'I am,' Archie replied. 'I'm here to see Mr. Jempson.'

'Would you like to follow me, I'll show you to his room?' she offered.

Archie noted the plush décor and the quality carpet. Bob's room was the third on the left. The lady knocked his door and Bob called out,

'Please come in. Is that my friend, Archie Leggitt?'

The lady smiled at Archie and opened the door. Bob was sitting in an easy chair, he looked tired and considerably older than Archie had imagined. Bob got to his feet and welcomed him, saying,

'Archie, thanks so much for coming, I lost your address and phone number when I moved to my sisters. The twins are now thirty-nine years old, but still provide me with a few worries.'

'It's good to see you, Bob,' Archie replied. 'Would you like to chat here, or go out somewhere?'

'I thought we'd have a cup of tea, here and then perhaps we could go to the Pipemakers Arms, it's a nice little pub and they do a decent lunch at a reasonable cost. Will that suit you or do you need to get back?' He asked Archie.

Archie took a seat next to Bob and told him,

'I'm not in any hurry. Elsie sends her regards, by the way. I'm happy to go along with whatever you want, Bob.'

Bob pressed his call switch and a young girl knocked at the door and entered.

'You called, Mr. Jempson. Can I get you anything?' she asked.

Bob smiled at her,

'Sarah, this is my friend, Archie, from Wigglesworth, where I used to live. Now, I've told you to call me, 'Bob', so just because I have a visitor, there's no need to be formal.'

The girl blushed slightly,

'Sorry Bob, but Miss Collins told me to call you, 'Mr. Jempson' because you had an important visitor.'

Bob smiled at her and Archie and said,

'Sarah, we're all important, Miss Collins is right to tell you to respect the guests, but now we've introduced ourselves, we can defer to our first names. Is that OK with you, Archie?'

'Absolutely fine, I'm pleased to meet you, Sarah.' He said.

'Well, Sarah,' Bob continued, 'do you think we could have some tea, please? We'll be going out for a while later on, but we'd like to sit and have a catch up chat before we go.'

Sarah smiled, Archie guessed she was about eighteen or twenty years old. She was a very attractive young lady and seemed to be naturally friendly.

'No problem, Bob,' she said. 'I'll see to it now. You will be sure to let us know where you're going, won't you?'

'I can tell you that now, Sarah,' said Bob. 'We'll be at the Pipemakers, in the village and I won't be requiring lunch today.'

Sarah nodded her approval,

'I think that's a good idea, Bob, you deserve a treat. I wish I could join you, it's a nice pub. I sometimes go there with my boyfriend. The food's good and its not too expensive.' Sarah smiled at them both and left.

Bob settled back in his chair and began telling Archie his concerns.

'Both of the girls are still nursing. Hilda is in Lincoln and Hannah was with her until a month ago. You know she married that Jeffery Davies? Well she finally got sensible and left him at the end of September. He was as nice as pie when they married, but he gradually began to get more like his father. He coerced me into changing my will, to an equal three way split between the twins and him. When Hannah found out, she left him. It won't be a fortune, Arch, but there's the house and the money I got from the sale of the business, so it amounts to about four hundred thousand altogether.'

Archie raised his eyebrows,

'I'd say that was a fortune for some people, Bob. Does he still have a claim to a third of it?'

Bob stroked his chin, thoughtfully before replying.

'Let me tell you what happened. I had a heart attack two years ago, Arch. They got me into hospital in time and I had a triple by pass operation. That stabilised me from a physical point of view, but it made me think about life a bit more deeply. I changed my diet and took some gentle exercise. I lost a couple of stone, which they said was good, but there was still an underlying problem. I've not been good these past few months, so I booked myself in here. My sister died last year, and she left me her house, but about half of the value went in death duties.'

There was a knock at the door and Sarah arrived with a tray of tea and biscuits. She set the tray on a low table and asked,

'Would you like me to pour, Bob?'

'Yes, please, Sarah. No sugar for me but I believe Archie likes a couple.' He raised his eyebrows enquiringly.

Archie nodded,

'Yes please, Sarah. I'd like two spoonfuls and a little milk. Thank you very much.'

She poured two cups and handed them to Bob and Archie.

'If there's anything else you need, just ring,' she said to Bob. 'I'll be working in the kitchen today, so it's no trouble.' She left the room, closing the door quietly.

The two friends sipped their tea, Bob said,

'She's a very nice young lady, Arch. I think she's the niece of the owner, Paula Collins. Paula used to be the matron of the old cottage hospital. She took this place when they closed it in1983. She has a brother who is a surgeon at Chichelster General. I think he has helped her a bit on the financial side.'

Archie smiled,

'Was it Miss Collins who showed me in?' he asked.

'Yes, Arch,' said Bob. 'She's a very professional lady, all the residents admire her. However, you haven't come all this way to find out about the staff at the nursing home!' He laughed.

'Now, where did I get to? Oh yes, on the seventh of October, Jeff Davies found the flat in Lincoln, where Hannah had been living with her sister. He assaulted Hilda and threatened her with a knife. It transpired that the knife, a 'Stanley' knife had no blade, which reduced the charge to assault with menaces. One of Hilda's neighbours fortunately came to her aid and called the police.

To cut a long story short, Hilda phoned me and gave me all the details. Incidentally, Davies' case comes up in Lincoln, next week. Once Hilda had told me what happened, I went to another solicitor, one who was not known to Davies, and changed my will to exclude him as a beneficiary.'

Archie put his cup and saucer on the tray,

'Bob,' he said, 'pause for a minute and drink your tea, or it will be stone cold.'

'Yes, thanks, Arch,' Bob picked up his tea and began to drink. Archie waited 'til he'd finished and then began pouring a second cup for each of them. Bob sighed and took a deep breath,

'Now I'm coming to the crux of the matter, Archie. Davies still thinks he's entitled to a third of the legacy. I want to name you as one of the executors. His solicitor will try to fight the new will, but I'm told he won't succeed. What he'll probably try to do is get back at Hannah. I don't want her to get her share until after she has divorced him. You see, he could claim half, if they were still married. He's stolen her passport, to prevent her from leaving the country, but Hannah is made of some good stuff, Arch. Hilda wouldn't tell Davies where Hannah was, but she told me. Hannah is in Belgium, working in a local hospital.'

Archie sat up and asked,

'How did she get to Belgium without a passport?'
Bob smiled,

'Hilda has a passport, Arch. They're identical twins, remember, or to all outward appearances they are. Obviously, I know the difference, probably so does Davies, but the border agencies wouldn't.'

'So her employers think she's 'Hilda'?' Archie asked.

'No, they know that she is Hannah, she was only Hilda on the journey.
The problem now is that Davies has reported her missing, to the police. He's told them that she must be in the U.K. because she left her passport at home, when she went. The police now have her passport to use as an identity picture, so Hannah can't come back without getting into trouble.'

'Hmm, A tricky one,' Archie said. 'In fact, it's probably two tricky ones, Bob, the will and the passport.' He chuckled to himself.

'What's funny?' Bob asked.

'I was just thinking it would make a good title for a mystery thriller.' Archie continued in a mock theatrical tone, 'And now for your entertainment the latest blockbuster,

'The Will and The Passport' adapted from the novel by Bob Jempson, in glorious technicolour!'
This brought a smile to Bob's face, which had carried a worried look since he began his story.

'Starring the famous twins, Hannah and Hilda Jempson, of Lincoln and Belgium.' Archie added with a flourish.
Bob's face lightened as he suggested,

'I wonder, is there a part for Jeff Davies, the evil villain?'
Archie thought for a moment, then said,

'Maybe a past president of the U.S.A. wasn't he a, 'Jeff Davies'? We might even get his sidekick, Bettis, to play the part of General Lee?'
They both laughed loudly, which lifted the atmosphere.
There was a knock at the door,

'Come on in,' Bob called.
Sarah entered, seeing their faces, she smiled and asked,

'Is everything alright, Bob?'

. 'Yes and getting better by the minute, thank you, Sarah,' Bob told her. 'Would you like to take the tray back for us, please, and tell Miss Collins that we will be leaving shortly. I think we will be gone for an hour or two.'

'Thank you,' Sarah replied as she left the room. 'I hope you will both enjoy your lunch.'

Archie had been thinking and now made his suggestion.

'I've got an idea, Bob. You can change your will to add a condition or a codicil, to cover Hannah's inheritance. Your solicitor will explain if you tell him what the problem is.'
Bob looked at Archie with concern in his eyes,

'Arch, I can't keep changing my will every few days. They'll think I'm going senile.'
Archie replied,

'You can change it as often as you like, especially if there's a valid reason. In this case, it's that your soon to be, ex-son in law is putting pressure on a sick man, for his personal gain and greed.

I'll come with you if you want me to. Now, there is an easy solution to Hannah's problem.'

'Is there?' Bob asked, 'What do you think we should do about it then?'

'Let's just re-cap for a moment, Bob.' Archie said. 'You said that Davies had taken her passport, to prevent her from going abroad, correct?'

'That's right, Arch'
Archie continued,

'But now, Davies has handed it in to the police, so he hasn't got it any more. You say he's up in court in Lincoln next week, so he won't be here, will he?'

'No, he can't be in two places at the same time and if the police are watching him, he'd be foolish to try to hurt her.'

'Can you contact Hannah, in Belgium?' Archie asked.
Bob shook his head, he thought for a moment, then said,

'I can't, but Hilda probably can, shall I try her number now? What were you going to suggest, Arch?'

'About fifteen years ago, when Hannah was a staff nurse at Chichelster General, Elsie was her ward sister. So she knows her and I would guess that she trusts her. If you can contact Hannah and tell her to come back in the next day or so, she can collect her passport from the police. They don't need to know she has been to Belgium. She can stay with us, we have a spare room. Davies won't know she's there. Once she has her passport, she can return legitimately to her job in Belgium, if that's what she wanted to do. What do you think she'll say to that, Bob?'
The smile returned to Bob's face.

'I think I'll phone Hilda and then treat you to a pint and some lunch,' he said.

CHAPTER 17.

The mobile vibrated in Jeffery Davies' pocket. He ignored it.
At Chichelster Police Station, he was being interviewed by DI
Tony Church and DS Ian Stuart.
Tony Church began,

'Thank you for coming in so promptly, Mr. Davies. We'll try
not to keep you for too long.'

'I understand, Inspector, you have your job to do and I have
mine. You mentioned that you also wished to speak with Martin
Bettis. I called to pick him up on my way here, but there was
nobody at home.'

'Thank you for trying, don't worry about it, we'll go to his
home later. Perhaps they went shopping or something.'

'Yes, probably, I think Elaine has her hair done on a Saturday
morning, I expect Martin has to wait for her.'
The DI continued,

'Can we get you a coffee or anything, before we begin?'
Davies shook his head,

'No thank you, I'm fine. Let's just get to why you wanted me
to come in.'

'OK Mr. Davies,' the DI continued,

'Well, this is an informal interview. You are not under arrest, but we need you to answer some questions in connection with events at your construction site. Can you explain your involvement in the attempts to hide or destroy the human remains which were found at your construction site this week?'

'I had no involvement with anything of that nature, whatsoever.' Davies lied.
DS Stuart then said,
'Are you also aware that these remains were discovered at a distance of some twenty feet beyond the approved boundary of the construction site?'

'No, but it doesn't matter, the land belongs to my father, Mr. Jason Davies.'

'That land is the subject of a tenancy agreement, between your father and the tenant farmer, Mr. Peter Bailley. As the law stands, neither you, nor your father, have any right to trespass on it.' Ian told him.

'I can go wherever I like on my father's land,' said Davies truculently.

'I can assure you that you are wrong in that assumption, Mr. Davies.' Ian continued. 'But that is not the issue we need to discuss at this juncture.'

'May we continue, please?' The DI asked. 'We have a very busy morning ahead of us and I'm sure we'd all rather be doing something else.'

'Well, let's stop now and all go home,' Davies said with a sneer.
Tony Church was getting a little tired of this charade.

'Mr. Davies,' he said, 'you are not under arrest, you are merely helping us with our enquiries. I would not normally wish to arrest you at this stage, but since you seem to be treating this enquiry frivolously, I am prepared to make an exception in your case. Now, I'll ask you once more, do you wish to co-operate with us or not?'

Davies appeared to realise that he was not doing himself any favours. He nodded his head in the affirmative.

'Yes, OK' said Davies. 'I will co-operate with you. You're right, inspector, we would all rather be somewhere else.'

'Thank you,' said Tony. 'Now will you please tell us what your response was to Mr. Bettis' telephone call to you on Thursday, when he told you that they had found some bones?'

'I thought they were probably animal bones, so I told him to bag them up and put them in the tunnel which they had just exposed.' Davies told them. 'When he said they looked as though they might be human, I said they were probably bones of a Neolithic flint miner. There are a lot of these old flint mines around here, it wouldn't be the first time relics of bones and deer antlers have been found.'

'Are you an expert at discerning the age and origin of bones and human remains?' The DI asked.

Davies looked a little flustered, as he replied,

'No, but they're only old bones, aren't they? There's no point in making a fuss about them. The best thing to do is just forget about them, they don't mean anything.'

'Perhaps the bones of the dead don't mean anything to you, Mr. Davies, but I can assure you that we are always interested in the discovery of human remains. Were you aware that some of these human remains have only been in the ground for thirty years?' DS Ian Stuart asked.

Davies looked surprised, he asked,

'How can you be sure of that?'

'We have something called, 'forensic science', Mr. Davies. We can date human remains to within five or ten years. We can also determine whether the remains are male or female and at what age they became deceased.'

Davies shrugged,

'So what do you know about these bones at the site?' He asked.

'We'll come to that, all in good time,' the DI said. 'But for the moment, please allow us to ask the questions. Why did you feel it necessary to set a blasting charge to destroy them?'

Davies thought for a moment before replying.

'I don't remember telling anyone to set a charge. I know I told him to bag them up and place them in the tunnel. Maybe it was Martin's idea to set a charge. Because Palmer had to stick his nose in and disobey Bettis' orders, we've got all this unnecessary hassle. If it wasn't for that, we wouldn't be here now, arguing about it, would we?'

DS Stuart shook his head in disbelief.

'There is no guarantee of that,' he told Davies. 'The blast sent bits of hessian, some bones and deer antler, up through one of the old mine shafts into Mr. Skrobe's garden. Were you aware of that?'

'No,' he said.

Ian continued,

'Are you aware that the discovery of human remains should always be reported to the police? Were you also aware that an audible warning must be sounded prior to blasting and that the area must be cleared of all personnel except those licensed to handle explosives?'

Davies shrugged and said,

'I suppose a lot of it is common sense, but I didn't know it was law.'

DI. Church then asked him.

'Your site manager, Martin Bettis should have been aware of the legal requirements with regard to health and safety and duty of care. As the site manager he should also have sufficient knowledge of the building regulations, to prevent loose spoil becoming a danger to persons working in the vicinity.

All of these areas are his direct responsibility, as the site manager. What are his qualifications, Mr. Davies?'

Davies looked uncomfortable as he tried to answer,

'Martin Bettis was the site foreman when I had my house built. He was very efficient and seemed to know all the right people. I don't think he has any formal qualifications as a site manager, but he can control a project. He keeps a discipline with the workforce and arranges deliveries of materials and equipment. I have had no problems with him, to date and believe that he has acted in the best interests of maintaining the build schedule.'

'Even if that has included breaking the law or putting his own interpretation on your instructions,' DI Church added.
He made a few notes and then looked up at Davies,

'Thank you, Mr. Davies, I think that's all for now but we may need to speak with you again, when we have more details from our forensics department.'
Davies nodded, but told him,

'I'll be away on business for a couple of days, next week. Shall I give you my mobile number, in case you need to contact me? I was also wondering if you had made any progress in locating my wife, Hannah?'

'We're still in the process of searching for her, Mr. Davies.' The DI said. 'Our colleagues in Lincoln are going to try to contact her sister in the next day or so. We'll let you know if there are any developments. We have her passport here, so any leads can quickly be checked against that. Thank you for your time, today. I hope you will enjoy what's left of the week-end.'
The detectives stood and Ian opened the door to show Davies out.

'Cup of coffee, and then we'll see if we can find this Bettis character.' Tony said. 'We'll see what we can draw out of him, if anything. Perhaps he's home now.'

CHAPTER 18.

Archie arrived home at around two o'clock, to find Joe Skrobe's van parked outside his house. He put the car in the garage and locked up. Elsie had heard him and was waiting at the kitchen door.

'We'd almost given up on you, Arch,' she said. 'Joe's been here for almost an hour. How was Bob?'

'I'll tell you all about it presently,' he said. 'Any chance of a cuppa, I'm as dry as dust.'

He went in and greeted Joe, as Elsie made a pot of tea.

'I've got some news for you, Arch,' Joe told him. 'Here's a copy of the letter Stephen has written to Tickners and he's written this one to Davies and copied it to the planning department at Arun District Council. There's a copy of the surveyor's report to go with it.'

'That's good, Joe,' Archie said. 'Give us a few minutes and I'll have a look. I just want to tell Elsie what happened at Bob's.' Archie hung up his jacket and went back into the kitchen to talk with Elsie.

'Joe,' she called out. 'Would you like another cup of tea, I've just made a fresh pot.'

'Yes, thanks Elsie,' Joe replied. 'I'll wait until Arch has finished telling you about his visit to Bob Jempson, then I'll tell you both what's happening in my neck of the woods.'

Archie explained about Hannah and that Davies had threatened Hilda at her flat in Lincoln.

'He's up in court on Wednesday on an assault charge, so he won't be around here. Bob's going to have a chat with Hilda, so he'll let us know what's happening after that.'

'So we may have a house guest for a few days next week?' Elsie said. 'It will be good if they can work it out. I always liked Hannah, when she was at the hospital with me. Hilda is probably very much like her, but she worked on a different ward, so I didn't see her very much. Oh, well, we'll see what happens after Bob's phoned. I hope it all works out fine for her. That Jeffery Davies sounds as though he's a bit like his father, a very nasty, spiteful man.' Elsie thought for a moment and then asked, 'Have they said any more about the bones they found?'

'Not as far as I know,' Archie told her. 'I think the DI is taking a keen interest in the whole situation. Tony Church doesn't like bullies, so he won't be taking prisoners.'

Archie picked up the tray with the tea, milk and sugar on it.

'Come on Else, let's go and hear what old Joe's got to tell us.' They went into the living room, where Joe stood looking out of the window.

'I'll pour, whilst you read Joe's letters, shall I?' Elsie suggested.

'Yes, thanks, Else,' Archie said. 'Now, Joe, let's have a look at Stephen's handiwork.'

The first one gave Tickners twenty eight days to settle the account for damage to the fence. It stated that failure to do so would result in a prosecution for criminal damage. The letter also stated that further evidence of this would be made available by the police and other independent witnesses.

Archie passed the letter back to Joe.

'I'd love to be a fly on the wall, when Mr. Grover opens that,' Archie said with a twinkle in his eye.

Joe smiled.

'Now here's the best bit,' he said, as he passed the second letter to Archie.

Archie read the letter first. It made a number of references to the enclosed surveyor's report, which he studied for several minutes. Archie finally looked up at Joe and said,

'So, the site is classed as a quarry? That must be what makes it subject to these extra regulations.'

'Yes,' Joe answered. 'Stephen phoned the borough surveyor yesterday. He was very helpful and he's coming out on Monday to do an official inspection. He told our surveyor to press for a cessation of works, on the grounds that the slopes to the adjoining land had been left in an unstable state. That's a Health and Safety Executive dictat. Whilst he's here, he will inspect the damage to my land and the subsidence of my foundations.'

Archie nodded,

'I've just read that bit. The letter also says that they must remove all plant and materials from the former farm shop site. What about repairing the greenhouse? I s'pose they could say that you can't prove it was damaged by them?'

'They can say that,' Joe said. 'It won't do them any good though. I've got it all on video tape. I've also got some footage of them entering the old farm shop shed and fitting a new padlock to it.'

'I s'pose they'll get these letters on Monday,' Archie said. 'That gives us tonight and tomorrow to get your stuff back from the farm shop. They'll be pretty mad when they find they've got to build retaining walls against your garden and the field, before they can continue with their project.'

'Stephen has also contacted Peter Bailley and advised him to re-negotiate the lease,' Joe said. 'He's lost almost half an acre and Stephen told him it would be dangerous to go too near to the excavated section, especially on a heavy tractor.'

'I think I'll come down tonight,' Archie said. 'You can watch me through your window, with your lights off, to be on the safe side. I'll just go in and get your bits back, if they get upset and spiteful about it afterwards, it won't matter.'

Joe thought for a moment,

'Wouldn't it be better to do it in the daylight?'

'No,' Archie said. 'When it's dark, you can see the headlights of any vehicles coming in. I don't want anyone surprising me whilst I'm in the farm shop looking for your stuff. You can keep a lookout from your house and call me on my mobile if anyone is coming. Once I'm in there, I'll pull the door shut until I've found your stuff. I can just walk back with it and they won't even know I've been there.'

'You've got a point, I suppose,' Joe admitted. 'Bettis came back whilst Stephen was visiting today. The police tape is still there and a notice stating that it is a crime scene. The notice says that any person found to be contaminating it would face police prosecution. He was going to tear the notice down, but then he looked around and saw Stephen watching him, so he just got back in his car and drove off.'

'Joe, refresh my memory as to what you think they've pinched,' Archie asked. 'A brief description will do, I know what these things look like, but the size and colour would be a help.'

Joe thought about it, he couldn't be sure about some of the things. He'd seen the strimmer go in the farm shop, and the heavy duty pruner. Joe wasn't one hundred per cent sure about the spade, but he was sure he'd seen the sledge hammer go in.

'I'd better do a list, Arch,' he said. 'I'll have it ready for you when you come. What time will be best?'

'Oh, I'll have my dinner first, Joe.' Archie said. 'I'll be there about half past seven. I'll take my bike. It'll save getting the car out again and if it gets lively, I can be away quickly and quietly.'

116

CHAPTER 19.

Not one, but two detectives called on Martin Bettis at his home in Wallerton. It was just after two-thirty on Saturday afternoon. The wind had picked up a little, from the east and the air had a distinct chill.

'Good afternoon sir,' said DS Ian Stuart, showing his warrant card. 'I'm Detective Sergeant Stuart and this is Detective Inspector Church. We'd like you to come with us to answer some questions please.'

'And if I don't want to come with you, or answer any questions, then what?' Bettis countered.

'I would hope that won't be the case, Mr. Bettis,' the DI replied. 'You see, we're asking you to help us with our enquiries, but if you refuse, we will have to detain you. That probably means that you would eventually be arrested for obstructing us. We don't want to play it that way, it means a lot of form filling and you'd be lucky to get home again until later this evening.' Bettis looked alarmed.

'So how long will it take if I come with you now?' He asked.

'That would be the most sensible thing to do, Mr. Bettis,' said Tony Church. 'Assuming you have nothing to hide, it probably

117

won't take very long at all. We don't like working on Saturdays, any more than you, but this is about the accident on Thursday morning. You understand, we have to try to get as much information as we can?'

'But the accident was nothing to do with me,' Bettis protested. 'I told the police that, when they came on Thursday.' Tony Church smiled at him, as he continued,

'No, of course not, we know that, but we need to find out from someone with a bit of savvy, whether there had been any events preceding the actual accident. Maybe some of the drivers were arguing or had a problem of some sort. You know the sort of things which can sometimes play on one's mind.'

'OK. I'll come down to Chichelster, but I'll use my car.'

'Oh, there's no need to use your car, sir. We're grateful for your help, we'll bring you straight home as soon as we're done. We're a very reliable taxi service to people who help us.'
Bettis called out to his wife, who came out into the front hallway. She seemed a well spoken lady, and smiled at the two policemen.

'I heard most of what was said,' she told Tony. 'It was terrible, what happened to that poor boy. I'll bet his parents were worried sick, I know I would have been. If you're too busy to bring Martin home, just call me, I can come and fetch him.

'Thank you, Mrs. Bettis. It is Mrs. Bettis, isn't it?'

'Yes, Elaine Bettis,' she held out her hand which Tony shook.

'Don't you worry, love,' He told her. 'We'll bring him home safe and sound. You don't want to go out driving, it's cold out there and it'll be dark in an hour or so.'
Bettis appeared behind her wearing a camel coloured top coat. He bent and gave her a kiss on the cheek. 'I don't think this will take long, love. I'll call you when we're on our way back.'
The back seat of the police Volvo was very comfortable and Bettis felt quite relaxed. They seemed a decent couple for policemen, and the big one, Inspector Church, was chatting to him as they drove.

'Have you lived in Wallerton for long, Mr. Bettis?'

118

He asked.

'About six years, now,' Bettis said. 'We only moved to this house last year, we had one of the cottages in Branks Lane before. It was a bit basic when we first moved in, but I spent a lot of time and money on it. It's like a little palace now. A retired bank manager bought it from me. I got more than three times what I paid for it.'

'We had a chat with your boss earlier, he was going to call for you on his way in, but there was nobody home.' Tony told him. 'Pity, really, it would have saved you having to come out now.'

'That's the road where Jeff Davies lives,' Bettis said, pointing to their right. 'It's exactly two miles from my place. I had to go out this morning, and then I had to pick Elaine up from the hairdressers. I expect that's where we were when Jeff called.'

It had begun to drizzle, the fine rain was smearing on the windscreen. Ian, who was driving, observed,

'I hate it when it's like this, not enough for the wipers, but too much not to use them.'

Bettis agreed, saying,

'It's just another thing which makes life difficult at this time of year. When you leave the car for more than a few minutes, you return to find all the windows have steamed up. I'm not a happy person in the winter, what with the cold weather, the price of coal and the expense of Christmas, just around the corner.'

Tony laughed,

'We've only just met and you're depressing me already. Why don't you just say, 'sod it' and clear off to somewhere warm until it's all over?' he asked.

They arrived at the police station just before three-thirty. The DI and Bettis went directly to the interview room. Ian Stuart went to the office to check their phone for messages. He had tried to call Rex Perrington, who was Bettis' part time clerk. There was a message from this gentleman, but it was very short and not especially helpful

Ian pressed the play button on his recorder and heard,

119

'If this is about the drivers being offered payment to damage next door's fence, I'm not interested. If it's about Palmer, he only has himself to blame, he shot his mouth off and got the sack for it.'

Ian Stuart grinned and thought,

'I can't very well play that in the interview room. It's not exactly a witness statement, because he doesn't identify himself. He obviously has a grudge against Don Palmer, but that's about it. On the other hand, it seems to be a fact that someone offered incentives to cause damage to Mr. Skrobe's property.'

He took the tape from the recorder and replaced it with a new one. He then put it into his jacket pocket and joined his boss in the interview room.

The DI had waited for his colleague, he and Bettis had a cup of coffee each and there was one on the table for Ian. Tony Church began by asking Bettis for his full name.

'Martin Donald Bettis,' he replied. 'Can we please get to the point of this? I'll try to give you whatever information you want, but I'd like to get done here as quickly as possible. What is all this about, the accident on Thursday?'

Ian raised his eyebrows,

'Why do you ask that, Mr. Bettis? Have you got some information which is relevant to it?'

'I don't think so, but if it's not that, why am I here?' Bettis asked.

DI Church smiled,

'We need to find out about these bones, Mr. Bettis,' he explained. 'But if you have any further information which may help our investigation into the accident, we'd be pleased to hear it. The young victim, who was knocked off his moped, is still in a serious condition in hospital. Can you tell us when you first heard that the workmen were finding bones at the site?'

Bettis thought for a few seconds and then he said,

'I think it was at the beginning of last week, it was bits of antler or goat horn as well to begin with. They were very old bones, looked as though they had woodworm, lots of tiny holes all over them.'

'You mean they were porous?' Ian asked him.

'Exactly,' said Bettis, 'prehistoric, I would guess.'

'So what did you do about it?' DI church asked. 'Did you notify anybody that you had found human remains at your site?' Bettis looked astounded,

'Is that what the law requires? I didn't know they were human bones, anyway.'

'The law requires that you notify the police if you discover human bones. In the event that they are ancient bones, we would not take any more action, except to notify the local history or archaeology society.'

Bettis sat back in his chair,

'So, that's it then, isn't it? You tell the local societies and I go home.'

'No, Mr. Bettis, that most certainly is not 'it', 'Tony said, sternly. 'Let me elucidate. Some of the human remains found at your site, have been buried in the ground for less than thirty years. These bones, and a complete skull, did not have little tiny holes in them. The skull, in particular had two larger holes in it, made by a point two, two bullet.'

Bettis gasped,

'You mean he was murdered?' he asked. 'In the last thirty years?'

'I can see that we are beginning to make our point.' The DI continued. 'Did you examine any of these bones, Mr. Bettis? Did you consult with anyone at all, as to what you should do about this gruesome find? Or did you think of the murder victim as a bloody inconvenience and do your best to dispose of the evidence to avoid a delay to your schedule?'

Mr. Martin Bettis was looking decidedly worried.

121

'Will I be prosecuted for my decision?' He asked. 'I did notify Jeff Davies, he said to just put them in a sack.'

'But you did more than that, didn't you?' Ian told him. 'You decided to try to destroy them in their entirety, didn't you? Put them in the hole and blow them to smithereens!'

Bettis was deep in thought. He was beginning to realise that there could be even more problems than Joe Skrobe's property.

'What do you think has happened to the rest of this person's skeleton?' DI Church asked. 'Loaded onto a tipper lorry and dumped?'

Bettis frowned,

'I suppose that's possible, I'm sorry. How did you find the skull? I just thought they were all ancient flint miners' bones. I'm told they often find them around here. Will I be charged with anything?'

Tony Church said,

'There are several charges which we could bring, contaminating evidence, suppressing evidence in a murder investigation, conspiring to pervert the course of justice and possibly a few more. Your worker, the one you fired because he argued with you, had more integrity than his boss.'

Bettis had picked up on the possible charges,

'A murder investigation?' He said incredulously. 'You mean he was murdered?'

'With two holes in the skull and a couple of bullets in amongst the soil and chalk inside it, wouldn't you guess it was a murder subject?' Tony asked him. 'What makes you think it was a 'him'? Is there something else you know, that you're not telling us, Mr. Bettis?'

'You mean it was a woman's skull, how can you tell that?' He asked.

Tony gave a wry smile,

'As I told your boss earlier today, we have something called 'forensic science'. At this stage, I can't say whether it was a male or female, but within a day or so we will know for certain.

There's another new tool in our box, it's called 'D.N.A' and it's more accurate than fingerprints, when we need to identify someone.'

'So you will be able to find out who this person was?' Bettis asked.

'Yes, eventually, I expect.' Tony told him. 'What can you tell us about a campaign to try to force your neighbour to sell up and move out of his home?'

Bettis' complexion took on a subtle shade of pale ivory.

'No, I don't know anything about that, Inspector.' He protested. 'Whoever told you that is just trying to get back at me. I guess you heard it from Palmer?'

'What makes you say that? Did Palmer hear you talking about it?' Ian asked. 'Or was it someone else? I can tell you that we've heard it from more than one source, Mr. Bettis.'

'Do I need a lawyer?' Bettis asked.

Tony stood up, saying,

'That will be your decision, Mr. Bettis. I don't think you'll need one today. Best to wait until all our enquiries are complete and then decide.

Thank you for your assistance today, now, would you like to go home?'

CHAPTER 20.

At seven o'clock, Archie got his bike from the shed and wheeled it through the passageway between the garage and the kitchen. It was a chilly night, so he had a thick pullover on under his navy blue anorak. He took the precaution of switching his mobile phone to silent, vibrate.

Elsie stood at the kitchen door,

'Be careful, Arch,' she told him. 'Don't take any risks, if there's trouble just come straight back. Are you sure you don't want me to take you? You'll have to push your bike up Grumbles Hill.'

'I'm not going that way, Else,' He said. I'll go up Forge Lane and along the top road, its flatter that way. I've got my mobile phone in my pocket. I'll call you if I get delayed.'

He checked his lights and scooted down the path to the road. Twenty minutes later he arrived at Joe's bungalow. He leaned his bike just inside Joe's fence and went to the kitchen door.

'You sure you want to do this, Arch?' Joe asked him.

'It'll all be over in about ten minutes,' Archie assured him. 'You've got my mobile number haven't you? Keep your house lights turned off, you'll be able to see the yard better. Just be sure to call me on your mobile if any cars turn up. If it looks as though there's trouble, phone the police on your main phone.'

Archie pocketed the screwdriver and walked around to the old farm shop. All was quiet, there was a JCB digger parked at the end of the car park, furthest from Joe's home. It was in darkness. Before Archie tried the farm shop door, he walked over to the machine and opened the cab door. The keys were in the starting switch.

'That's asking for trouble,' he said to himself.

He walked back to the farm shop and checked the padlock. Joe was right. It was a brand new one. Archie pushed the large screwdriver behind the top of the hasp and pulled back firmly. The wood splintered, but the hasp didn't pull clear. He gave it another try, this time from underneath. It swung clear and he opened the door and went in. There was not much of a moon, but he could see the strimmer, leaning against the end wall. There was a bench at the end of the old shed, where he found the pruners and a pair of wire strainers.

Joe was watching from his window, and saw headlights turning into the farm shop car park. He phoned Archie, before the vehicle had stopped.

'There's a car coming in,' he said. 'Its turning round, now he's stopped.'

'I can hear it,' Archie said.

'He's getting out. Now he's walking towards the gates. He's left his driver's door open. He's got the wrong key for the gates, Arch.'

'The lorry drivers changed the padlock, remember?' Archie reminded him.

'Oh yes,' Joe said. 'You're right, I forgot about that. Hang on. He's climbing over the gates. He's gone round the back to that shed next to the portakabin.

Archie looked through the slightly open door of the shed. The car was a red Toyota pick-up. The door had been left open, as Joe had said. Archie thought perhaps he wanted to make a quick exit. His phone buzzed again.

No response.

'Archie, can you hear me?'

No response.

'He's coming back, Arch. It looks like he's got a petrol can. He's climbed back over the gates. He's coming towards you Arch.'

Joe watched horrified as the man began dousing the bottom of the shed with petrol.

He tried Archie's phone again.

'Arch, quick, he's going to set fire to the hut! Get out!'

No response.

'ARCHIE' he shouted. ARCH! Get out NOW! I'll phone the police!

'Stop panicking, Joe!' he heard Archie say. 'I'm not in the shed. I'm in the cab of the JCB! I'm watching him. Use your house phone to call the police, keep the mobile open.'

He heard Joe's voice again,

'It looks like he's taking the empty can back. No, he's thrown it over the fence and he's walking back. He's going to do it, Arch! He's lit a whole box of matches and....

Blimey!

Archie saw the flames leap into the air with a loud 'whoosh'. He saw the man run to the pick-up and jump in. He closed the door, but didn't move.

Joe came back on line,

'Are you alright Arch? Then, 'Looks like he's having a problem starting his car, I think.'

'Yes, Joe,' Archie chuckled. 'He would have, I've got his keys in my pocket!'

'I've phoned the police, Arch. They should be here soon.' Joe told him. 'You didn't manage to get my stuff out, but never mind. At least you didn't get hurt.'

'Your strimmer, a pair of pruners and a pair of wire strainers are in your front garden by the new bit of fence' He heard Archie say.

'I've had the heater plugs going on this thing,' Archie told him. 'Now we'll see if it starts.'

It started!

With headlights and working spotlights blazing, Archie lifted the front bucket just clear of the ground and began rumbling his way towards the Toyota. He was about to lift the back end and push it into the soil bank, when he saw the blue lights of the fire engine. It pulled into the car park, closely followed by the police car.

Archie reversed the JCB back to where it had been parked and stopped the engine. As he walked towards the police car, he saw the man being hauled out of the pick-up. Joe came down his front garden and put his hands on Archie's shoulders.

'Thank God you're safe,' he whispered. 'You had me worried there, Archie. I thought you were still in the shed.'

'Not me,' Archie replied. 'When you said he'd gone round the back, I nipped out and tossed your bits over the fence. Then I looked for somewhere to hide. The JCB was an ideal vantage point. I pinched the keys out of his pick-up on the way back. I could see everything he was doing, from the cab of the machine. It was like a grandstand view.'

'What are 'wire strainers' Arch?' Joe enquired.

'They're for keeping fence wire tight, while it's secured to the post.' Archie explained.

'They're not mine.' Joe told him.

'Well they are now!' Archie laughed, 'I'm not takin' 'em back.'

The old farm hut was a blackened shell. The fire was out and one of the firemen was approaching them, together with a policeman.

'Are you both OK?' The policeman asked them.

'Yes, thanks' said Archie. He put his hand in his pocket and pulled out the keys to the Toyota. He held them out towards the policeman and dropped them into his outstretched hand.

'I 'spect you'd rather drive that out of the way, than push it,' he said.

'Where did you find them?' The policeman asked.

'They were in the ignition switch, I thought I'd better hang on to them, in case he did anything silly' Archie was grinning as he said it.

'Looks as though he's already done that,' said the policeman. 'We'll take him back with us and find him a room for the night at 'Hotel Nick'. He'll be facing several charges. We'll let him know when we've worked out what they'll be.'

The team leader of the fire brigade approached them, he asked,

'Can either of you two gentlemen, tell me who the shed belongs to?'

'Yes,' said Joe. 'It's mine, all the front plot is mine, including the greenhouse at the end, which the site workers have destroyed for me.'

'Did you know that someone had broken into it? The hasp has been pulled off the door.'

'I just did that,' Archie told him. 'The developers had taken possession of it, along with some of Joe's tools, and fitted a new padlock to prevent us getting in.'

'It didn't though, did it?' the policeman said, 'prevent you, that is. Did you know you were going to be interrupted this evening?'

Both Joe and Archie said, 'No' at the same time.

Joe continued with his explanation,

'It's like this officer I've had nothing but problems with the developers, ever since the job started. They want me to sell up to them and move out. They've damaged my fence several times, they have left the excavations unstable and their blasting has cause subsidence to my foundations. There was a serious accident here last week. One of their drivers reversed into my fence,

128

apparently deliberately and then almost killed a young man when he knocked him off his moped. So, I asked my friend, here to help me get back the garden tools which the workers had stolen from my garden a couple of weeks ago. I saw him put the strimmer, this one here,' (Joe pointed to where it lay on his lawn.) 'into the shed and then lock it with a new padlock.'

'So you went and got it back for him?' The policeman asked Archie.

'Yes, you see, we know they can be a difficult lot, so we thought it might not be a good idea for just one of us to sort it. Joe watched from his kitchen window, while I went and got his property back.
He rang me on my mobile, when the vehicle was coming and he kept me informed as to what was happening. It's a good job we'd planned the operation, otherwise I could have been in the shed, when he set fire to it.'

'Do you know who he is?' The officer asked them.

'No,' Joe told him. 'I didn't really get a good look at him. It was pretty dark. It wasn't Bettis, he's taller than that. Maybe it was one of the other workers. He seemed to know his way around. He knew where to find the petrol can. He tried the gate padlock first, but one of the lorry drivers had added another one, so he climbed over. I saw him go to the shed, next to the portacabin, which they use as an office. When I saw what he was going to do, I told Archie to get out of the shed.'
Archie continued to explain,

'I picked up the tools and dropped them over Joe's fence. I'd seen the keys were still in the Toyota, so I took them out on my way back. I'd checked that the JCB was unlocked, before I broke in to the shed. I hid in the cab and watched him sprinkling petrol all over the shed and then set fire to it.'

'And that's where we came in!' The fireman said with a smile.
The policeman's radio crackled and his colleague said,

'We'd better get this one back and get him processed, John. We don't want to make it last all night. If you get these gentlemen's details, we can get someone out to take statements tomorrow or Monday.'

'Yes, OK. will do, wait there for me, I'll be right over,' he said into his mic.

Joe gave him his name and address, which he wrote in his notebook.

'We'll probably get our local man to come out for the statements,' he said.

Archie interrupted,

'We know Bill Pickering,' he told the officer.

'And he knows us!' Joe added. 'Archie lives in the village, Slindon Road. Mr. Pickering has his telephone number.'

The officer put his notebook back into his pocket and shook their hands.

'I think we can wrap it up for tonight, gentlemen. Thank you for your help. I'll leave a note at the station, for them to contact Bill. He can let you know when he's coming. I take it you will be claiming on your insurance for the shed, so I'll let you sort it out.'

They shook hands again and he left.

The fire engine was just leaving, so the police waited until it passed in front of them. Archie ran down to the driver's side and tapped the window.

The driver wound the window down,

'Yes, sir,' he asked, 'was there something else?'

Archie pointed over to the Toyota and asked,

'What's happening about the pick-up?'

'Sorry,' said the driver, 'I meant to tell you. Our transporter will be out presently to load it up and bring it in. It will be held for evidence and examination.' He chuckled as he said, 'You never know, we might be able to do him for a bald tyre or something as well!'

The pair went back indoors. Joe put the kettle on, while Archie phoned Elsie and gave her a brief account of their mission.

As they drank their tea, Joe said,

'Pity about the old farm hut, but at least they can't use it any more.'

'You'll get a brand new one from the insurance, Joe.' Archie consoled him.

'I won't,' said Joe. 'I didn't have it insured. I bet someone will have to pay for it though, don't you?'

CHAPTER 21.

Jason Davies liked to lie in bed on a Sunday and read the newspapers. He had recovered a little from his unpleasant surprise on Friday. He had tried to phone his son yesterday morning, but without success.

'I wonder what the problem can be,' he was thinking.
'It must be something that's just happened. I haven't spoken with him for months. Perhaps I'll try to call him again later.' He went back to perusing his newspapers.
An article on the second page of the Telegraph caught his eye.

'Woman's remains found at Sussex building site.'
'Human skeletal remains were discovered on Friday, at a
building site close to Wigglesworth, in West Sussex.
They are believed to be those of a woman, aged
approximately thirty years, at the time of her death.
Forensic officers of the West Sussex force are currently
treating the discovery as an unsolved crime.
A police   spokesperson stated that the remains appear
to have lain undiscovered, in the chalk and flint soil of
the South Downs, for the past twenty five to thirty years.
Police are hopeful that more details will emerge from
their ongoing investigations, in the very near future.

Jason read it again!

'That's his development,' he said out loud. He sat on the edge of his bed, still looking at his paper. 'Oh my God, Friday, it says, that's when the case was left on the doorstep. So bloody Gorse found out before me, but how?'

He buried his head in his hands and said to himself,

'What can I do? I can't say anything to Jeff, or he'll be suspicious. Gorse says he's coming on Monday. I can't have him here at the same time as Jeffery. Who's taken the bloody rifle? I doubt it would be Duncan Dobbs. He's been delivering my logs for years.'

His thoughts began to race, heading inevitably to a confused jumble.

'He had a younger lad helping him this time, 'Kenneth' something or other. I wonder if he knows anything about it.'

He was about to take his shower, when the telephone rang.

'Oh, shit!' he said. He was half afraid to pick it up, in case it was Gorse. His hand hovered over the hand set. He finally picked up and cautiously held it to his ear without uttering a word. He heard no sound at all for a few seconds and then a click, followed by the dialing tone.

Was somebody watching him? Maybe they were watching the house? No, he was probably just being paranoid. Had there been somebody watching him, he would have noticed, wouldn't he?

Jason went into his bathroom, collecting a clean bath towel from the airing cupboard on his way. He thought he heard the telephone again as he got out of the shower. He checked, but there were no messages. The number was withheld, probably indicating that the call was made from a mobile.

He dressed and then made some toast and put on a fresh pot of coffee. Today was Armistice Day. He could get rid of the case of Mary's clothes from the log store. Cathy was not due to come today, so he could work at a slower pace. Jason remembered that he had seen a 'Humana' clothing bin at the car park in Hangleton, he would 'donate' them there. He decided he could dump the empty case in a skip somewhere on the way back. There were always a few of them outside houses where building work was in progress. Most people would be either at home or at one of the remembrance services at village war memorials. As long as he wasn't seen, it should be quite easy.

He switched the radio on and listened to the commentary from the Cenotaph, in Whitehall, where preparations were under way for the parade and the annual Service of Remembrance. When he had finished his toast, he took his plate into the kitchen and returned to the lounge. It was just after nine-thirty, not too early now, to phone Jeffery.

He picked up the phone and dialled the number.

'Hello,' said a male voice.

'Good morning, is that you, Jeff?'

'Yes, at last!' he said. 'What took you so long, Father? I left a message with Cathy on Friday, didn't she say?'

'Yes, Jeffery, I got the message, I tried to phone you on Friday and again yesterday, but there was no answer. What do you want?'

'You know Hannah has left me?' Jeff said.

'I had heard,' his father confirmed. 'How is that anything to do with me?'

'I remember you telling me that when my mother ran away, you hired a private investigator to try to find her, right?'

'Yes, that's right. What about it?' Jason asked.

'I want the name and phone number of the investigator, he may be able to find where Hannah has gone.'

'Waste of time, Jeff,' Jason told him. 'He's either retired or dead by now. I'd just find one in the phone book, if I were you. Someone told me you're up in court this week, is that true?'

'It is, father, but like you just said, 'how is it anything to do with you?'

'OK, Jeff, is there any more information about these human remains? The Telegraph says the police are treating it as an unsolved crime, does that mean murder?'

134

'I was asked about it yesterday, at the police station in Chichelster. That's probably where I was when you tried to phone me. I didn't see anything, Martin Bettis was on the site. He thought they were some more old bones like the ones we found before. When we asked about those, the archaeologists examined them and said they were remains of ancient flint miners', like the ones they found at Cissbury. So when he asked me what to do, I just told him to bag them up and carry on.'

Jason asked him,

'So how did the police get involved?'

'Martin told one of the men to push them back in the hole and set a charge behind them. That Donald Palmer collected them in a sack and hid them in the generator shed. He went back for 'em later and that's how the police got hold of them. He'd had a row with Martin earlier and Martin had sacked him.'

'So there was a bit of bad blood between them before all this? What was the accident on Thursday? I heard they're still holding the driver of your lorry.' Jason asked.

'I don't know much about that either. Martin was questioned by the police yesterday, but I haven't heard from him since. It's not our lorry, it's one of Grover's. Tickners Transport, you remember, don't you? Anyway, I must get on. I've got to book a room in Lincoln for Tuesday night.' Jeff told his father.

'Right, I'll let you go then, good luck for Tuesday.'

'Tuesday will be fine, its Wednesday I'm in court. I'll come and see you when I get back.'

Jason could tell that his son was either lying to him, or leaving something out of his account.

Jeffery Davies wondered why his father was so interested in the bones. He didn't usually have anything much to say, just comments about the weather. He never got involved in the business side of things. The last time he'd asked him for financial help, he'd flatly refused.

'I've baled you out for the last time, Jeff,' he had said.

It was true that he had wasted most of the money his father had given him over the years. Theirs was not a good relationship.

'I suppose it will all sort itself out eventually,' he thought. 'I'll need to have a chat with Martin, see what he knows that he hasn't told me and find out exactly what he's told the police.'

Jason Davies was still wondering who had tried to phone him earlier. It obviously wasn't Jeff. Was it Gorse? And who had taken the rifle from the log store? Nobody else knew where he had kept it all these years. Another sudden thought occurred to him.

'My shotgun!'

In a state of high anxiety, he hurried to the cabinet. To his immediate relief, he saw that it was still secured with the chain.

'At least that's still OK,' he thought.'

He was about to close the cabinet, when he spotted half a box of point two-two ammunition.

'I'd better hide that somewhere, in case someone comes snooping,' he decided. He picked it up and closed and re-locked the cabinet. In the kitchen he opened one of the lower cupboards and placed the small box of ammunition in a cast iron enameled casserole dish. He replaced the lid and closed the cupboard door.

'I'll go and get the suitcase and put it in the car,' he decided. Jason put on his old jacket and went out to the log store. As he began moving the logs to get to the suitcase, he noticed that someone had been here before him. There were a couple of dozen logs from the top half of the pile, which had been tossed onto the muddy ground in front of the shelter. He peered beneath the lean-to roof and could see the black plastic soil pipe, still fastened to the back wall.

'That's a bit strange,' he thought. 'I wonder who's been here.' More in hope than anticipation, he put his hand into the open end of the pipe. There was a rifle there!

Jason pulled it out and checked it. It was definitely his rifle, a Martini action point two-two target rifle.

'Who's been using it and when did they put it back?'
Jason checked that the breach was empty and carefully replaced it in the pipe. He retrieved the suitcase and re-stacked the logs, filling the house log basket at the same time. It took two trips back to the house, the suitcase first and then the log basket, which was heavier than he had thought. He left the logs in the back porch and carried the suitcase round the side of the house, leaving it behind the Audi which was still in his garage.

He went back indoors, took off his old jacket and washed his hands. He poured himself the remainder of the coffee and switched the machine off. He sat in his favourite arm chair and using a clean handkerchief, polished his spectacles. He switched off the radio and put on his new jacket and a tie. He found a small safety pin to secure his poppy, checked that the back door was locked and left the house through the front door. A short while later he was driving towards Hangleton with Mary's suitcase on the back seat of his beloved Audi convertible. He had left the kitchen in a bit of a mess, but he would tidy it up when he returned. Cathy wouldn't complain when she came in the morning, but he would still feel guilty.

CHAPTER 22.

Sunday morning was cold, but dry for a change. Archie was up early and had taken Jimbo for a walk up to his allotment. He dug a few parsnips and washed them off in the water butt. The sprouts needed another frost to sweeten them, so he cut a savoy cabbage instead. The ground was a bit sticky from the week's rain, so he decided not to do any more. On the way back, he saw Bill Pickering in his car, going towards his home. Bill stopped and wound his window down.

'I hear you've been causing mayhem again last night, Arch,' he said. I expect you'd rather leave the statements until tomorrow, wouldn't you?'
Archie crossed the road to speak with him, keeping Jimbo on a short lead.

'Yes, we'll be going to the service at the war memorial later, Bill. Will you be there?'

'I will, Arch, I'll have to stop the traffic for the scouts and the British Legion parade. I hear there's tea and biscuits available in the hall afterwards, for anyone who wants it.'

'I'll pass on that, thanks, Bill,' Archie told him. 'I think we'll probably favour a drink at the Old Bell, instead. When d'you want us to do these statements? Would it be better if we did them together, me and Joe?'

Bill thought for a minute before replying,

'Yes, that would save a bit of time and you would be less likely to miss anything out. Let me know in the morning, where you'd rather do 'em. I can fit my time to suit you two.'

'OK, Bill, I'll have a word with Joe and call you in the morning.' Archie agreed. 'We'd better get home and have our breakfast, hadn't we Jimbo?'

The dog appeared to understand the word, 'breakfast,' he wagged his tail and tugged Archie back to the footpath.

As they turned the corner into Slindon Road, Archie saw the newspaper boy mount his bike and pedal away. The aroma of bacon cooking, welcomed them both as they reached the kitchen door.

'That smells good, Else,' Archie said as they entered. 'I'll just feed Jimbo and wash my hands. There's a couple of parsnips and a cabbage in the carrier bag outside. I'll deal with them after breakfast.'

'I don't suppose the parsnips will be all that sweet yet,' Elsie remarked.

'No,' Archie replied, 'that's why I didn't pick any sprouts. They really need a couple of frosts to sweeten 'em up.'

'I've had a telephone call from Belgium, while you were out,' she told him. 'Hannah Jempson will be here on Tuesday. She doesn't know what time, but it will be afternoon.'

'You mean Hannah Davies,' Archie reminded her.

'Yes, Arch, you know who I mean. She asked if you would take her to Chichelster police station, to get her passport back. Apparently she will need to prove her identity and she thought you would help. She said she'll have to be careful about letting them know where she's been. She thought she would be in trouble if they discovered she'd been working in Belgium.'

Archie rubbed his neck with his hand as he tilted his head back and said,

'You mean travelling on her sister's passport?'

'I expect that's what she was referring to, Arch, but there's no need to mention that, is there? What's the matter with your neck?'

'Must've lain awkward I s'pose, feels a bit stiff, that's all,' he said as he sat down at the table.

Archie had to agree, but couldn't see how they would know about Hannah working in Belgium. There were no border passport stamps between the UK and Europe, these days.

'Did she say how long she might be staying?' He asked.

'Not in so many words, Arch,' Elsie explained. 'She said she'd like to spend a bit of time with her dad and was hoping that Hilda might come down for a few days, whilst she was here.'

'Good job there's twin beds in the spare room. Does she know they'll have to share?'

'I told her that, but she didn't seem to mind, I think she was grateful to have somewhere to stay, without needing to pay hotel prices,' Elsie said.

They continued chatting whilst they ate their breakfast. Archie told her that Bill wanted to get the statements done tomorrow.

'I think I'll phone Joe and suggest we do them at his place. Bill will be able to see the state of the old farm hut and by then, Bettis or Davies will have received Stephen's letter.' Archie said. 'They have to move all their materials and equipment from Joe's property.'

Archie thought for a few moments and then continued.

'It could be entertaining to watch. The lorry drivers put a different lock on their gate, so they won't have a key for it. I don't know whether the drivers will even turn up, I think they were in dispute with Grover, so there could be some industrial strife involved there.'

Elsie nodded that she understood.

'You're going to change before we go up the war memorial, aren't you?' She asked.

Archie grinned as he said,

'Oh yes, Else, Best straw hat and a clean pair of overalls. I might even wear my new green wellies!'

'And don't forget to change your poppy over from your work jacket,' she chided.

CHAPTER 23.

Jason Davies was feeling pleased with himself. He had deposited the clothes into the Humana box and found a council rubbish skip where he got rid of the suitcase.

'Better than getting caught dumping it in someone's private skip,' he thought to himself, and no need to watch out for the twitching curtains!'

He decided that he would treat himself to a pub lunch, instead of cooking for one, when he got home. As he drove through Tarring, he glanced at the instrument panel. The digital clock told him it was 12.17 so the next pub he came to would be open.

'Sunday lunches'
It said on the blackboard. Underneath was the menu.
Choice of Beef, Lamb or Pork from our carvery, with roast potatoes, parsnip sprouts and carrots.
Choice of puddings, Tea or Coffee and mints.
Just, £6.50

'That'll do me,' he thought as he pulled in to the car park and found a space.

He went up to the bar and asked,

'Do you have a table for one, please?'

The young lady answered him,

'The best I can offer is a table for four, sir, one of those over by the window. Perhaps you would like to choose which one you prefer? Can I get you a drink whilst you wait for your meal sir?' She asked.

Davies liked this he was being treated like a proper gentleman.

'Thank you,' he said, smiling at her. 'I think I'd like a glass of your house red, please.'

'I'll bring it to your table, sir,' she said. 'I can take your food order at the same time, if you wish.'

'That sounds just right, thank you.' He walked over towards the front of the bar and selected a table furthest from the door. He had noted the way that the wind had made the tablecloths flutter when he entered. Here he was out of the draught and with a view of the car park and the road. The young lady brought his drink and placed it on a coaster. She pulled a pad from her pocket and asked,

'What would you like for your main, sir?'

Jason had studied the menu on the large chalkboard and had decided almost before he sat down.

'I think I'd like the beef, please,' he said.

The young lady wrote on her pad,

'It will be around ten minutes, sir. Will that be alright?'

He was in no hurry now, his mission was accomplished. He could afford to relax.

'Yes, thank you, that will be fine,' he replied. 'You may find you'll get busy today,' he remarked.

'Yes,' the waitress replied. 'We're usually quite busy at weekends, but its Armistice Day, so perhaps some of the mums might have a day off from cooking.'

She thanked him for his order and returned to the kitchen.

While he waited for his meal, Davies looked out of the window. The volume of traffic was fairly light. Every now and then a car would pull into the pub car park. Davies noted that some went to the side of the pub,

'There must be another car park at the rear,' he thought.
He got up from his chair and went towards the rear of the bar. Along a short passageway were the toilets and at the end a door led to the car park. Davies opened it and went outside. The car park was even larger than the one on the forecourt. He used the gents toilet on his way back to his table where he sat and waited for his meal. The front car park was filling rapidly, which he decided was possibly due to the remembrance services coming to an end. The young waitress brought his meal and asked if he required any horseradish sauce or mustard.

'I'd like some mustard, please,' he said, adding, 'you seem to be getting busy already.'

'Yes,' she said, 'I may need to ask you to share your table presently. Would you mind?'

'Not at all, my dear,' Davies replied. 'I didn't expect to have a table for four people all to myself.'
She smiled and said,

'Thank you, sir. I'll go and get your mustard.'
The meal was good, all nicely cooked and the beef was very tasty. He was about half way through when the waitress returned with a young couple. She turned to them and said,

'Will this be OK for you? I asked this gentleman if he would mind sharing his table and he said he didn't.'

'That'll be fine by us,' the young man said. 'Thank you sir,' he said, smiling at Jason. 'The place fills up quite quickly on a Sunday. I expect there are a few more in today because its Armistice day, don't you?'

'I think you could well be right in your assumption,' Davies replied. He nodded to the young lady and offered his hand to her companion.

'Since we're enjoying each other's company for a while, my name is 'Jason',' he said.
The young man returned his smile, saying,

144

'I'm David, and this is my wife 'Susan', we've only been living here since June.'

'I'm very pleased to meet you both,' Davies told them. 'So you live in the village here, do you?'

'Not quite in the village,' Susan replied. 'We actually live in Angmering, but some of our friends told us about this pub, when we first moved in. It's excellent value here and the food is always good quality. We treat ourselves occasionally, usually on a weekday evening, when we've done our grocery shopping.'

'I must confess, I haven't been here before,' Davies told them. 'It was a spur of the minute decision. I saw the sign, felt hungry and pulled in to the car park.'

The young couple smiled at his explanation. The waitress brought their drinks and told the man,

'Your meals will be a few more minutes, would you like mint sauce with your lamb, or cranberry jelly?'

Susan looked up at David,

'I think I'd like mint sauce please, how about you?'

He nodded,

'Yes please,' he said to the waitress, 'mint sauce for both of us, please.'

Davies was idly watching the front car park, through the window. A very low, very red and very loud sports car zoomed in and shot into the only space available. It had barely stopped, when its lone female occupant got out. The petite brunette, in stiletto heels and carrying a very large shiny handbag, began walking briskly towards the pub. Before she had reached the door, a black Volvo saloon drove in and stopped in the centre of the entrance. Two men and a woman got out and ran towards her. The woman caught her by the wrist and seized her handbag. One of the men reached into his breast pocket and showed her an identity of some sort.

Davies had by now recovered from his initial surprise and had decided that her pursuers were probably police officers. Several of the customers were also staring out of the windows at the

145

drama unfolding in the car park. Two of the male customers went out to investigate, but soon returned to their tables. The young woman was escorted back to her car, but the woman police officer had retained her handbag. The Volvo reversed out onto the road and waited while the sports car drove out. They then appeared to follow her in the direction of Worthing.

Jason's table companions were speculating as to what the incident could be about. One of the men who had been outside, came over from the next table and said,

'They were policemen, I know the girl they were speaking with. She's a regular customer here, her first name is, 'Patricia'. I asked her if everything was alright and one of the men said to me, 'This is police business, sir. Please return to your table and enjoy your meal'. I don't know what it was all about, but they took her handbag and it looks as though they're following her to the police station in Worthing.'

There was a muted discussion from several of the other tables, but the atmosphere quickly returned to normal. Davies finished his meal, declined the sweet course and paid his bill. He shook hands with his two companions, thanking them for their company over lunch and left for home. As he got into the car, he noticed that the back seat was wet.

'I expect that suitcase was wet,' he thought. 'The log store roof has always leaked a bit.'

It was a bit warmer than first thing and the weak November sun was out. He put the roof down and buttoned his coat.

'That will probably dry out by the time I get home,' he thought. 'I'll leave it open until tomorrow, the garage is dry enough.'

He arrived home to find the garage doors open, as he had left them. He turned the car round in the driveway and got out. Davies then went into the garage to retrieve something he needed, before reversing the car into the garage. He left the keys in the ignition lock, having set the gear shift into the 'Park' position. He closed the wooden garage doors and entered his home. He was both surprised and irritated to see a second, smaller suitcase in the front porch.

'A day earlier than he said,' Jason thought.

He took the case into the hallway and opened it. There was an envelope on top of the clothes. He opened it and tipped the contents into his other hand. It was a bank key to a deposit box. Written on the envelope were the details and number of the box. Jason put the envelope and key into his jacket pocket, closed the case and replaced it in the porch.

He made some coffee, poured himself a cup and then went and sat in his armchair. Ten minutes later he was asleep.

CHAPTER 24.

At about ten fifteen that morning, Archie, in a clean pair of trousers and his new blazer, came downstairs so that Elsie could vet him!

'Will this do?' He asked her.

She looked him up and down,

'Turn round,' she said.

Archie did a complete 'three-sixty', spinning on one foot.

'I meant so that I could see your back,' she scolded. 'Stand still, I'll get the brush. You've got dog hairs all over the back of your trousers. Hold your jacket up, so I can brush them.'

He did as requested and when she had finished she smacked his behind with the back of the brush.

'Ouch!' he said, 'what was that for?'

Elsie was laughing.

'Now lets have a look at the front again, where's your poppy?'

'Still in my work coat, I expect,' Archie said, grinning. 'I'll go and get it. Shall we take the car? I know it's dry, but that wind is cold.'

'Yes, I thought the same, Arch,' Elsie agreed. 'I'll drive, I'll come in the pub with you afterwards, but only for one drink, if you want to stay, you'll have to walk back home.'

They left for the service at the war memorial and were surprised to see Andy and Jan Clarke walking up Forge Lane. Elsie slowed the car and wound her window down.

'Would you two like a lift up to the village?' She asked them.

'Yes, thanks, Else,' Andy replied. 'I didn't realise how cold the wind was until we turned the corner into Forge Lane.'
The pair got in and Jan began chatting with Elsie about the W.I. Christmas bazaar, which was planned for the next Saturday. They parked in the High street and walked across to the war memorial, where several villagers were milling about. Reg and Jenny Tobin and their son Chris, chatted with Alec and Valerie Gillham. Jimmy Ingram, the ironmonger was there, with his wife and their two boys. Bert Brooks was holding their attention with one of his tales. It seemed that the whole village had turned out for the occasion. Some were in small groups chatting and several couples marshalling their children, in readiness for the parade. Bill Pickering, in uniform, was preparing to stop any traffic, whilst the parade marched from the hall car park up to the memorial. Archie spotted Joe Skrobe, standing by himself and went over to greet him.

'Morning, Joe,' he began. 'Bill wants us to do our statements tomorrow, is it OK if we do them at your place?'
Joe nodded his agreement,

'What time is he coming?' He asked.

'I said I'd phone him later today,' Archie explained. 'Are you coming back to the pub with us after the service?'

'I'd like to, but it's a long walk home from there, Arch,' Joe said. 'I walked here today, if I had realised we were going for a drink, I'd have brought the van.'

'I'll take you home afterwards,' Elsie offered. 'I won't be staying long, but it'll give you two a chance for a chat.'

'In that case, I accept your very kind offer, Elsie,' said Joe.
The parade and the remembrance service were quite moving. The standard bearers of the British Legion and of the Scouts, were

well rehearsed and added meaning to the two minutes silence. The ceremony was followed by an address from the vicar. After it had ended, Elsie, who had been chatting with their little group, announced the transport arrangements which she had made. The wind had dropped a little and the sun was trying to break through.

'Joe, you and Bert Brooks will be going back to the pub with Alec and Val Gillham. Andy and Jan will come with us. Jan doesn't want to stay long, neither do I, we'll go back home and get our lunches ready. When you're ready to go home, Joe, Jenny will take you. She's not drinking today because she had a tooth out on Monday and she's been on anti-biotics all week. Is that OK with everyone?'

There was a chorus of, 'Yes, Else, that sounds fine, thank you.'

'Lunch is at half past one,' she told Archie loudly, so they would hear her above their banter. 'If you're any later, yours will be in Jimbo!'

The others laughed as Archie, hung his head in mock shame.

By the time Archie got to the pub, Bert Brooks was in his usual place at the bar.

'Better get the first round in, Arthur,' he said to the landlord. 'I don't want 'em talkin' about me all the week. Come on all of you. Tell Arthur what you'd like to drink. Better let Arch go first, else his dinner will be in the dog!'

A good discussion over a few beers was the ideal finale to the occasion. After about an hour, suitably refreshed, Archie and Andy took a gentle stroll home, leaving the others to continue their socialising.

Jimbo was barking excitedly as Archie went in through his front gate. He always seemed to sense the impending arrival of his 'best pal', which also served as a reminder to Elsie!

'You just made it in time,' Elsie told him as he came through the kitchen door. 'There's a phone message for you, from Bob

150

Jempson. He says there's been a development which he wants to talk to you about.'

'Shall I phone him now, or after lunch?' Archie asked.
Elsie looked at the clock,

'You've got time now, Arch. Lunch will be another few minutes,' she said.
He took off his blazer and shoes and changed into his slippers. Checking that there was a pen by the phone pad, he dialled Bob's mobile number.

'Hello,' Bob answered.

'It's Archie Leggitt. I got your message, Bob. What can I do for you?' Archie asked him.

'Thanks for phoning back, Archie,' Bob said. 'Have you got a few minutes, while I explain what's happened'

'Yes, Bob, fire away!'
Bob Jempson began to explain.

'I had a visitor this morning, a young lady who said that she was a friend of Hannah's. She said her name was Sharon Ellis. I don't know all of Hannah's friends, but I couldn't remember her name being mentioned, so I asked her where she knew Hannah from. She said they had worked together at the hospital. I asked her if she knew Hilda, and she was hesitant, but said that she did. When I asked what she wanted, she said she needed Hannah's address, so that she could write to her.'
Archie was thinking about what Bob had told him yesterday.

'Did she say why, after all that time, she needed her address now?' Archie asked.

'You're thinking the same as me, Arch,' Bob said. 'Anyway, as luck would have it, Hilda chose that precise moment to phone me. I said to this Sharon Ellis, 'You'll have to excuse me. My daughter is on the line. I'll take this call and then I'll listen to what you have to say.' You remember young Sarah, the young lady who brought our tea yesterday?'

'Yes, of course I do, Bob,' Archie assured him.

151

'Well, just then she knocked on my door to ask whether we would like some tea. I was holding Hilda on the phone and I wasn't quite sure who this young woman was, so I said, 'No thank you, Sarah.' Sharon Ellis then said,

'I think I would like a cup of tea, please.'
I shook my head at Sarah and she understood, she smiled and left the room.'

'This Sharon had a bit of a nerve, didn't she?' Archie remarked. 'So then what happened, Bob?'

'What happened was that I spoke with Hilda and asked her whether she could recall the name, 'Sharon Ellis'. I said that she had told me that she worked with Hannah at the hospital.'
Hilda said,

'Ask her which hospital that would have been, see what she says.'
So I did, and guess what she replied.

'Why, Sussex Royal County Hospital, in Brighton, of course!'
I knew then that I was right to be suspicious, so I said to Hilda, 'She knew Hannah from the Sussex Royal County Hospital.' She wants to have Hannah's address, so that she can write to her. I don't know her address at present, so it was fortunate that you phoned when you did. Perhaps you'd have a word with her Hilda, she says she knew you as well.' I handed the phone to this Ellis woman, so that Hilda could talk to her.'

'But both your girls were at Chichelster General, same as Elsie, weren't they?' Archie said.

'Yes, Arch, neither of the twins ever worked at any of the Brighton hospitals. I heard Hilda raise her voice on the phone, 'Give the phone back to my father, immediately please.' She shouted. I grabbed the phone from her and spoke with Hilda, 'She's an imposter, Dad,' Hilda told me. 'Get rid of her and don't tell her anything. I believe she's working for Jeff Davies, but she's not who she says she is.'

152

Sarah came in whilst I was shouting at her to leave. She called security and they evicted her. I heard her car start up, it sounded very loud, almost like a racing car. When she'd gone, I noticed that she'd taken my little notebook. That's where I keep all my addresses and phone numbers. Thankfully there are none of Hannah's details in there. The last address I had for Hannah, was when she was living with Hilda, in Lincoln.

Before I disconnected from Hilda, she said something which worried me. This Sharon Ellis, or whoever she really is, said to Hilda, 'It doesn't matter how you try to protect her, we'll get to her in the end, you know that, don't you?'

Hilda told me so that we can warn Hannah, that's why I needed you to know how it is.'

'Did you find out who she really is and who she's working for?' Archie asked his friend,

'Not yet, Arch, but Sarah told security what had happened and they've called the police. Sarah had taken the registration number of her car. It was a red sports car. Sarah said she left in such a hurry that the tyres threw gravel against the windows.'

'Try not to worry, Bob,' Archie said. 'I'm sure the police will catch her before she has a chance to do anything with the notebook. I'm going to have my lunch now, give me a call if there are any further problems.'

'Thanks Archie, sorry to lumber you with it, but Hilda's coming down tomorrow. I think she's already spoken with Elsie about it, but it may be a day earlier than planned. Oh, hang on, there's a police car in the driveway, I'd better go.'

'I don't suppose Hilda's early arrival will be a problem, but I'll mention it to Elsie. I'll have to go now Bob, or else I might be wearing my lunch instead of eating it!'

They said their 'goodbyes'. Bob said he'd phone later if there were any further developments.

They had finished their lunch and Archie was about to take Jimbo for a walk, when the phone rang. Archie picked up the receiver and heard Bob Jempson's voice.

'Hello, Arch,' he said. 'They've brought my book back. That woman was a private investigator. She was working for Davies, as I guessed she probably was. She's been ticked off by the police and they suggested they would be prepared to prosecute her for theft by deception. I told them not to bother, but they said if I change my mind or anything comes from it as a result of her information, to let them know. I explained that Hannah had left him and that he had assaulted Hilda in Lincoln. I told them he's up in court on Wednesday for that. The policeman said it might be a good idea to talk to a solicitor and get a restraining order against him.'

'It's worth thinking about, if he tries any more nasty tricks,' Archie suggested. 'Let's wait until we can have a chat with Hannah, it'll be up to her to decide the best course of action, won't it?'

Bob agreed,

'Will you phone me when both the girls have arrived with you, please Arch?' he asked. 'I'd like to have a chat with them together, somewhere neutral, perhaps that pub we went to.'

'Don't worry any more, Bob,' Archie told him. 'We'll sort something out as soon as they get here. I think the priority is to get Hannah her passport back from the police station. Once we've done that she can decide what she wants to do about the legal side of the separation.'

Bob thanked Archie again for his help and bade him 'goodnight'.

CHAPTER 25.

At Chichelster police station, Graham Fuller woke in his cell on Sunday morning at around 6.30am. The custody officer had brought him a mug of tea and was engaging in light conversation.

'Did you manage any sleep?' PC Peter Hayles asked him.

'Yes, I think I eventually went off for a while,' Fuller replied. 'What time will the interview begin?'

'I expect it will be fairly early,' said the officer. 'DI. Church will want to get to the remembrance service, I expect.'

'What's happened to my truck?' Fuller asked.

'I expect it'll be safely locked in the pound,' the officer told him. 'It will be thoroughly examined tomorrow, a full safety check, it won't be released until that's completed. I'll get you some toast and a cup of tea presently and then you can spend a few minutes deciding what you're going to say and whether you want us to call you a solicitor.'

'Are they just charging me with arson?' He asked as the officer was leaving.

'They'll read the charges to you before they ask you any questions, Mr. Fuller.' The officer added, 'I'm afraid I'm not privy to any charge related information. I'll get your tea and toast.'

He returned to the desk and told Sergeant Mike Hodd what Fuller had said.

'He obviously doesn't realise that 'just' arson, is about as serious it gets,' said the desk Sergeant. 'I think it depends on whether life was endangered as well, but in some circumstances, arson can carry a life sentence. Go and get his tea and toast, Pete, make sure it's 'well done',' Mike Hodd grinned as PC Haylos sauntered off towards the rest room.

Graham Fuller was permitted use of the shower and provided with soap and a towel. His wife had been contacted last night, but advised that he would be held in custody and would not be permitted visitors until the DI had seen him in the morning. He was returned to his cell after his shower and requested the attendance of a solicitor, during his interview.

DS Ian Stuart was the first detective to arrive at the station. He checked his watch and signed in at 7.42 am.

'Tony's just parking his car, Mike,' he said. 'Has our guest had some tea and toast?'

'First class hotel we run here, Ian,' Mike told him. 'I've put the heating on in room one for you. It was a bit nippy in there at six, but it should be more comfortable now.'

'Thanks Mike, oh, here's Tony now.'

'Good morning gentlemen,' DI Church said, smiling.

'Mike's put the heating on in one and our guest has had tea, toast and a shower. How's that for efficiency?' Ian told him. Sergeant Hodd lifted the address book from the shelf below the counter, saying,

'You might need this, Inspector. Pete Hayles said he was asking for a solicitor.'

DI Church took the book from him and said,

'Thanks, would you ask PC Hayles to bring Mr. Fuller to the interview room for us please, Mike? He can sit with him until we get there. I've just got to pick up a few bits from my office. We'll be there in a few minutes.'

Graham Fuller was already seated when the two detectives got there.

'Good morning Mr. Fuller,' the DI greeted him. He shook hands with the man and introduced Ian.

'I'm Detective Inspector Church and this is my colleague, Detective Sergeant Stuart. I'd like us to have an informal chat, to begin with, no tape recordings, just the three of us. Are you OK with that?'

Fuller seemed taken aback by the apparently relaxed approach.

'Yes, I suppose so. Do I need a solicitor to be present?'

Tony looked him in the eye and replied,

'I'm not recording this, so whatever you decide to tell us is at your discretion. Obviously we would like you to tell us the truth, but we are not at this stage trying to trick you into saying something which you think you may later regret. I believe you realise that you are in serious trouble, and you are aware that we have witnesses to your actions last evening, so your guilt is already established. What I am puzzled about is your reason for doing what you did. Are you willing to co-operate with us in this preliminary interview?'

'When can I see my wife?' Fuller asked.

'We can arrange something later today, I expect.' DI Church told him. 'It's unlikely that you will be formally charged until tomorrow. So at this moment you have been arrested on suspicion of arson. You are, as the statement will say, 'helping us with our enquiries'. Do you understand?'

'I think so, Inspector. Can we stop if I think I'm saying too much?'

'We can stop whenever you like, Mr. Fuller, but when we resume the interview it will be on a formal footing. This is your chance to explain, off the record, what prompted your rather extreme actions of last evening. Are you willing to do that?'

'OK,' Fuller agreed, I've got nothing much to lose by telling you why I did it, have I?'.

'Thank you,' said Tony. 'Can we get you a cup of tea or coffee, whilst we talk?'

Fuller seemed to brighten a little, saying,

'I've just had some tea and toast, thanks, but a cup of coffee would be nice.'

'Milk and sugar?' Tony asked him.

'Please, just two sugars, thank you,' Fuller added.

Ian nodded to him as he opened the door of the interview room and walked quickly down the corridor to the front desk. Peter Hayles was nearing the end of his shift.

Ian called to him as he was about to leave the reception area. He turned and began to approach the DS.

'Would you do us a favour before you bugger off home, please Pete?' Ian asked. 'We'd like three cups of coffee, and a few 'bickies' delivered by your good self, to room one please.' Peter Hayles smiled,

'I always hoped I'd be selected for CID eventually,' he quipped. 'I suppose everyone begins as the 'tea boy' and progresses from there! I'm grateful for the start though, DS Stuart, you can depend on me!' He went on his way to get their refreshments.

Ian saw that Sergeant Mike Hodd was chuckling to himself.

'Bloody kids,' he said to Ian. 'They always try to seem smarter than they really are!'

Ian shook his head and smiled at Mike as he returned to the interview room. Fuller looked up as he entered,

'Thank you,' he said to Ian.

'I just caught PC Hayles before he went off duty,' he told Tony. 'He'll be back in a few minutes.'

The DI began the interview, whilst Ian took a few notes on his pad. Fuller tried to look at what Ian was writing.

'Don't worry about what DS Stuart is writing, Mr. Fuller. We'll show you at the end of our chat and you can delete anything you don't like. Now, just so that we all know, please can you confirm your name and address and place of employment for us?'

Graham Fuller obliged, giving his occupation as lorry driver for Tickners Transport.

The DI continued,

'Now, perhaps, in your own words, you'd like to tell us what motivated you to take such drastic action last evening?'
Fuller placed his hands on the table, either side of his coffee cup and began trying to explain his actions.

'I just got so riled up about what those bastards were doing, that I just completely lost it. That Bettis is denying everything. He knows he set Steve Foggarty up by promising fifty quid if he damaged the old boy next door's fence. Then Bloody Grover makes out he knows nothing about it. They're all in league with each other. OK I know Steve was wrong. He's almost suicidal over that poor lad he hit. Bettis and his cronies couldn't give a shit. We, that is, the rest of us drivers at Tickners, are bloody angry. We thought we'd go on strike, but it's getting near Christmas and money's a bit tight. We have a whip round for Steve's 'missus' every week, but it's not the same as her getting a regular wage, is it?'

'No, of course not,' said the DI. 'Tell us how burning Mr. Skrobe's shed helps with all this?'

'What!' Fuller said with incredulity. 'It's Bettis' shed, he told us so. He said his stuff was in there and he didn't want it stolen. He told that creep Rex Perrington to put a new padlock on it. I think you've got that bit wrong, Inspector.'
It began to dawn on Tony Church that although his offence was still arson, which can carry a long jail sentence, the intended victim was not Joe Skrobe, but Martin Bettis.

'I'm beginning to see this in a slightly different light, if you'll pardon the unintentional play on words,' said the DI. 'I can, however assure you that the shed, and the forecourt and the greenhouse at the end, are all the property of Mr. Skrobe. You say that Bettis said it was his shed, with his stuff in there. Do you know what of his, 'stuff', he was referring to?'

'Not all of it,' Fuller said. 'He had a strimmer and some other tools in there, I don't know what else there was. He's a nasty piece of work, but the others all seem afraid of him. He even

159

sacked Don Palmer for arguing with him over a bag of old bones. He's a lovely man, old Don, always willing to help anybody. He used to check our twin rear tyres for brickbats before we left the site. Nobody asked him to, he was just thoughtful like that.'

'I can tell you now that the yellow petrol strimmer, which was in there, also belonged to Mr. Skrobe.'

'So I've destroyed that as well! I feel really bad about this, Inspector. I honestly thought I was hurting Bettis, not the old chap next door. I got really worried when the digger driver started coming at me. I suppose Bettis had him watching the site, in case anyone tried to break in.'

The DI looked up at Fuller, a wry smile on his face.

'I'm afraid you got that bit wrong as well,' he told him. The man driving the digger was looking out for Mr. Skrobe, not Bettis. Fortunately he was able to remove Mr. Skrobe's tools before you set the shed alight.'

Tony paused, he had had a sudden thought.

'Mr. Fuller, in the event that we discovered sufficient evidence to make a case against Bettis, would you be willing to give evidence?' The DI asked.

'Yes,' Fuller replied, almost eagerly. 'Why? Do you think it's possible that he's broken the law?'

Tony Church looked at his DS and said,

'Well, it's early days yet, but I can say that we are aware of some irregularities concerning his business methods. Until we have had time to gather and analyse all of the information, it is just speculation at this stage. As far as you are concerned, Mr. Fuller, we will be obtaining statements from witnesses tomorrow. That is when you will be formally charged, do you have a solicitor, or would you like us to provide you with one?'

Fuller thought briefly before replying,

'I don't have a solicitor, so I'd like you to help me on that. When can I phone my wife?'

'Your wife has been informed of your whereabouts,' the DI told him. 'You may phone her from here, when we have ended this chat. I'll also have a word with the duty Sergeant and ask him to allow you fifteen minutes or so with her, if she would like to come in. This is a privilege for your wife only, not for a family group.

Now, before we close this informal interview, is there anything you would like to ask?'

'Yes,' said Fuller. 'Is there any way that I can apologise to Mr. Skrobe?'

Tony Church thought for a moment before replying.

'I'll have a word with him tomorrow, but whatever he decides, you will still be charged with the offence. There is nothing I can do to stop that now, you understand, don't you?'

Fuller said that he did and the interview was terminated.

CHAPTER 26.

Monday morning was dry but cold. Archie had his cooked breakfast and picked up Jimbo's lead. The dog came excitedly to him and stood while Archie put on his jacket and boots. There was a thin layer of ice on the bird bath, but the grass was just wet. He walked over to the mill and then along the path beside the mill pond. Jimbo ran on ahead of him, returning to Archie's side every few seconds. Archie reckoned that the dog covered at least three times the distance he did. As he reached the weir, he heard the two tone sirens of an emergency vehicle as it sped through the village. He reminded himself that he and Joe needed to give their statements to Bill Pickering this morning. He wondered how the arsonist was feeling now, in the cold light of day.

The pair arrived back home. Archie left his muddy boots outside the kitchen door and reached in to grab the old towel which was kept for the dog. Elsie appeared in the kitchen doorway,

'Do you want a cup of coffee, before you go up to Joe's?' she asked him.

'Yes please, Else.' He replied. 'I'll phone Joe first, we can phone Bill from his place.'

'I'll take you up there, Arch, but perhaps Joe will bring you back? I've told Joan I would meet her in 'Chi', after she's been to

162

the opticians. I should be home by about three. We'll probably have some lunch, so I won't want a full dinner tonight.'
Archie took his coffee through to the lounge and sat in his arm chair.

'There's a 'Marks and Sparks' steak pie in the fridge, isn't there?' he called out to Elsie.

'Yes, Arch,' she said. 'Are you going to eat all of it?'

'I'll save a bit for you, if you want me to, or you could have bacon and eggs instead. What do you think?'
Elsie refilled Jimbo's water bowl, which he drank from almost immediately, splashing water all over the floor.
Elsie waited until he'd finished drinking and then mopped it up. She looked at Archie thoughtfully.

'I don't think I want bacon and eggs, Arch. I might get myself something in 'Chi' instead. Are you nearly ready to go to Joe's?'
The telephone rang. Archie answered it,

'Hello?'

'Archie, it's me, Joe. There's a problem up at Ridge Farm, behind the building site. I just saw Bill on his way up there. He said leave the statements until this afternoon, so I'll come down to you later on. Do you want me to phone before I come?'

'OK.' Archie said. 'Elsie's going to Chi to meet up with her sister Joan. She could drop me at your place, if you don't mind running me home when we're done.'

'So now what's happening?' Elsie asked him.

'Wait a minute, Else,' he said, 'I can't hear both of you at once. Sorry Joe, say that bit again please, Elsie was talking to me.'
Joe continued to explain.

'Peter Bailley came down from the field and asked to use my phone,' he said. 'He's got his tractor stuck and the ground's giving way. He says something's up at Ridge Farm, as well, old Davies' place. I'm not quite ready yet Arch, so I'll come and get you in a little while, if that's OK?'

163

'Yes, Joe,' Archie said. 'Use my mobile number. I'm going over to the mill to finish a little job when I've had this cup of coffee. I'll take Jimbo with me, so I'll need to take him home before I come up with you. I'll see you later, Bye for now.'

Elsie stood listening to Archie's side of the conversation. Now he had finished and put the phone back in its cradle, she asked again,

'Tell me what's happening now, Arch?'

Archie picked up his coffee and took a sip.

'Something's up at Ridge Farm. Peter Bailley's got his tractor sinking in the field behind Joe's and there's something going on at old 'Diddler's' farm house.'

'What's going on at the farm house?' Elsie asked.

Archie sighed,

'Joe doesn't know, I don't know, so I can't help you there. I'm going over the mill with Jimbo. Joe will pick me up later, so you can go straight to Chichelster when you're ready. He'll bring me home when we're done.'

'What about Jimbo?' Elsie asked.

'I'll bring him home before I go to Joe's. Don't worry about us, just go and enjoy your day.'

He finished his coffee, put on his coat and grabbed his hat.

'Come on Jimbo, we've got a bit of woodwork to finish,' he said as he picked up the dog lead and left through the back door.

CHAPTER 27.

Cathy Simons arrived at the farm at about half past eight on Monday morning. She was surprised to see a suitcase in the front porch. She left it where it was. Using her key, she let herself in and called out,

'Morning Mr. Davies, I'm here. Shall I make some fresh coffee? This one is almost stone cold.'

She looked at the jug on the kitchen worktop. It was almost empty. She emptied the filter and re-filled the coffee maker. She switched it on and looked out of the kitchen window.

'Perhaps he's out there getting logs again,' she thought.

She opened the back door and called out,

'Are you out there, Mr. Davies?'

There was no answer. Cathy had noticed that the lounge curtains were opened, as she came up the drive. There was no sign of his coffee cup in the kitchen, so he probably got up early and made the coffee.

'I bet he's nodded off in his chair,' she thought. 'I'll take him a fresh coffee and wake him up.'

Jason Davies was in his Parker-Knoll armchair. He did not seem to hear Cathy enter the room with his coffee.

Jason Davies was dead.

A single small hole in the centre of his forehead was almost certainly the cause of his sudden and totally unexpected demise. Cathy dropped the cup and saucer and screamed in horror. She ran out of the room and picked up the telephone from the hall table. Her shaking hands tried to dial the emergency number, but in her agitated state, she dropped the phone after dialing the second nine. Frantically she picked it up and listened for the dialing tone. A voice was repeating, somewhat impatiently,

'Are you there caller? This is the emergency service! Emergency! Which service do you require, please?'
Through her sobs, she managed to say,

'Police, I think he's dead. Oh dear, it's awful.'

'One moment please.' Then, a different voice,

'Hello caller, this is the police. Can you tell me? What is your emergency?'

'Oh dear, I just told the lady, I think he's dead. No, he must be dead!

'Try to calm down, caller. First, please tell me your name and where you are calling from?

'Yes, yes, I'm sorry, Cathy Simons, I'm at Ridge Farmhouse in Wigglesworth. You go along through the village and past the new hotel site ....'

'We know how to get there, thank you. Can you tell me who you think is dead?'

'Mr. Davies. He's sitting in his chair. I think he's been shot. Please get here quickly.'

'Are you in the house with him?'

'Yes, of course, I got here about twenty minutes ago.'

'And you've just noticed he appears to be dead?' The policeman asked. 'What makes you think he's dead, where has he been shot?'

'I told you, in his chair, in the lounge.'

'The police are on their way to you now, Cathy. Where on his body do you think he's been shot?'

'No, not on his body, he's been shot in the head!'

166

'Are you saying that you shot him, Cathy?' he asked.

'No, no, no!' Cathy almost screamed at him in her terror. 'I work for him. I thought perhaps he was out in the back yard. I called out, but there was no answer.'

'Thank you Cathy, now please try to stay calm. I'm not accusing you of anything, but we have to ask these questions. Don't touch anything and don't leave the house. We'll be with you very soon. Would you like to stay on the line until our officers get to you?'

Cathy had managed to pull herself together after her initial shock,

'Yes, please,' she answered. 'Whoever did this might still be around! Oh! This is terrible.......'

The controller managed to keep her calm and lucid until at length Cathy told her,

'The police car is here. Thank you very much, I'll go and let them in.'

Cathy replaced the handset and opened the front door to the two uniformed officers. The female officer entered first and put an arm on Cathy's shoulder.

'I'm PC Carol Hickson,' she said. 'Try not to worry. We'll help you through this. Now, first tell us who you think is dead and where we can find him.'

The male officer began walking through the hall. PC Carol Hickson called to him,

'PC Mercer, come back here, now!'

He paused and looked around at his colleague.

'I'm checking that there's nobody else here,' he said.

Carol Hickson was obviously the more senior officer, she then said to him, in a stern voice,

'You're trampling all over a potential crime scene, you haven't been invited into this lady's home and your manners need improvement.'

He addressed Cathy,

'Would you like me to take a look around, madam?'

Before Cathy could answer, PC Hickson said,

'What you had better do, PC Mercer, is go back out to the car, call forensics and then bring some latex gloves and plastic overshoes. When you have done that, you can wait with me, to hear what this poor, traumatised lady has to tell us. Understood?' Mercer retraced his steps and with a scowl at PC Hickson, went back outside, leaving the door slightly open.

'I'm so sorry about that, my dear,' Carol Hickson told her. 'He's new to our force, transferred from the 'Met' about a month ago. It will take him some time to get used to our methods. Now, you were about to tell me what you found this morning. Can you begin from the moment you got here, please?'

'It's Mr. Davies, he's dead! Don't you want to see for yourself?' Cathy asked, still in shock at her discovery. Carol Hickson took the gloves and overshoes which Mercer had handed to her, saying,

'Thank you. Now please wait with me until this lady has explained the situation. Did you call forensics?'

'Yes, someone called 'Brineplace' is coming out. They said not to do anything until he gets here. He'll have someone with him,' PC Mercer told her. Carol attempted a smile at Cathy as she said to Mercer,

'I believe you'll find that was 'Detective Sergeant Brian Pace', not as you misinterpreted, 'Brineplace'. So we will do as they ask and leave the forensics to them.' Mercer attempted to defend his actions, he said,

'It's not like the 'Met'. I'm finding it difficult dealing with the country accents. She should have said it in plain English. Anyway, in the 'Met', we'd be expected to check the premises for intruders, before we did anything else. The safety of the occupants is always paramount.' Carol Hickson said,

'PC Mercer, go outside now. Wait in the car until a senior officer arrives. Thank you.' He turned and went, slamming the front door on his way out.

Cathy was becoming anxious, she was crying and trembling. Carol Hickson put an arm round her shoulders and helped her to the chair by the hall telephone.

'I'm sorry about that,' she said to Cathy. 'Now, it's just us two. My colleague is still a probationer with our force and has a lot to learn about our methods. Perhaps you could begin to tell me now, what you found when you got here this morning?'

Cathy tried to compose herself,

'I got here at about half past eight, I think,' she began. 'There was a suitcase on the doorstep, which I hadn't seen before, so I left it there.'

Carol Hickson nodded as she wrote in her notebook.

'How long have you worked for Mr.'Davis?' She asked.

'Its not Davis, its spelled, 'DAVIES', pronounced as, 'Davees'. I don't know, probably getting on for fifteen years, maybe longer. He gave me a key, so that I can still do my job if he's not at home.'

Carol Hickson continued to write in her notebook. She said to Cathy,

'Shall we begin as we should, by asking you for your full name and address, please, Cathy?'

Cathy provided the details with no trouble, and then asked,

'Would you like a cup of tea?'

'I was afraid you would ask me that, but it would be really be better to wait until the scientific brigade have checked everything first. They'll be looking for fingerprints everywhere I expect, so the less we contaminate their evidence, the better.'

Cathy's face showed alarm again.

'Is there a problem, Cathy?' Carol asked.

'But I've touched everything in the kitchen. I made him a fresh pot of coffee.' She explained. 'That's when I found him, when I took the coffee in to him. Oh, and I've got to clean up the mess in there, I dropped his cup of coffee, it's all over the carpet.'

'That's fine, Cathy,' Carol explained. 'Its best if we leave any cleaning up for now. They'll take your fingerprints, to eliminate them from any others they might find. You're not a suspect, you're my star witness. Now please carry on, you noticed the suitcase, then what?'

Cathy put her hand to her forehead and continued speaking,

'I let myself in and called out to him to let him know I was here. Then I went through to the kitchen and put my bag down. There was a half full pot of stale coffee on the worktop. I felt it but it was almost stone cold, so I tipped it away and re-filled the coffee maker. I think that's when I called out to him again. He's getting on a bit and sometimes he goes to sleep in his chair. Last week when I got here I couldn't make him hear and eventually I found him out the back stacking logs.'

Carol nodded sympathetically, she asked,

'Did you check if he was out the back this morning?'

'Yes.' Cathy said, 'I opened the back door and called out, but there was no answer. I made the coffee and poured out two cups, well a mug for me and a cup for Mr. Davies. He doesn't like the thick china mugs. I thought he was probably asleep, so I took it into the lounge. I knew he had been up, because the curtains were open when I came up the drive. Anyway, that's when I saw him sitting there. It's awful, it's absolutely awful!' Cathy burst into tears again as she recounted her experience.

'Now, now, Cathy,' Carol soothed. 'We'll get through this gently. How did you know he was dead? Did you check for a pulse?'

'No, nothing like that,' Cathy sobbed. 'There's a small, round hole, in the middle of his forehead and his eyes are open, but dull. Who's going to tell Mr. Jeffery? That's his son. I don't even know where he lives. They didn't have much to do with each other, but I think that's his only living relative.'

Carol Hickson looked up from her notes,

'Cathy,' she said, 'you've been very brave and very helpful, thank you. Don't worry about who will break the news to his son, we will see to that.'

There was a tap on the front door and a male voice called out,

'Are you there, PC Hickson?'

'That's Brian Pace,' she explained to Cathy. 'He's a Detective Sergeant, a very nice man.'

Carol unlocked the door and admitted him. He was followed into the house by another officer. Both wore white paper coveralls and blue latex gloves. DS Pace smiled at Cathy and introduced himself.

'Good morning, I'm Brian Pace and this is DC Adam Morton.'

Adam smiled and nodded to both of the women. Brian Pace spoke next,

'Carol, Tell me please, why is your trainee sitting in the car looking like sour milk?'

'I'll explain later, DS Pace,' she replied. 'This is Cathy Simons. She's worked for Mr. Davies for more than fifteen years. You'll find him in the lounge, first right. Do you want Cathy to come with you?'

DS Pace smiled at Cathy,

'I think I can find him, thank you, but you look as though you need a cup of tea. Let me have a quick look in the kitchen, first and then I suspect it will be a good idea if we all have one. I'm afraid we can't do very much until Doctor Gibbs arrives. He's the pathologist and I really mustn't touch the body until he's seen him. I understand that this has been a terrible shock for you, Cathy, but would you mind staying for a while? I may need your knowledge of the place, if you would be so kind.'

Cathy seemed to brighten a little,

'No, Inspector,' she said, 'I don't mind. Shall I wait here until you've checked the kitchen?'

'Yes please Cathy and thank you for the promotion, I'm a detective Sergeant, not an Inspector, but you never know, maybe one day?' His mobile phone began to buzz. He pulled it from his pocket and opened it.

'Pace here,' he said and then, 'Oh, hello Bill, you've found what?'

His expression changed to one of bewilderment as he continued,

'I'm already at Ridge Farm. I'm in the farmhouse. Is this about the death?' He paused to listen. 'Bill, I can't come just now, I'm waiting for Duncan Gibbs to arrive. Would you mind just securing the scene, without disturbing too much? I'll ask young Adam Morton to come up to the field to meet you. He's my trainee DC. He's here now, will he need boots?'

DS Pace looked at his young colleague,

'That was an affirmative from PC Bill Pickering,' he told him. 'He says it's thick and sticky up there.' He spoke into his mobile again. 'Thanks Bill, it'll probably be an hour or so before I can let him go, but I'll try to be as quick as I can.'

DS Pace turned to his assistant and said,

'Adam, before we forget, would you make sure to take Cathy's fingerprints, so that we can eliminate them from whatever else we may find. First though, I need you to assist me in the kitchen. Put on a clean pair of gloves and overshoes and make sure you've got a biro. Bring the kit with you and remember, don't touch anything except the evidence bags and labels.'

The two forensics men went into the kitchen. The two ladies could hear Brian Pace explaining the right way to check a scene.

'Imagine the room drawn up into grid squares, Adam. Always begin at the entry point, in this case the internal door from the hallway,' he explained. 'Right, Adam, we'll begin by looking at the whole scene from here, before we go into more detail. Try to establish whether there are any marks or fibres, visible to the naked eye. See if anything may look damaged or out of place. Next we dust for fingerprints, we know that Cathy Simons has been in and made coffee, so we'll find hers. Any others which are not Davies' could belong to our perpetrator. We'll begin with obvious places like door handles and door frames'

They dusted the door and found several prints. There was nothing in the way of obvious footprints on the floor, but Brian got onto his hands and knees and looked along the kitchen at floor level.

'There are some marks, maybe footprints by the kitchen bin,' he told Adam. 'No, don't go over there just yet, remember our grid search.' Together they dusted the worktops and cupboards for prints, finding several sets. Next they lifted some fingerprints from the drawer handles. Brian checked the taps and found prints on both the hot and cold tap tops. Another set on the door to the back porch and an almost complete set from the top of the plastic kitchen bin.

'This is always a good place to check, Adam,' he said as he carefully opened the bin, removing the lid for better access.

'Large evidence bag please,' he called out as he lifted a blood stained tea towel from the bin. 'See this,' he held the towel up for Adam to inspect. 'That's blood, probably Davies', but this looks like a powder burn,' he pointed with his pencil. 'There's probably some other evidence on here, maybe sweat, for DNA comparison, possibly even some hairs.' He dropped the towel into the bag and continued his search of the bin contents.

'Make sure you identify the object and where it was located, Adam,' he said. Never mix two items in the same evidence bag.' On top of the recent rubbish, he found a broken table knife wrapped in some kitchen paper. 'Ah! This may be useful,' he said as he dropped it into another bag.

'Now, please pass me some tweezers or forceps, Adam.' He held up the tweezers which gripped the shiny backing plastic from a sticking plaster.

'If our suspect cut himself on the broken knife, he probably used this. Smooth plastic is usually a good source for fingerprints. We'll check the bathroom cabinet later. He probably got the band aid from in there. Now tell me Adam, have you formed any thoughts about our suspect, so far?' Adam thought carefully before answering, his response might hold the key to his future as a forensics officer.

'He's careless, for a start,' he said. 'He wasn't in a hurry, or he'd have just left as quickly as he could. He probably left through the back door, with his holdall.'

'Why do you say, his holdall?' Brian queried. 'How do you know he had a holdall?'

Adam smiled as he replied,

'It's a blue one, Mr. Pace,' he said confidently. 'The zip's broken, look down there by the kitchen bin, it fell out of that tea towel as you dropped it into the bag.'

Brian looked to where Adam was pointing his biro. On the floor were some coarse, dark blue fibres with part of a zip fastener attached, next to it was the broken brass pull tag. Using the tweezers again, Brian picked it up and examined it. He read the maker's name embossed on the brass tag, 'Carlton'.

'Full marks, Adam,' he said. 'Forensics are more often than not, fifty per cent science and fifty per cent observation. You just passed the observation part, we'll teach you the 'science' as we go.'

Adam looked pleased,

'Thank you, Mr. Pace,' Adam said to his boss. 'This is the sort of police work I was most interested in. I hope we don't miss anything important.'

'No matter how carefully we search, there is always the possibility we'll miss something,' Brian explained. 'That's one of the main reasons we use the grid method instead of diving after the first thing we may notice.'

Adam nodded that he understood.

When they had completed their check of the kitchen, they spent a few minutes making sure that all the evidence and fingerprints were correctly identified.

'I want to quickly check the bathroom for any evidence,' DS Pace continued. 'Perhaps whilst we're upstairs, we'll have a cursory look at the bedrooms.'

Together they checked the bathroom. A couple of small spots of dried blood were on the tiled floor in front of the wash basin. Brian carefully scraped them from the tiles and placed them in a small bag which Adam then identified. They had found more prints on the handle of the bathroom cabinet and the glazed surface of the basin and the toilet lid. Adam waited on the upstairs landing, while Brian checked the main bedroom. The bed was made and didn't look as though it had been slept in. On the dressing table he found some envelopes. One was addressed simply to, 'Cathy Simons'. He put this in his pocket, to give to her when they returned back downstairs. They returned to the kitchen, where Brian took a cloth and wiped up some spilled coffee from the worktop. He emptied the coffee maker, switched it off at the wall socket and filled the electric kettle. Whilst it was boiling he took some clean cups from the cupboard and placed them on a tray with the sugar basin, some spoons and a jug of milk from the supply in the refrigerator. He found a teapot and tea bags and left them on the worktop in readiness.

Adam had collected his evidence kit and was ready to leave for his next assignment in the field, where PC Pickering would be waiting for him.

'How do I get to this field, Mr. Pace?' He asked.

Brian turned to him and explained,

If you go on up to the top of this lane you'll probably see PC Pickering. He's with Mr. Peter Bailley, in the field on the left. It's pretty muddy, he tells me so you'll need to put your boots on before you leave here. I should put your coat on, as well, Adam. It'll be a bit chilly up there, I shouldn't wonder. Take a few evidence bags with you and some latex gloves. You'd better make sure you've got a few pairs of larger ones for Bill. He's a good sort, if you need any help, just ask him. Are you OK with that, Adam?'

'Yes, Thank you Mr. Pace,' he said. 'What's going on up there? Is it connected to this incident?'

'Not directly,' Brian told him. 'I'll come up there after I've had a word with the doctor, he should be here by now, but I don't suppose he'll be much longer.'

He followed Adam to the front hallway, where Cathy sat with PC Carol Hickson. He took the envelope from his pocket and handed it to Cathy.

'I believe this is for you, Cathy. I found it on Mr. Davies'
dressing table. There are others for his son and someone named
Bernice Tenham,' he said. 'Does the name mean anything to
you?'

'He has a sister called, Bernice,' Cathy told him. 'I think they
live in Worthing.'
She took the envelope from him and read the address. She
recognised Jason Davies' handwriting.

F.A.O.

Miss Cathy, Simons.

To be opened only upon the occasion of my death.
Jason W. Davies.

'Do you want to open it whilst we're here?'
'I don't know,' Cathy said in some distress. 'Do you think I
should?'
Carol Hickson looked at DS Pace and said,
'It's your decision Cathy, but the 'occasion' is now, isn't it?
Cathy took the envelope and slid her finger along the flap. There
was a short letter from Jason Davies. She showed it to DS Pace.

'It's from him, from Mr. Davies,' she said in some alarm.
'Would you read it for me please?'
DS Pace took the letter and began to read it aloud.

'It's dated yesterday,' he said. 'Remembrance Day.'
He began to read, his voice was soft and he kept an eye on Cathy
as he read.

'Dear Cathy,
Today has been a day of reflection for me. I had a drive out this
morning, it was Armistice Day. I saw people gathered around the
war memorials of several villages. I stopped for some lunch at a
pub in Tarring, where I met a delightful young couple who shared
my table. They were most courteous and I enjoyed their company

176

for an hour or so. I began to think that perhaps if I had been a more considerate man, I would not have led such a lonely life. It is true that I have never wanted for the material things, but there is no substitute for friendship. You have been a good friend to me and have kept house and cooked for me for a great many years. Such loyalty should not go unrewarded. I know that I have not always shown my appreciation, but I have made arrangements with my solicitor to ensure that you are not forgotten.

You may have noticed that I have not been a well man just lately and I fear it may signal a recurrence of my heart trouble. I do not wish to distress you, but just to thank you for your eternal kindness.

I have had two sets of visitors this evening. The first was from my sister, Bernice and her husband. They provided me with some information which lifted a great burden from me. For years I blamed myself for the loss of my late wife, Mary. In that I was not as kind to her as I should have been. I learned this evening that another person was guilty of ending her life, not me.

My second visitor of the evening was my son, Jeffery, who was accompanied by a female companion. Maybe it was her presence which influenced him, but he was unusually pleasant, which was good. Perhaps he has finally come to realise that he can accomplish more by treating people with respect, than by bullying or threatening them. I do hope so.

With my sincere and heartfelt thanks,

Jason Davies.'

Brian Pace looked up as he finished reading, there were tears in PC Carol Hickson's eyes. She had a comforting arm around Cathy's shoulders. Cathy was sobbing uncontrollably.

'To hell with protocol,' said Brian Pace, 'I think we all need a cup of tea after that.' He went back into the kitchen and Carol heard the kettle boiling. As he made the tea, he could feel a lump in his throat. Cathy was obviously dedicated to looking after old Jason. He returned to the ladies whilst the tea brewed.

It took several minutes for Cathy to regain her composure, or at least some of it. She had been shaking as she took her letter from Brian Pace's hand

'It's almost as though he knew he was dying, isn't it?' Cathy had said, tearfully.

Brian nodded, in agreement.

'I don't think he anticipated being shot, though.' He said.

Adam had returned in the middle of all this, he read the situation. 'Back in a minute or two,' he said and mouthed silently to Brian, 'Fingerprints' as he pointed to Cathy and disappeared back outside for a while.

Brian brought a tray of cups and saucers and placed it on the hall table.

'Tea, milk and sugar coming up,' he said. 'I recommend at least three sugars, Cathy, it will help with the shock you've just had. Do you feel cold? Perhaps you'd like a blanket round you. Shock sometimes affects people like this.'

Carol Hickson poured the tea for them and a cup for Adam

Adam returned for the second time, with his fingerprint kit.

'Shall we leave this until we've had a cup of tea?' He asked.

Brian smiled at the ladies as he said to Adam,

'Did you say 'we'? You mean you want a cup of tea as well?' Brian teased him. 'We get the trauma and you get the tea! Damn cheek, you didn't even have the good grace to make it for us!'

The girls looked up and smiled through their tear stains.

'Thank you Mr. Pace,' Carol said, sipping her tea. 'How much longer do you think we'll have to wait for Doctor Gibbs?'

They heard a car pull up in the driveway and a few minutes later the pathologist tapped gently on the front door.

'I expect that'll be him now,' said DS Pace, as he opened the door to admit him.

'Sorry about the delay, Brian,' he apologised. 'I wasn't sure where I was supposed to be. I stopped and asked at the bungalow,

178

along the road and they began directing me to a field at the top of this lane. I saw your car in the driveway and thought I'd try here first.'

Brian shook his hand and introduced him to the others.

'You're in the right place, Doc,' he told him. 'You'll find the deceased in there,' he indicated the lounge. 'I'll leave you to it for now, but you may be required up at the field later. They've found some human remains, young Adam is about to join the others, up there, as soon as he's obtained this young lady's fingerprints.'

The Doctor followed Brian to the door of the room and went over to where Jason Davies was seated in his armchair.

'Oh dear,' said Gibbs. 'Who discovered him?'

'His housekeeper, Miss Cathy Simons,' Brian told him. 'She's out in the hall with Carol Hickson. I've given her a cup of sweet tea, but she's pretty shaken by her experience.'

Doctor Gibbs went back out to her,

'I'm sorry for your loss, Miss Simons,' he said to her. 'If you'll just give me a moment, I'll get you something from my car, to help you to cope. I can't do anything to help Mr. Davies, but the least I can do is to try to relieve some of your pain and anxiety.'

'Thank you,' said Cathy, as he left, leaving the front door slightly open, in readiness for his return.

CHAPTER 28.

Archie had been at the mill for about an hour, when Joe called his mobile.

'Can I come and get you now, Arch?' he asked.

'Yes, OK.' Archie replied. 'Pick me up from home, I'm over at the mill but I've got Jimbo with me. I'll take him home and feed him and then I'll be ready. Is Bill there now?'

'No, not yet,' Joe explained. 'There was a problem in the field behind my house, you know, Ridge Farm. It's on the bit of ground Peter Bailley rents from Davies.'

'What sort of a problem, Joe?' Archie asked.

'I'll tell you about it when I pick you up,' Joe said. 'Be about ten minutes, OK?'

Archie put his phone away and went down the stairs. He picked up his Barbour jacket from the bench and went out of the mill. Jimbo waited while Archie locked up and then trotted along with him back to the house. Archie put a bowl of biscuits down and changed Jimbo's water.

'I won't be too long, boy,' he explained to the dog. 'I'll see you later, be a good boy.' He patted and rubbed Jimbo's head and went out through the kitchen door. Joe had just stopped in his van as Archie went out of the gate.

'That was good timing,' Archie said as he got in the van.

'Better than some, I suppose,' Joe told him. 'I'd just finished my breakfast when Peter Bailley came banging on my kitchen door. He was a bit shaken and covered in mud and grass.
He said he was replacing the fence where they'd been blasting at the back of the site next door. He jumped off the tractor and began walking round to the back of the trailer. He noticed a large hole a few feet away, towards the edge of the field. It was quite a big hole, more like a crack in the ground, as though the ground had sort of caved in all by itself. He went to have a closer look and saw a skull lying on some loose soil near the top of the hole. He went to touch it with his gloved hand, but it sunk a bit lower in the hole. The sides were loose and beginning to cave in, so he stepped back from the edge. He said it was a bit like a bottomless pit, the soil just kept moving.'

'So he thought he'd better tell someone, I suppose?' Archie suggested. 'I was wondering, Joe, how deep is a bottomless pit?'
Joe laughed.

'You mean it might go right down to Australia?'

'Even further than that if it's bottomless,' Archie grinned.

'So there'd be another bottomless pit there, I suppose?'
Archie began laughing.

'Of course, a 'perfect' bottomless pit would be flawless, or should that be, 'floorless'? I know it's not really a laughing matter, but that would all depend on which end you were standing close to, wouldn't it?' he said. 'Anyway, I suppose he called Bill from your place, to come and have a look?'
Joe nodded,

'Well, yes and then he phoned his farm and got hold of his tractor driver, John Tindall. You see, as he looked around, his tractor started sinking into the ground near to the edge of the field. He said he tried to get in the cab and move it away from the edge, but it was tilting too quickly, so for his own safety he jumped out again. He said that as he jumped, the place he landed was also unstable and his right foot went down a hole.'

'Is he OK?' Archie asked anxiously.

'Just about,' Joe said. 'He asked John Tindall to put the buck rake on that big Ford County tractor and bring half a dozen sleepers up to the field.'

Archie nodded,

'I expect he wants to try to make it safe, before he tries to recover it. Which tractor has he got up at the field?'

'I haven't been up there yet,' Joe replied. 'I think it's the little one, a 'Dexta' or something. Anyway, Bill turned up and went into the field through my garden. He wants us to call in his house on the way back and ask his wife for his wellies. By that time, Bill said it looked as though the tractor might be going over the edge into the building site below. They're both up there now, trying to work out what to do when John arrives with the sleepers.'

Joe stopped the van outside the police house and Archie went to the back door and knocked loudly. Kate opened it and said,

'Hello Archie, I haven't seen you since the summer. What can I do for you? I'm afraid Bill's not here. He's been called out to a problem up at Ridge Farm.'

'Yes, Kate,' Archie said. 'I'm with old Joe Skrobe, we're parked out the front. We're on our way back to the field now, but Bill asked us to call in and collect his wellies. It's a bit on the sticky side up there, with all the rain we've had.'

Kate went back into the house and came back with Bill's boots.

'There you are, Archie,' she gave him the boots and asked, 'Do you think he'll be home for lunch?'

Archie grinned at her,

'I never was much good as a clairvoyant, Kate. Your guess is as good as mine on that one. Thanks for the boots, I'll ask him to give you a call and let you know.'

Kate smiled as she replied,

'I can't imagine anyone paying you for a reading, Archie. Yes, if you wouldn't mind, ask him to let me know. Bye Archie, give my best wishes to Elsie.'

182

Archie got back into the van and they carried on to Joe's bungalow.

The pair climbed over the low fence at the back of Joe's garden. Archie waved the boots at Bill and shouted,

'Bill, come and get these, they weigh a ton before you've got 'em muddy!'

Bill Pickering strode over to where they stood and leaned on a fence post while he changed into them.

'Thank you gents,' he said, then to Joe, 'Can I leave these shoes in your kitchen, please?'

Joe took the shoes and walked back to the kitchen door. He put them inside and closed the door again.

'I'd better leave old Thunder indoors,' he called to Bill. 'He's rather partial to a few bones and we don't want him eating all the evidence, do we?'

'It's not just the evidence on offer, Joe,' Bill told him. 'We've got a shiny new police forensics man here for him to sniff, as well.'

Bill introduced them to Adam, who had just arrived on the scene. He had walked up the lane from the farmhouse and was feeling hot in his top coat. He was glad that he had worn his boots though. They now weighed almost double, with the mud which had collected on them on his way across the field. He had briefed Bill about the death at the farm, but told him to keep it to himself until they had a few more facts.

Peter Bailley stood assessing the situation with his tractor. It was leaning at a dangerous angle. Archie noted that the left hand rear wheel had sunk almost a foot into the soft ground.

'Hello Arch,' he said as they approached him. 'What d'you think about this then Arch? Any sensible suggestions welcome at this stage.'

Archie cautiously approached the tractor from the field side.

'I think the first thing is to get the trailer unhooked, Peter,' he said.

'I didn't want to risk disturbing it any more, in case it all went over the edge,' Peter told him. 'How would you suggest we go about it?'

'We really need those sleepers,' Archie said. 'We might be in with a chance once they arrive. Joe told me that John is on his way with them.'

'I thought he'd be here by now,' Peter replied, checking his watch/ 'It's only a five minute job to stick the buck rake on and there's a new stack of sleepers down by the yard gate.'
The two policemen were inspecting the hole where the skeletal remains were located.

'I think this is a job for a team, Bill,' Adam said. 'It looks as though there's more here than just a skull. If we start poking about too much, we could send the whole thing downwards. The whole area looks as though it could collapse at any minute.'
Bill nodded,

'I believe you're right, young Adam,' he agreed. 'I'll get on old Joe's phone again and ask Dixie Dean for a digging crew.'

'Use my mobile, Bill,' said Adam Morton. 'I'll just phone Brian Pace first, to let him know the situation.'
He punched in Brian's number and explained what was happening. Brian listened intently and then he said,

'It sounds a bit hairy, especially with a tractor about to go off the edge! Is there anyone below that could suffer injury if it goes?'

'I don't know, hang on, I'll ask the others.' He turned to Bill and Archie for an answer and then responded to Brian's question.

'No, Mr. Pace, the site is closed, pending a decision by the courts. There is a major problem with the remains which have been discovered.' He went on to explain the unstable conditions. 'I don't know whether it's because of all the rain, or if it's got some connection to the building site next to us. Bill Pickering says there are a lot of old flint mines around here and they do give way from time to time. This is not the first time that large holes have mysteriously appeared. He's going to phone Sergeant Dean and request a digging team, will that be OK?'

'It sounds to me to be the best and safest way to move forwards, Adam. The doctor has just arrived, so I'll have to go now. I'll try to pop up and see you later on. I've suggested that Carol Hickson should stay here, but her probationer can go and help the digging team when they get here.'

Adam passed the phone to Bill, when he had finished.

'He thinks that sounds like a good plan, Bill, he's going to send that new bloke, Mercer, to help with the digging team. He's already upset Carol Hickson and the lady at the farm house. She's sent him to wait in the car, out of their way.'

Bill took the phone,

'Thanks,' he said. 'I'll see what Dixie says about it.'

'The number's already on there, under HQ,' Adam explained. 'If you tell them it's my mobile, they've got the number listed.' He selected the number and passed the phone to Bill.

'Thanks,' said Bill as he began explaining the situation to the desk constable.

'He'll tell Dixie and get him to call us back,' he told Adam as he passed his phone back to him.

Archie could see exhaust smoke over the hedge in the farm lane, but it didn't seem to be moving,

'Perhaps he's got stuck,' he suggested to Peter Bailley.

Bill came over to them,

'What's up chaps?' he asked.

'I think something's up with John,' Peter told him. 'It looks as though he's stuck in the lane. We can see the exhaust smoke from the big old County, but it hasn't moved for the past five minutes.'

'I can't do anything until the diggers get here,' said Bill. 'I'll go and find out what the problem might be.' He clomped off towards the gate and the lane.

Outside the driveway to the farmhouse, John Tindall was sitting in the cab of the big four wheel drive tractor. Standing between the diameters of the two huge tyres, was PC. Eric Mercer. He didn't hear Bill Pickering approaching over the noise of the huge diesel engine, so when Bill tapped him on the shoulder, he jumped!

'What! Who are you' he asked Bill.

'I'm a policeman, son,' Bill told him. 'Why are you delaying this man? Don't you realise we're all waiting for these sleepers to try to prevent a major disaster'

Mercer didn't like to be addressed as, 'son'. He turned to face Bill and with a scowl on his face, pulled himself up to his full and most important height and said,

'I'm not happy about his load of old railway sleepers. He's come all the way from Wigglesworth like this. They're not secured and could cause a nasty accident.'

Bill smiled at John Tindall and then he turned to face the other officer.

'I think I heard that you were told to sit in the car and wait. Is that right?' Bill asked him.

'Yes, but if I see something which could present a danger, or looks unsafe, it is my duty to act in the interests of public safety and the law.'

Bill ignored him and said to John Tindall,

'Off you go John, get up there, but don't go anywhere near the edge, its all unstable ground.'

Bill then beckoned Eric Mercer over to the grass verge as John Tindall continued on his way.

'You deliberately undermined my authority,' Mercer said to Bill. 'I intend to report your conduct to a senior officer at the first opportunity.'

'Yes,' said Bill. 'You do that, at your first opportunity. In the meantime, DS Brian Pace has told me that you can come with me to assist in the recovery of some human remains and a little 'Dexta' on the verge of a suicidal leap into the unknown!'

Mercer looked puzzled.

'What's a 'Dexta'?' he asked.

'It's like that one's little brother,' Bill said, 'Now, have you got any wellies with you?'

'Wellies, no, why do I need wellies? He asked.

Bill sighed,

'Take a look at my feet,' he said. 'Your nice shiny shoes won't last long in the field. Were you issued with gum boots?'

'Yes, but I didn't think I'd need them today,' he said.

'So they're at the station,' Bill suggested. 'That's no problem. We can get the others to bring them, when they come. Where are they, in your locker?'

'No, they're at home,' Mercer replied.

Bill fixed him with a straight look and said,

'Look, maybe we got off on the wrong foot, what's your name?'

'Mercer,' he replied.

'No your first name? I'm Bill Pickering, the village policeman.' Bill held out a hand to Mercer, who shook it. For the first time since their encounter Mercer half smiled.

'Eric Mercer,' he said. 'I transferred from the 'Met' a few weeks ago. I haven't made any friends in the force here yet, they seem to have taken a dislike to me.'

'If you don't mind me asking, how old are you, Eric?'

'I'm twenty six, I'll be twenty seven in March,' he replied. 'Why do you ask?'

Bill walked with him back towards the farmhouse and the police car, parked in the drive. DS Pace's car was parked behind it, Bill leaned against the police car and said to Mercer,

'I'll tell you something, Eric and I'm trying to help you when I say this. You don't need to waste all your efforts looking for problems here. Try to relax a bit, people will notice and you'll find they'll come to you and begin to tell you things. They won't do that if you appear to be prickly or hostile to them.'

'But in the Met you had to be alert to problems all the time. You've no idea how dangerous it can get. You can't afford to relax, even for a few minutes.'

187

Bill smiled and said,

'When you were about twelve years old, I was in the Falkland Islands firing shells at the 'Argies' from a Royal Navy Warship. I did eighteen years in the 'Andrew' and joined the police when I came out. I've only been a 'copper' for seven years, so about the same length of time as you, Eric. Although I can promise you one thing, it did get just a tad dangerous out there, on more than one occasion.'

'Yes, I can imagine it did,' Eric Mercer agreed. 'I've seen some of the news film about the Falklands war. I watched it on the 'telly' while it was still going on. It looked exciting to me as a boy, but I can believe it was pretty scary to actually be there.'

'So you can see that there's always a bit of danger in whatever we do, but it doesn't help to keep yourself on, 'high alert' all the time. Why did you leave the 'Met'?' Bill asked. Mercer frowned,

'My wife couldn't put up with it,' he explained. 'All the hassle and gangs really got to her. She was afraid to go out on her own, even just shopping. It was probably made worse because of my job. Once they find out your old man's a copper, they pick on you even more. It was a case of get out of London, or get out of the force altogether.'

'Well, Eric, you're not in the 'Met' any more. It's a totally different style of policing down here in Sussex. Why did you choose Chichelster?'

'I suppose I thought I'd fit in better because it's a city.' Bill nodded,

'But it's not a capital city, Eric. We don't have gangs of muggers or fights in the street. It's safe for ladies to go shopping without an escort and the neighbours won't treat your wife any differently because you happen to be a policeman. You need to adapt and survive, Eric. I can understand that if John Tindall had been driving that precarious load of sleepers down Oxford Street, you would need to stop him. But this is a private farm track in the

Sussex countryside, which makes it very, very different. Understand what I'm saying?'

Eric Mercer was thoughtful for a moment before he replied.

'I thought they were against me because I was a former 'Met' officer, but I'm beginning to see your point. It's going to take some time for me to get used to it, but we worked on the principle of 'zero' tolerance. You know, nip it in the bud, before it escalates.'

Bill smiled,

'The best advice I can give you is to forget the 'zero' bit and emphasise the 'tolerance' element. Don't go jumping into a situation, watch and learn. There may be instances when you find you need to be the big, hard policeman, but they're a bit thin on the ground in this neck of the woods. It's a great help to have the public on your side when there's a crisis. You won't get that if you're officious and unapproachable, will you? My advice, for what it's worth, is just to 'back off a bit'. After a while, people will begin to confide in you and help you'

'Thanks, Bill,' said Eric Mercer. 'I'll try to do that, maybe things will begin to work for us, instead of against us.'

'Right,' said Bill, 'Now it's no good you coming with me if you've got no boots. What size do you take?'

'Eleven.'

'Is Carol Hickson still in there?' Bill indicated the front door with his head.

'Yes,' Mercer replied. 'She's with the young lady who found the body.'

'The body!' Bill exclaimed. 'What, old Diddler's popped his clogs?'

'There I go again,' said Mercer. 'I was told not to say anything to anyone until the details have been announced. Now I'll get another bollicking for that.'

'No, you won't,' Bill assured him. 'We'll keep that just between you and me. I'll go and ask Carol to organise some boots for you. I'd better not go in there in these boots though, ask her to come out, would you?'

Eric went to the front door and knocked. The door opened and Carol's face appeared in the gap. Bill saw Mercer begin to talk to her. The door opened wider and Carol put her hand up to Bill.

'I'll just be a minute, Bill,' she said and went back inside. She re-appeared a few moments later with her top coat on and came out to meet him.

Bill spoke with her and she got in the car and radio'd Chi to arrange for a pair of boots to be brought out. He told her what the situation was in the field whilst she was waiting for a response. Bill heard the voice of Sergeant Dean on the radio,

'Tell Bill, we've got three diggers coming out with tools, and an extra pair of boots for the 'Met apprentice!' Tell him to wait in the lane by the farmhouse. It'll be about half an hour before they get there. I've already told young Morton and he said Bill had gone to deal with another issue. Can Mercer get a cuppa while he's waiting? And tell Bill Pickering not to find any more bodies, he'll be getting us a bad name!'

Carol looked at Bill and Eric Mercer and grinned,

'Yes Sarge, I'll get them both a drink before they go back to the field. Bill heard what you said. He's here at the car with me.' She handed the microphone to Bill.

'I'm not finding 'em, Dixie, just diggin' 'em up!' He said. They finished their conversation as DS Pace came over to them.

'Hello Bill,' he said, as he shook hands, 'I'm going to be tied up here for a while yet. Did you know Jason Davies?'

'I know of him,' Bill told him. 'Rumour has it that he's not one of the kindest men on the planet, I'm sorry to say.'

'Well, he won't be causing anyone offence now,' Brian Pace said. 'It looks like a murder, but we won't know for sure until the post mortem. Doc Gibbs has just gone. The removal team should be here soon. Young Adam should be able to manage your problem and it will be good experience for him. I'll come up to find you if I get through here in time. Cathy Simons has been a real godsend, she's a very nice young lady. Do you know her?'

'No, I'm afraid not,' Bill said. 'I've seen her now and then, in the village shops, but not to talk to. I expect Archie Leggitt will know her. He seems to know everybody.'

Brian Pace returned to his forensic duties, leaving the others in the driveway.

CHAPTER 29.

Archie, Joe and Peter Bailley pondered on the best and safest way to uncouple the trailer. It was a most precarious situation, if the tractor slipped over the edge of the escarpment, the trailer would go with it. They were somewhat relieved when John Tindall arrived with the big County and six railway sleepers. John stopped the tractor some way from the edge of the field and walked over to where they stood. He told them about the young policeman and how Bill had come along at just the right moment.

'I've brought that long chain as well,' he told Peter. 'I thought we might need it to drag the Dexta away from the edge.'

'Thanks, John,' Peter said, 'We want to begin by unhooking the trailer. Archie reckons if we use a couple of sleepers to take the weight of the drawbar, we could pull it round sideways. It will probably slide on the sleepers, enough to hitch it to the County and get it out of the way.'

'Keep well clear of that hole,' Archie called out as he pointed. 'That's where the skeleton is and we don't want it to sink any further.'

Adam Morton was standing close to the hole, as if guarding his 'treasure'.

'I don't think it's moved any more since I've been here,' he called out. 'I wonder what else we might find when we start digging. There might be a whole skeleton down there.'
Archie grinned as he said,

'Just let's hope we don't find another bloody tractor down there as well!'
They had been standing around for long enough to begin to feel cold. Joe offered to go and make up a couple of flasks of coffee.

'I'd better let old Thunder have a run whilst I'm down there,' he said as he climbed over his fence. 'I'll keep him away from here, it's a dangerous enough as it is, without a big friendly Alsatian jumping at everyone.'
The others cautiously studied the scene from a closer viewpoint.
Archie was thinking aloud as he said,

'We'll put a sleeper behind the trailer wheels first, to stop it running back when we pull the pin from the drawbar.'
John nodded his agreement and began unloading the sleepers from the buck rake. Archie worked with him and together they decided on a plan which they thought would offer the best chance of a safe and successful outcome.
The pair first carried a sleeper over to the back of the trailer wheels and wedged it against the tyres. Archie then took the chain and passed the hook through the 'A' frame of the trailer drawbar, hooking it back on itself. John attached the steel ring on the other end, to the front towing hitch on the County. Peter and Archie slid a couple of sleepers under the trailer's drawbar, leaving a small gap between the top of the sleepers and the bottom of the steel angle iron 'A' frame.

'That's good enough,' Archie said. 'Now, John, can you gently take up the slack in the chain? Don't pull the trailer yet, just go gently back until the chain is almost tight.'
John was a skilled driver of the big machine and just crept backwards until Archie signaled that the chain was taut enough.

'Be careful, Arch,' Peter called out as Archie approached the drawbar in readiness to pull the towing pin. The trailer moved slightly as the pin came out, but the chain held it.

'Everybody, stand clear,' Archie called out. 'The tractor might shift a bit once the weight comes off the drawbar.' He turned to look at John, still in the seat of the County. 'Go back as gently as you can, John.' Archie called out. 'Whatever you do don't go forwards. We don't want the trailer to slide the wrong side of the hitch.'

There was a jolt as the trailer came free and landed on the two sleepers. The little Dexta moved slightly, causing Peter to gasp!

'I thought it was going then,' he said.'

Carefully John pulled the trailer well clear of the edge of the escarpment. Archie and Peter picked up the sleeper they had used as a wheel chock and replaced it behind the wheels again.

'Now for the tricky bit,' said Archie. 'I've got a plan which I think will work, it involves a bit of geometry.'

Joe returned from his home with a carrier bag containing the flasks and some mugs.

'Oh, you've got the trailer off, well done!' He said to Peter. 'Do you want this now, or after you've made the tractor safe?'

They began a brief discussion, which was cut short by the tractor's back wheel sinking another inch into the soft ground.

'I think we'd better try to get it secured first,' Archie said. 'Another inch or two of subsidence and there won't be any tractor to rescue.'

He began to explain his plan to them all.

'We need to lift that left hand back wheel, to try to get a sleeper or two under it. If we try to just drag the Dexta back, it will probably tip over, so we've got to get it as level as we can, before we try to move it. My plan is to attach the chain to the left side of the axle casing, as close to the hub as possible. Working from behind it, I want to drop the hook down in front of the axle and then pass it underneath and catch the main length of the chain, to 'choke' it, as we did with the trailer. When we've got it

194

attached, we'll secure the ring on the other end to the front hitch on the county. Leaving the chain slack, we can take the longest sleeper and stand it on its end, leaning against the wheel on this side. I think if we then pass the chain over the top end of it, we can use the upright sleeper as a fulcrum. John can then reverse the county to gently take up the slack. We can re-position the sleeper to a better angle if we need to, before we begin to try to level the tractor. Are we all OK with that, so far?'

They all nodded.

'What if the chain slips off the sleeper?' Peter asked.

'Once it's under tension, it will probably dig into the end of the sleeper, as long as we can keep it in line,' Archie explained. 'The only thing we've got to do is make sure that the sleeper is being pulled up towards the vertical. That's why we have to begin with it leaning towards the Dexta. We'll have more sleepers ready to slide underneath the axle, they should support it while we re-adjust everything for a second lift. Shall we give it a try?'

'Just be bloody careful, Arch,' Peter said. 'Don't get too near the edge, I don't want you getting hurt. I'd rather lose the tractor.' Archie took the end of the chain and cautiously dropped it over the axle casing. On his knees, he reached underneath, picked up the hook and attached it to the main length of chain. He crawled back away from the tractor, still holding the chain to keep it under a little tension. Standing up, he was able to guide the slack up behind the seat and pass it to Peter, who stood by the upright sleeper. Joe supported the sleeper at approximately the right angle, as Peter slid the chain over the top end, letting it settle at about mid width. Archie scrambled out from behind the little Dexta and held the chain as tight as he could over the sleeper, while Peter took the ring and attached it to the front of the County.

'Take it gently, John,' he called out as he stepped away from the chain.

John Tindall slowly eased the powerful machine backwards until the chain began to creak under load.

195

'Hold it there a minute, John,' Archie called. 'I just want to check the upright sleeper.'

He saw that the bottom end had begun to bed into the ground and the angle looked about right. Peter and Joe let go their hold on the sleeper. It remained in position.

'Get ready with a couple of sleepers to put under the wheel or the axle, once there's enough of a space under it,' Archie said to Joe and Peter. Then to John, he said, 'Are you ready? Take it very, very slowly John. Keep your eye on the top of that sleeper, as you go.'

Several creaks, pops and soil grinding noises later, the left hand wheel began to rise. There was just room to slide a sleeper under it, but the upright sleeper was almost at vertical.

'Stop!' Archie shouted. 'Can you get that sleeper in there?'

'I think we can with a bit of wiggling,' Peter called back. 'We could do with another inch really.'

'If we take it any further, the sleeper will begin to go down towards John,' Archie warned.

He looked over at the heap of sleepers and noted one which was slightly thinner than the rest.

'Here, Peter,' he called out. 'There's a slightly thinner one here, see if that will go.'

They came and picked it up and slid it under the wheel with ease.

'We'll slacken off the chain and re-position the upright sleeper,' Archie announced. 'That should give us another seven or eight inches, which will bring the wheel level with the other side.'

They repeated the operation and added another sleeper under the wheel. The little Dexta was almost sitting level now. Peter wore a satisfied look on his face.

'I think we're almost there, Archie,' he called out. Archie went to take a closer look.

'Let the chain go slack, John,' he shouted. The tractor remained roughly level. John jumped down from his lofty seat and removed the pin from the front hitch, the chain dropped onto the ground.

'I'll line up with the Dexta again,' John called out. 'I think we can pull it away backwards. I won't get too close, just in case the ground gives way again.'

Archie reached underneath and retrieved the hook, which he then attached to the Dexta's rear drawbar. He walked over to where John had positioned the County and re-attached the ring to the front hitch. The huge powerful machine gradually eased the little tractor clear of the unstable ground. John stopped his engine, walked over to the Dexta and applied the handbrake. Peter Bailley thanked them all for their help.

'Thanks Archie,' he said shaking his hand. 'I didn't fully understand what you meant when you said it would involve a 'bit of geometry', but I certainly do now.'

'A cup of coffee now, I think,' said Joe as he came over to the pile of sleepers where they all sat.

'Well done, Arch,' Peter said as he patted him on the back. 'I've always admired your ingenuity, ever since you used a fishing rod to lift that water wheel.'

'What?' John exclaimed. 'How did you manage that?'

Peter entertained them with the story, whilst they drank their coffee.

'I hope you've saved some for us,' Bill Pickering shouted as he trudged across the field towards them. He was accompanied by another four gum booted officers, carrying an assortment of gardening tools.

Archie looked over at them as they approached. He shouted back to Bill,

'You know where my allotment is, what are you doing up here? I told you to start at the bottom end, but don't dig past the rhubarb!'

Joe went to make some more coffee for the new arrivals, while Bill briefed them to follow Adam Morton's instructions, to avoid the possibility of destroying any evidence. He then approached Archie and said,

'I didn't anticipate any of this, mate. Perhaps it would be better if you and Joe write your statements when you've got time. Give me a ring when you're ready and I'll come and help you to tidy 'em up in the morning. How does that sound?'
Archie agreed and then asked Bill,

'What gives down at old 'Diddlers' place?'
Bill raised his eyebrows and placed a forefinger against his nose.

'Not here, not now, Arch,' he said. 'Tony Church and Ian Stuart are down there now. We'll know a bit more later in the week I expect.'
Adam Morton was busy attending to his diggers, but had looked up when he heard Archie ask the question. He now continued with renewed fervor and they heard him say,

'There's more, look, see that bit of clothing? Dig to the side of the hole, we'll maybe get down a bit lower without the sides caving in again.'
Joe returned with another two flasks of coffee and some clean mugs. He approached the diggers and said,

'There's some coffee here for you chaps, bring the flasks back when you're done. We're going indoors now, just climb over the fence there,' he pointed towards his garden.

'Don't worry if the dog's out,' he told them. 'He'll bark, but he won't hurt you.' He crossed to where Bill and Archie were standing. Bill suggested to Joe, that they could write their statements together. Bill explained what he'd told Archie, he could check them when he called to pick them up. He said to Joe,

'Just let me know when you think you're done and I'll come up and check them through before you sign them.'
Archie and Joe sat in the kitchen with mugs of tea, notepads and pencils. They compared notes several times and discussed the odd discrepancy between their different viewpoints. By the time they had finished, they looked a bit like a schoolboy's essay, so they decided to write them out again, this time in ink. They put the

198

revised copies into an envelope, which Joe placed behind the clock on his kitchen unit.

'I'll let Bill know we've done them,' Archie said. 'I'll give him a call later, from my home phone.'

'What do you think they've found up there in the field?' Joe asked. 'It gives you the creeps just thinking about it, doesn't it?

'I'm guessing it will turn out to be another one which is only twenty or thirty years old,' Archie suggested. 'If it was another flint miner, the bones would be deeper than that. I 'spect we'll find out sooner or later.'

'Do you want another cup of tea, Arch?' Joe asked him. Archie really wanted to get home, he could phone Bill later and probably find out what had happened at the farm.

'No thanks, Joe,' he replied.

'In that case,' Joe said, 'I'd better take you home. Thanks for your help and for getting these statements done.'
Joe stood up and picked his van keys from the hook.

'Come on, Thunder,' he called to the big Alsatian. 'You can come for a ride and then we'll have a stroll along the mill path.

CHAPTER 30.

DI. Tony Church was having a very busy Monday morning. After a lengthy interview with the arsonist, Graham Fuller, in the presence of the duty solicitor, he had left him to prepare his statement. He arranged for a hearing at the Magistrates court, for later today. He had decided not to oppose bail. Fuller seemed contrite and whilst his actions had been both rash and extreme, the DI. now had a better understanding of his frustration and anger at Bettis.

There was more to this then met the eye, Tony Church was in no doubt that both Bettis and Davies had been economical with the truth at their respective interviews. There seemed to be more than a little injustice in the way they had treated their employees. There was still the possible issue of incentives being offered for damage to Mr. Skrobe's property, to try to force him to sell up.

The DI was surprised to receive a telephone call from the front desk, informing him that Mr. Jason Davies had been found shot dead at his farmhouse. Tony had asked DS Brian Pace to attend the scene, with his trainee, DC Adam Morton. He also requested that Dr. Gibbs attend the scene as soon as he could. Acting in the capacity of police surgeon, the doctor could certify death and arrange for the removal. It seemed that a post mortem would be inevitable, under the circumstances. Once the forensics officer had collected evidence and samples from the scene and established the nature of Davies' demise, he would contact the DI. with a brief appraisal.

Tony called DS Ian Stuart to his office, whilst they waited for the call from Brian Pace. They discussed Fuller's situation. Tony had hoped the statements from the eye witnesses, Archie Leggitt and Joe Skrobe, would be available before the court hearing, but this now appeared unlikely. They were not strictly necessary for the hearing at the Magistrate's court, but would certainly be needed for the County Court trial which would ensue at a later date.

'I suppose that now old Jason's dead the estate will go to his son, Jeffery, won't it?' Ian asked his boss.

'We'll have to wait and see on that one, Ian. It's always dangerous to assume anything in this business. I believe Jason has a sister, somewhere. She may have offspring who could also be beneficiaries. It's no secret that Jeffery didn't get on with his father. They're a strange pair. Both wife beaters without a shred of shame and they both have all the bluster of political dictators. Whenever there's a problem, they always manage to distance themselves from it, with several layers of insulation'

Ian smiled as he said,

'And that, I take it, is your own complete and totally unbiased opinion, is it?'

The DI laughed.

'Did it come out as heavily disguised as that? I must be getting better at hiding my feelings, Ian!'

The telephone buzzed and Tony Church answered it. It was DS Brian Pace, speaking from his car phone.

'I'll give you the situation as far as I know,' Brian said. 'It looks like a murder. There's a small calibre, probably point two-two, entry hole in the centre of his forehead. It was fired from a few feet away, as he sat in an easy chair. The strange thing is that there is no blood. The wound appears to have been cleaned, maybe with damp tissue or toilet paper. We'll know more when we check it at the lab. I've called Doctor Gibbs to check that he's still going to attend and he said he'll be here within the hour. I've done a quick check of the areas in the kitchen which the cleaning lady had touched. She didn't realise anything was wrong until she found him. She took him a cup of coffee, then realised that he wasn't asleep, but dead. Carol Hickson is with her, she's still in shock. Her name is Cathy Simons. She's been very helpful in spite of her ordeal. I don't want to disturb the corpse any more, until Doc.Gibbs gets here. I have found some evidence of a recent visitor. We'll have our work cut out on this one. I've got a feeling it's going to be a tough one to crack. I'll start with a list of any items which may have been removed since Cathy was last here.'

'Thanks, Brian,' the DI responded. 'Have you got any news of the skull on the hill?'

'Apparently it's more than just a skull, possibly even a whole skeleton. Adam's gone up there to supervise but I haven't got any feedback yet. I'll try to keep you posted.'

'Thanks,' said Tony, 'I think we'll go and pick up Mr. Jeffery Davies for starters. We should be back here in an hour or so. We'll make sure he comes back with us, that should keep him outside his comfort zone and out of the way of the investigation. We'll talk again later, Brian, cheerio for now.'

On their way out, Tony asked Sergeant Hodd, at the desk, to prepare interview room one, in readiness for their return with their 'guest'.

They arrived at Davies' home to find a red Porsche nine eleven parked in his driveway.

'Flashy sod,' Ian observed as they walked past it to the front door. Ian pressed the bell push and heard an elaborate set of chimes from inside the house. They waited a minute or so and then Tony banged on the door with his fist.

'Open the door please, Mr. Davies,' he shouted. 'It's the police and we need to speak with you urgently.'

The door was opened a little until the safety chain restricted it. A young woman peered at them through the gap. She was wearing a dressing gown but had bare feet. Ian guessed that she was probably not wearing much else!

'Why do you want him?' she asked Tony. 'He can't have done anything he's been here all night with me.'

'We'll discuss it with Mr. Davies, please,' Tony said firmly. 'Will you please tell him to come and speak with us, now?'
The door closed abruptly and they heard voices from the rear of the house.

'I don't know,' the woman protested. 'They won't tell me, they just want to talk to you.'
Then a male voice, which they took to be Davies,

'They'll have to wait for me to get dressed, go and tell 'em I'll be ten minutes.'
Ian looked at his boss,

'Is there a back entrance to this place?'
Tony frowned,

'I dunno, Ian. D'you want to take a gander and find out?'
Ian walked round the block to the service road at the rear of the houses and counted them in from the corner of the road. It was the fifth house from the corner. He saw a close boarded fence about five feet high, in the centre of which was an oak gate. He tried the ring of the handle and it opened easily. He slipped inside and watched the back of the house from where he stood.
The curtains were closed upstairs, but open on the ground floor. There was a small patio outside a modern conservatory and Ian saw that the French doors which led to it were open wide. The young woman was getting dressed in what Ian took to be the lounge, but there was no sign of Davies. Perhaps he was upstairs. Ian felt a bit like a 'peeping tom' so he retraced his steps, closing the gate behind him. He rejoined Tony Church at the front door.

'There's a back gate, Tony,' he told him. 'The service road is a dead end, so if they went out that way, they'd need to pass the corner there,' he pointed to where he had just come from. 'The woman was getting dressed in the lounge, downstairs, but all the curtains upstairs were closed, so I couldn't see him.'

A few seconds later, the door opened and Davies and his companion came out. Davies was dressed in jeans, polo shirt and a leather bomber jacket. His lady friend wore a mid green v neck sweater and a grey and black pencil skirt, with a large check pattern. She had on a pale green anorak coat with a fur trimmed collar.

'Good morning, Mr. Davies,' the DI said. 'We need you to accompany us to Chichelster police station please. The situation demands your most urgent co-operation.'

He turned to the woman and said,

'Move your car, Trish, so I can get mine out. We'll take the Land Rover. I want to go to the farm on the way back.'

Tony put his hand up in a signal to Davies,

'We will be providing the transport, Mr. Davies,' he told him. 'I'm afraid we have some bad news for you and you won't be going to the farm on your way back. It is at this moment a crime scene, and there will be no visits by any member of the public until further notice.'

Davies' face paled.

'What's happened?' he asked.

'We'll explain that in good time, Mr. Davies,' the DI said. Please get in the Volvo, your companion is welcome to come with you. We will bring you both back as soon as we have finished the interview and have your statement.'

Davies opened the rear door of the police Volvo, to allow his companion to get in first.

'Can you tell me what this is all about?' he asked the detectives. 'Why is the farm a crime scene?'

'We'll explain everything back at the police station,' Ian told him. 'You are not under arrest, but we would appreciate your full co-operation.'

He got in and began to fasten his seat belt. Ian was driving and watched them in his rear view mirror. They looked at each other several times and smiled, but said nothing.

Back at the station, they were booked in at the front desk. The young lady gave her name as, 'Patricia Walker' with an address in Worthing. She gave her occupation as, 'Locator of missing persons'.

'Is that really a sort of, 'private investigator'?' Ian asked her.

'Yes, sort of, I suppose,' she agreed. 'I work for several local agencies in a consultancy role.'

'And you found Mr. Davies?' Ian smiled.

'I did,' she said.

'Was that for an agency or did you find this one for yourself?' He suggested, grinning broadly.

She decided not to respond any more, but Ian noted that she was wearing a slightly embarrassed smile.

'If you would like to wait here, whilst we interview your 'find', I'll organise some refreshment for you,' Ian offered.

'Can't I stay with him?' she asked.

'I'm afraid that would not be permitted in this instance.' Ian explained. 'I'm sure you are aware of privacy laws and there may be questions of a personal nature. Interviews are always conducted in confidence. We could find ourselves on the wrong side of the law if we broke that confidence. By the same token, if you were being interviewed, Miss Walker, we would be in breach of regulations if your personal information was made available to Mr. Davies, without your consent. Do you understand?'

'Yes, of course,' she said.

'Now, can I get you a cup of tea or coffee?' Ian asked.

'Thank you,' she replied. 'A cup of coffee please.'

Ian smiled and asked the constable at the desk to,

'Please bring Miss Walker a cup of coffee, whilst we have a chat with her companion. Thank you.'

He went to join his boss in the interview room. Tony had not begun the interview but had arranged the refreshments and a few biscuits. Davies sat opposite the DI and acknowledged Ian as he joined them.

'Shall we get on with it?' DI Church suggested.

Davies nodded his approval, so Tony placed two new tapes in the recorder and set it going.

'Monday the thirteenth of November interview in room one. Present are DI Tony Church, DS Ian Stuart and Mr. Jeffery Davies. I have explained that Mr. Davies is not under caution and is helping us with our enquiries, of his own volition.' Tony stopped the tape and said to Davies,

'Mr. Davies, before we begin, it is my sad duty to inform you that your father died in the early hours of this morning. Please accept our sincere condolences.'

Davies gasped. 'Dead! My father is dead? Is that what you've brought me here for?'

'No, Mr. Davies,' Tony continued. 'We also need to talk with you on an entirely unrelated matter. Please accept our sympathy and condolences in your loss. Do you need a few minutes alone, or in the company of your companion, before we continue?'

'Yes, just let me ask a few questions about the circumstances please,' Davies responded. 'He seemed OK last evening, when Trish and I visited him. Was it his heart?'

Tony saw that Davies was genuinely shocked and saddened by the news. He took a sip of the coffee and looked up at Tony, as if to expect an answer from him.

'I can't provide you with any details at this stage, I'm afraid.' Tony explained. 'I hope you will understand that it would be more than we'd dare to do, to issue any statements based on just speculation or first impressions. Apart from the distress it could cause to family members and friends, there could be severe legal repercussions if we got it wrong.'

Davies nodded that he understood, but appeared still puzzled.

'I'm getting the feeling that you might know a little more than you're telling me, Inspector,' he said.

Tony looked at Ian before he spoke again.

'You are an intelligent man, Mr. Davies. I can give you a little more information, but it is unconfirmed at this time. Will you give me an undertaking not to mention this to anyone, and I mean anyone, until we have issued an official statement?'

Davies sat back in his chair.

'I'm wondering what you might tell me, but yes, I'll keep it to myself until you issue your official statement. Are there some complications?'

Tony consulted his notes before he replied.

'All I can tell you from my information is that the cause of death may not have been purely natural causes. A small calibre firearm was used, but from our forensic officer's report, it would seem that there was no blood.'

'How could there be no blood, if he was shot?' Davies asked.

Tony consulted his notes again.

'In the event that his heart was failing before he was shot, there may not have been much, if any, blood pressure. To put it into purely mechanical terms, if the pump stops, the leak stops. We won't be able to confirm this until we have the findings of the post mortem. If it is of any consolation to you, and I can understand this has come as a terrible shock, I'm assured that his death would almost certainly have been pretty much painless.'

He paused to let Davies recover some of his composure.

'I'm sorry we had to break it to you like this, Mr. Davies. Of course, we now have to try to establish some relevant facts and most importantly, bring the perpetrator to justice. I can promise you that we will be relentless in our investigations of this terrible crime. Perhaps we'll get some more refreshments to give you a few minutes to come to terms with your loss. Would you like another coffee?'

'Yes please,' Davies replied, 'then perhaps I can find out the real reason you have brought me here.'

The interview resumed a few minutes later, when Ian returned with fresh coffees. He told Davies that his companion was going to pick up some shopping. She said she would return in about twenty minutes and wait for him in the front office.

Tony re-started the tape.

'Thank you, Mr. Stuart,' said Davies as they all sat down again. 'I'll admit that my father and I didn't always see eye to eye on a number of issues, Inspector,' he said. 'I went to see him last evening, to try to mend fences. I tried to contact him on Saturday, by phone and left a message with Cathy, asking him to call me back. He phoned me yesterday morning and was rather offhand with me. I think he thought I was going to ask for more money. I told him that I was upset because my wife had left me and he said, 'How is that anything to do with me?' I told him that I had to appear in court in Lincoln on Wednesday, because I had tried to find where Hannah was, by asking her sister. There was a neighbour of hers involved, he heard me shouting at Hilda and intervened. I know I was overwrought and should have been more diplomatic. But now I'm being prosecuted for assault, just for trying to find my wife.'

DI Church nodded and said,

'Mr. Davies, I understand what you are saying, but that is not why you are here now. We are trying to establish some facts leading up to your father's death. I'm sorry that you are finding it difficult without your wife, but perhaps you have found some comfort with your companion who came here with you.'

Ian interrupted at this point and asked,

'When you saw your father last evening, did he seem to be unwell in any way?'

'No,' Davies replied emphatically. 'He was in a better frame of mind than when he phoned me in the morning. He offered us both a drink and said he hoped things went as well as possible for me on Wednesday.'

'He offered you both a drink?' Tony queried. 'Does that mean that you took Miss Walker with you on your visit?'

'Yes, we went together,' Davies said. 'Trish, Miss Walker, is trying to help me to find my wife. I need her to sign some papers.'

'Divorce papers?' Ian queried.

'No, not divorce papers,' Davies answered, somewhat forcefully. 'Financial papers, the house is in her name, it should be in our joint names. That's all, I don't want a divorce.'

'We're back to you and your marital problems again, Mr. Davies,' the DI said. 'Perhaps your wife is the one who wants a divorce, I don't know. I don't want to know, but it's not getting us any nearer to finding out who may have killed your father, is it? Can we please concentrate on that aspect just for now?'

'Yes, sorry,' he said. 'Anyway, as I said, he was in quite a good frame of mind when we left.'

'What time would that have been?' Ian asked.

Davies thought for a few seconds and then said,

'Somewhere between eight and nine, we were home by nine thirty. Martin phoned me just after nine, so we must have been back by then.'

'Did you see anyone around the farm, when you left?' Tony asked him. 'Did you see or hear anyone or anything that seemed out of the ordinary, either around the house or in the lane? Did your father appear to have had a visitor? Were there any signs that someone else had been there, like an extra cup or glass in the kitchen, for instance?'

Davies was thinking hard.

'I see what you're getting at, Inspector, but no, I don't think so. It's not the sort of thing I would have been looking for though, is it? I'm sure I would have noticed anything obvious, but not any of those small details which you would possibly have noticed, as a policeman.'

The DI nodded to Davies,

'Well, thank you for your help, Mr. Davies. I wonder perhaps whether your companion could possibly have noticed anything. Sometimes a passenger notices things which a driver may not see, except perhaps in peripheral areas of vision. I will ask her to spare us a few minutes just to enquire. Do you think she would mind?'

There's just one other thing which my forensics man has mentioned. Do you know if your father had a lady friend?'

'Not to my knowledge, Inspector. Why do you ask?'

'There are some recent letters from someone called, 'Bernie', and their tone seems to indicate that they are from a female, not another male.'

Davies smiled, and explained,

'That would be his sister, Bernice. She's married to a man named Ronald Tenham and they live in Worthing. They didn't communicate for years, but they patched up their differences a couple of years ago. I think they are quite close again now.'

'Thank you,' said the DI. 'That's another mystery cleared up. Would you like us to contact her and let her know of her brother's death? Or would you prefer to deal with it yourself?'

'I think it would be better if you did that, please,' Davies said. 'I haven't had much to do with them since I was a kid.'

'OK that's not a problem, we'll attend to it. Just let us have her address before you go home,' said the DI. He continued, 'I'm satisfied that what you have told us is the truth, but you realise it means that somebody was there after you two left. Our forensics man has collected an assortment of prints and DNA evidence, so we will need to take a DNA swab from you both, so that we can eliminate you from our list of suspects. Would you have any objection to us doing that?'

'You took my fingerprints on Friday, Inspector. Surely you won't need them again, will you?'

Tony smiled and said,

'No, of course not, not unless you've had a double hand transplant over the week-end!'

Davies grinned,

'No, I didn't have the time this week, but I don't mind providing a DNA swab, it's not a painful process is it?'

'Not at all, and thank you again. We'll be as quick as possible with Miss Walker. I'll give you a few minutes to explain to her what has occurred, before we talk with her. As soon as we're done, we'll take you both home.' He paused for a moment and then said, 'For the benefit of the tape, this interview is now terminated.' He switched the machine off.

'The standard procedure now is for me to give you one copy, which we will both sign and we'll retain the other copy, with both signatures as with the first. You may wish to keep it, or pass it to your solicitor for safe keeping. I'll leave that decision to you.'

Davies signed the tapes and put his in the envelope provided.

The two detectives walked together with Davies back out to reception. Patricia Walker was looking through a magazine which one of the female officers had lent her. She looked up as they entered and took the magazine back to the front desk.

'Please thank your colleague very much, she said to Sergeant Hodd. It saved me from becoming bored, whilst I was waiting.'

Davies quietly explained to her what had happened. She appeared both shocked and saddened, but said she would do anything she could to help.

Ian took Jeffery Davies through to forensics and left him with one of the team to take his DNA swab. Ian then returned to the reception area, where Tony Church was asking Patricia Walker if she would mind helping with their investigation.

'No, Inspector,' she smiled. 'I don't know if I'll be of much use to you, but I have nothing to hide.'

The three of them walked back to the interview room. Tony told her that she was not under arrest and would be helping the police voluntarily. He explained that the interview would be recorded and that one copy of the tape would be given to her at the end of the interview.

'Why do I need a copy?' she asked.

Tony smiled,

'It's just police procedure, Miss Walker. It safeguards you as much as us. Before this was adopted, there were often disputes over details in statements. This method ensures that there will be no misrepresentation by either side.'

Patricia Walker nodded that she understood.

'Have you known Mr. Davies for long?' Tony asked her.

She thought for a moment,

'I suppose I have, when I think about it, but we only recently renewed our acquaintance,' she said. 'We were casual friends when we were teenagers. He used to come to the dances on Worthing pier, with some other lads from out in the sticks. We used to chat in the coffee bar afterwards, while they waited for their bus. In those days they ran a 'dance special' to some of the outlying districts.'

'So you hadn't seen him since then, until when?' Tony asked.

'Until he phoned the agency on Friday, he was asking for help in tracing his wife. The agency passed the job to me and I contacted him by phone. It was only when I visited him at his home that I realised that we had known each other from way back then.'

Tony smiled at her as he asked,

'Was it a joyful reunion, Miss Walker?'

Patricia smiled,

'I suppose you could say that it was,' she said. 'We chatted about old times, and then he gave me some information to help to find his wife.'

'Before we continue, I have to tell you that I have just given Mr. Davies some rather sad news.' Tony told her. 'His father, Mr. Jason Davies, whom I believe you met only last evening, was found dead this morning.'

'Oh my God!' she exclaimed. 'How did he die? Jeff just told me you wanted to ask me about our visit last night. I hope we're not suspects or anything like that. He was perfectly alright when we left him. I thought he was a very nice man. I thought Jeffery looked a bit pale when he came out from your room. Jeff told me he had suffered with his heart in the past, was it a heart attack?'

'I'm sorry to break it to you like this,' Tony said. We're of the opinion that there was an intruder, I expect Mr. Davies will explain to you later. We'd like to ask you whether you happened to notice anyone or anything unusual whilst you were visiting

212

him, last evening. Did you notice anyone or perhaps something unusual as you were returning to Mr. Jeffery Davies' home afterwards?' Were you with him all day yesterday?' The DI asked.

She replied quickly,

'No, I got there late in the afternoon. I had to go and confess!'

'Confess what?' Tony asked.

Patricia blushed as she began to explain.

'I'm afraid I made a bit of a bad mistake when I followed up the inquiry. I went to visit his wife's father yesterday. Mr. Jempson is now in a care home. I pretended to be a friend of Hannah's to try to find out where she was living. Unfortunately for me, Hannah's sister, Hilda, phoned her father whilst I was there and denied any knowledge of me. I gathered up my notes and excused myself. It was all rather embarrassing for both of us. I had inadvertently picked up Mr. Jempson's notebook, with my maps and notepads. He noticed it a short while after I had gone and the matron called the police. They caught up with me just as I was going into the hotel for my lunch. I had to leave my car in the pub car park whilst they took me to Worthing police station. I was treated like a criminal. They took my fingerprints and everything. After about an hour they told me that Mr. Jempson accepted that it was accidental and did not wish to press charges. I was let off with a caution and then I had to wait for another hour before they had a car to take me back to the pub in Tarring, where I'd had to leave my car. By the time I got there, the pub was shut, so I didn't get any lunch.'

Tony looked her in the eye and said,

'Not the best beginning for a missing person enquiry, then? What did Mr. Davies say about it?'

She smiled again as she said,

'He fortunately saw the funny side of it, although I admit that I screwed up my assignment. He told me that he had gone to the agency because he had screwed up himself. He'd gone in too heavy when he was trying to get the information from Hannah's sister in Lincoln. He's got to appear in court on Wednesday on an assault charge. He said, 'at least you only got a caution, so that was better than my methods.'

Tony smiled and said,

'You've probably had enough of police stations for one weekend, but hopefully this won't cause you any more stress.'

'So can we continue?' she asked. 'I expect Jeff will want to talk about his father.'

'Yes, of course,' Tony replied, 'I'll just set the machine and we can proceed.'

He recited the names of those present and the time and date of the recording. He began by asking her,

'Did you visit Mr. Jason Davies last evening?'

'Yes,' she replied, 'with Jeff. We arrived at about a quarter past seven.'

'Did he seem well?'

'He did, yes, in fact he was not in the least as I had imagined him to be from what Jeff had said.'

Tony raised his eyebrows and asked,

'What had Jeff said about him which made you form an opinion of him?'

'He told me that they not had a good relationship for a number of years. He'd borrowed money from his father and not repaid it. He said that his father had written off most of the debts but refused to lend or give him any more.'

Tony smiled,

'So he was more or less telling Jeff that he must stand on his own two feet and not rely on the 'bank of father'?'

'I guess that's probably the crux of it,' she said.

'So you found him to be quite amiable and pleasant?'

Yes, he offered us a drink, but I said nothing alcoholic, thanks. He said 'there's always tea or coffee, but you'll have to make it yourself'. He was chuckling as he said it, so I asked him if he would like one as well. 'Why thank you, my dear,' he said. 'You'll find all the equipment in the kitchen'. So I did.'

'Do you know what he and Jeffery were chatting about?' Tony asked her.

Patricia frowned as she replied,

'I think Jeff was telling him what had happened in Lincoln to begin with. When I brought the coffee in, his father was saying that he'd been out to lunch. The strange thing is that he was having his lunch at the same hotel in Tarring, where the police caught up with me.'

'Did he indicate that he had seen you or the police whilst he was having his meal?' Tony asked her.

'No! Not a word, either he hadn't seen me or perhaps he just didn't recognise me,' she said, adding, 'or maybe he was being extremely discreet. I suppose we'll never know now, will we?'

Ian Stuart then asked her,

'Think about what you may have seen or heard whilst you were coming or going from the farmhouse. We've asked Mr. Davies but he was driving, so he may not have noticed small details. Another aspect of this question is that Mr. Davies is used to the surroundings and to rural driving, whereas you are most probably used to town driving. You will naturally both notice different things when you are out of your normal environs.'

Patricia was thinking about her trip to the farm. She understood what Ian had meant.

'It had been drizzling earlier, but it was dry when we went to the farm,' she said. When we got there, there was one dry area, the size of a car on the tarmac part of the driveway. I would say that someone had parked there and moved away less than an hour before we arrived.'

'Good!' said Tony, 'that's the sort of thing we mean. So there had possibly been another visitor before you both arrived. Can you think of anything else which seemed unusual?'

'Unusual, perhaps no,' she said, 'but there was a dead fox on the grass just beyond the farmhouse entrance. It was still there when we came out to go back to Jeff's.'

Tony thought for a moment before asking,

'Had it been hit by a car, do you think?'
Patricia looked up at him,
'No, not as far as I could see and the headlights shone right on it on our way there. It wasn't mangled or bloody. Maybe it had just died or been poisoned, but it wasn't wet like the grass.'
'Perhaps it had been turned over, so you couldn't see any damage.' Ian suggested.
Tony raised an eyebrow at him.
'Who would run a fox over and then place it on the grass by the side of the lane? No, that doesn't seem likely, Ian. On the other hand, it could have been shot, I suppose.'
Patricia asked,
'I didn't hear any loud bangs, and wouldn't that have left blood all over it?'
'It depends what it was shot with,' Tony said. 'A twelve bore would have made a bit of a mess, but a rifle wouldn't.'
Ian interrupted his thoughts,
'On the assumption that it was lying where it was shot and that the weapon was a rifle, don't you think that was a bit close to the house to discharge a firearm safely?'
Tony nodded,
'Well done, Miss Walker,' he said. 'I think we'll have a look for this fox and find out how it died. I'll get one of our lads to go out with a couple of bin bags and retrieve the carcass, if it's still there. The lab can check it out when they've got a few minutes to spare.'
'Can you see what I meant about being familiar with an area and failing to see these things' Ian asked.
She nodded,
'I live in the town, but if I'm on my way to work and a neighbour happened to ask me whether the binmen have been, I probably wouldn't have noticed one way or the other.'
Ian nodded in agreement, he continued,
'So we have the dry space where a vehicle had been parked and a dead fox, anything else that you can think of?'

'No, nothing else on the way back, we got to Jeff's at about half past eight.'

'And that was the end of the evening's entertainment?' asked Tony.

She thought hard for a few seconds and then said,

'Yes, apart from the telephone call from Jeff's site manager, I think his name is 'Bettys or something. Jeff got quite angry with him because he wanted to come round and sort out some problem face to face. Jeff said, 'No!' he didn't want any more of his attitude tonight. He told him to just keep a low profile until Thursday. Jeff said he would deal with it when he got back from Lincoln. We sat chatting about his father, he seemed very upset. We had a bottle of wine and some food. After that we watched the television and went to bed.'

Tony looked at Ian and said,

'I think that was a very full and frank statement, don't you?'

'Yes, I must congratulate you on your memory, Miss Walker.' Ian agreed. 'Are you willing to provide a DNA mouth swab, to help us exclude your DNA from whatever others we may find at the house?'

She nodded her acceptance. Tony thanked her and terminated the interview. They each signed both tapes and Patricia Walker was escorted to the forensic team's office where her swab was taken.

A short while later they were returned to Jeffery Davies' home by two uniformed officers, PC's Frank Burton and Peter Hayles. The two officers chatted amiably with them on the journey. As they dropped them outside Davies' home, Frank Burton told them,

'That was the most pleasant part of today's work. Now we've got to try to find a dead fox up a muddy old farm track and try to get it into a black bag without retching!'

Peter Hayles laughed and thanked Davies and Miss Walker for their company, before they drove off to find their quarry!

CHAPTER 31.

Elsie arrived home from shopping at half past two. She let Jimbo out into the garden and then gave him a fresh bone which she had got from the butchers in Pulborough. She unpacked her bags and put the shopping away and then looked at the kitchen clock,

'Twenty to three,' she said to herself. 'Plenty of time, Hilda said she would be here between about five and six. I hope she likes lamb.' She put the kettle on and picked up the phone to dial Archie's mobile.

It rang several times before he answered it. She heard a large dog barking and someone shouting.

'Thank you very much, that was most welcome.'

Archie answered,

'Hello?'

'Archie?' she said. 'Where are you and how long will you be before you're home?'

'Joe's and half an hour,' he told her.

'You haven't forgotten that Hilda's coming, have you?'

'No, Else, I hadn't forgotten. What's for dinner?'

'Men!' she exclaimed. 'I got a shoulder of lamb, I hope Hilda likes lamb.'

'I'll see you presently,' Archie said. 'Joe's bringing me back. We've had a very busy morning. I'll tell you about it when I get there.'

Elsie put the phone back on its rest. She went back to the kitchen and poured herself a cup of tea.

'I suppose I'd better get the lamb in and get some vegetables done.' she thought.

She rinsed the lamb and placed it in the roasting tin with some oil and a few sprigs of rosemary. She peeled the potatoes and carrots and prepared some sprouts. The telephone rang. Elsie took her cup of tea into the lounge and sat down to answer it. It was Hilda.

'Hello, Hilda,' Elsie said. 'How are you?'

'I'm fine, thank you, Elsie. I'm with Dad for an hour. I got away a bit earlier than I thought, so I decided to visit him on my way to you. Are you sure you don't mind us both coming?'

Elsie smiled to herself, she replied,

'Hilda, it will be an absolute pleasure to see you after all this time. Of course we don't mind you both being here with us. Archie will be home soon, I've got us roast lamb for our meal, do you like lamb?'

'Ooh, my favourite,' Hilda said. 'What time do you want me there?'

'Whenever you like,' Elsie said. 'You know how to find us, don't you?'

'Dad said turn left by the church, before I get to the village. He said to keep going until I get to the main road and then turn right and your house is just along on the right. Is that correct, Elsie?'

Elsie thought for a moment before replying,

'Yes, that sounds right, you can park in the driveway. Our car is in the garage, Archie is getting a lift home. Perhaps you might find it easier in the daylight, that's all I was thinking.'

Hilda hadn't thought of that,

'Oh, yes,' she said. 'What time does it get dark?'

'Usually about half past four or five o'clock,' Elsie said. 'It depends how bright the day has been, today has been dull and cloudy so it will be dark earlier I would think.'

'I'll be there by half past four, Elsie', Hilda told her. 'I'm really looking forward to seeing you again.'

'That will be good,' Elsie replied. 'Bye for now, Hilda, drive safely, it doesn't matter if you're a bit later. Just get here safely.'
Jimbo began to bark at the back door.

'Your 'dad's' home, I expect,' Elsie said to him.
A few moments later, Archie came into the kitchen. He made a fuss of Jimbo and then said,

'What a day, Else,' he said. 'I'll take Jimbo for a walk and then I'll tell you all about it.'
He clipped Jimbo's lead on and set off towards the mill. The light rain had stopped but the wind was beginning to pick up a bit. As they got to the mill, Archie noticed that Joes van had gone, so it was safe to let Jimbo off the lead. He heard a police siren in the distance, it sounded as though it was up on the main road. They reached the weir and Jimbo decided to go for a quick dip. The water was cold, but absolutely gin clear, so Archie wasn't concerned about the smell. After a short while Jimbo came out and shook himself dry. Archie laughed as he caught most of it in the face! He picked up a stick and threw it along the bank. Jimbo ran after it and brought it back again, laying it at Archie's feet. All the way back towards the mill, the exercise was repeated, Jimbo was well and truly tired by the time Archie clipped the lead back on his collar. As they approached the main road, PC Bill Pickering came along in his car. He stopped and lowered his window to chat with Archie,

'Thanks for your help with old Peter's problem this morning, Arch,' he said. 'I didn't want to say too much whilst we were in company, I'm sure you understood my meaning.'

'Yes, Bill, too many ears and then a whole lot of questions which you didn't have answers to, I guess.'

Bill nodded.

'You got it in one, pal,' he said. 'The top and bottom of it is that old Jason's dead. It looks like a murder, shot in the head with a small bore bullet. Brian Pace was a bit cagey but I think that was because the new boy from the 'Met' was within earshot. I did manage to find out that DI Church had pulled Davies' son Jeffery in for questioning. He also let slip that judging by the degree of livor mortis, death had occurred somewhere between one and three in the morning. This is all sensitive information, Arch, so for your ears only until it's made public.'

'When d'you reckon that will be?' Archie asked.

Bill thought about it,

'Probably sometime tomorrow, I expect. They'll be asking whether anybody heard anything in the early hours. That will be as good as a statement regarding the time of death to any newshound worth his salt.'

'Who found him, Bill? Not poor young Cathy Simons, his cleaner?'

'Yes, Arch,' Bill confirmed. 'Do you know her?'

'Known her for years, mate. She looked after her old mum until she died. She had Parkinson's, but Cathy never once complained about not having a life. She's been cleaning for old 'Diddler' for about fifteen years, maybe even longer.'

'Brian Pace reckoned she was a great help this morning. A 'godsend' he called her. She was still in shock, but gave them all the information they needed,' Bill told him. 'The problem was that she'd brought the milk in and gone through to the kitchen without realising anything was wrong. She'd called out to him, even went out the back looking for him when he didn't answer. She caught a quick glimpse of him in his chair and thought he'd probably nodded off. Then she made a fresh pot of coffee and took him a cup. That's when she realised what had happened. She dropped the coffee and called three nines.'

'Has she got someone with her, Bill?' Archie asked in a concerned tone.

'Yes, Arch, we're not that hard on people in shock,' Bill assured him. 'Carol Hickson stayed with her all the while the police were there. She's taken her to her brother's house, somewhere over at Slindon. We'll need to talk with her again tomorrow, I dare say. Anyhow, I'll come and pick up yours and Joe's statements sometime tomorrow, unless we get another dose of panic and mayhem!' He laughed as he waved goodbye and drove away.

Archie and Jimbo walked briskly home. Standing talking with Bill had made him feel a bit chilly, so he was pleased to feel the warmth of the kitchen.

'That's a fresh pot of tea, Arch,' Elsie called from the lounge. 'I didn't pour yours out. I wasn't sure how long you'd be. Does Jimbo need his towel?'

'No, he's not too bad, Else,' Archie said. 'I'll get my tea and then tell you about my day, before Hilda turns up.
He went into the lounge and sat in his armchair.

'The 'bottom line' is that old 'Diddler' Davies has been shot,' He told her.

'Oh!' she exclaimed, 'is he going to be alright?'

'Well, apart from being dead, I s'pose,' Archie said.

'You didn't say he was dead, Arch, just that he was shot.'
Archie smiled,

'I must have forgotten to put that bit in, then. He's been shot dead. Is that better?'

'Where was he shot, Arch?'

'In his armchair, in the lounge, apparently.'

'No, I mean where on his body?'

'Oh,' Archie said, with a silly grin. 'Not on his body, he was shot in the head!'

'Do the police know who did it? What was he shot with Arch?'

222

'I didn't get an invitation to the forensic examination, or taken into the pathologist's confidence, so I don't know much more about it yet, other than what I've just told you.' Archie said. 'As you can imagine there were more policemen than villagers up there this morning, what with the diggers and all.'

'Diggers? What diggers? Who found him, Arch? Was it Cathy? Cathy Simons, I mean?' Elsie asked.

'Yes, that's what Bill told me just now. I saw him on my way back with Jimbo. He said that nice police lady, what was her name?'

'Lesley Stevens?' Elsie queried.

'No, not her, the other one,' he said frowning and scratching his head. 'Hickton, or Hickman,'

'Carol Hickson,' Elsie said.

'That's the one, Else, yes, Carol Hickson. Anyway she was staying with Cathy, I expect the poor girl's in shock. Bill said that Brian Pace had told him that she'd been a great help.'

'Who had, Carol Hickson or Cathy Simons?'
Archie sighed,

'Cathy, not Carol, although I suppose Carol was a great help to Cathy. I 'spect they were both a help to him. Brian Pace told Bill that Cathy had provided a lot of information and she'd been kept busy making tea and coffee for the others. There was a new bloke up there, PC Mercer, he's ex Metropolitan Police. Bill said he was trying to throw his weight around at first. Carol had sent him out to sit in the car, Bill had to have a word with him. He seemed OK by the time he came up with the diggers.'

'What do you mean, 'diggers'? Elsie asked him.
He told Elsie about Peter Bailley's tractor rescue and how the police were digging up another lot of bones.

'I could only see a skull, but Brian Pace has got a young assistant now. His name is Adam, something! He reckoned there was more than just a skull, possibly even a whole skeleton. That's why they had to dig carefully. It was beginning to get chilly and began to spit with rain, so once we'd got the tractor safe, Joe and

I went into his place and wrote our statements about Friday night. Bill's going to pick them up, probably tomorrow.' He paused and stood up, 'I don't know about you, but I could go another cup of tea, do you want one, Else?'

'Yes please and then I think it would be a good idea if you went and had a wash and got a bit tidy, before Hilda gets here.'

'That Lamb smells good, Else,' he said. 'It must be nearly ready to come out of the oven.'

Elsie smiled at him,

'You mean so that you can try a slice, before you get showered and changed! Nice try, Arch, but the answer's 'no', it needs another hour. When it comes out it will need to rest for a while.'

Archie grinned at her and said,

'I didn't know that cooking it made it feel tired! I thought it was only while it was still part of a lamb, running about in the field, that would make it feel tired.

'Just go and get cleaned up.' Elsie said, raising her eyebrows in exasperation.

CHAPTER 32.

Later on Monday afternoon, Graham Charles Fuller was in the waiting room at the Magistrates Court. His companion was Michael J. Johnstone, one of the duty solicitors. The court had been specially convened following a request from the Chichelster police. Fuller was seated on the hard wooden bench. Michael J. Johnstone stood next to Fuller, with his left foot on the seat. He was writing on a legal pad, balanced on his knee. He put his pen back in the top pocket of his jacket, turned to his client and said,

'I believe you have been a very foolish man, Mr. Fuller. Under the circumstances, I also believe that you have been an extremely fortunate man. Let me just explain something which has brought me to this conclusion.'

Fuller looked up at his legal representative,

'Yes, Mr. Johnstone,' he said. 'I'm very grateful to you for your help. I heard what the magistrate said and I was bracing myself for the worst.'

Johnstone continued,

'This is, I believe, the first instance that I can recall, in my twenty odd years as a solicitor, that an arsonist has been granted police bail. Detective Inspector Church is nobody's fool and must have felt some sympathy for your situation. I suggest that you also remember to thank him for his report. You realise, I hope, that you must remain at your home address and be available to the police at all times. In the unlikely event that you are permitted to return to your job, you are required to obtain the authorisation of the court prior to you commencing that work. You may do this by application to the clerk to the court, or, failing that, submitting your application to the police, for approval by the bench.'

Fuller sat, head bowed, as he said,

'I don't think that is very likely, Mr. Johnstone. My boss is in cahoots with Bettis, who was the main cause of all the problems. I'm not blaming anyone but myself, for this. I should have listened to my wife, when she told me to do nothing, but wait and see what the eventual outcome of the enquiry would be.'

Michael Johnstone nodded his agreement,

'Men are by nature, somewhat headstrong, I must confess that on occasions I have 'jumped the gun', when it would have been more prudent to sit it out.'

He changed his bag over to his left hand and proffered his right to Graham Fuller, who shook it.

'I wish you all the best, Mr. Fuller. I am still your appointed solicitor, so you may contact me for advice on this, if you need to. Now get along home, and try to relax for a while.'

'Thank you very much,' said Fuller as they left the Court building together, Johnstone to return to his practice and Fuller to rejoin his wife in their car.

Steven Foggarty, the driver who had been responsible for the accident on Thursday the ninth, had also been released on police bail. It had not yet been determined whether the damage to Joe's fence was a deliberate act, or an accident. Certainly the collision with the young lad on his moped, was accidental, albeit the result of careless, reckless or dangerous driving. The police would be taking action in respect of this element.

Both Archie and Joe Skrobe, were convinced that Bettis had instigated a campaign of destruction of Joe's property. They had intimated this to Bill Pickering, and also to Sergeant Dean, whilst he was at the scene. Now that both lorry drivers were released from custody, perhaps they would either corroborate or refute this supposition. Before the hearing, Ian Stuart had subtly suggested to Fuller, that he and Mr. Foggarty could do worse than to compare their situations.

He explained that this advice was strictly 'off the record' and as such he could not be quoted. He said to Fuller,

'I am not suggesting that you and your colleague should embark upon any kind of revenge strategy. I will just make an observation, which may already have occurred to you. In the event that you are released on police bail your conduct will need to be exemplary. However, if either of you believe that there are any mitigating circumstances which may have affected your rash and extreme actions, you now have the opportunity to discuss them with your colleague. Should you decide that your employer, or his associates are complicit in the offence of, 'incitement to commit criminal damage, it may be in your best interests to bring it to our notice. You would need to provide evidence to the court and it would be beneficial to your case, if other witnesses were also willing to testify.'

Ian noted that Graham Fuller had absorbed his suggestion. As they parted company, Fuller had thanked him for his help and advice.

CHAPTER 33.

Hilda Jempson arrived at the Leggitt house at around a quarter to five. Archie went out to meet her and bring her small suitcase in.

'Come into the lounge, Hilda,' said Elsie, 'let me look at you.' Jimbo, always keen to be a part of any social occasion, followed Hilda in and then sat in front of her, holding his paw up.

'Oh, hello,' Hilda said, as she bent towards him, 'and who are you, you gorgeous furry beast?'

'That's Jimbo,' Elsie told her. 'He found Archie last year! But please sit down and tell me your news.'
Hilda smiled at her,

'Don't you mean, 'Archie found him? You said, 'he found Archie!' Hilda was laughing.
Elsie smiled at her,

'No, I said it right, Hilda. Jimbo found us.' She began to explain. 'Archie came home from the mill and Jimbo was lying on the front path. Archie stroked him and gave him a drink. The rest is history. He just followed Archie everywhere he went. He's a lovely dog, very friendly and obedient. Everybody loves him.'

'I can see why,' and then to Jimbo, 'You are absolutely gorgeous, aren't you?'

'I wouldn't say I was gorgeous, Hilda,' Archie said as he came into the lounge. 'I'm house trained, but not quite as furry as him. No, I'd just describe myself as kind of useful, mostly!'
Elsie shook her head in mock disbelief,

'Don't listen to him, Hilda. I believe he gets sillier as he gets older. Tell me all about you and Hannah. You don't mind sharing the room, do you?'
Hilda shook her head,

'Of course we don't,' she said. 'We're grateful to you both for your kindness. Elsie, it's so good to see you after all this time and thank you both for letting us stay with you. Dad sends his Best Wishes, he was very happy to see me this afternoon. The home he's in is really nice. I met the matron, a Miss Collins. She told me he's a very easy man to look after. She said that Mr. Leggitt had been to see him. Dad's asked him to be an executor of his will, but I hope that won't be for a few years yet.'

'Tea or coffee, Hilda?' Archie called out from the kitchen.

'Oh, I think I'd like a cup of tea, please Mr. Leggitt,' she replied.
Elsie stood up,

'While Archie, not 'Mr. Leggitt', makes a pot of tea, let me show you your room,' she said to Hilda. 'I'm sorry you'll have to share, but the only alternative was to make up a camp bed in the dining room.'
Hilda picked up her suitcase and followed Elsie up the stairs.

'We don't mind sharing, Elsie,' she said. 'We only had the one bedroom at Lincoln, whilst Hannah was living with me when she left Jeff. Oh, this is lovely, thank you,' Hilda put her case on the chair next to the window and surveyed the room. As they went back down the stairs, Elsie said to her,

'I expect you'll be tired tonight, you've had all that driving and it's been a long day for you. Just let us know when you want to retire, we won't be offended.'

'You're right about that, Elsie,' Hilda replied. 'I've been working night shifts for the past month, so I used the week-end to catch up on my sleep. I don't think I'll be too tired tonight. It makes a lovely change to have a meal cooked for me, instead of having to cook when I wake up in the afternoons.'

They returned to the lounge just as Archie came in with a tray of tea and the biscuit tin.

'Just one thing, Miss Jempson,' he smiled as he said, 'don't keep calling me 'Mister'. If you want to be, 'Hilda', then please let me be, 'Archie' or 'Arch', which is what most of my other friends call me.'

'Sorry,' she said. 'Elsie already told me off for that, it's just that even when we worked together, when I was just a staff nurse, Elsie and I were always on first name terms. It was never, 'Sister Leggitt' but always just, 'Elsie'. So I'll try to remember to call you, 'Archie' in future.'

The ladies had so much to talk about, Hilda enquired about the other nursing staff who they had both known. She told them about Jeffery Davies' visit to her flat in Lincoln and how her neighbour, Doug Fielding had come to her rescue at just the right moment.

'So that's why I have to be back in Lincoln on Wednesday morning. It takes about four hours from here, so I really need to leave by about four o'clock tomorrow. Hannah phoned while I was at Dad's. She'll be here by late morning. I was hoping perhaps you could take us both through to the police station, Archie. There shouldn't be any problems if we're both there, should there?'

'No, Hilda,' he replied. 'I think it will be straightforward enough. It sounds as though young Davies has got himself more problems than he needs.'

'How do you mean Archie?'

'I was over by the farm yesterday morning,' he told her. 'By all accounts his father, old Jason Davies, was shot dead at sometime during the night.'

'What, murdered?' Hilda asked with alarm.

'They're looking at it that way, love. Apparently he was sitting in his armchair with a bullet through the middle of his forehead. Cathy Simons found him, when she went to begin her little cleaning job.'

'Oh, my God! The poor girl,' Hilda said. 'Poor Cathy, has she got someone with her? She lost her mother to Parkinson's, didn't she?'

Elsie nodded,

'Yes, that's right,' she said. 'She hasn't had much of a life, has she? I think old Jason mellowed a bit as he got older though. She used to say he was very good to her, when I saw her in the village. I think even his sister had a soft spot for Cathy. She used to send her little gifts now and then. I don't suppose you can remember Bernice, can you?'

'Only vaguely,' Hilda replied. 'She was a lot younger than old Jason, wasn't she?'

'About ten or twelve years younger,' Elsie confirmed. 'She married a Worthing man. What was his name, Arch?'

Archie thought for a minute and then said,

'Tenham, I think, yes, Ronald Tenham, that was it. I think he worked in an office at Shoreham docks. Bernice use to work at the Westminster Bank. I think she fell out with her brother over his money management. That was years ago though, of course she shouldn't have known anything about it, so she couldn't report anything.'

Hilda looked puzzled,

'What was there to report?' she asked Archie. 'Was there something illegal going on?'

Elsie looked at Archie, then back at Hilda,

'Don't ask me how,' she said, 'but he always knows more than he lets on. What was it Arch?'

Archie smiled to himself,

'Well, it's all so long ago now, and old 'Diddler's' dead, so I s'pose it don't matter. I can only tell you what I heard from Ron Tenham. He used to come to the Old Bell, in those days, after

231

he'd done a bit of courtin' up at Myrtle Grange. Anyway, Diddler' used to bank with the old National Provincial. In those days you could get a cheque book on a current account, without paying bank charges. When the bank was taken over by the Westminster and became, 'NatWest', Bernie was one of the clerks involved with transferring the accounts to the Westminster Bank system. That's how she saw all his dealings and didn't think much to 'em.'

'Was that before he married Mary Eldridge?' Hilda asked.

'No, they'd married a couple of years before that,' Archie told her. 'Old Harry was still alive then. 'Diddler' and Mary lived in the old farm cottage up until he died. Harry Eldridge didn't like him. He was against Mary marrying him, but he couldn't stop her. Nobody was surprised when Mary left him. He was a nasty piece of work when he was younger.'

'Perhaps his son, Jeffery was cast from the same mould,' Hilda suggested. 'Was Jason's father still alive then?' she asked Archie.

Elsie smiled at her, saying,

'His father was a real 'gent', I don't know where Jason got his attitude from, but it wasn't from Gilbert.'

'Was that his name? Gilbert?' Hilda asked. 'So he was still alive when Jason married Mary?'

'Yes, Hilda, Gilbert Arnot Davies was still very much alive then. He owned the glass works in Popham. He was a First World War hero you know. I don't remember exactly what he did, but he was decorated for it.'

The women both sat watching Archie, as though waiting for him to continue.

'I'll tell you as much as I can remember, but it was a long time ago and I can't even recall exactly who told me,' he said thoughtfully.

'I believe it was an article in a magazine or something. One of the blokes had spotted it and read it out to us in our lunch break. I think it was while we were building the new library in 'Chi'. That

must have been thirty or forty years ago. Anyway, he was wounded and got left behind when his platoon retreated. He was crawling away in the darkness, when he came to a barn. He thought it would provide some shelter from the rain, if he could get in without being spotted by the soldier guarding the main doors. He managed to crawl towards the back of the barn, where he pulled away some of the half rotten wood and got inside. There were several German vehicles, some loaded with munitions. Stacked up along the side of the barn was a large quantity of petrol and oil in cans and large drums. The only guards he had seen were outside the front door of the barn, under a lean to shelter. Quietly, using the charges from some of the ammunition and one of the vehicle's ignition systems as a makeshift detonator, he set about arranging a surprise party for them! Once he was satisfied with his sabotage, he realised that he couldn't afford the luxury of his shelter any longer, unless he wanted to become a part of the inferno! He left through the same hole he hade made to get inside and somehow managed to get back to his own lines, a couple of miles away. He told his Sergeant what he had done and the officer in charge decided to delay the planned counter attack, until after the 'fireworks' began at first light. Gilbert later said that he had felt sorry for the German driver who had started his engine and lit up the sky! He was patched up and sent home to recuperate. His leg was so badly mutilated and infected, that they had to amputate it once he got to the military hospital in Dover.'
Hilda had listened wide eyed to Archie's story,

'So that was Jeffery's grandfather, was it?' she said. 'It seems a pity that his grandson doesn't have the same moral values, doesn't it?'

'I'm afraid to say that even his own son, Jason, was a little short on moral fibre as well,' Archie told her. 'Old Gilbert wanted to retire, so he asked Jason to take over the management of the glass works. He set it all up and signed the business over to him. Less than six months later, Jason sold up to the big glass works in Worthing, and kept the proceeds of the sale for himself. The only positive thing he did was to secure the continued employment of the seven staff. They all transferred to the Worthing Glass Works and as far as I know, they were kept on.'

'After Harry Eldridge died, Jason and Mary moved into the farmhouse.' Elsie added. 'He thought Mary had inherited the whole farm, but what he didn't know at the time, was that Harry had sold those three acres and the cottage to your father. He tried to get it back, but it was too late.'

Hilda was enraptured at hearing this local history from her older friends. She sat quietly pondering for a while and then she asked,

'Do you think perhaps it was Jeffery's father who set fire to our home all those years ago? The night our mother died?'

Archie shook his head,

'No, Hilda, he wasn't brave enough to do anything like that. He was being watched by the police because of the domestic abuse he had been giving Mary. There was an intensive police investigation.

There was a young hooligan around at that time. He'd been caught breaking into the farm shop a couple of times in the months before the fire. Afterwards, nobody ever saw him again. The police had him on their books, from the young offender's lists at the remand home at Findon. His name was listed as, 'Robert Bourner' After he was released, the 'rehab' people had installed him in a flat in Pudborough, with another young offender. When they went to pick him up, his flat mate told them he had gone back to his folks somewhere in Essex. They did wonder if perhaps he'd got wind of the fact that your father had begun to take the cash box home at night, instead of leaving it in the filing cabinet in the Farm Shop. They believed that the fire was started by the thief as a diversion. Paraffin had been splashed about in the back porch and the kitchen. The paraffin heater in the back room had been knocked over. The fire investigation team found no trace of the steel cash box. They did find a charred remnant of a leather glove. These days they would probably have

234

pursued it more vigorously. There were probably boot prints. The thing is there were so many firemen and policemen there and the ground was all churned up, water from the hoses had turned it into a sea of mud.

Elsie stood up and smiled at Hilda,

'I hope we're not upsetting you with all this history, my dear,' she apologised.

Hilda sat upright in her armchair and smiled at them both,

'No, not at all,' she told them. 'There are still so many unanswered questions about it and I don't like to ask Dad. He gets very emotional whenever we reminisce about when we were kids.'

Elsie went into the kitchen and called out,

'Dinner will be another half an hour, would you like to unpack your case and hang some of your clothes up, Hilda? It may save a bit of ironing time tomorrow.'

'Yes, good idea,' Hilda said as she began to get up. 'I'll still probably need to run the iron over a skirt. Perhaps you wouldn't mind if I do that after we've had our dinner?'

'No, of course I don't mind, Hilda,' Elsie called up the stairs. 'Just say when you want to do it and I'll get the ironing board out from the cupboard under the stairs,'

They all enjoyed their roast dinner. The lamb was particularly good and was accompanied by Elsie's home made mint jelly.

'There's apple crumble with custard, or if you prefer it, with ice cream,' Elsie said to Hilda.

'Have you already made the custard?' Hilda asked.

'No, not yet, but it'll only take a few minutes,' Elsie told her. 'It's up to you, Hilda, Archie won't care which it is, just as long as it's food!'

They settled for ice cream eventually and afterwards adjourned to the lounge with the coffee pot. They spent a pleasant couple of hours, in conversation and then Hilda asked for the iron to press her skirt. Archie decided it was time he took Jimbo for his walk.

It was turning colder, so he pulled on a sweater before putting his coat on. The grass was very wet, so he stayed on the hard ground to save having to dry Jimbo when they got back. He wondered whether there would be any mention of old Jason's death on the news, but it was probably too soon to have the details published. They watched the television for a while and Archie noticed that Hilda was having difficulty staying awake. At around eleven, they decided it was time to turn in. They were all tired and Hilda had a busy couple of days ahead of her.

CHAPTER 34.

Martin Bettis was worried. He had met with the borough surveyor on Monday morning. Jeffery Davies had not shown up at their appointment, so he had to deal with things on his own. He'd tried to contact his business partner, but without success.

'Where is Mr. Davies?' the surveyor's clerk asked him. 'He assured me that he would attend this meeting. Do you think he may have forgotten?'

'I'm very sorry,' Bettis replied, 'but I've been trying to contact him on both his home phone and also on his mobile. I can only assume that he has been detained on a matter of some urgency. Under the circumstances, I realise that I have no choice, but to accept your findings, on behalf of our partnership

Bettis was, at this stage, unaware of the developments at the farm, or of the drama unfolding in the field behind the site.

The clerk nodded and raised an eyebrow at the surveyor, who had been conversing with members of the Planning Committee. He nodded his head and the clerk took a seat. The borough surveyor rose from his chair. He held a sheaf of papers in his hands and referred to the top sheet as he began to address Martin Bettis.

'Mr. Bettis,' he began. 'Firstly, I think I speak for us all when I say that we are disappointed that your partner, Mr. Davies, has for whatever reason, seen fit not to attend this meeting. We will reconvene at another time, so that we may discuss with him the actions which your partnership proposes to take. I will now try, briefly, but accurately, to explain our findings, which in the event of your non-compliance, are enforceable by law.

You will be presented with a copy of this report, which you may discuss with your partner and any other interested parties, before our next meeting. Do you wish me to continue?'

'Yes, please,' Bettis replied.

The surveyor continued,

'I'm sure that you are aware of the lengthy and thorough procedures undertaken by us, whenever a new development is proposed.'

Bettis nodded, 'Yes, Sir,' he agreed. 'I understand how necessary that procedure is and accept that we have strayed outside the official parameters against which the plans were approved.'

'That's a start, Mr. Bettis,' said the surveyor. 'At least you are prepared to recognise that fact. I have here letters from your neighbours and their solicitors. I have police reports, which quite frankly I find most disturbing. I have a letter from the tenant farmer who states that your development has deprived him of approximately half an acre of the land which he rents from Mr. Jason Davies. Do you accept this to be the case?'

'I know that we have encroached on adjoining land in the process of excavating the site,' Bettis acknowledged. 'I haven't checked on the exact areas, but I will not contest Mr. Bailley's claim.'

The surveyor continued,

'The Health and Safety Executive have advised us that excavations on two sides adjoining your site, have been left in an unstable and potentially dangerous state. As the developers, you and your partner, must have been aware of the angles of repose of

238

loose spoil. Did you consider this in the course of your preparations?'

'I was not aware that the site was left in a dangerous state,' said Bettis. 'I'm sure this would have been rectified, had we been permitted to complete the project.'

There was a mumbled response from the committee members at the table. The surveyor referred to another of his notes before continuing.

'I must emphasise this point, Mr. Bettis. The site must, by law, be left in a safe and stable condition at all times. This is not the same as tidying up after the job is finished. Do you employ a qualified civil engineer at your site in Wigglesworth?'

'Not all the time,' Bettis told him. 'We get one in to advise us on a sub contract basis, as and when we deem it necessary.'

'Not the right answer, I'm afraid.' The surveyor told him. 'A project such as this, needs a chartered civil engineer available at all times. By that, I don't mean that he has always to be on the site. I do mean that he should be the person responsible for the safety elements of the site. Under the terms of the Health and Safety at Work act, you have a legal duty of care. This applies not just to your workforce, but to any third parties who may be affected by your bad working practice, or your negligence.'

Bettis tried to appear contrite, but the surveyor seemed not to notice. He turned a few more sheets from the collection he held in his hand. Reading from the sheet he had placed on top of the sheaf, he continued,

'Mr. Bettis, you may already be aware that I together with another chartered surveyor, who was appointed by your neighbour, checked your site, in some detail on Friday. The police gave us special dispensation to carry out this inspection, since the entire site has been designated as a crime scene, since an incident on Thursday last. Together we also inspected the foundations supporting Mr. Skrobe's home. The ground beneath and surrounding his home has been disturbed by your blasting operations. A qualified civil engineer would have prohibited the

239

use of explosives on the site, given the unstable nature of the subsoil. The whole site is in an area of historic interest. Ancient flint mines are still being discovered every few years. They must be preserved until properly examined, not blown to smithereens by reckless cowboy builders!'

His clerk was stifling a giggle, but dare not let his boss see him. He bent as though to retrieve a pencil from the floor behind his desk. Bettis was attempting to look offended, but the surveyor continued apace.

'Furthermore, the loose spoil and shale, against Mr. Skrobe's land, to the West and to the agricultural land, to the North, was left at an angle of repose approaching 85 degrees. The prescribed angle of repose for loose chalk/loam is 60 degrees. A certified engineer would have provided you with this information. Had you checked a few basic details, you could have prevented most of the problems which you now face. The building regulations are most explicit regarding the health and safety aspects of site work. You have chosen to ignore or contravene these regulations. You have broken the law and must now accept the consequences.'

The surveyor handed Bettis an envelope,

'This is an order prohibiting any further building on your Wigglesworth site, until the perimeters have been stabilised and rendered safe. As the developers, you and your business partner will be charged with 'Corporate Negligence'. I must warn you that the court can and probably will, award costs in respect of damage caused by you to neighbouring properties.'

A crestfallen Bettis nodded his acceptance.

'Will we be charged in respect of the accident, or the human skeletal remains, as well?' he asked.

The surveyor looked at his documents before replying,

'I'm afraid that is something which falls outside our remit. I don't appear to have any details of any other matters, but no doubt the police will be able to advise you of their intentions. The only other matter which concerns this office is the original planning permission, which is now withdrawn. I'm afraid that before you can resume your activities at that location, you will need to submit a completely revised set of plans, for approval by the Planning Committee. I'm afraid that is how it is, Mr. Bettis and that concludes our meeting for today. We will be in touch with you shortly.'

They shook hands and Bettis left the office.

To put the situation in a 'nutshell', Bettis was now 'broke'!
He had to find a way through this dilemma. Elaine would be unwilling to offer any further financial help. She was a wealthy woman in her own right, her father had left her more than half a million and that was after Death Duty and 'Inheritance Tax' had been paid. At the time when they were married, she had owned a small chain of shops, selling cosmetics and beauty products. Bettis had persuaded her to sell all but two of these, to invest in his business. Elaine still owned the house in which they lived and this was secured for her future by a pre-nuptial agreement.
He had to get some cash urgently. There would be no more stage payments from their client and the likelihood of a cash injection from any other source seemed remote. Where was Jeff Davies? Why hadn't he been in touch? He must have known the situation was desperate, yet he had snubbed the Borough Surveyor, by refusing to attend this meeting.

Bettis stopped off at the off license on his way home for a bottle of vodka. He let himself in and took off his coat. Elaine's car was not there, she must have gone to one of her friends. In the kitchen, he selected a half pint tumbler and half filled it with neat vodka and then topped it up with tonic water from the fridge.
He took it into the lounge and flipped the television on to catch the local mid-day news.
The newsreader had almost finished his lunchtime bulletin. Bettis was just in time to hear the last bit. Police had confirmed that a second set of skeletal remains had been discovered at a farm site in Wigglesworth. They were thought to have lain undiscovered

for approximately thirty years. The report went on to say that the area was thought to have been the site of Neolithic flint mines. Archaeological groups had found many remains and ancient relics over the past hundred years.

The weather forecast followed. It would remain cloudy with strong winds in the south. Further north there would be some wintry showers. Heavy rain was expected later in the week. Now thoroughly depressed, he switched the television off.

Minutes later, the telephone rang. It was Jeffery Davies.

'Martin, sorry I couldn't make it this morning, I've been with the police. My father was found shot dead this morning!'

'What?' Bettis exclaimed. 'I'm sorry to hear that, Jeff. I thought I was having a bad morning, but I can't compete with that. D'you want me to come over to your place?'

'That would be good, Martin, I've got to go to Lincoln tomorrow for this damned court hearing. Trish is here at the moment, but she won't mind if you don't.'

'Who's 'Trish'?' Bettis asked.

'She's a private investigator, but also an old friend, from way back. She's been trying to help me find Hannah.' Davies explained.

'I'll leave a note for Elaine and then I'll be over. See you in about a quarter of an hour.'

'OK thanks, Martin,' said Davies.

Bettis arrived at Davies' home and was invited into the lounge. He was introduced to Patricia Walker, who asked them if they would like her to make them some coffee.

'Yes please, Trish,' Davies said and then turning to Bettis, he asked, 'What happened at the meeting?'

'I'll tell you about it later, Jeff. What happened at your dad's place?'

'Cathy found him,' Davies said. 'I think it gave her quite a fright. She stayed all day, trying to help. I think she was quite fond of the old boy. She seems to know more about him than I do, in certain areas. I can't go up to the house until the police tell me. It's cordoned off with crime scene tape at present. Cathy told them the name of his solicitor. I believe they'll contact him first. Bettis explained the content of his meeting at the Borough Surveyor's office and showed Davies the order which he had been given. Bettis explained to him.

'He wasn't very happy about you not turning up. In fact he wasn't very happy about any of it. He reckons the police will also be following up on the accident and those bones they took away,' he said. 'I was going to say that the accident was nothing to do with us, but then I don't trust that bastard, Grover. He wouldn't think twice about dropping us in it.'

'You didn't mention him to the planners, did you?' Davies asked him.

'No, Jeff, of course I didn't. I thought the best thing would be for me to say as little as possible, but to keep agreeing with him. He seemed to mellow a bit towards the end, but it looks as though we're screwed, Jeff. We've got to stabilise the site and make restitution to old Skrobe, before we can do anything else. There will need to be a new set of plans drawn up and presented to the planners for approval. I don't know how we'll survive this one.' Davies read the documents which Bettis had given him. He placed them on the coffee table and looked up at Bettis.

'Well, Martin, it looks as though he was right about the building regulations. We only have ourselves to blame on that front. We both thought we could get the old boy to sell up. There's one thing I hadn't realised, that whole frontage is his. Even our access road is on his property.'

I'm surprised the planners never noticed that,' Bettis said. 'I think our architect should have noticed it too, don't you?' Davies thought for a few moments and then he said,

'Yes, I think they should both have picked up on that, but they didn't. Now we've got to try to persuade old Skrobe to sell us access rights over it. We've tried using force, now we need to go back to gentle persuasion.'

243

'I've done a rough calculation on the cost of the extra work,' Bettis told him. 'The shuttering and the concrete against the field and Skrobe's garden will come to about fifteen thousand. After that, we need to try to keep everyone on side and sweet.'
Davies was looking thoughtful.

'There won't be any more stage payments from our client,' he said. 'Not until we can resume work on the project at any rate. Our investors won't be keen to contribute to the cost of our screw up either. I daren't go to the house yet, not before my court case in Lincoln, anyway. I'll be back on Thursday, Martin. My solicitor thinks I'll either get a suspended sentence or one of those community service orders. I'll still have a fine to pay, but I don't know how much it will be.'
Bettis asked him,

'Will you inherit all of your dad's property?'

'I won't know that until his will is read,' Davies told him. 'There should be enough to get us out of this hole, but it may be several weeks before we know. They usually have to notify all of the people who are mentioned, whether there is anything left to them or not. Then when the date is set, they are all invited to attend the reading of the will.'
Bettis was becoming agitated.

'We really need some cash now, to get things moving, Jeff,' he said. 'We can't afford to wait weeks and weeks on 'spec', can we?'

'If we go in there before the police tell us we can, we'll be lining up the next load of trouble for ourselves,' Davies told him. 'I know my father kept a few thousand in a safe in his cellar, but that's about all I would dare to touch until after the will was read. That would be his 'secret stash', so it wouldn't be listed in the will.'

'If it's in a safe, how would you get it?' Bettis asked.
Davies laughed at him,

'How do you think I'd get it?' he said, still laughing. 'I'd unlock the safe and take the money out of course. What did you have in mind, dynamite? I think that might be a bit too noisy, don't you?'

Bettis was grinning at his own thoughtlessness.

'Yes, I suppose it would destroy the element of stealth and surprise. So you have a key to this safe, Jeff, do you?'

'Not personally,' he replied, 'but I know where he keeps it. There's a loose paving slab in the garage floor, it's in a box under that.'

Bettis was thinking perhaps they could get it sooner,

'Won't the garage be locked as well?' he asked.

Davies laughed again.

'What's funny, Jeff?' Bettis asked.

'You've obviously not seen father's garage,' Davies said. 'The brickwork is fine and the roof doesn't leak. The window is not broken and the floor is as clean as the day it was built. The double doors however, are the originals. Good quality timber and well made, but now they're more than fifty years old. They're still fairly solid, but there's a two inch wide gap when they are closed. The vertical plank which used to shut against the right hand door is missing. I believe my dad left them open once when he went out. The wind caught them and when he returned, that piece of wood had smashed and split. It dragged on the ground for a few weeks, but in the end he just pulled it off and threw it away.'

Bettis was smiling as he asked,

'Doesn't the wind still blow them about?'

'Only if he forgets to tie them together with the baler twine,' Davies said. 'The staple is still on the right hand door but the hasp went with the piece of split wood. Now there's just a steel eye on the other door, with a length of baler twine tied to it. He only used to tie it after he'd put the Audi away. He couldn't leave the car outside, it's a 'soft top' and it used to leak a bit. Father was not good on security. He always left the keys in the car even when he parked in a car park. He reckoned if someone was going

245

to pinch it, he was in with a better chance of getting it back in working order. He used to say,

'It's a rag top, Jeffery, anyone can get into it with a penknife. If I take the keys they'll just as likely smash the lock and then hot wire it, so I'd have all that extra expense if the police got it back for me.'

I suppose he was right in a way, but I think I'd have still preferred to lock it and take the keys, if it was mine.'

Bettis said,

'So it should be fairly easy to get in and pick up the money from the safe?'

'In theory it should, once we got into the house,' Davies agreed. 'But we'd still have to wait until the police have cleared it as a crime scene. We'll have a think about it when I get back. Cathy Simons has got a key to the house. I expect she would lend it to me.'

Patricia Walker had been listening to their discussion. She held up a forefinger and said to Bettis,

'Don't try to act this one out on your own, Martin. Do as Jeff says and wait until he's back from Lincoln.'

'Yes, yes, of course,' Bettis said as he held his open hands up in surrender. 'Of course I will.'

CHAPTER 35.

Hilda had woken early. She searched frantically for her mobile phone, which was where the loud whistling was coming from. She had increased the volume of the ringtone last evening, to be sure she would hear it when Hannah called.

The whistling stopped. Hilda looked at her watch on the bedside cabinet. It was six minutes after six.

'Damn!' She muttered to herself. 'I'll have to find it now, so I can call her back.'

The whistling tone began again, just as she located the mobile.

'Hannah?' she said quietly, 'Where are you?'

'I'm just driving through Arundel,' she replied. 'I should be with you in about half an hour. Put the kettle on, 'Sis'. I haven't had a drink since I was on the ferry and I'm parched.'

Hilda was worried that she may have woken Elsie and Archie. She put on a dressing gown and went down the stairs as quietly as she could. Archie was already in the kitchen, getting ready to take Jimbo for his early walk. He was startled to see her.

'Good morning, Hilda,' he said. 'Didn't you sleep very well?'

She smiled at him as she explained,

'Yes, thank you, Archie, I slept very well. I was woken by my mobile phone. Hannah is much earlier than she thought. She said she was just driving through Arundel, she will be here soon. I hope I didn't wake Elsie.'

Archie laughed quietly,

'She wakes early, Hilda, I've just taken her second cup of tea. You'll probably be able to squeeze another one out of the pot, but you'd better make a fresh one for Hannah. I'll be back in about twenty minutes. I just take him over the mill field, as soon as he's had a 'pee' we'll come back.'

As Archie went out of the back door, Hilda saw the dog's lead on the hook. She opened the door and called after him,

'Archie, you've forgotten his lead.'

'He won't need that for this walk, Hilda.' Archie explained. 'There's hardly any traffic about this early and he waits for me at the kerb anyway. See you in a little while.' He waved as he went out of the front gate.

Hilda returned to the kitchen and filled the kettle. She had poured herself a cup of tea, but it was beginning to 'stew' so she didn't drink it. She emptied the remains of the pot into the sink and transferred the spent tea bags to the bin. She began searching for the tea bags which she eventually found in a white jar, with the word, 'Coffee' embossed on it! She smiled to herself,

'Just like it used to be at home,' she thought, 'a place for everything and nothing in the right place.' Out of curiosity she looked into another jar marked 'Tea', it contained sugar. 'I suppose that's logical,' she thought, 'the coffee will be in the sugar jar.'

Wrong again! The sugar jar contained rice!

Elsie was watching her from the doorway,

'Good morning Hilda,' she said, 'Have you found everything you need yet?' Elsie was laughing. 'That's Archie, he never looks at the labels, just uses whichever jar is empty.'

The kettle had boiled so Hilda made the tea.

248

'I'm sorry if I disturbed you, Elsie,' she said. 'I had a call from Hannah on my mobile. She'll be here very soon now. She's a lot earlier than I expected her, I hope everything's alright.'
Elsie rinsed the cups under the tap and tipped away half a cup of cold tea from Archie's mug.

'He'll be back soon,' Elsie told her. 'He just gives Jimbo a short walk in the mornings, so that he can stretch his legs and have a pee. Arch will feed him when they get back.'

'He's a lovely dog, Elsie,' Hilda said. 'Tell me what you meant when you said that he found Archie?'

Elsie told her how Archie had come home to find him on their doorstep one day.

'We tried to find out who owned him and eventually Bill Pickering, the village bobby, found out. The young family who had him from a puppy, were going to live abroad and they'd asked one of their relatives to have him. Unfortunately, she already had an Alsatian.
Jimbo wasn't comfortable with it and kept escaping. He took a real shine to Archie and Bill arranged for us to keep him. So you see, it was Jimbo who found us, not us who found him.'
Archie returned from his walk with the dog and began preparing Jimbo's meal.

'What's the weather like Arch?' Elsie asked.

'It's a bit chilly, but it's not raining,' he replied. 'The grass is still wet and the mill pond weir is doing its stuff. He put a couple of partridges up on the way there. That's the first time I've seen any English partridge for months. They're usually the French ones, with the red legs.'
Hilda looked up at him, she asked Elsie,

'Is he pulling my leg, Elsie? Do they really have red legs?'

'No, Hilda, he's not joking. The French partridges were brought here when our native species was in decline and yes, they do have red legs.'
Archie grinned at her and sat down with the tea which Elsie had poured for him.

'What sort of time do you two want to go to Chichelster today?' Elsie asked. 'I expect Hannah will have some breakfast with us, she'll be tired as well if she's been travelling all night.' Hilda nodded in agreement,

'She should be here any minute, unless she's forgotten the way,' she said. 'I asked her if she knew exactly where you lived this morning and she said she did.'

Jimbo had eaten his meal and was noisily slurping from his water bowl. When he had finished drinking, he went to Hilda and rested his head on her knee.

'Oh, Jimbo,' she said in surprise, 'look at my dressing gown, it's soaked!' She was rubbing his ears and laughing at him as he tried to place a damp and muddy paw on her knee.

'Don't worry about it,' Elsie told her. 'We can have that washed and dried whilst you're in Chichelster, unless you were planning to wear it at the police station!'

There was a very gentle tap on the glass of the kitchen door. Archie got up and opened it. A rather exhausted looking Hannah stood outside. Her face lit up as she saw her sister sitting at the kitchen table with a cup of tea.

'Oh, thank goodness,' she said. 'I still wasn't sure if I had come to the right house. Hello Elsie and you must be Mr. Leggitt,' she said as she looked at Archie.

'Me?' Archie replied, with a shocked look on his face. 'No, not me, I'm just 'Archie'. I'm only, 'Mr. Leggitt' to people who don't know me, Hannah,' he told her. 'It's good to see you, again after so many years. You must be worn out with your journey, come and sit down. You have a cup of tea, whilst I get your bag from your car. Would you like to give me the keys?'

Hannah opened her bag and gave Archie her car keys.

'Thank you, Archie,' she said smiling. 'There's a small gift and a bunch of flowers in the luggage boot. My case is on the back seat.'

Archie returned a few minutes later with Hannah's case and the flowers.

250

'These are for you, Elsie,' Hannah said, handing her the bouquet. 'Did you find the gift, Archie?' she asked him.

'Is this it?' He asked as he pulled a small gift wrapped box from his pocket.

Hilda smiled as she took it from him, 'Thanks Archie, yes, that's it.'

'I hope you'll like it, Elsie,' she said as she presented it to her. Elsie stood up as she accepted the box. She hugged Hannah and said,

'Thank you Hannah, you shouldn't have bought me anything else. These flowers are lovely. I know things are not easy for you just now, but you're always welcome here, both of you.'

She sat back at the table and began to unwrap her gift. It was a silver necklace, with a pearl dropper.

'Oh, it's lovely, Hannah,' she said, smiling. 'It really is, but you still shouldn't have spent your money on me.'

She gave Hannah a big hug and kissed her cheek.

While Hannah went and freshened up, Elsie prepared the breakfast. They chatted all the while about old times and the old farm shop. Hannah returned to the kitchen looking a little less weary, and they continued chatting through their meal. Archie told them about old Joe and the problems he had been having with the hotel building site next door. They appeared shocked when he mentioned the skull which had been found and were even more surprised when Archie told them about the other set of remains which they had discovered yesterday morning.

'Do they know any more about them yet?' Hilda asked.

Archie smiled,

'There's every possibility that they do by now,' he said, but they won't be advertising their findings. I'll make a few discreet enquiries when we're up there this morning.'

'Will they tell you?' Hannah asked him.

Elsie nodded to the girls, and raised her eyebrows.

'They probably will,' she told them. 'Archie has a very good relationship with the police locally. They seem to rely on him for his help and local knowledge. He's been one of their part time helpers ever since he retired.'

Archie helped Elsie to clear the breakfast things whilst the girls relaxed in the lounge with Jimbo. They heard Hannah gasp,

'What? You're telling me he's dead? Are you sure?' She came out into the kitchen and asked Archie,

'Hilda says that Jeffery's father was murdered yesterday, Archie. Is that right?'

'That's as far as I know at the moment,' Archie replied as he followed her back into the lounge. 'Though it isn't official yet, so don't broadcast it. We may find out a bit more this morning. What time were you thinking of going through to Chichelster?'

Hilda looked at her watch and said,

'Goodness! I hadn't realised the time was going so quickly. It's ten o'clock already.' She turned to Hannah and asked, 'Are you going to see Dad before you go back?'

'Yes, but not today,' Hannah replied. She went into the kitchen, where Elsie was tidying up.

'Elsie, would you mind if I stayed a little longer than I first said?' She asked. 'It's just that I need to see a solicitor to get a restraining order on Jeffery and there are a few other things I need to do.'

Elsie smiled at her, saying,

'Hannah, you can stay for as long as you like, you don't need to give us a reason. Just make sure you don't try to do too much until you've had a good rest. I know you need to go to the police station whilst Hilda is here, but when you come back from there, make sure you take some time for yourself.'

'Thank you, Elsie,' she said, smiling. 'I do really need a good sleep, so I'll take your advice.' She returned to where Hilda was still sitting with Jimbo.

'Elsie says I can stay a bit longer, Hilda,' she told her. 'Would you mind driving us into the police station? I'm really tired, so I hoped I could leave my car here. You'll need yours later, if you're driving back to Lincoln tonight.'

'Yes, OK. Just leave your keys here, in case Elsie needs to use their car whilst we're out,' Hilda suggested. She walked out into the hallway and called out,

'Archie, is it alright if we go in about ten minutes?'

'Yes,' said Archie, from half way down the stairs. 'I'm ready when you are, but first, I think you should phone your dad, Hannah. I promised him I'd let him know when you had arrived safely. Whose car are we using to go to Chi?'

'Mine,' Hilda told him, 'We need to swap them round, so mine is at the front, ready to go back this afternoon. I've told Hannah to leave her keys with Elsie, in case she needs to move it, before we get back. Do I need to take anything with me, Archie?'

'Only your sister, wait until she's phoned your dad and then we'll swap the cars round. It might be a good idea to get your passport back from Hannah before we go,' he suggested. 'I know you're pretty much identical, but it might look better if you have your own passports instead of each others!'

Hannah had finished her phone call.

'Gosh, I forgot about that,' Hilda laughed as she called to her sister. 'Hannah, before you go to reclaim your passport, do you think I could have mine back, please?'

Hannah laughed as she said,

'I was going to hang on to it to prove my identity at the police station.' She opened her bag and took out the passport, passing it to her sister. 'Thanks Hilda,' she said. 'It really got me out of harms way, I'm just sorry he tried to hurt you. I told dad I'd phone him again later.'

Less than an hour later they were in the front office of Chichelster police station. Sergeant Dean looked up as they entered and smiled at Archie and the two ladies.

'Good morning, young Archie,' he said. 'To what do we owe the pleasure of your company on this fine morning? Could it be an official 'state visit' or just another 'social occasion'?' He laughed as Archie replied,

253

'Heard you were on the front desk, Dixie and just couldn't keep away!' They shook hands and Archie introduced the two sisters to him.

'I'm guessing that you've come to claim the passport which you left behind when you went away, is that why you're here?' He asked.

'Yes, Sergeant,' Hannah answered. 'The fact is however, that I didn't leave it behind. Jeff took it from me, thinking it would stop me from leaving him. I didn't forget it. He said he was going to burn it.'

'Oh, I'm sorry,' Sergeant Dean said. 'I was quoting from your husband's statement. I believe DI Church would like a word with you. He has your passport in his office. I'll see if I can find him for you.'

Whilst they were waiting for DI Church, Archie asked Sergeant Dean whether there had been any further developments on the forensics front.

'I wouldn't know about that, Arch,' said the Sergeant. 'You'd need to ask Brian Pace or his young protégé, Adam Morton. I believe you met him briefly whilst you were rescuing a tractor. That's the story I got from Bill Pickering, is that right?'

'It's close,' Archie said. 'It was a bit of a 'hairy' job, that one. We were lucky not to lose it over the edge. The ground was very unstable, but we got lucky.'

DI Tony Church entered the front office. He was smiling at the two sisters.

'Good morning,' he said. 'I'm Detective Inspector Church.' He shook hands with them both. 'Do I have to guess which one of you is, Mrs. Hannah Davies?' He asked as he looked at Hannah's passport photograph and then at the twins.

'I'll own up to that,' Hannah said, seeing her passport in Tony's hand. 'I'm just pleased that he didn't do as he threatened and burn it.'

'Yes, I'll bet you are,' he said, 'but I'd just like a quick word with you, in private, if you wouldn't mind.'

254

Hanna smiled at him and replied,

'Not at all, Inspector, my sister has to be in Lincoln later today. It won't take long, will it?'

'I'm sure young Archie will look after her,' the DI assured her.

Their informal chat helped Tony Church to understand the situation a little better.

'So the alleged assault on your sister at her home is somewhat typical of your husband's behaviour when he loses his temper?' He suggested.

Hanna nodded,

'He can be quite violent and he's extremely controlling,' she told him. 'That's why I left him and later today I'm going to a solicitor to try to get a restraining order. I don't want him anywhere near me or my family. I just want a divorce and to be rid of him for good.'

The DI was sympathetic in his reply,

'I can imagine him to be a bit impetuous,' he said. 'I believe he has a few money worries, because of the development project he's running on the Arundel Road. He said that he needed you to sign some documents, do you know what he meant?'

'I haven't the faintest idea,' she told him. 'Didn't he tell you?'

'I'm not really supposed to say anything, but I'm sure I can rely on your discretion, Mrs. Davies,' Tony placed his forefinger along the side of his nose and raised an eyebrow.

Hannah understood his meaning,

'Thank you, yes Inspector,' she said quietly. 'I understand completely. I'll be staying for a few days with Archie and Elsie Leggitt. If you need to contact me, I can give you my mobile number.'

The DI leaned towards her and in a soft voice, he said,

'He told me that the house is in your name and that there is a pre-nuptial agreement. He wants to make you sign it over as joint ownership, so that he can borrow money using the house as collateral. I'll take a note of your mobile number, but if you feel

in the least threatened by him, please don't hesitate to call us.'
The DI picked up a pencil to note Hannah's mobile number. He
noticed the change in her expression and asked,

'What is it that's bothering you?'

'Oh,' she said, 'that old chestnut again! He's already tried to
forge my signature on the Land Registry documents, but not
everyone is a stupid or as arrogant as him. They queried it with
me by letter and when I told them what he'd done, they marked
the file. Before any transfer can take place, they now require me
to apply in person, with two independent witnesses and my Birth
Certificate, N.I. number and my passport. So, you see, now that I
have my passport safely returned, he can do no more forging.'
The DI was happy to have cleared up the confusion created by
Jeffery Davies' misleading statement. Hannah thanked him for
his help as they returned to the front office.

'I'm pleased to have been of service to you Mrs. Davies,'
Tony said as he shook her hand once more. 'Don't hesitate to let
me know if you need any help or advice. Can you bear to wait
just a few minutes while I have a quick word with Mr. Leggitt?'
Archie came towards the DI,

'Over here, Archie,' he said. 'There's no need to go into the
office, just a quiet word will do.'
Archie followed the DI towards the back wall, away from the
desk and telephones.

'I haven't got very much yet, Archie,' he began. 'There's
some which I can tell you, and some which I can't, well, not just
yet anyway. I don't suppose you'd know yet, but there was a fox
shot dead, just the other side of Ridge Farm. Jeffery Davies'
young lady companion spotted it when he visited his father on
Sunday evening. I'm telling you this in confidence. Perhaps it
would be wise not to mention any of this to your two lady guests
just yet.'
Archie nodded his agreement.
The DI continued.

'To keep it brief, our lads collected the corpse of the fox, a smelly business, to say the least. Anyway, the forensic boys recovered the bullet from it and our boffins tell us that it is a match for the two found in the skull, last week. Brian Pace was impressed with the way you noticed them amongst all the other soil and debris and in the poor light.'

'So the gun which killed the lady whose skull we found, is still in use and still local?' Archie said.
The DI nodded,

'It looks that way, doesn't it? There's more, Archie,' he continued. 'It's definitely not a match for the bullet which killed Jason Davies. He was shot with a point two-two or two-five bullet, but not from the same weapon. Now for the delicate bit, as far as your house guests are concerned.'

'Yes?' Archie leaned closer and said, 'Please tell me.'

'Ian is not here just now, Archie,' the DI told him. 'He's with their father, Bob Jempson. The skeletal remains which we managed to extract yesterday, whilst you were busy rescuing a traumatised tractor, were most interesting. It seems that the poor lad was crushed to death. As near as we can tell, from the forensic evidence, he was in a wide crack in the ground, trying to recover a stolen cash box. We believe he may have deliberately hidden it there and gone back for it later. We haven't been able to identify him as yet, but he was in his early twenties when he died. I can tell you that in the same location as his remains, apart from the cash box, we discovered a few remnants of clothing. As you may imagine, most were in an advanced state of decay, but one glove was still recognisable. It matched the charred glove which was found after the house fire which caused the death of Bob's wife, Sally. The cashbox, although somewhat waterlogged, still held some money and delivery notes relating to the farm shop which Bob owned.'
Archie's eyes opened wide as he asked,

'D'you reckon he was the arsonist?'

257

'It's beginning to look as though he had something to do with the fire, but we don't know whether it was arson or accident. We'll need to identify him, if we can, so that we can inform his next of kin, if he had any. The problem is that it was all about thirty years ago, so we'll be lucky to find anyone who can help us. We may get lucky with dental records, we'll just have to wait and see.'

The DI stood and looked at Archie, who was digesting the information. He could almost predict that he would be processing it for the next hour or two.

'That's about it, for the time being,' Tony Church told him. 'Jason Davies' house is still taped as a crime scene, but we can't spare the manpower to put a guard on it. You can pretty much see the house from where Joe's old greenhouse stands, so if you happen to be along that way and notice anything untoward, perhaps you'd let us know.'

'Yes, of course I will,' Archie replied. 'But who is likely to want to gain access to his farm house, now a crime scene?'

The DI lowered his voice again as he spoke,

'There's Jeffery, his 'accomplice', sorry, partner, or there's his sister, Bernice and her family. I dare say that they all believe old Jason owes them something. They will have to wait until the body is released, before his solicitor can read the will. Between you and me, I think there may well be a few surprises when that day comes. We'd better leave it there for now, if anything comes to your ears, which you think may be useful to us, we'd be glad of your help, as usual.'

'Thanks, Inspector,' Archie said, as they shook hands. 'It looks as though my companions are ready to make tracks, so I'll get them home. Hilda is going back to Lincoln today, ready for Davies' court appearance tomorrow. Hannah is staying for a few days. She has some other business to attend to, whilst she is here.'

'Yes, Archie, she told me so, herself,' said the DI. 'I wish her every success and I hope that Hilda has a good result in court tomorrow. I'll leave you now, and thank you for your help, past, present and future.' He smiled as they shook hands and went their separate ways.

'Are you ladies ready to get back home for some lunch?' He asked.

'And a lovely sleep for me, this afternoon,' said Hannah.

CHAPTER 36.

After an uneventful drive back to Wigglesworth, they enjoyed a light lunch of ham, eggs and chips, which Elsie prepared shortly after they arrived home. Hannah apologised, but said that if she didn't have a sleep soon, she would go to sleep standing up.

'Wake me before you leave, Hilda,' she asked as she went up to the bedroom.

Hilda told Elsie about their visit to the police station.

'I liked that Inspector Church,' she told her. 'Hannah said he was a very kind man. He couldn't give her all the information, but he did tell her that Jeffery had said Hannah had forgotten to take her passport when she left. Hannah said that he didn't seem surprised when she told him that Jeffery had taken it from her and threatened to burn it.'

Elsie smiled,

'I think he's a good man, Hilda,' she said. 'So is his Detective Sergeant, his name is Ian Stuart. Did you see him, Archie?'

'Not this morning, Else, he was out on business,' Archie said. 'I found out a couple of things though, from Tony Church. There was a fox that had been shot, somewhere further up Ridge Farm Lane. The police recovered the corpse and guess what!'

'It had a rabbit inside it?' Elsie suggested, 'A white one perhaps?'

Archie laughed, he noticed Hilda was also giggling.

'Not quite, but it had a couple of point two-two bullets in it.' He told her. 'And they are a match for those they found in that skull last week.'

Elsie looked startled,

'So whoever killed that woman thirty odd years ago is still around?' She asked incredulously.

'Not necessarily,' said Archie, 'but the rifle is.'

'What about the other skull?' Elsie asked him. 'Did they say anything about that?'

'Yes,' Archie replied. 'They found almost the entire skeleton of that one. It seems that he was trapped in a fissure and crushed to death.'

Elsie pulled a face,

'How awful, Arch,' she said. 'It must have been a terrible death. I can almost imagine him screaming.'

Archie nodded,

'The thing is that once Bob's house had gone, in the fire, there would be nobody around to hear him. Perhaps he couldn't even scream or shout, because of the pressure of the earth on his chest. That ground has always been unstable. It's riddled with old flint workings and even the vibrations of heavy traffic can set it all moving. I think it's gradually slipping down the hill, a sort of slow motion landslide. There are always fresh cracks and holes appearing up there, especially after we've had heavy rain. That's how Peter Bailley almost lost his tractor yesterday. It wasn't that close to the edge, when it began to sink in.'

'Was the other skeleton close to where the tractor was sinking?' Hilda asked.

'Quite close,' Archie told her, 'about thirty or forty yards, I suppose.'

'Was it the same rifle that was used to shoot old Jason?' Elsie asked him.

'Not as far as I know,' Archie replied. 'I'm sure Tony Church would have said if that were the case. It's a bit worrying to think that there are people here, in our peaceful community, who carry lethal weapons. I just hope it won't be too long before they find whoever it is.'

Jimbo had been sitting next to Hilda, in fact he was almost leaning on her.

'Tell him to move if he's pressing on your legs,' Elsie said to her. 'He often does that when we have visitors. I think it's his way of saying, 'I like you', but I'm sure you know that by now.'

He's alright,' Hilda said, rubbing Jimbo's ears. 'I was wondering perhaps if we could go and have a look at your watermill before I go back, Archie. Would you mind showing me?'

'No, Hilda,' said Archie, smiling. 'We can take Jimbo with us. He'll enjoy a walk along the field. Do you fancy a stroll, Else?'

'No, thanks, Arch,' she said. 'I'll stay here, if Hannah wakes up and finds everyone gone, she'll wonder what's happening!'

They chatted as they walked over to the mill. Once they had crossed the road, Archie let Jimbo off his lead. He ran along in front of them, stopping every now and then to wait for them to catch up.

'How long did it take you to get it back into full working order, Archie?' Hilda asked as they walked through the grass footpath towards the mill.

He looked at Hilda, while he thought about her question.

'From start to finish, it was almost a year,' he said. 'There was a lot of research which we had to do before we began any actual work. There were bits of machinery and some of the wooden gears missing. It was a bit like a three dimensional jig saw puzzle.'

Hilda smiled. She was obviously both interested and impressed.

'How did you manage to replace the missing parts, Archie?' She asked. 'Did you get them from another mill which had been left to decay?'

'No, Hilda, we had some new ones made,' he told her. 'You'll see presently, when we go up to the top of the mill. Do you think you'd like to see it all working? I can't grind any corn, because it's all been cleaned, ready to begin again next year. Reg, that's the owner, uses it to generate electricity through the winter. It saves him quite a bit on his bill and it keeps the waterwheel in good trim.'

'Doesn't it put extra strain on the machinery?' Hilda asked. 'Surely it needs a rest from work, the same as we do.'
Archie smiled as he explained,

'You would be amazed at the way machinery in general can deteriorate when it's not used for a while. Even us humans need to keep active, to remain fit. Try to imagine if the water wheel was left static for a few months. The part which was in the water would swell and become saturated. The rest of it would tend to dry out altogether. When it was re-started after it had had its 'rest', it would be out of balance. That would make it surge instead of rotating smoothly, wouldn't it?'
Hilda thought for a moment, before replying,

'I hadn't thought of that, of course the bottom of the wheel, where it was stopped, would be continuously immersed in water. I can see that would make it sort of, 'oscillate' when it was re-started.'
They had reached the water wheel now and paused to look at it.

'You see, it's stopped now, but the bit that is out of the water is still wet, from last night, when it was turning,' he said. 'Of course it's not just the water wheel that would suffer, if it was run out of balance. The bearings would take some of the strain and the wooden gears would run and wear unevenly.'

'I understand what you're saying, Archie,' she said, smiling. 'It's the same when you have a car which you don't use for a few months. It usually won't start when you need it urgently.'

'Come in and have a look round,' he said as he unlocked the big door and called Jimbo, who was busy sniffing by the sleeper bridge. 'I'll put the lights on. There aren't too many windows, so even in the summer we need lights some days.'
He gave her the full guided tour. On the milling floor, she saw the partly finished guard rail that he had been making.
'Oh, you're still working on it, are you?' She asked.
'I suppose you have to be careful that people don't get too close to the moving parts, whilst they're being shown around?'
Archie nodded as he replied,
'Yes, health and safety's everyone's responsibility. You'd be surprised how silly and reckless some people can be. I've seen parents with young children, letting them reach out towards the gear wheels whilst they're turning!'
'No!' she said. 'Surely they think more of their children's safety to do a thing like that?'
'The trouble is, Hilda,' he went on. 'These days, some parents think that because they paid to look around anywhere, be it watermills, castles or steam museums, the responsibility for their children's safety suddenly transfers from them as parents, to the owner or the operator of the attraction. They don't even bother to supervise their kids. I've even seen them watch their children while they draw on some of the walls with crayons.'
'That much I can believe, Archie,' Hilda said. 'We've had the same sort of thing at the hospital in Lincoln. The parents have no manners or respect, so the children go the same way. You wouldn't believe some of the abuse we have to put up with, especially in 'A and E'. A few years ago it was unheard of to have to call the police, but these days it's almost a daily occurrence.'

Jimbo suddenly barked loudly and startled them both.
'What's up, Jimbo?' Archie called down the stairway.

264

He continued to bark, so they went down to take a look. Archie opened the oak front door, to find PC Bill Pickering standing there.

'Hello, Jimbo,' he said as he rubbed the dog's head and chest. Jimbo was always happy to see anybody he knew. He sat in front of Bill, with a look of expectation.

'I haven't brought any biscuits, Jim,' Bill explained, showing the dog two empty hands.

'Hello Bill!' Archie said in surprise. 'What can I do for you this fine afternoon?'

Bill smiled and nodded to Hilda,

'Let me introduce you,' Archie said. 'This is Miss Hilda Jempson, her twin sister, Mrs. Hannah Davies, is at home with Elsie. She's having a sleep after her journey.'

Bill held out his hand to her,

'I'm very pleased to meet you, Hilda,' he said. 'I'm Bill Pickering, your local police force.' He grinned as he continued, 'I don't suppose Archie has told you anything about me, but we have been known to help each other out, now and then.'

Hilda smiled, saying,

'I believe he did mention your name in connection with his tractor escapade yesterday, Mr. Pickering. I'm pleased to have met you and put a face to the name.'

Bill looked at Archie and said,

'There's no urgency, but Joe asked me to give you a message, next time I saw you. He's had a letter from Davies' solicitor, asking for an estimate to repair the greenhouse. He wants you to inspect it with him first. Make sure the framework is still intact and then make a list of the glass and clips that will be needed. He'll be happy to pay you for it. He said he can add that to his bill.

He's got another letter from the court requesting the cost of a replacement for the farm hut, but he says he can do that by himself.. They are two separate issues, but it looks as though Davies is accepting responsibility for the greenhouse. We

265

allowed them back onto the site this morning to assess the materials needed to shore up the bank next to Joe's garden. They have also agreed to make safe all the support pillars under his bungalow. They really didn't have much choice in the matter. The court has ruled that no further work can be done until restitution has been made for the damage which they caused. I noticed that all their machinery and equipment has been cleared from Joe's property. It's all been moved to the other side of their site fence.'

Archie smiled at Hilda,

'That's what Bill meant when he said we sometimes help each other out,' he said. He looked at Bill and explained.

'Hilda has to be back in Lincoln later today, so we can't waste too much time just now. I'll phone old Joe later and have a chat. How did you know I was over here?'

'The usual method, Arch,' Bill grinned. 'I asked Elsie and she tried your mobile. We could hear it ringing in your jacket pocket, hanging in the hall.'

Archie laughed, I had my good jacket on this morning,' he said. 'We had to go to 'Chi' to collect Hannah's passport from Tony Church. I forgot to change it over when we got back.'

'I'll leave you in peace,' said Bill. 'Nice to meet you, Hilda, I wish you a safe journey back to Lincoln.'

Bill went on his way and Archie locked up the mill, He and Hilda walked along the bank of the mill pond, up to the weir. Jimbo had a good walk, continually running back and forth until they returned to the road. He sat at the kerb and waited for Archie to clip his lead back on. They arrived home to find that Hannah had woken from her sleep and was sitting with Elsie in the kitchen.

'Come in Hilda,' Elsie called out. 'I've just made a pot of tea. I expect you'd like one after being bored by Archie for an hour or two!'

Hilda smiled at Elsie and her sister,

266

'I'm going to be perfectly honest,' she said. 'I found the mill extremely interesting, we've had a good chat about all sorts of things and I've met Mr. Pickering. Jimbo has entertained me the whole time and I don't really want to go home.'

Hannah was laughing,

'Well,' she said, 'if it was that good, perhaps I'll go with Archie tomorrow.'

Archie gave a theatrical bow, saying,

'It would be my pleasure to have your company, Hannah. Just say the word and we'll do our best to accommodate you. I think perhaps you'd better go and see your dad first though.'

Hilda had a cup of tea with them and then went upstairs to collect her belongings. She promised to let them know the outcome of the court case.

'I'll phone you tomorrow, Elsie,' she said. 'I know it's a bit of a cheek, but do you think I could come down again on Thursday? I've got this week off and Dad said he'd like to see us both together. Hannah has already told me she's staying for a few days longer. Will that be alright with you and Archie?'

Elsie looked at Archie who was already nodding and smiling.

'Yes, Hilda, that will be absolutely fine by us. Now, I've made you a couple of ham sandwiches for the journey. Would you like to take a flask with you?'

'No, thank you, Elsie,' she replied. 'The sandwiches will do just fine. I can eat on the way, but I don't like to stop if I can avoid it. The motorway places are awful. The food is terrible and the prices are too high.

I'll use the bathroom before I go and I'll phone you when I'm safely home in my flat.'

The sisters hugged each other and then Hilda gave Elsie and Archie a hug and a kiss on the cheek.

'Thank you both, so much,' she said. 'Dad told us that you were good people, and you're even better than that. When I come back, we'll all go out for dinner somewhere a bit special.

267

I think I'd better go now, with luck, I may get close to home
before it gets properly dark.'
Archie saw her back out into the road and they all waved her off.
Back in the kitchen, Elsie cleared the table and asked Hannah,
'Would you prefer pheasant or fish and chips for our meal
tonight, Hannah? We don't mind either way, but I'll have to cook
the pheasant by tomorrow at the latest. We don't hang our game,
but it was shot yesterday. Arch has plucked and dressed it. It's in
the fridge in the garage.'

'Ooh!' exclaimed Hannah, 'Pheasant, please Elsie. I haven't
had pheasant for years. It doesn't often feature on the hospital
menu, as you can well imagine!'

'Just boring old caviar and asparagus, I s'pose,' Archie said,
with just a hint of sarcasm. 'Right, Else, I'll go and fetch it and
then I'd better phone old Joe. Bill said he wants to see me.'
He went out to the garage, returning less than a minute later with
the pheasant, which he passed to Elsie, who rested it on the
draining board.

'There may still be a couple of bits of shot in it, but most of it
was in the left wing.'
He went through to the hall and began to phone Joe Skrobe.

CHAPTER 37.

At the police station in Chichelster, DI Tony Church, together with his DS. Ian Stuart, tried to piece together the information before them. They had established that the bullets in the female skull and the fox had been fired from the same rifle.

The bullet extracted from Jason Davies' head, had been from a different weapon.

The DNA provided by Jeffery Davies had been checked by the lab against the sample from the female skull. The result left them in no doubt that it was Jeffery Davies' mother, Mrs. Mary Davies. She had been shot, of that there was no doubt, but had it been murder, or an accident? The fact that her body had been buried in Jason Davies' field indicated that someone knew more of her disappearance than they had been willing to say at the time.

The suitcase which had been left on the farm house doorstep was filled with women's clothes. This suggested that a third party was still involved. But who could it be?

'I wonder whether we should begin by asking his sister to come and help us with our enquiries,' Tony Church suggested. Ian Stuart thought for a moment before replying.

'We had no luck with DNA from the clothes, but Jason Davies' fingerprints were on the suitcase,' he said. 'I must confess that I was surprised by that. It's almost as though the clothing had been professionally sterilised.'

'Maybe it had,' the DI replied. 'We're obviously dealing with someone who thinks they're clever. Whether they were aware of the DNA element, I wouldn't like to guess. Probably if the clothes had been dry-cleaned, it would have destroyed any DNA.' He re-read the statements from Davies and his female companion, Patricia Walker.

'I'm still a bit baffled by the dry patch left by the mystery car which Davies' lady companion told us about.'

'I think she was being truthful, Tony,' Ian ventured. 'She told us about the dead fox up the lane and Davies didn't see it or even know about that.'

Tony Church agreed.

'Let's try his sister, Bernice, see what we can discover from her,' he said. 'What was her surname, Ian?'

'Tenham, I think,' said Ian, still reading Jeff Davies' statement. 'Yes, Bernice and Ronald Tenham, they have a son, Barry. Do we want to talk with him as well?'

'How old is he, Ian?' Tony asked.

'Born in nineteen seventy seven,' Ian read from the report. 'That makes him nineteen.' He looked up at Tony.

'Yes, get him in as well,' he said. 'Make it a family outing for them. He might have seen or heard something useful, you never know.'

There was a knock at the door,

'Yes? Come in,' called the DI.

It was DS Brian Pace, from forensics. He nodded to the detectives and said,

'I've got a bit more info, if you're interested.' He addressed Ian and asked him, 'How did you get on this morning with old Mr. Jempson?'

Ian smiled as he told them both,

'He's a nice old boy, but still bitter about whoever was responsible for his wife's death. I told him the news, that we had found a thirty year old skeleton of the man we believed to have been the perpetrator. When I mentioned Robert Bourner's name, he was astonished.

'That young man was a bad lot,' Bob Jempson said. 'He used to deliver mushrooms from Fairways Nurseries, at Pudborough. He came early one morning, I mean much earlier than usual. The farm shop wasn't properly open, so I sent him to the house for the money. Sally paid him, but didn't get a receipt. When I phoned the nursery about it, they told me we hadn't paid yet. Eventually he wriggled out of it by saying that he'd left the receipt book in his van and forgot about it until he was asked for the money. I'm assuming that's probably how he found out where we kept the cash box.'

'I guessed he was right in that assumption.' Ian continued. 'Bob Jempson didn't have his address and neither did the people at the nursery. 'Fairways' has changed hands several times since those days. So I didn't expect to glean much from them. When I left Mr. Jempson, he was waiting for a telephone call from his daughter, Hannah, the one who's married to Jeffery Davies.' Ian paused to look at his notes. 'I contacted the remand home and told them who I was and told them I was trying to trace Robert Bourner. They invited me to go over to Findon, so I did. The records at the remand home showed that Bourner was released with another young man, a 'Peter Dennison'. They were set up in a flat in Pudborough, as part of their rehab. Dennison got himself a job with one of the local undertakers and kept his nose clean. Bourner was in and out of trouble for the next few years. The last arrest was for shoplifting in 1964, but he gave a different address at that time.'

The DS paused again, to judge their reaction to his somewhat lengthy diatribe.

'So now we need to find his fellow former inmate, Peter Dennison?' Tony suggested.

Ian smiled as he replied,

'I've already started on that road. I'll let you know in a day or two.'

'Have you got anything startling to impart?' The DI asked Brian Pace.

The forensics man grinned as he replied,

'I have both mundane and startling, in that order,' he said. 'First the mundane, there is a clear fingerprint on Jason Davies' front doorbell, which I have no link to. It may belong to his sister or her husband, but it's not anywhere in our records, and doesn't match any of those whom we have interviewed since. That's the mundane bit.' Brian Pace looked up from his notebook and then resumed his report.

'The startling element is that Jason Davies' murderer may not have killed him!'

Brian Pace waited until the surprise had registered on their faces and then began to explain.

'At the precise time that Davies was shot in the head, he was close to death or possibly even already dead,' he said bluntly. The pathologist has established that Davies was at the very best, semi-conscious when he was shot. The actual cause of death may have been a heart attack which occurred within minutes of him being shot.'

'Give us that in layman's terms please Brian,' said the DI.

'A blood clot the size of a large pea was found in his aorta, the main blood vessel of the heart,' Brian explained. 'His heart was not in a healthy condition, probably the result of years of abuse. That would explain the lack of blood at the bullet wound site. Once the pump stops, gravity takes over. Blood drains away from the highest point first.'

Tony Church leaned back in his chair and put his hands behind his head.

'So if we find out who shot him, do we charge them with murder, attempted murder, or tampering with evidence? I think it all hinges on whether the perpetrator thought that he was alive or dead.'

272

'I think we'll need to take advice on that one, Guv,' said Ian. DI Tony Church thought about the situation. It seemed obvious to him that the person who shot Davies had believed him to be alive. Why waste a bullet and risk a murder charge, for shooting a dead man? As Tony saw it, it was either murder or attempted murder. He looked up at his two colleagues and said,

'Whichever way we play this, there's somebody out there with a weapon, who is prepared to use it to kill. I'm proposing that we treat it as a murder hunt until we have the perpetrator under lock and key. We can take advice on the possible charges whilst we locate the suspect or suspects. What do you think, gentlemen?'

Both the detective Sergeants nodded their agreement.

Ian said,

'We have to remember that our first duty is to protect the public and the best way we can do this is to treat it as a murder. We also have to remember that there is another rifle out there, unrelated to this crime. We need to track down the person who is using it, before we find another corpse on our patch.'

Brian Pace asked the DI,

'What's the latest on the other two cases? The lorry drivers, I mean.'

'They're both pleading guilty,' the DI told him. 'There's more to it than that though, Bettis has got something to do with it. Do you remember, Don Palmer? The man who preserved the bones and the skull for us? He's willing to give evidence that Bettis had offered rewards for anyone damaging Mr. Skrobe's property. I just hope he gets the support he deserves from the other drivers. Bettis could be charged with, 'Incitement to commit criminal damage'. It won't help our Mr. Foggarty much, but it at least explains his recklessness. Fuller just hated Bettis for the way he had used people. He wouldn't have burnt the farm shed if he'd known it was Mr. Skrobe's. He had thought it belonged to Bettis. Even Bettis had told him that. He's still guilty of arson though. There's no 'get out of jail free' card on that one.'

Ian was smiling,

'So it's, 'Hello, Mr. Bettis, would you like to come in and try to wriggle your way out of this one?' I'll bet my eye teeth he'll deny any knowledge of it, but we're going to have a word with a Mr. Grover of Tickner's Transport, first. If we can crack him, then Bettis will be on a very 'sticky wicket'. It's all up to the CPS at the end of the day.'

'That's it for now,' Brian said as he turned to go. 'I promise to keep you in the loop. If I find anything important you'll be the last to know!' He winked and grinned as he left. Tony Church was laughing, he threw a ball of screwed up paper at the door as Brian Pace closed it.

'And don't come back 'til you've got something!' He shouted after him.

CHAPTER 38.

Archie telephoned Joe Skrobe on the land line. It rang for several minutes before it was answered by Joe, who sounded a little breathless.

'Are you alright, Joe?' Archie enquired.

'Yes, Arch,' he replied, 'I was at the top of the garden and I heard the phone. I came as quickly as I could.'

'Bill Pickering said you'd like me to help you with something. He said it wasn't urgent, so I thought tomorrow would be OK.' Joe had regained his breath.

'Tomorrow's fine, Arch,' he told him. 'I've had letters from all over the place. I'll tell you all about it when you get here. Stephen's letters have certainly set the ball rolling. There's even one from Mr. Grover, telling me he has passed the bill for the fence to his insurers.'

Archie gave a chuckle,

'He's changed his tune a bit since we saw him last, then?' Archie observed. 'Bill said you'd got one from Davies' solicitor as well. Is he accepting liability for the greenhouse?'

'It seems that way, Arch,' Joe said. 'He wants to know the cost of replacing the glass that his men have smashed. That's really what I need your help with.'

'What were you going to do with it once it was repaired?' Archie asked him.

'I thought I might try to grow a few tomatoes and cucumbers. Maybe even use some of the space for some flowers and early potatoes. What d'you think? would it be worth it?'

'Yes, Joe, you could do that,' Archie agreed. 'I don't mind giving you a bit of advice on that, once you've got it functional.'

'I was hoping you'd offer,' said his friend. 'It'll be more of a hobby than a business, but since I've got it back, I might as well try to use it. They've got to shore up the garden with concrete and repair and stabilise the piers holding the bungalow up.'
Archie thought for a few seconds before he replied,

'It wouldn't surprise me if this bankrupts them as developers, Joe. The site's no good to anyone without revised planning permission. It won't be a cheap fix for them. They must be well over budget on it already.'

'There's something else, Arch,' Joe almost whispered. 'I'm sure I've had a prowler around my house and garden.'

'What makes you think that?' Archie asked.

'It's like this,' Joe continued. 'You remember yesterday when everybody was using my garden a s a short cut to the house and the road?'

''Course I remember yesterday,' said Archie. 'I 'aven't gone senile overnight and you told 'em to use your garden. How does that mean you've got a prowler?'

'I was just coming to that, Arch. When they'd all gone, I went and raked it all over, whilst the ground was still soft. Well, I thought I heard someone about last night at about nine o'clock. I grabbed my torch and put the lead on old Thunder and opened the back door without putting the light on. Thunder barked and I switched on the torch. The top strand of wire on the fence was still vibrating as though someone had just been over it. I'm sure I could hear someone panting, but I didn't see anything else.'

'Could have been a fox or something,' Archie suggested. 'Or maybe a badger, they're quite big.'

'Badgers are quite intelligent animals, Archie,' Joe said. 'They wouldn't be silly enough to have an earth in loose ground like that is. It wasn't a fox, either.'

'I don't see how you can be so sure about that, Joe. They sometimes make quite a lot of noise and the scent would be enough to alert Thunder.'

'Have you ever known a fox to be wearing size twelve wellington boots, Arch?' Joe asked, laughing.
Archie was laughing now,

'If you'd mentioned that to begin with, I wouldn't have suggested a fox,' he said. 'I mean, size twelve 'wellies' are a bit big, even for a badger!'
Joe was imagining a badger wearing gumboots.

'This is as good as, 'Tales from the Riverbank' Arch. I'll have to tell Lakshmi and Stephen about it now.'

'Well, Joe,' Archie said, 'don't go stompin' about on the ground now, I'll have a look when I come up in the morning. I'll be there by about ten or half past, OK?'

'Thanks, Archie,' said Joe. 'I'll say 'goodnight' and let you go, see you in the morning.'

CHAPTER 39.

The Tenham family arrived at the Chichelster police station, as requested. DI Tony Church had contacted Bernice and offered to bring them from their Worthing home, but she had assured him that they would prefer to drive over in their own car. He had explained that it was a somewhat delicate matter with regard to her brother, Mr. Jason Davies.

Bernice had told the desk Sergeant who they were. Sergeant Mike Hodd, had thanked her and said,

'We're most grateful to you for sparing us your time, Mrs. Tenham. I'll let the DI know you're here, I expect he will be out to see you in a few minutes.'

DI Church, came into the front office, he was smiling as he approached Bernice,

'Mrs. Tenham?' he asked.

'Yes, Inspector Church,' she confirmed. 'This is my husband, Ronald Tenham, and our son, Barry.'

The DI shook hands with all three of them.

'I'm so pleased that you could come,' he told her. 'I hope this won't be too painful for you, but I'm afraid I have some bad news to begin with. Would you like to come to my office? I'll arrange some refreshments for you presently. It's this way, please.'

He held the door open for her and the family followed him to his office, where Ian Stuart was waiting.

'This is Detective Sergeant Ian Stuart,' he told them. 'Ian, can we get some tea or coffee for Mr. and Mrs. Tenham and, um, Barry, wasn't it?'

'Yes, that's right, Inspector,' the young man replied.

'Yes, of course,' said Ian, getting up from his chair. 'What would you folks like to drink?'

'Coffee, please,' said both parents.

'I'd prefer a cold drink, please,' Barry said. 'Anything will do, water if there's nothing else.'

'We save the 'bread and water for our convicts, Barry,' Ian told him, with a smile. 'There'll be fruit juice, lemonade or coke, I expect.'

Barry smiled, 'I'd like a glass of lemonade, please.' He said. 'I wouldn't wish to deprive the convicts of their water.'

They smiled at the lad, who, Tony noted, had a good sense of humour.

'I'd like a coffee, please, Ian,' he said, 'oh, and one for yourself, of course.'

Ian laughed as he went out of the office,

'Do I get a packet of crisps for going, Guv?' he asked.

Once the Tenhams were seated, Tony explained to Bernice, as gently as he could, that her brother was dead.

'I'm really sorry to have to break it to you like this,' he said. I had to tell your nephew, Jeffery, yesterday, but I didn't have your address then.'

Bernice seemed to be more upset than shocked.

'Jason has had a heart problem for several years, it could have happened at any time, I suppose. It's just that I was only chatting with him on Sunday evening. I hope it wasn't anything I told him that brought it on.'

279

'I wouldn't have thought so, but what did you tell him that makes you think on those lines, Mrs. Tenham?' The DI asked her. She looked at her husband briefly, before she replied.

Have you heard of a private investigator named, Gorse? He lives in Worthing. It was connected with something he did that Jason didn't know of.'

'That name rings a distant bell, but I don't think I know the man,' Tony told her. 'What do you think he's done, Mrs. Tenham?'

'It's 'Bernice' inspector or, 'Bernie' please. I'm glad you asked us to come to see you, I was thinking of going to the Worthing police, but I don't think they would have done anything.' She seemed agitated as she went on, 'You know about Mary, don't you?'

'Mrs. Tenham, sorry, Bernice, you obviously have the advantage of me regarding this information.' Tony said. 'Would you mind waiting until my Sergeant returns, and then if you have no objection, we'll run a tape. I can assure you that you have nothing to fear, you are not under caution and we are most grateful to you all for your help.'

She looked at her husband and asked,

'What do you think, Ron?'

He replied quickly,

'I can't see that there is any problem, Bernie. You were going to tell them the full story anyway and I think you'll feel happier once you've explained what you found out. As you just said, I don't think the Worthing police would have been in the least interested.'

She smiled and nodded to Tony,

'Yes, inspector, I'll do that.' She said. 'I'll try not to forget anything, but perhaps we can listen to what I've said afterwards, just in case?'

DI Church nodded his approval,

'Yes, of course,' he said. 'It won't be an official statement. I just thought it would be easier for us to refer to it and less bother for you than writing it all down on paper. There's just one thing you could do for us, which would be most helpful. We have a fingerprint taken from the bell push at the farm, which we can't identify. Perhaps you wouldn't mind letting us take yours, for elimination purposes?'

'I understand, no, no, I don't mind at all,' she replied.
Ian had returned with their drinks and the DI explained to him what they had agreed. They set up the tape machine and Tony asked Bernice,

'Would you like to finish your coffee before you begin?'

'Yes, I think that would be best,' she agreed. 'Ron may decide to interrupt me anyway, if it looks as though I've forgotten something, or got it in the wrong order.'

'How did you gather this information, Bernice?' Tony asked. 'What made you curious about this man 'Gorse'?'
She smiled as she replied,

'It was strictly speaking, a bit underhand and if my employers had got wind of it, I would have been disciplined for what I did.'

'Did it involve breaking the law?' Tony asked her.

'I don't believe I broke the law, but I'm sure I broke the bank's rules of confidentiality,' she admitted. 'Shall we start the tape? A lot of this will be relevant to what I want to tell you.'

'Good idea,' Tony agreed, as he pressed the 'record' switch on the machine. 'Just speak normally, Bernice,' he told her, 'it balances itself to the volume, so there's no need for you to speak any louder than you are now. If you want to pause for a while, that's OK. We'll just leave it running unless you feel you need several minutes.'

'Thank you,' she said, 'I'll begin now.
I worked for the National Westminster Bank, as it now is. It used to just be called the Westminster Bank Approximately thirty years ago there was another bank, 'The National Provincial' which was absorbed into my bank. At the time of the merger, I, together with several others, was engaged in the transfer of customers accounts from National Provincial, to the Westminster

281

Bank's system. My brother, Jason, had been a National Provincial customer, and I found myself transferring his details to the new system. I should really have declared an interest and they would have put another clerk in my place to deal with his account, but I didn't do that. At that particular time, I was not getting along too well with Jason. I thought he was becoming a bully, not just to Mary, but to some of the people who were working for him. He suspected that Mary was having an affair. Jeffery was away at boarding school, so they didn't need to look after him, except during school holidays. He told me he had received a leaflet in the post advertising a detective agency, 'Gorse Associates' of Worthing. The leaflet emphasised confidentiality and discretion, so Jason decided he would put it to the test. He telephoned the number and arranged for someone to call at the farm. Gorse listened while Jason told him everything. When I say, everything, that's exactly what I mean. He told him of his suspicions, his financial status, nothing was held back. He even told this man how he had married Mary and inherited the house and the farm.

Gorse was a clever manipulator and a real 'con' artist.He already knew that Mary was having an affair, since he was the one she was having it with!

That was how he was able to target Jason with his leaflet, in the knowledge that he would probably draw a response. Mary, of course was oblivious to this, she had no idea that Jason had employed her 'lover' to check on her.

Mary confided in me, that Jason was a control freak, which I had already surmised. She told me she was going to leave him and that she had found a very kind man, named, 'Leon', who was going to find a house for them to live in together.

I began to put two and two together and re-checked the details of their account. By a stroke of chance, or luck, Gorse also banked with Westminster, so when I heard that Jason had engaged his services, I had a look at his account. I could have got into real trouble if anyone had found out, but nobody did.

To cut a long story short, Jason had two separate accounts, the farm account and a joint current account. There were two large cash withdrawals from the current account. One was for five thousand pounds, withdrawn by Mary and another for one thousand pounds withdrawn by Jason. Three days later, both of these sums were deposited into Gorse's account. The one thousand was paid into his business account and the five thousand into his personal current account. I noted that Gorse's wife also had her own personal account with us, but this appeared to be 'clean', with no unusual transactions.

Of course, I couldn't do anything with my information at this stage, but I focused on Mr. Gorse and his somewhat dubious dealings.

I confided in a girl friend of mine, not one of the bank's workers, and I asked her what she thought I should do. I hadn't even mentioned anything to Ron at that stage.

She advised me to have a quiet chat with Mary, to see what she was proposing to do. I arranged to meet Mary, she seemed very 'cagey' and insisted that Gorse was just arranging things for her, so that she could be with her new man. She was emphatic that the new man in her life was not Gorse, but someone she had met independently. She said that Gorse was just dealing with the financial side. When I asked her what she meant, she told me that her new lover had a wife who wanted to keep everything and leave him with nothing. Gorse was acting as a go-between and trying to arrange an amicable settlement.

Mary was becoming suspicious of me by then. She was almost hostile, so I would have found it difficult to get any more information from her. I knew that she had an old school friend in whom she placed her trust. Her name is 'Olive Duxon' and she now lives in Slindon. She has a daughter, Angela, who joined the Bank as a 'teller' in 1991. I got to know her quite well, we used to take our lunch breaks at the same times and we would chat about all sorts of things. One day she began talking about her, 'Aunt Mary', she had disappeared when Angela was a child. Her mother and Aunt Mary were very friendly. 'She wasn't a real, aunt, just one of mum's friends' she once said to me. I think that's when the 'penny dropped'.

I had to be careful how I asked her my questions. I was afraid that, like Mary, she would become suspicious and just stop telling me anything. She'd asked her mother what happened to 'aunt Mary' and her mother had shown her a letter which Mary had written to her. In the letter, she said that she was leaving Jason and going to live with her new man, 'Leon'. They had hatched a plan which involved her catching the train at Pudborough. She was to buy a single ticket to London, Victoria, but get off the train at Haywards Heath. There Leon would meet her and take her to their new home. She said she would let Olive have her new address, but she must promise not to give it to another soul. Angela said that her mother never heard from her again.

The police were called in after she had been missing for about a week, but after extensive enquiries, they eventually had to abandon their search. She was listed as a 'missing person' from that day onwards.'

Bernice paused and shifted in her chair.

'Can we take a little break, please inspector?' Bernice asked.

'Yes, of course,' Tony said as he stopped the tape.

'Some more refreshments, I think,' Ian suggested, 'same again for everybody? Perhaps some sandwiches, as well?' He asked

'Yes, please, Ian,' said the DI. The others all smiled and nodded their approval. He looked at Bernice and asked,

'Would you like to have your prints taken now? It will save you having to wait about when we're done here.'

'Yes, good idea, she said. Do you need Ron's as well?'

'Did you all go into the house on Sunday, or just you, Bernice?' the DI asked.

'We both went in, Barry waited in the car,' she told him.

'I've never had my fingerprints taken,' said Barry. 'You can do mine as well, if you like.'

284

Tony smiled and replied,

'I'm honoured, I'm sure, Barry, we'll take them if you wish, but it really isn't necessary.' He turned to Ronald Tenham and said, 'We don't often get volunteers for this procedure, most of our customers are reluctant, in case it incriminates them!'
The Tenhams laughed,

'At least it indicates his openness,' Tony said. 'If he has nothing to hide he also has nothing to fear.'

CHAPTER 40.

Whilst they took their break, they chatted freely. The atmosphere was relaxed and both parents obviously felt at ease. Ian was chatting with their son, Barry. The talk was mainly about football and also about him, (Barry) who would soon be going ski-ing with his friends, in Canada.

'Shall we continue?' Bernice asked. 'We're not in much of a hurry but it would be nice to get home in the daylight.'
They agreed and Ian re-started the tape and nodded to her,
'Whenever you're ready,' he said quietly.
Bernice continued with her story,

'I decided that I needed more information about Gorse. He obviously wasn't living with Mary. When the coast was clear, I checked the accounts again. I had to be careful, I picked a day when Angie was off, so she wouldn't know what I was doing. There had been no more withdrawals in Mary's name, since she had 'run away' all those years ago. Jason however, continued to withdraw fairly substantial sums, both on the farm account and on the joint current account. The majority of these withdrawals were mirrored in deposits to Gorse's accounts. These deposits alternated between his personal account and the business account. But invariably they were in identical sums to Jason's withdrawals. I decided that something was not right. Why would Jason keep paying Gorse to search for Mary after more than twenty five years? My guess was that it was some form of 'hush' money. In other words, Gorse was blackmailing him over something that had happened.

It was time to get some help from my friend, I won't give her real name here, let's call her, 'Jane'. She had left her husband and was anticipating a messy divorce. She has been lodging with her sister, but is looking to rent a flat until the house is sold. Thankfully there are no children involved. 'Jane's' husband is purposely delaying putting the house on the market. She needs her share of the proceeds of the sale, to begin to rebuild her life. She's convinced that he now has at least two women living with him, in their former matrimonial home. She's almost sure that his extravagant lifestyle is supported by a drugs connection. Anyway, to get back to the Gorse business, I'd already confided in her about my brother, and she knew that I was becoming increasingly worried. Something was very wrong and my guess was that Gorse was probably at the centre of it. She'd asked me what she could do to help. I warned her that Gorse was a devious character, so it would not be a good idea to give him too much information. She suggested that she could put her case to him, to see just what lengths he would go to. Jane is an attractive lady who knows how to play her cards. She went to Gorse's office and asked the young receptionist for an appointment. She waited a few minutes whilst the receptionist went into Gorse's office. She came out and said to Jane,

'Mr. Gorse is very busy, but if you can be quick, he'll see you now.'

Jane, not her real name, I repeat, explained her problem to him in some detail, stressing the confidential nature of her case. For the purpose of her visit, Jane carried a hand held battery dictaphone in her lightweight bag. To safeguard herself she had left it

switched to record. The last thing she wanted was for it to begin clicking, as they do when voice only recording is selected.'
Bernice reached into her bag and produced the dictaphone.

'This is what she got,' Bernice said, 'there's a lot of crackle and white noise, from the contents of her bag.'
Bernice switched the machine to 'play' and placed it on the desk. Tony put his hand up to halt the proceedings.

'I think we can switch our tape off whilst we listen to yours, Bernice,' he said. 'We can make a copy of that later, so you can return the original to your friend.' He stopped the tape, the dictaphone recording was about to begin. The rather poor sound quality did not detract from the spoken content.
This is roughly what they all heard,

'Thank you for seeing me at short notice. He's being a real pig, Mr. Gorse. He wants the house, which I put the deposit up for and have paid half the mortgage. He's got two young girls living with him and I'm sure he's got some sort of drugs racket going. That's why I moved out four months ago.

'Close the door please. I think we need to discuss this in grater privacy. I trust my receptionist, but in these matters, one can't be too careful.'
The door closed with a click.

'Thank you, now, Mrs. *****, (Some words had been erased or 'smudged' by Jane, to protect her identity)
Please give me you name and address and then write down your husband's name and address.'
(Pause)

'And this is the house which you jointly own and which he refuses to sell?'

'Yes, Mr. Gorse. I'm at my wits end with worry. I can't see a way out of this situation.'

'Oh, don't you worry, there are always ways out of any situation. I'm sure I can think of something to help you. There will be a fee, of course. I take it that you have some funds available to you?'

'I have a few thousand, but how much will it cost? The house is worth around seventy thousand and we only have about seven thousand outstanding on the mortgage.'

'So approximately ten per cent of the value is outstanding? Why settle for half the value for your settlement, when with a little careful planning you could take the whole house?'

'What sort of planning do you mean? Selling the house without telling him? I've thought of that, but it would be illegal and he would find out and probably kill me.'

'No, no, my dear lady, I'm not suggesting anything illegal. My plan would be a simple case of you inheriting the house. Your husband wouldn't come after you if say, for argument's sake, he were to suffer a heart attack.'

'I don't know about that, Mr. Gorse. I don't want to find myself on a murder charge, thank you.'

'Who mentioned anything about, murder? I certainly did not. Perish the thought! What I said was that perhaps he could suffer a heart attack. With his current life style, drugs, call girls, probably excesses of drink, he can't be in such good shape as you obviously are. That's all I meant, oh no, we don't murder people.'

'I'm sorry, Mr. Gorse, I must have misunderstood you. If he were to die naturally, I'd be very upset, but I can see how you think that it would resolve the problem. There would be a post mortem, when they would be sure to find any contributing factors.'

'On the basis that he is a habitual user of drugs, there could be nothing unusual to find, it would be a heart attack, brought on by his lifestyle of excesses. He is probably unfit, due to the drugs and possible over exertion with his young female companions. We could apply a little pressure by making his lifestyle public knowledge. He could be made to feel so uncomfortable that he might decide to just disappear without a trace.'

'They would still find him eventually, they always do. It wouldn't matter where in the world he was hiding, they would still find him sooner or later.'

'Have you any idea how many people disappear every year in this country? Most of the South Downs is riddled with ancient flint mines, they are full of bones, both ancient and modern. There would be no need of a post mortem, if there was no evidence of foul play.'

'I'm not sure about this, perhaps I should think about it and come back to you. How much is your fee, just for advice?'

*'Yes, Mrs. *****, you may do that, just remember that I have not proposed anything unlawful, I just outlined a couple of purely hypothetical instances.'*

'Yes, Mr. Gorse, I understand, that you wouldn't propose just burying a body on the Downs, flint mines or not.'

*'I can promise you that I could arrange for such a scenario, Mrs. *****, I say that with confidence and I speak from experience. My fee for today's consultation is one hundred pounds, please. I prefer cash, if you have it, if not I can call on you tomorrow evening to collect it.'*

'That won't be necessary, I shall call in here tomorrow morning to pay you myself. Thank you for your help, I'll bid you good afternoon, Mr. Gorse.'

The sound of the door opening and closing, and then the receptionist's voice,

*'Bye, Mrs. *****!*

Sounds of traffic and an outer door closing.

Bernice switched the machine off and passed it to Ian for copying.

'It was obvious that the receptionist had heard most of what was said,' Bernice observed. 'Otherwise she would not have known my friend's name. She had refused to give her name or any other details to her on her way in. When she was asked, she just said, 'it's confidential, as it says on your leaflet.'

290

The receptionist just nodded her acceptance. After she left, Jane had the feeling that she was being followed. She stopped to look at a menu in one of the Indian restaurants windows and in the reflection, she caught a glimpse of Gorse's receptionist, on the opposite side of the road. Jane told me that just then, she had got lucky. The Hove bus was coming to a stop outside the restaurant and it temporarily obscured the receptionist's view of her. Jane got on the bus, leaving her 'tail' on the opposite pavement. She travelled for a couple of stops and then got off and walked quickly to the car park, where she had left her car.'
Tony Church nodded his acceptance of her statement.

'That, in effect makes the receptionist an accessory to any crimes which Gorse decides to commit. I don't suppose she is aware of the fact that she could face a prison sentence, just for knowing his proposals and failing to make the police aware. Of course, he hasn't, as far as we know, committed any crime yet, but I had wondered what he was implying when he said he was speaking from experience. Thank you for this,' he said, indicating the cassette recorder. 'You were going to say something else, please continue.'
Bernice resumed her explanation,

'My friend returned the next day,' Bernice added. 'Gorse had already confirmed her husband's address and intimated to her that he knew of his involvement with the local drugs scene.
Now here's the part I found most important. He told her that there was no possibility of any comeback on her or him. He said that he had been instrumental in the disappearance of a woman some thirty years ago. Then he actually said,
'Her bones have only just been found and a bullet found with her came from a point two-two rifle. Her husband owns such a rifle, as do I, come to that. He thought he had accidentally shot her, two days after her death by air embolism! He used to use one of his barns for target practice, with a paper target attached to the hay bales.'

Gorse told my friend that he had placed her body behind the bales, with a book in her hands. He had previously taken the insurance of shooting her in the back of the head with his own rifle. Her distraught husband was convinced that he had killed her. He confided in Gorse that he didn't realise that she had returned and was in the barn, much less, sitting the other side of the hay bale barrier.

Her husband was desperate not to get the police involved and at Gorse's suggestion, he even helped to lay her to rest in one of his fields. Gorse stated,

'There was absolutely no connection with me or any of my associates.'

Bernice continued,

'I believe that he was referring to Mary, my brother's wife. I told Jason about it on Sunday, when I went to visit him. He seemed relieved at first, as though a great weight had been lifted from him. Later he seemed consumed by anger that Gorse had been deceiving him for all those years. I believe that if he could have got hold of Gorse, he would have killed him there and then. That's what I meant when I said that I hoped his heart attack wasn't the result of something which I had said.'

Both detectives looked at each other, Tony spoke first.

'Bernice, firstly, I must thank you for your very concise account of your experience and your findings, via your friend, Jane. I must ask you to prepare yourself for a shock. Your brother did not die from a heart attack, as you may have suspected. He was shot with a small bore weapon. We are treating his death as a murder. There is one consolation I can offer you. Mr. Davies was semi conscious when he was shot. Your assumption was partly correct. Our pathologist discovered that he was having a heart attack when he was shot. In the opinion of our pathologist, there was a possibility that he could have recovered, had he been given first aid, instead of being shot.

I hope this information, though distressing, will alleviate any feelings of guilt, which you may have been experiencing.'

'Oh, my God,' Bernice exclaimed. 'Poor Jason, I still feel bad because I had maligned him for years, believing that he had done something to Mary. I accept that he was no angel, especially in his younger days, but now he can't even defend himself against any accusations.'

Tony looked at her and said,

'You may rest assured that we will be looking into the activities of your Mr. Gorse. We will be careful not to alert him to our observations, so that he will not realise that he is under surveillance. I wonder if you would ask your friend, Jane to contact me, personally. I'm sure we will be able to help her in some way and it won't involve any nefarious activity. We will respect her privacy and anything she wishes to tell me, will be treated in the strictest confidence.'

He gave her his card, with his home number and his mobile telephone number on it.

'She can call me on either of these numbers,' he told her. 'I can coach her in any future dealings with Mr. Gorse. He sounds a very dangerous man. Someone we would refer to as, 'a slippery customer.' I can tell you that whilst we have been chatting, a colleague has been doing some research. Gorse was charged with 'fraudulent conversion' a couple of years ago. His case was dismissed as there was insufficient evidence. I can tell you that we believe he had found a way to tamper with our evidence, but we couldn't prove it. I promise you that we will pursue this with all due diligence. Mr. Gorse is not fireproof, any more than the shrub of the same name.'

The Tenhams shook hands with the detectives and began to leave. As they walked towards the front office, Tony said to her,

'If you remember anything else which you think may be relevant, please call me.'

'Thank you inspector,' she said, smiling. 'There is just one more thing. Jason gave me two letters to post on Sunday. I didn't look at the addresses. They already had stamps on, so I just posted them on our way home.'

293

Her husband and son had walked on a little as she turned to Tony and said quietly,

'He also gave me a key to a safe deposit box at the bank. He told me it contained Mary's jewellery which he wanted me to have.'

'Have you checked the box yet?' Tony asked.

'No, do you think I should do it now?'

Tony thought for a moment,

'I think you should do it as soon as you can and make sure you have someone reliable with you, in case you're being watched. You can call me if there seems to be anything unusual or if you're worried. My mobile number is on the card. Please use it if you need to.'

I'm glad I told you instead of the Worthing police. I wouldn't mind betting he's got some connection with them. I don't want to find my family is next on his 'hit list'.'

They all shook hands and Ian walked with them to the car park.

'We'll be in touch with you shortly,' he told them all. 'Thanks for all your help, have a safe journey home.'

CHAPTER 41.

In the Leggitt household, Hannah had enjoyed the best night's sleep she'd had for weeks. It was half past seven before she came downstairs. Elsie had taken her a cup of tea at about seven o'clock. She hadn't knocked, so when she saw Hannah was still sleeping, she had retreated quietly.

'Good morning, Elsie,' she said, in a still sleepy voice, as she entered the kitchen. Elsie looked up from her newspaper and smiled at her.

'Did you sleep well?' she asked.

'The best, Elsie,' she said. 'I know I was very tired, but I also felt extremely relaxed. I must have been asleep within a few minutes of my head touching the pillow. Where's Archie?'

'He'll be back presently, he's taken Jimbo for his walk,' Elsie explained. 'Because you were still sleeping when I brought you a cup of tea at about seven, he decided he'd wait and have his breakfast when he got back. There you are, Hannah, it's a fresh one, I made it just before you came down.' She pushed the cup and saucer towards where Hannah sat at the kitchen table.

'Thanks, Elsie,' she said, 'I think I'll go and see Dad later today. Archie said he'd show me the watermill, perhaps I'll take him up on that first.'

'Archie is going up to Joe's later this morning,' Elsie said. 'Perhaps you could drop him off on your way to your dad's? I expect Joe will bring him home, when he's finished whatever they're doing together.'

'Yes, of course, Elsie,' Hannah replied. 'I'll probably take dad out to lunch. He said Archie took him to a little pub near the care home. I expect he'd like that.'

They heard Jimbo at the kitchen door.

'I expect he's run in front of Arch,' Elsie speculated. 'I'll start getting the breakfast presently. There's plenty of hot water, Hannah, if you wanted to shower before breakfast.'

'Have I got time for another cup of tea, first?' Hannah asked.

'Yes, there's no strict timetable here, my dear. Just tell me when you're ready for your breakfast. We usually have a cooked breakfast, in case we get busy around lunch time. Will that suit you?'

Hannah passed her cup and saucer to Elsie,

'I really am being spoilt, Elsie.' She said. 'I usually have a bit of toast on my way to work. A cooked breakfast is a luxury for me. I usually only have one on special occasions, so it sounds really good to me, thank you. I'll go for my shower when I've drunk this tea. Will I need old clothes to go over to the mill?'

Archie came in through the back door, a panting Jimbo at his side.

'I heard that!' He said. 'Of course you won't need old clothes, Hannah. It's not dirty. It's a flour mill, so it has to be clean. There's not even any flour dust at this time of year.'

Jimbo sat next to Hannah, his head on her knee and began leaning against her legs.

'It's no good getting too comfortable, Jimbo,' Hannah told him. 'I'm going for my shower presently.'

'I'll get his breakfast now, Else,' Archie said. 'He's had a good old run about. He put up a couple of pheasants along by the pond. We could have had 'em for dinner if I'd had the old 'four-ten' with me.'

Elsie laughed.

'You'd just as likely have missed the birds and frightened Jimbo out of his wits,' she said. 'Anyhow, you can't go walking about like John Wayne, with a dog and a shotgun. This is rural, peaceful Sussex, not 'Dodge City'.'

Hannah was laughing. Elsie raised her eyebrows in a questioning way.

'What?' she asked.

'I was just thinking, if Archie was the sheriff, then Jimbo could be, 'Deputy Dawg' couldn't he?' Hannah said, giggling. Archie was smiling,

'I don't think Bill would be too happy in the role of 'Officer Dibble' though.'

Hannah went upstairs to shower and get dressed. Jimbo ate his breakfast with his usual gusto and then proceeded to soak half of the kitchen floor, with water from his drinking bowl. With his tail wagging excitedly, he went over to where Archie was sitting and dried his face on Archie's trousers. Elsie made a fresh pot of tea, while Archie sat at the kitchen table, reading the newspaper. After about ten minutes, they heard Hannah moving about upstairs.

'Hannah,' Elsie called out to her, 'I'm starting the breakfast now. How much longer will you be?'

'Another five minutes, and I'll be ready,' Hannah called back.

'One egg or two?' Elsie asked her.

'Oh, one is plenty, thank you,' Hannah said. 'I'm just coming down, now.'

After breakfast, Archie asked Hannah if she was ready to go over to the mill.

'Yes please, Archie,' she said. 'Will I need a top coat, or do you think I'll be warm enough in this jumper?'

'I think you'll probably need a jacket, Hannah,' he told her. 'Although the sun is shining, it's a cold wind. The anorak you had on yesterday will probably be enough.'
Hannah went up to her room and returned carrying her grey anorak.

'Right,' she said, 'I'm ready when you are. Are we taking Jimbo?'

'Not this time,' Archie said. 'I thought if we took your car over to the mill, perhaps we could go straight from there up to Joe's. Elsie said you didn't mind dropping me off on your way to your dad's.'

'No, that's fine by me, Archie,' she said.

'Give our love to your dad, please,' Elsie reminded her.
Hannah said, of course she would, and she and Archie set off for the mill.

'Wow!' Hannah exclaimed as they stopped outside the mill. She got out of her car and put on her anorak. 'It's bigger than I had imagined, does the water wheel turn? Do you really grind the corn into flour?'

'Yes and yes, to both questions, Hannah,' Archie replied. 'Be patient, you'll see how it all happens in a minute. I might even find a small bag of flour for you as a souvenir.'
He gave her the full guided tour, as he would have for a group of visitors. He explained the processes of each part of the operation. Hannah was most interested in the milling floor.

'I'd love to see it all working,' she said. 'When will it be milling flour again?'
Archie explained that most of the milling was done during the spring and summer, when the tourist parties were visiting.
They were on their way back down the stairs when they heard a woman's voice.

'Archie, Is everything alright?'

'Its all fine, thank you Jen,' he called back. 'We're just coming back down the stairs.'

298

They reached the ground floor, Archie first and Hannah following.

'Good morning Jen,' he said. 'This is Hannah, an old friend of mine's daughter. She's staying with us for a few days and I've just been showing her the mill.' He turned to Hannah and said. 'This is Jenny Tobin, her husband, Reg, owns the mill.'

The two ladies shook hands and smiled at each other.

'I'm absolutely amazed at this building,' Hannah told her. 'I've never seen the inside of a mill before. Archie has explained how everything works. I'd love to come back and see it all running.'

Jenny smiled and nodded to her.

'Well, why don't you just do that, Hannah? Of course, I don't suppose he's told you that we wouldn't have a watermill if it hadn't been for him. He's the one who has built it back up from a collection of what looked like old junk.'

'Yes, but I had a lot of help, Jen, didn't I?' Archie parried. 'It's been a joint venture, Reg has done his bit as well, don't forget.'

'Archie, you know as well as I do, that Reg didn't know where or how to begin this project,' Jenny said. 'It was you who kept writing to the Mills Trust until they approved the grant. It was you who organised the new waterwheel and got it all fitted.'

'Yes, alright Jen,' Archie said as he smiled at both of the ladies. 'But Reg had the new gears made and helped build the new weir. He was also doing a full time job, don't forget. It was a joint effort, Hannah. Even some of the village tradesmen helped at a vastly reduced rate of remuneration.'

Jenny Tobin shrugged as she said,

'I suppose you're right, Archie. But we all know it was referred to as, 'Archie's watermill job', all the time you were working on it.'

They were still smiling as they left the mill. Archie had explained to Jenny that he had to get to Joe Skrobe's this morning.

'I said I'd be there by half past ten, but it's already twenty to eleven.'

They said goodbye to Jenny and got back into Hannah's car.

CHAPTER 42.

It had been impossible to determine the exact cause of Robert Bourner's death. Whether he had starved or succumbed to hypothermia before he was crushed in the ground subsidence, the forensic people were unable to say.

Efforts were made to locate his next of kin, but it soon became apparent that both parents were deceased. The addresses of both of the young men who were released from the remand home at that time were made available to the police.

DI Tony Church followed up on the information and whilst he drew a blank on Bourner, he was able to locate the other man, Peter Dennison. He was working at 'County Caskets', a firm of coffin makers in Billingshurst. The DI pre-empted his visit with a telephone call, to avoid the possibility of a wasted journey.

'I'll be here all day, Inspector,' Dennison told him, 'so no need to make an appointment.'

Peter Dennison smiled as he shook hands with the DI.

'Good morning Inspector,' he said. 'Please tell me how I can help you.

The DI thanked him, saying,

'I'm afraid I have some news regarding your former flat mate, Robert Bourner.'

Dennison looked startled.

'I haven't seen him for more than twenty five years,' he said. 'Frankly, it wouldn't bother me if I never saw him again.'

'You won't!' Tony Church told him. 'We found his skeleton last week, trapped in an underground crevice on the Downs at Wigglesworth. We just wondered whether you could tell us anything about him. We've discovered that his parents are both deceased. Do you know whether he had any siblings?' Dennison began to explain.

'As you will be aware, we had both been 'naughty boys' and were at the remand home together. Bourner was a real oddball. He didn't want to make friends, or make any effort to better himself. I think he fancied himself as a sort of celebrity criminal. He was put with me in the hope that I could use my influence to help him see the folly of his ways. That's not how it worked out though. He was just a sly and spiteful lad and he blamed the police for his problems. It wasn't long before he began stealing from me.
I had a job with a firm of undertakers in Pudborough. I kept my nose clean and began to take an interest in the way coffins were made. I saved a bit, when I could. There was no way I wanted to go back to that home again.'

'Did Bourner have a job at that time?' Tony asked. Dennison thought for a moment,

'I believe he was working for a delivery company for a while, until he got the sack for stealing. He never had a steady job for long but to answer your first question, he did have a sister. As far as I can remember she worked at the old Manston airport, in Kent, as a clerk or some sort of administrator.'

'I don't suppose you can remember her name?' Tony asked him. 'Do you know whether she was older or younger than Robert?'

'Older, I think,' Dennison replied, 'I'm sure her first name was Rachael and I know she was married. I don't think I ever knew her married name. She disowned him because he stole her credit card and used it to buy drugs. She reported it to the police at the time, but then decided not to follow it up with a prosecution. I think he got to her and said that he would be locked up for years.'

'So, what happened with your flat?' Tony asked.

'Oh, the flat,' Dennison began, 'I had to move out because of him. It was a bit 'spartan', so I began to buy a few small bits, just to make it more like home. You know the sort of thing, an easy chair, a coffee table, that sort of thing. I bought a radio cassette player, for a bit of music in the evenings. He stole that and sold it for half what I'd paid for it! The next thing was he came home with a big television set. 'I got that from a mate of mine,' he told me. Well, I knew that was a lie, he didn't have any mates who were better off than he was, for a start. When I asked him who was paying for the license, he just shrugged and said it worked OK without the license. I mentioned it to my boss at work and he said,

'The best thing you can do, Peter, is miles.' I asked him what he meant and he said, 'Put as many as you can between him and you.'

He offered me the cottage next to the undertakers, for a modest rent, provided I promised to keep it clean and not allow Bourner anywhere near it. I moved out of the flat that week-end, without telling Robert where I was going. That was the last of him, the last of the flat and the last of my problems. All my troubles were finally behind me.'

Tony Church looked pleased,

'Thank you, Mr. Dennison,' he said. 'I'm please to hear that you took heed of the warning in time to turn your life around. Are you married?'

'Yes,' he replied. 'We had our Silver wedding anniversary last week and we're expecting our first grandchild in March next year.'

'How long have you worked at 'County Caskets'? Tony asked. 'I'm always interested when somebody makes good. I

303

know nothing about your particular business, but I'm sure there will always be a need for coffins.'

'I founded the company twenty one years ago,' Dennison said, proudly. I worked for 'Linus' the coffin makers in Pudborough for a couple of years, after I left the undertakers. He was a lovely old boy and taught me a lot. He had nobody to take on the business and he was reluctant to invest any more money in it. He still did almost everything by hand. He was expensive, but he wouldn't use any of the cheaper alternatives to wood. The big firms were undercutting his prices and he began to think of nothing but retirement. He offered me the business on condition that I honoured the existing contracts. I knew if I was going to make a go of it, I would need to see for myself, how the bigger firms were operating. I arranged a couple of visits to different casket makers and noted the methods which they were employing. I went to see my bank manager and together we came up with this place. I shipped all the materials over here and invested in some new equipment. I continued to live in the cottage in Pudborough for a while, until the bungalow opposite came onto the market. I went back to the bank and asked for a loan and a mortgage. It was a bit cheeky really, but they saw that I was doing well with the business and it all went ahead.

'You say that his sister reported the theft of her credit card to the police,' Tony said. 'Can you give me any idea when that would have been? They may still have it on record, which could lead me to his sister's address.'
Peter Dennison was thinking hard,

'I think, as near as I can remember, it was towards the end of nineteen sixty six or maybe sixty seven. I know it was about this time of year, because the case was dropped just before Christmas.'

'Thank you, Mr. Dennison,' Tony said. 'I'll try to get some information from our colleagues in Kent. We need to do our best to find at least one member of his family. We have a burial to organise and it always seems a little sad when there are no mourners.'

'What happens in a case like this?' Dennison asked. 'I suppose the funeral expenses are paid from public funds?'

'Yes,' Tony agreed. 'It all gets a bit basic I'm afraid. We don't like arranging funerals without some sort of contact with the deceased's family members.'

'Well, Inspector, if you are able to locate his sister and she needs help to arrange his funeral, I'll be pleased to be of help to her if she wishes.' Dennison offered. 'Perhaps you would like to take one of my cards. I can recommend one or two funeral directors locally.'

The DI thanked Dennison for his time and for the help he had both provided and offered. They shook hands and Tony got back into his car and drove back to Chichelster.

CHAPTER 44.

Hannah dropped Archie off at Joe's front gate,

'I'll be back sometime this afternoon, Archie,' she said. 'Tell Elsie I'm only having a light lunch, so I'll be ready for my dinner this evening.' She added, 'I hope I'm invited?'

Archie laughed,

'Yes, Hannah, you're more than invited,' he said, 'you're expected. Give your Dad my best regards, I'll see you later.'

Hannah smiled and waved as she drove away on the Arundel road..

Joe Skrobe was in high spirits and met Archie in the front garden.

'Hello, Arch,' he said, 'thanks for coming. I can't believe how much a letter or two from Stephen has changed things. It seems that both Davies and Grover want to put their damage right. I'm sure that's not how they really feel, but as long as the end result is satisfactory, I don't mind.'

Archie grinned at his friend,

'What's all this about repairing the old greenhouse, Joe?' He asked. 'You won't be using it for growing plants, will you?'

'Well, probably not, Arch,' he replied. 'Would you like to have it at your allotment?'

306

Archie began to laugh,

'It would take up half the allotment and I bet it would be smashed by the kids before I'd had a chance to plant anything in it.'

'Well then, why not use it here, where it is?' Joe suggested. 'I could keep an eye on it, I can see it from my hall window.'
Archie thought about this, it could work. He just didn't think he'd have the time to attend to it regularly.

'I'd like to have a greenhouse, Joe,' he told him, but I wouldn't have the time to look after it properly. Even if I got it planted up, it would need watering every day. Then there's the shading in the summer, no, I think I'd better say 'no thanks'.
Joe was still smiling,

'If that's the way it is, why don't you tell me how to do it? I'll pay for whatever plants and compost we need. I'll look after it and water it. I just need you to advise me. Of course there'll be problems, but you're the gardener. You could have a look at it from time to time and let me know what I need to do to put them right.'
Archie sighed,

'We could give it a try, I suppose,' he said. 'Shall we get a pencil and paper and a tape measure, then we can have a look and see just how much glass it needs?'

'Come in and have a cup of tea, first, Arch. Old Thunder will be pleased to see you. We can take him with us he could do with a walk. There's something I want to show you first, out the back. We'll go there first, the kitchen door is unlocked, so we can get our tea on the way back in.'
The pair walked around the bungalow towards the top of the back garden. Joe was wearing his gum boots,

'You'll be OK if you stay on the grass, Arch,' he said. 'It's a bit sticky round the workshop area.'
Archie walked carefully, looking all the time at the loose soil which Joe had raked level.

'See those boot marks, Arch?' Joe asked as he pointed at them in the soil.

'Size eleven, so he's a big lad, I reckon. He tried to get into my workshop, but I think he heard old Thunder start to bark and growl and changed his mind.'

Archie bent to take a closer look,

'They're not his boots, Joe,' he said emphatically.

'Whose boots are they then? Jo asked, puzzled.

'You're wearing wellies, Joe,' said Archie. 'Walk over the ground next to those footprints and I'll show you the difference.'

Joe did as asked and then followed Archie back to the edge of the raked ground.

'See where your heel first touches the soil it digs in quite cleanly, doesn't it? Now look at those footprints. See how the soil is dragged into the heel mark?'

'Yes,' said Joe, 'what about it?'

Archie smiled and said,

'When you're wearing heavy wellies which are a couple of sizes too large, you can't put your heel down firmly. The weight of the boot makes it drag on the ground before you can put your weight on it.'

'So he's wearing wellies which were too big for him?'

Archie nodded.

'He's wearing brown woolly gloves too,' he stated. 'See the strands of wool on your workshop door, where he tried to prise the hasp and staple off? He's caught another bit of wool on the rough wood at the bottom of your window. He was probably trying to see what was in there. From where he's wiped the glass, I'd say he was a bit shorter than you.'

Joe looked up at Archie,

'Why, thank you, 'Mr. Holmes', he said, with a smile. 'Your powers of observation do you credit'.

Archie laughed,

'It's elementary, my dear Skrobe,' he replied. 'So now your prowler is a five foot six giant, in someone else's wellies!'

'Let's go and have this cuppa' Joe said.

They went in through the kitchen door. Archie got a grand welcome from Thunder, who kept rubbing his head against Archie's legs.

'Hello old boy,' Archie said as he stroked and tousled the big German Shepherd.

'Who was that young lady who dropped you off, Arch' Joe asked from the kitchen.

'She used to live here, when she was a little girl,' Archie replied. 'She's Bob Jempson's daughter, she's staying with us for a few days. She married Jeffery Davies, but she left him a few months ago.'

'Where does she live now, Arch? Didn't you say she had a twin sister?'

'Yes, Joe,' Archie replied, 'Hannah's sister lives in Lincoln. Hannah's been working in Belgium, but from some of the things she's been saying, I think perhaps she would like to return here. She's gone to see her dad this morning. He's in a care home near Salvington. She offered to drop me off on her way.'

Joe brought two mugs of tea into the lounge, where Archie was sitting with Thunder.

'Will all the glass be a standard size, Arch?' he asked.

'I don't know whether its still a standard size, but I expect they'll all be the same width.' Archie told him. 'The corner panes and the door glass may be different. They're usually held in place with spring clips on aluminium framed greenhouses. That will be where we need to be careful. I expect there are different styles of clip for each different make of greenhouse frame. Probably we'll need to bring a clip back with us, if we can find a whole one, to make sure we get the right ones from the garden centre.'

'Will the garden centre sell us the glass as well?' Joe asked.

Archie thought for a moment, before replying,

'They'd probably like to, but it might be cheaper and quicker to go to a glass works, or the greenhouse manufacturer direct. It will all depend on how much we need. We can't do anything until we know the size and how much we need. We'll have this cuppa and then go and take a look, shall we?'

A few minutes later they were sauntering along the old farm shop frontage to the greenhouse at the far end. As they passed the charred remains of the old hut, Joe reminded his friend of the night he had thought Archie was still inside, when Fuller was about to set fire to it. Thunder bounded along in front and then returned enthusiastically to them. The Greenhouse was quite a large one and was sited only a few feet from the lane which led up to Ridge Farm. They began by measuring the standard sized panes. Archie called out the dimensions and Joe wrote them on his pad.

'I think we'd better draw a sketch of the greenhouse,' Archie suggested. 'In fact two would be better. Sketch the left hand side and front, to show the door. Then sketch the right hand side and the back. We can mark where the angled panes are needed. We'll have to measure them separately. It might be a good idea to make a few cardboard templates for those, to make sure we get the angles correct.'

Joe began to make a rough sketch,

'It's a good job I can draw a straight line reasonably well,' he remarked. 'Otherwise we'd need some peculiar shaped panes to fill in the framework!'

'Just a minute, Joe,' Archie said quietly. 'There's a Range Rover parked in the field gateway, just up the lane. I'm going to take a quick look. You wait here, while I stroll up behind the hedge and get a bit closer to it.'

The vehicle was parked facing away from the house and there was a young woman sitting in the driver's seat. As he got closer, he saw the number plate, 'BET15'. He retraced his steps and said to Joe,

'Something fishy is going on there, Joe. The Range Rover belongs to Bettis. There's a woman sitting in the driver's seat, pretending to read a magazine. I should think she's acting as a lookout for Bettis, whatever he's up to.'

'What do you think we should do?' Joe asked him.
Archie thought for a few moments,

'You and Thunder go back home and phone Bill. You've got his number, haven't you?'

'Yes,' Joe confirmed, 'but what if he's not there?'

'Then you'd better phone Chichelster and tell them that there's something suspicious going on at the Ridge farmhouse.'

'Shall I tell them it's Bettis?'

'No, just say it looks as though someone is prowling about round the house and grounds.' Archie told him. 'We don't know for sure if it is Bettis. Bill told me that its still taped off as a crime scene, so whoever it is, shouldn't be there. You can tell them that I've gone to have a look and I'll be able to tell them more, when I come back.'

'OK Arch,' Joe said, 'but be careful, won't you? You know what a nasty piece of work Bettis can be. Don't take any chances.'

'Don't worry, Joe,' Archie assured him. 'I'll be fine. I'll go up in the field before I cross the lane. His lookout, if that's what she is, won't even see me.'

CHAPTER 45

Archie kept low as he walked up the hedgerow, next to the lane. Just before the entrance to the farm house, he quickly checked that the Range Rover was out of his sight line and crossed the lane opposite the driveway. Straight ahead was the garage, with old Jason's car parked outside. To the right was the house, with a large parking area in front of it. The car engine was idling and the roof was down, as thought it was a summer's day! He noticed that the left hand door of the garage was in the closed position. The right hand door was opened right back and was obstructing his view along the side towards the rear of the house. As quietly as he could, keeping tight to the left hand hedge, Archie crept towards the garage. The sound of the car engine was masking his footsteps on the gravel. He reached the closed left hand door and peered round it into the garage. There was a man on the floor in an unconscious state. He had a gash on his head, above his right ear, which was bleeding profusely. Archie went into the garage and bent over the man. Then suddenly everything went black!

He wasn't sure how long he had been out, but when he came to the garage doors were both closed and the car had been backed up against them. The engine was still running and the garage was beginning to fill with exhaust fumes. The man on the floor next to him began to stir. He looked up at Archie with some alarm.

'Who are you?' He almost shouted. 'What are you doing here?'

'Be quiet,' Archie told him. 'You've got a bad cut on your head. Have you got a handkerchief?'

The man pulled a handkerchief from his coat pocket and handed it to Archie.

'Who are you?' He repeated loudly. 'Why did you hit me?'

'Hold the handkerchief firmly there,' Archie said as he made a pad and placed it over the wound. 'I didn't hit you. You're losing blood too quickly. Keep your voice down, there's some lunatic out there. He's clobbered me as well.'

'I won't ask you again,' the man, who Archie now recognised as Bettis, said. 'Who are you and what are you doing here?'

Archie had to make him keep quiet.

'Listen. right now, I'm your rescuer, what I'm doing here is trying to find a way out of this bloody garage before the exhaust fumes finish us both off. Now, shut up, sit still and keep the pressure on that wound.'

Bettis tried to lean against the wall, but was obviously still dazed and fell back to the floor. He was watching Archie's every move.

'What did you hit me with?' He asked, quieter this time.

Archie went over to him, his face a few inches away and said,

'Listen to me. I didn't hit you at all. Someone else did and then they hit me. I didn't see what I was hit with either, the only difference is that I don't appear to be bleeding all over the place. I suggest you save your energy and let me try to get us both out of here.'

'OK, OK, I'm sorry,' Bettis said. 'How can you get us out?'

'I'm thinking,' Archie told him.

'What are you thinking?' he asked.

'Among other things,' Archie said, firmly, 'I'm thinking that if I was semi conscious and bleeding, I'd keep quiet and show a bit of patience with someone who was trying to help me.'

Bettis nodded and managed to pull himself up to a sitting position as he watched Archie. He coughed and then began to be sick all down the front and sleeve of his coat.

Archie looked around to see if there was anything he could use. There was the usual assortment of clutter in the garage, some flower pots, a few tomato canes, half used tins of paint, some lengths of orange baler twine, hung on a nail, obviously cut from bales of hay. There were no garden tools or anything heavy enough to break the stout wooden doors. Archie had noticed that there was a two or three inch wide gap between the closed doors. It looked as though a board was missing, possibly it had rotted and been discarded. The exhaust was gently pumping the garage full of carbon monoxide, so he needed to do something urgently. Over the folded down roof of the old convertible, he could see the car's gear shift. The automatic transmission had been left in 'P' but Archie could not tell whether the handbrake was on or not.. The fumes were beginning to hurt his eyes. He pushed as hard as he could, but the weight of the car was holding the doors firmly closed.

Archie checked on his fellow prisoner and noticed that he had again lost consciousness.

He looked at the assortment of clutter against the wall and then he had an idea.

'It just might work,' he thought to himself. Picking up one of the tomato canes, he took his pocket knife and made a split in the end of it. Into this he forced a piece of baler twine. The distance from the garage door to the gear lever, he reckoned to be about twelve or fourteen feet. By overlapping and binding four canes together, he had a makeshift, 'fishing rod' of a suitable length. He began to join lengths of baler twine together, until he had more than twice the length of the canes. Very carefully, he began to poke his 'fishing rod' through the gap in the doors. He held the other end of the twine in his teeth. After a couple of failed attempts, he was able to wrap the twine around the gear shift. He drew his makeshift fishing rod back through the gap, paying out the slack twine, until he held both ends in his hands. Gently, very gently, he tensioned it. Wrapping the twine around his hands, he exerted a firm, steady pull on both ends of the twine. The gear shift moved back one space into 'D' for drive!

The effect was immediate.

The old Saab took off down the drive, towards the farm lane. Archie shoved open the doors and ran after it. He caught it just as it got to the junction with the farm lane. He opened the driver's door, stood on the brake and returned the lever to the 'P' position. Archie switched the engine off and removed the keys. The taste of fresh air worked its magic on him and he ran back to the now open garage. Bettis was beginning to come round as Archie got back to him.

'How did you do that?' he asked Archie. 'Where's the man who hit me?'

Archie looked at him. He was in a mess. He wouldn't be able to do anything useful for a while.

'Just stay here and keep some pressure on that head wound.' Archie told him. 'I'm going to find whoever it was slugged us both. The police have been called, they should be here soon.' Archie closed the left hand door, to shield Bettis from any passers by. He left the other door open to clear the fumes.

Archie was beginning to feel angry now, as silently as he could, he crept along the side of the garage towards the back door of the house. He tripped and almost fell over a log, which had been dropped on the pathway. He picked it up and looked at it. It was around three inches in diameter and he saw that there was a bit of blood and a tuft of grey hair on one end.

'That's what the bugger hit me with, I expect,' Archie thought to himself. 'I'll keep hold of it for now.'

Stealthily, almost like a cartoon cat, he tiptoed along against the house wall. He was alert in spite of his headache. He reached the back porch of the house. Someone was breathing heavily and grunting, probably on the porch steps. Archie leaned his log against the wall and using his fingers to grip the side window ledge, he slowly pulled himself up so that he could see through the window.

The young man had his back to him. He was sitting on one of the steps changing his wellington boots for a pair of trainers. Archie lowered himself to the ground, picked up his log and shifted it to his left hand. The door at the bottom of the porch steps was open. Archie gently nudged it so that it creaked and swung slightly and then it stopped.

'Who's that?' He heard the man say from his seat on the porch steps.

Archie panted loudly, like a large dog. It had the desired effect! His assailant came quietly down the steps and Archie saw a set of right handed fingers come round to grip the edge of the porch door.

WHACK!

Archie's left handed log contacted the fingers against the edge of the door. There followed a loud scream from their owner, who fell to the ground in front of him.

'Don't hit me!' he shouted at Archie, who now stood over him, his log raised in both hands as though ready to launch it at the man's head.

'Please, please, I'm sorry, don't hit me!'

Archie heard three blasts on a car horn, some way down the farm lane.

'That's a good sign,' he said to the man on the ground. 'It means that the police are coming up the lane. You'd better stay down there until they get here.'

He tried to grab Archie's left leg, but was rewarded with a kick in the ribs from his right one! At that moment the other victim, still holding his handkerchief to his head wound, appeared at Archie's back. He was accompanied by Bill Pickering, who was wearing his usual 'not you again' grin. Archie thought later that it must have looked a bit comical. A young man wearing a trainer on one foot and just a muddy sock on the other.. He was holding his right hand under his left arm and he was crying like a baby.

'I'm sorry, I'm sorry, you've broken my hand. It's bleeding. Oh! My fingers! I think you've broken my ribs as well. I'm sorry, oh oh, please don't hit me again!'

Bill Pickering was looking at this sorry individual as he said to Archie,

'I think you'd better tell me what's happened Mr. Leggitt. I don't think I'm going to get much sense out of him just yet.'

Archie looked down at the man,

'Stop your 'mytherin' and sit quiet, before I start dancin' on you.' Archie said. 'You're lucky you're still conscious, which is not how you left us two.' Archie then turned to Bill and said,

'I thought the cavalry would never get here! Better late than never, though, I s'pose'

'I think you'd better sit down, Mr. Bettis,' Bill advised. 'You seem to have quite a nasty wound there and you've lost a bit of blood.'

Bettis sat on the second step of the porch. He looked quite pale and was still shaking.

'I think he needs an ambulance, don't you, officer?' Archie suggested.

'Yes,' Bill agreed, 'what about you? You've got a small cut and a lump on the back of your head. Perhaps you'd both better go to the hospital for a check up.'

'No, thanks, officer,' Archie protested. 'I took most of the blow on my shoulder. I was only dazed for a few minutes. When I came sensible, I thought Mr. Bettis was dead, but then I saw he was trying to sit up. I got his handkerchief and made him hold it firmly on his head wound. I've got a bit of a headache, but Elsie will soon patch me up.'

Bill Pickering looked at Archie and said,

'I'm going to call for a police van and an ambulance first. I'll be as quick as I can, I don't think he'll give you any more trouble.

When I come back here, I'll caution him and arrest him. He may need medical attention as well, the ambulance people will decide, when they get here.' Bill walked briskly back to his car and got on the radio.

Archie looked down at the man on the ground and said to him,

'Before you go, tell me where you put the rifle?'

'What rifle?' he protested.

'The one you slugged Mr. Bettis with, unless you've got two rifles. In which case, we'll have 'em both!'

Bill returned from his car, he had heard 'rifle' mentioned. He looked at Archie.

'Did he have a rifle?' Bill asked.

Archie was still looking at the man. He said to Bill,

'Yes, and a pair of brown woollen gloves, and a pair of someone else's wellington boots, which he wore to visit Joe's garden last night.'

'I suppose you know everything about me, do you?' He said to Archie, with a sneer.

Bill smiled at Archie and said,

'I'll leave you to look after him, Mr. Leggitt, while I check on Mr. Bettis. Will you be alright for a few minutes?'

'Oh, yes, officer,' Archie said with relish, 'I'll be absolutely delighted to oblige you.'

'Don't leave me with him,' pleaded the young man. 'It's in the log store by that barn. I've run out of ammunition, the empty box is in my jacket pocket, next to it.'

Bill turned around from where Bettis was sitting on the steps.

'Is it your rifle?' Bill asked him as he strode past them towards the log store.

'No, I borrowed it from a friend,'

'Do you have a firearms certificate?' Bill called out.

'No, but my friend has one,' he said defensively.

'Not for much longer, though,' Bill replied as he returned with a bolt action point two-two rifle. He wore gloves and carried the weapon by the end of its barrel.

318

'What's the name and address of this friend of yours?' Bill asked him.

'You can tell me before I caution you if you like. It might help the judge to look a bit more kindly on your case.'

'I'll tell you, officer, but get me away from him,' he said, indicating Archie with a nod of his head. 'He's like a mad man.' Bill took some details and then cautioned and arrested him. Two ambulance men walked around the corner of the house. They had a wheelchair with them and got Bettis into it, ready to take him to A and E.

'Do you want us to notify anyone, sir?' One of them asked him.

'How long will I be at the hospital?' Bettis asked him.

'Hard to say, sir, it looks as though you've got a nasty gash there. They'll probably want to check for concussion.' The ambulance man told him.

Better tell my wife, she'll be at work now. Leave it until she gets home, I'll give you the phone number.

'I can call round and tell her, if you'd prefer,' Bill offered. 'I thought that was her sitting in your car just down the lane. She hooted at me as I passed, but she didn't wave.'

'We'll come back and have a look at these two, before we go.' The senior of the two ambulance men said to Bill. When they returned, Bill had the young man handcuffed. He held his arm in one hand and the rifle in the other.

Bill asked them to check Archie first. He was asked to sit in the ambulance whilst they checked him over. Bettis looked at Archie and mouthed a silent, 'Thank you.'

Archie could have helped to make things a lot worse!

Instead, he looked at Bettis and just winked. It hurt his head. He made a mental note to get some aspirin on the way home. Archie would be alright to go home, the ambulance men decided.

'Just take it easy for the rest of today,' they advised him. They heard a vehicle coming up the lane.

'That'll be our police van,' Bill said to the ambulance men. It wasn't! It was Joe Skrobe in his A35 van, he had Thunder with him. Joe got out, he held Thunder on a short lead. The dog barked once and strained on his lead to get to Archie.

'Don't let him bite me!' The young man screamed. 'He remembers me from last night. He can smell me!'

'We can all smell you,' Archie said, grinning. 'Not for much longer though, someone else will have to put up with it.'

'Will I have to go to hospital?' The man in handcuffs asked, hopefully.

'I don't think so,' said the senior man. 'Your fingers are just bloody and bruised, not broken. Whatever you did to cause it, I seriously recommend you not to try it again.'

Moments later the police van arrived with two PC's. They opened the side door to reveal a weldmesh wire cage. A steel seat was bolted to the floor and a rail each side of the seat provided an anchor point for handcuffs.

'This is your passenger for Chichelster central,' Bill told the driver. 'He's been cautioned and bandaged. Keep him isolated until I get there, please. I'm just going to have a quick word with these two gentlemen and I'll come straight over to 'Chi' when I'm done.'

Bill came over to where Archie and Joe stood. He rubbed Thunder's head and said to Archie,

'I'll pop round later, Arch, about seven, after I've finished. Will that be OK?'

'Yes, Bill,' Archie replied. 'We've got a house guest at present, Bob Jempson's girl, Hannah. She's a very nice lady, I'm sure she won't mind having her meal a bit early.'

'How did you know he had a rifle?' Bill asked. Archie grinned at him,

'To be honest, I didn't. It was an educated guess. I saw the cut on Mr. Bettis' head and it looked as though it had been made by something sharper than a log. There were some spent two-two cases in the field where we were trying to rescue Peter's tractor.

320

This idiot had walked through the field on his way to Joe's back garden. There's another one down there, look,' Archie bent to look at the brass shell case. 'Bill, don't touch it, I'll pick it up by poking a twig inside it.' He held it up and looked at the cap. '0.25 ACP' it said around the rim. 'This one's different, Bill, it's not a two-two, it's a point two five. It might have a fingerprint on it, have you got an envelope?'

'Hang on a minute, Sherlock,' said Bill as he searched his pockets. 'Here's one,' he said as he removed the letter from it. 'pop it in here, I'll give it to Brian Pace later, it might be significant. I'm still impressed with your powers of observation, Arch.'

'I just saw it there and it didn't look quite the same colour as the others,' Archie said.

'So you put two and two together and came up with, a 'two point five'!' Bill laughed. 'But how did you know he had brown woollen gloves?'
Archie looked at Joe and smiled. I'll tell you, he said.

'He left some threads of 'em on Joe's shed door. He was wearing wellies which were too big for him, old 'Diddler's' I expect. He was changing out of 'em when I introduced myself to 'im just now!'

'Oh, that's the way you introduce yourself, is it?' Bill said. 'Archie, I think perhaps you should take the advice of the ambulance man and go home and take it easy. I'll drop by later. I suppose we'd better put old Jason's car back in his garage. He won't be using it, but if it stays out here with the roof down, it'll get pretty wet.'
Bill reversed the Audi back into the garage and tied the string 'lock' across the two doors. He came back over to Joe's van,

'That's a nice car,' he said to them. 'Almost a classic I'll bet. I wonder whether he'll have left it to his son. I hope not, I don't think he'd appreciate it, probably just sell it. Thanks for your help again Arch, now get home and have a rest.'

'I shan't be doing anything strenuous, Bill,' he said. 'Thanks for coming so quick, another few minutes and I might have got a bit cross with him!'
Bill shook his head in disbelief,

'Don't you think you're getting a bit old for this sort of thing, Arch? Most people your age are engaged in more peaceful pursuits.'

'I'll have plenty of time to practice sitting in a rockin' chair later on,' Archie told him. 'I'm not ready for the scrap heap yet!'
Bill shook his head.

'You seem to still think you're fit enough for a scrap, never mind the scrap heap,' he said, winking at Joe. 'Get him home for me, Joe. Elsie's the only one with any control over him.'
Archie got into the passenger seat of Joe's van. Thunder was let in via the back door. He came straight to the back of Archie's head and began to lick his wound.
That's the way dogs usually are!

CHAPTER 46.

'Do you want to go straight home, Arch, or shall we have a cup of tea first?' Joe asked as he started his van.

'I could certainly use a cup of tea and a couple of lightly buttered aspirins, if you've got any,' he replied.
Joe drove away slowly,

'Is that where the Range Rover was parked?' He asked, as they passed the field gateway.
Archie looked to his left,

'Yes, that's where it was,' he said. 'But it wasn't his wife in the car. I've seen his wife, she's got a make-up and perfume shop in Pudborough. I don't know who she is, but he was being very cagey about it.'

'Tell me what happened, Arch,' Joe asked. 'How did you get the bump on the head?'

'Let's get a cup of tea, first, Joe,' he said. 'I'm as dry as dust and I really need those aspirins, or whatever else you've got for headaches.'
They got back to Joe's and Archie sat in Joe's lounge with two anadin tablets, a glass of water and a cup of very sweet tea.

Joe had taken Thunder for a walk, to give Archie time to recover from his experience. He returned half an hour later, to find Archie asleep. Joe emptied the teapot and boiled the kettle ready to make some fresh. He heard Archie talking softly to Thunder.

'You're another lovely old boy, aren't you? I wonder if you'd like to meet my lovely boy, his name is 'Jimbo'. He's a very friendly dog, not quite as big as you. He lived with another dog before, but he didn't like it. I think the other dog used to be spiteful to him. He's alright now though, your 'dad' likes him.' Joe entered the room. He was smiling as he spoke,

'Sorry to interrupt the deep and meaningful conversation between you two, but I wondered if you might like another cuppa? How's the head, old friend?' he asked Archie.
Archie looked up from his furry companion,

'Hello, Joe,' he said. 'Thanks, I'd love one, the headache's almost gone. What's the time?'

'It's a quarter past one, Arch' Joe called from the kitchen.

'Is that all? Its amazing how much fun we can cram into a couple of hours, isn't it?'
He brought a tray with two mugs of tea, and a biscuit barrel..

'I'm going to stand outside and have a smoke, first,' Archie announced. 'When I come back in, I'll tell you all about it.' He went out through the kitchen and sat on the back door step. He finished his smoke and went back inside, closing the kitchen door on his way. Thunder had 'pinched' his seat on the settee.

'Move over a bit,' Archie said. 'If you play your cards right, you might even get a bit of biscuit.'
He gave Joe verse and chapter of his morning's adventure, the only gap being the few seconds while he was stunned.

'What was Bettis doing there, Arch?' Joe asked him.

'I told you, he was lying on the floor, bleeding,'

'I meant besides that.'

'I s'pose he might have been groanin' a bit as well!'
Joe laughed, 'You know what I mean, why was he there in the first place?'

Archie smiled,

'Why didn't you say that? I don't know what he was up to, Joe.' he said. 'But knowing the way he is, I expect it was something nefarious. I can tell you one thing which seemed strange. He mouthed a silent, 'thank you' to me whilst we were both sitting in the ambulance. I took that to mean, 'thank you for not saying too much'. I'll wait and see if he contacts me again, before I have to give a statement.'

'Would you tell the police what he was up to, Arch?' Joe asked him.

'I can't tell 'em what I don't know, can I? I just thought it was strange that old 'Diddler's' car was outside the garage, with the roof open and the engine running.' Archie replied

'D'you think perhaps he was going to pinch the car?' Joe asked.

Archie shook his head,

'No, he's not stupid, just greedy. I think he was after something from the garage and before you ask me what it might be, I don't know. For what its worth, I think the lad who bushwhacked us was probably the one who was after the car. It was certainly him who backed it up against the garage doors and tried to gas us both.'

The pair drank their tea and sat chatting for a while.

'I s'pose I'd better get home,' Archie said eventually. 'I'm not sure what time Hannah will be back.'

Joe got his jacket and together they went out to the van, leaving Thunder asleep on the lounge carpet.

CHAPTER 47.

At eleven am on Wednesday morning, the conference room at Chichelster police station was almost full. DI Tony Church addressed the meeting.

'Good morning, ladies and gentlemen. I have called this meeting to co-ordinate the investigation into the sudden death of Mr. Jason Davies, of Ridge Farm, Wigglesworth. There are, as usual, several lines of enquiry which we may find will overlap. Where and when this occurs, I want you to refer back to myself or DS Stuart. It will be a waste of our resources if we have two or more teams pursuing the same element of investigation, possibly even from the same source of information. The way forward here is by co-ordination. Information must be shared as it comes to light and not pursued independently by individual officers. In short, we must work as a team if we are going to get the right result.

I am now going to delegate particular areas of our investigation to specific officers or pairs of officers. We have received some specific information which will involve some of us operating outside our usual geographic areas. By necessity this will involve officers in plain clothes. These units will operate independently of the local uniformed force, but senior officers will be aware of their presence.

Before I divulge any further information, I must stress that any and all of the details made available to this meeting, are strictly confidential. The information is not to be made available to the public, neither is it to be shared with or sold to the media. Any serving officer who jeopardises the security of this investigation, will be severely disciplined.

Are there any questions, at this stage?'

There were none.

'I will now outline the facts of the case and disclose any specific information which we have obtained to date. You may make notes or ask questions as we go, but please try not to impede the flow of information in the process.

Fact one.

Mr. Jason Davies, from this point on, to be referred to as, 'JD.' was shot dead in the early hours of Monday morning. He was at his home and seated in an arm chair, he was also possibly in the throes of a heart attack.

Fact two.

The weapon, a small bore hand gun, has not yet been found.

JD had a number of visitors on Sunday evening, besides the one who took his life. We have interviewed those of whom we are aware and transcripts of those interviews can be made available to you if considered relevant to your specific line of enquiry. Their content is confidential and must not be divulged to any person not directly engaged in this investigation. I will remind you to take care that the case is not discussed in a public place, such as a café or hotel bar. Many a prosecution has failed as a result of an eavesdropper picking up on a casual conversation.

Fact three.

Certain events which may fall outside of this investigation should not be allowed to cloud the central issue. These range from the discovery of yet another set of human remains on farm land in the vicinity, to another individual, as yet unidentified, who is at large and carrying a point two-two rifle. Though this is not the weapon used to murder our victim, JD. It has been confirmed as one used in another local killing, some thirty years ago.

Fact four.

Items were stolen from the home of JD, presumably by the killer. I have listed these in the order in which they may be most readily identified. This list will be circulated to, jewellers, watch and clock repairers, pawnbrokers and gun shops, country-wide.

The list includes:

A double barreled twelve bore shot gun.

An engraved 14 carat gold pocket watch, taken from a sideboard drawer.

A solid silver tea service and galleried tray.

An antique French carriage clock.

A collection of old gold coins, including sovereigns, half sovereigns, Kruger rand and various commemorative gold and silver coins.

There are other items which have been taken, including a substantial amount of money and some items of jewellery.

Copies of the list are available to you, if required. Are there any questions, so far?' He asked the assembly.

PC Eric Mercer held up his hand.

'One moment, please,' said the DI. 'For those of you who have not yet had the pleasure let me introduce, our new arrival, PC. Eric Mercer. Eric has transferred to us from the Metropolitan Police. I hope you will all do your best to help him to fit in to our somewhat different operational style.

Yes, PC Mercer, you wished to ask a question?'

Mercer stood and looked around the room,

'Have we got any photographs of these missing items, Sir?' he asked.

'Good question,' Tony said. 'The answer, I'm afraid is a resounding, 'no'! We may eventually be able to produce some, but that will depend upon whether his family are able to help.

The best we can hope for is a more accurate description at this time.'

'Thank you, Sir.' Mercer replied.

'I suppose we could put out an appeal to ask the perpetrator to bring his spoils back for a photo shoot!' Tony said smiling.

'However, I imagine that would not yield a positive result. I will mention it to Mr. Jeffery Davies, the deceased's son, he may be able to provide us with some more details.

Before I continue, I suggest that you each take a copy of the list, just in case you should come across any of the items in the course of your enquiries.

Those of you who may have read the transcript of the interview with Mrs. Bernice Tenham, JD's sister, may have taken note of the man, 'Gorse'. I will require two plain clothes officers to investigate this man, who is a suspect. I do not want them to make direct contact with him, but I need to know everything about him. Where he lives, who his friends are, what are his hobbies and habits? The whole works. I want to know when he gets up in the mornings, what he has for breakfast and what car he drives. We believe he is married and has a son. I want to know everything about them as well.

I want all this information as quickly as you can get it. What I **don't** want is for him to guess, or even sniff that we are interested in him.'

'I'll volunteer for that, Sir,' Eric Mercer called out.

Tony smiled and replied,

'I appreciate your enthusiasm, PC Mercer, but I'll allocate the personnel for these jobs, if you don't mind.'

'Sorry, Sir,' Mercer mumbled.

Tony nodded to Ian, who seemed mildly amused.

'Right, so we'll start with that job, DS Ken Foster and DC Phil Travis, I'd like you to study what we've got and get yourselves over to Worthing. I'll get it cleared with our Worthing colleagues, by Superintendant Glover.

I'll need another pair of officers as back-up, to liaise between them and the local force. DS Lesley Stevens and DC Alan Bell, will you please arrange to rent a local holiday flat. Make sure it isn't too far from the town centre and large enough for the four of you to use as a base. You'll all need a bit of privacy and somewhere to get a bit of sleep. Just don't sleep on the job! Above all, don't break your cover by getting too friendly with the locals. I'll have a chat with you before you go, to answer any questions which you may have.'

Ken Foster raised his hand.

'Is it OK if we stay to hear the rest of your information, sir? The DI replied,

'Yes, please, Ken. I need you all to get as much from this update as possible. Now, getting back to the local scene, I'll make the direct appointments first, the rest of you will, 'wait in the wings' until we have more specific information. DS Brian Pace, you and your 'apprentice' DC Adam Morton, will go over the house and the farm with a fine tooth comb. There must be something else there which will point us in the right direction. Now to uniforms,

PC's Malcolm Foster and Brian Taylor, I want you to watch Martin Bettis and young Jeffery Davies. They must be kept away from JD's house and farm until we have finished our investigations. Young Davies is up in court in Lincoln today on another matter, but he'll be back tomorrow. We have to ensure that he keeps away from his estranged wife, Hannah, who is currently staying with our friends the Leggitts, in Wigglesworth. Jeffery Davies has a young lady named, 'Patricia Walker' in tow. She is a private investigator and Davies is trying to use her to persuade his wife into signing over her house to joint ownership. His business partner, Bettis, is a devious character and a bully boy. I wouldn't trust him anywhere I couldn't see him. He was at the farm earlier, when he shouldn't have been. There may well be an innocent explanation for this, but we won't know until we have discussed it with him. He was rendered unconscious by an assailant and was later taken by ambulance to the hospital. His young assailant also sustained a minor injury. He was treated to first aid at the scene and is currently our guest, awaiting an interview. We need to keep up regular patrols around their building site on the Arundel Road. It's next to the bungalow where Mr. Skrobe lives. They've already tried to drive him out, they may try again. Try to be discreet or they will be hollering, 'police harassment' from the rooftops.

The rest of us just need to keep our eyes and ears open. Remember, any information comes directly to me, however insignificant you may believe it to be.

Before we break up this meeting, are there any questions?' There were none.

'Thank you all for your attention, be discreet, and be observant. Good luck and good hunting. We'll re-convene when we have something new to share.'

The meeting over, they dispersed. The officers who were assigned to the Worthing based duties, went back to the DI's office for further information and instructions.

CHAPTER 48.

Archie arrived home a few minutes before Hannah returned from her father's.

'What have you been up to, Arch?' Elsie asked. 'You look awful. Your face is dirty, you've got dust all over your trousers and what's that on your head?' She rubbed his head with a towel.

'Ouch! Don't do that, Else,' he said. 'It's still a bit painful, the headache's gone, but the bump's still tender.'

'Let me look,' she said as he sat on a kitchen chair.

'Oh, Archie,' she said, 'you've got a small cut and there's a lump like half a ping pong ball!'

'I know,' he said, 'don't you think I can feel it? It's not bleeding and it'll soon go down. It don't need you rubbin' it with a towel, that's a sure thing.'

'What have you been doing? I thought you were only helping Joe to get his greenhouse sorted out.'

'There was something happening up at Ridge farm,' he told her. 'I went to have a look while Joe phoned the police. Some young hooligan smacked me with a log, whilst I was trying to help that Bettis man.'

'What do you mean? Why were you trying to help him? I thought you didn't like him.' Elsie asked.

'I don't particularly like him, Else, but he was on the ground unconscious. What did you expect me to do, spit on him and walk away?'

At that moment, Hannah arrived. She tapped on the back door and came straight in.

'Hello Hannah,' Archie said, 'had a good day?'

'Hello you two,' Hannah replied. 'Yes, I've had a lovely day, thank you. Dad sends his love and wants to thank you for letting us stay with you. Hilda phoned while I was there. Davies was lucky not to go to prison, instead, he got a hefty fine and has to pay a hundred and eighty pounds costs. Ninety for Hilda and sixty for Mr. Fielding, the rest was for the court. He's got to do forty hours community service, but he can do that here. He has to report to Chichelster first and then the local police, probably Mr. Pickering, until he's done it. It just serves him right!'

Hannah laughed. 'He'll think twice before he tries to bully either of us again.'

She noticed Archie sitting on the chair whilst Elsie bathed his head. She looked at his head and exclaimed,

'Oh, what's happened, Archie? Are you hurt? How did you do it? Oh, that looks painful.'

Archie began to giggle and then in 'Pink Pantheresque' humour, he mimicked Peter Sellers, as Jaques Clouseau.

'I have just recearved a burmp on ze head!'

'Hold still, you silly old fool,' Elsie said as sternly as she could manage. 'How can I bathe it if you can't keep still? There are bits of bark and grass and all sorts of dirt in here. Stop your silly giggling.'

'Stop.' Archie said as he burst out laughing. 'That's five questions from you two in less than a minute. Why do women do that? Keep firing off questions without letting you get a word in edgeways to reply?'

Both women were laughing,

'I'm sorry, Archie,' Hannah said. 'I was just concerned that you had hurt yourself. How did it happen? Was it while you were at Joe's? Did you knock yourself out?'

'Here we go again,' Archie said. 'I'll tell you how it happened. I was hit on the head with a log, by some young hooligan at Ridge farm. So, no, I wasn't at Joe's and no, I didn't knock myself out, but the log did. Not for many seconds, but it did knock me out. Now I've got a bump which if left alone, will subside in a day or two.'

Both women looked at each other in surprise.

'Well,' said Elsie, 'That's us told, I suppose. Alright Arch, we won't say another word about it.'

'Hilda's coming down again tomorrow, Elsie, Will that be alright?' Hannah asked.

'Yes, of course it will,' she said. 'I thought you had said something about making your separation legal and getting a restraining order on Jeffery. Will you do that whilst she's here?'

Hannah smiled and said,

'I don't think the restraining order will be too difficult, but I'm going to see dad's solicitor tomorrow. He reckons I've got enough grounds to begin divorce proceedings. Another thing, when I told dad that Jeffery's father was dead, he said that Jeffery will probably be left the farm house. He thinks I'll probably get my house back without too much trouble. Dad made me get a formal, pre-nuptial agreement, so that he couldn't claim the house as his. That Inspector at Chichelster, the one Archie knows, said that Jeffery wanted to find me to get me to sign the house over to joint ownership. I can tell you now, with certainty, that won't be happening!'

Archie looked up at Hannah,

'Would you want to live here again?' He asked her.

'I think I might,' Hannah replied. 'I could get my old job back at the General, I've been told that much by the nursing manager. Yes, I might give that some serious thought. It would mean I was closer to dad. He's not too bad, but the health scare with his heart last year had us all worried. Incidentally, he wants us all to have lunch with him on Saturday. I said I'd ask you and then let him know. He says he wants to book a table at the Aftonia, that's the big one, on the sea front.'

'There's no need to go overboard, Hannah,' Archie said. 'Is that where you went today?'

'No we went to the pub you took him to, last week. I think he just wanted to give us all a wider choice of menu, that's all,' she said.

'Yes,' Elsie said, 'we'd enjoy that, very much I think. We could eat our lunch with a sea view. How do you feel about it Arch?'

Archie nodded,

'Yes, I like the sound of that, Hannah,' he said. 'A nice ride out and lunch in style at the Aftonia.'

'With a sea view,' Elsie reminded him.

He laughed as he saw the puzzled look on Hannah's face.

'Lunch was the key word, Else,' he said. 'The Aftonia and the Sea view are all extras!'

'Typical,' Elsie said to Hannah, 'food and beer. They're the two elements that men exist for!'

CHAPTER 49.

DI Church was pleased to learn that he had the full co-operation of the Worthing force. Better than that, their Chief had actually endorsed the plan. He had privately acknowledged that some of his officers may be known to Gorse, which could have compromised the entire undercover operation. They jointly decided that their temporary accommodation should also remain confidential.

The two Detective Sergeants, Ken Foster and Lesley Stevens went ahead to arrange a rental on a holiday flat. They succeeded in their mission and returned to Chichelster with the details. They had paid a £50 deposit and a fortnight's rent. They had a choice of four locations, it being November and therefore not over busy with tourists!

The ground floor flat which they had selected was just off the sea front. There were two bedrooms, a lounge, a bathroom and a well equipped kitchen. Street parking was nearby and as yet, not subject to charges or restrictions.

'Just because there's a decent kitchen,' DS Stevens told the others, 'don't imagine for one minute that I'm doing the cooking.'

They laughed at the thought, Phil Travis responded with,

'Thank God for that, a fortnight on spaghetti bolognaise, would drive me into a bout of deep depression.'

'I can cook more than spaghetti bolognaise!' Lesley protested. 'I'm quite a good cook actually. You can ask my partner, he'll tell you.'

'It's all a bit academic, really,' said Ken Foster. 'Lesley says she's not cooking, so it'll be take-aways or microwave meals. We'd better get ourselves ready for a few days, and possibly nights, away from home comforts.'

Alan Bell and Lesley Stevens would be their 'public' faces, as and when required. They would pose as a couple of friends on their annual holiday. Ken Foster and Phil Travis would be engaged in the more obscure elements involved in the investigation.

They had taken photographs of the flat, mainly to give the DC's an idea what to expect. Alan Bell was impressed with the amount of room there seemed to be. Phil was a little more sceptical, with regard to the sleeping arrangements. Obviously Lesley would need a room of her own, so the men would need to share. There were two single beds in the second bedroom and the other bed was a pull out from the sofa in the living room.

'Don't worry about it, son,' Ken Foster advised. 'You won't be spending much time in your bed, whichever one it turns out to be.'

Their details were provided to DI Church, who would be able to mobilise more officers should assistance be required. They would be using hire cars from Chichelster, to avoid any direct links to the police. Their registration numbers were also provided to the Worthing chief as a safeguard against any adverse attention by local officers.

The operation commenced on Thursday afternoon. Ken Foster and his DC began with an observation of Gorse's town centre office. They checked the number of clients who came and went, taking photographs and logging the times. By five pm they had established that there were no longer any clients inside. This was confirmed by the young lady, whom they took to be his assistant, leaving at around five fifteen, with a handful of letters. She headed to the local post office, about a hundred yards along the road. At five thirty one, the office lights were switched off and Gorse came out. He checked his watch and looked up the road towards the High Street. A silver Mercedes SL came down the road at speed and screeched to a halt. Gorse opened the passenger door and got in. The car then moved off at a more realistic pace and turned right at the sea front. The driver was a young man, in his twenties. He had shoulder length hair, covered by a baseball cap which he wore backwards.

'I don't think much of his choice of chauffeur,' said Phil Travis. 'Proper scruffy looking character, wasn't he?'

'He needs to slow down a bit,' Ken added, 'or he'll come to grief sooner than he thinks. Right, young Philip, I need a cup of tea and a bun, how about you?'

Phil nodded, 'I'm glad you said that Sarge, I need to stretch my legs, shall we park up and take a stroll?'

'Don't get used to it, but whilst we're on this op, you'd better call me, 'Ken'. We don't want to blow our cover on the first day, do we?' He winked at Phil, 'I could do with a bit of a walk as well, so we'll lock up and find a tea shop, preferably one close to a gent's toilet. It goes almost straight through me this weather.'

Phil agreed. They left their car and buttoned up their top coats as they walked towards the sea front.

Back at the flat, Lesley and her DC, Alan Bell, were busy arranging some of the furniture and discovering where the controls for the heating system were located. Alan was filling the kettle, when there was a loud 'POP' and all the lights went out.

'What was that?' Lesley called out.

'Dunno!' Alan called back, 'fuse, I suppose. Have you got a torch?'

Lesley groped about to try to find her bag, she cursed softly as she stumbled over a dining chair.

'Got it,' she went into the kitchen where Alan still stood by the sink.

'Something's not right, Sarge, I got a shock off the tap whilst I was filling the kettle.'

'Put the kettle down and switch it off at the socket,' Lesley told him. 'I expect there's a short circuit in the kettle, possibly the element has gone. Another thing, Alan, whilst we're on this op, you'd better call me, Lesley. I don't suppose many couples on their holiday break, would address each other formally, do you?'

'Sorry, Sarge, shall I try to find the fuse box?'

'That would be a good place to start, and it's not bloody, Sarge! Try to remember or our operation will be over before it begins.'

He took the torch and a few minutes later the lights came back on. Alan returned to the kitchen and gave Lesley back her torch.

'Thanks Ss…. Lesley,' he said, sheepishly. 'I'll have to try harder, it doesn't come naturally. I'd better make sure it is the kettle, hadn't I?'

'No!' Lesley almost shouted. 'All that will achieve is putting all the lights out again. She looked at the kettle, a stainless steel jug, with a plastic handle. 'I can see how you got a shock from it, the screw holding the handle is level with the surface of the plastic. We'll phone the agents and have them bring us a new one.' She pulled her mobile from her bag and looked at the information card on the inside of the front door. Lesley dialled the number and a female voice answered.

'Coastal holiday lets, how can I help you?'

Lesley explained the problem and asked for a replacement kettle.

'I'm on my own here,' said the young lady, 'I won't be able to bring you a kettle until tomorrow morning.'

'Then I shall come to your office and collect it,' Lesley replied. 'You do have a spare kettle there, don't you?'

'I'm not sure, maybe Alex will have one somewhere, I've only been here a month,' she told Lesley.

'OK I'm on my way,' Lesley called out as she put her phone away. 'Don't lock me out, Alan. I'm going for another kettle. I'll take this dud one with me, so they can see for themselves.' She picked up the kettle, emptied it down the sink and left through the front door.

The office of the letting agents was almost in Shoreham. Lesley parked outside and went up the stairs to the reception, on the first floor. She noticed a small fridge in the outer office with tea and coffee making ingredients on a tray on the top. The young lady smiled as Lesley entered.

'Hello, Mrs. Stevens,' she said, 'I haven't been able to find another kettle, but you could take the one out there for the time being. I finish in about half an hour. I'll leave a note for Alex. He can sort it out when he comes in tomorrow.'

'Thank you,' said Lesley, smiling. 'Actually it's Miss Stevens at present. I'm taking a break with my partner, he's not my husband yet.

'I'm Gloria,' said the receptionist. 'I'm sorry about that, I shouldn't have assumed. Is everything else alright? You've worked out how to control the heating, I expect. I know all the instructions are there, but you'd be surprised at how many people either don't read them properly or don't understand them.'

'Yes, thank you, I think this was the only problem, my partner got a small shock from it when he touched the tap, so I expect there's a hole in the element. Perhaps you should include that in your note to your boss. I wouldn't like to think he would try to use it and get electrocuted.'

Gloria nodded, 'yes, I see what you mean. I'll add that to the note in case Alex does the same. I finish at five, so I've only got another twenty five minutes and I'll be on my way home.'

'Do you live far away?' Lesley asked.

'Not far, Hove, actually,' Gloria answered. 'It's not too bad at this time of the year, but in the summer I expect the traffic would be much worse.'

'Surely it can't pay to have a full time receptionist for the holiday lets at this time of year?' Lesley enquired.

'No, it wouldn't be enough on its own, but we do the bookings for several small hotels and the Gatwick coaches as well. I work two evenings a week at the bar in the casino,' Gloria continued, 'Fridays and Saturdays. Alex sends a taxi for me and another one to take me home afterwards. He's a very good boss.'

'Well, I'm sure you're a very good receptionist, Gloria. Does your boss own the casino?'

'No,' Gloria smiled, 'he's not that rich. He's the bar manager, so he has to order the stock and employ the bar staff. They had some trouble in the summer. A couple of the girls were giving free drinks to their men friends. Alex gave them the sack and then next time these men came in there was a fight. Several people were hurt and had to go to hospital. That's why he makes sure that all the bar girls have protection on their way into work and home again.'

'Well, I must get back to the flat,' Lesley said. 'Thank you for your help, Gloria. Have a safe journey home. I expect we will meet again, enjoy your evening, bye for now.'
With her 'nearly new' kettle, she got back into the car and drove back to Alan in the flat.

CHAPTER 50.

Hilda telephoned at nine am on Thursday morning.

'I'm just leaving,' she said. 'Is there anything you want me to bring? I should be there by about one o'clock.'

'Just yourself,' Elsie told her. 'There's no great hurry, so drive carefully and get here safely. Don't worry about the time.' Archie had taken Jimbo for his walk and had his breakfast. He was about to go over to the mill, when the phone rang again. Elsie answered it and he heard her say,

'Just a moment, he was going out, I'll see if he's left yet.' She came out into the kitchen, where Archie stood by the back door.

'It's for you, Arch,' she said handing him the phone. 'He says his name is Bettis and he needs to speak with you urgently.'

'Hello,' Archie said into the mouthpiece. 'Archie Leggitt speaking, how can I help you?'
Elsie saw a puzzled look appear on Archie's face as she listened to his side of the conversation.

'I wanted to thank you for helping me yesterday,' Bettis said to him. 'I wonder if we might meet somewhere, somewhere neutral, that is.'

'I don't see why it should be urgent,' Archie said. 'What do you mean by neutral?'

'Not where we would be overheard, somewhere a bit private. You could come to my house if you wish, but I don't want to put you out,' he said.

'Well, I'm just going over to the mill. You can come and find me there if you think that will do. There won't be anyone else there and I've got a job I want to finish,' Archie explained.

'How do I get there?' Bettis asked him. 'Will the door be unlocked?'

Archie gave him directions to the mill. 'Yes, the door will be shut, but not locked, I'm working upstairs,' he said. 'If you just hoot when you get here, I'll come down and let you in.'

'It'll be about half an hour, is that OK?' Bettis asked.

'Yes, I'll still be there,' Elsie heard him say.

Hannah had just come downstairs and was standing in the kitchen doorway. Archie turned to Elsie and said quietly,

'I don't know what he wants, or how he got our phone number, but I told him to come to the mill.' Elsie nodded as he looked past her to their guest and said,

'Good morning, Hannah. I'm glad to see you up and dressed, all ready for the action.'

Hannah laughed,

'I suppose you've been for a walk, had your breakfast and started on your first job of the day?'

'What d'you mean first job? This is about the fifth, counting the toast, isn't it Else?'

'Away with you Archie Leggitt,' said Elsie laughing. 'Will you be back for lunch?'

'Yes, of course, call me on my mobile when Hilda gets here,' he said as he went out of the door.

It was a cold morning with a chilly east wind, but at least it wasn't raining. He had just unlocked the mill, when Jenny Tobin came out to her car.

'Morning Arch,' she called out. 'I'm going into Chichelster, is there anything you need? I'll be back by mid afternoon if you wanted to see me.'

'I can see you from here,' Archie said, 'no need to wait until this afternoon. But no thanks Jen, I don't need anything. I'm only fiddling with that guard rail on the top floor. It shouldn't take me too long.' He waved as Jenny got in and set off down the lane. Archie had just reached the top floor and picked up where he had left the job last week, when he heard a car horn.

'This job is cursed,' he said to himself. 'If I ever get these measurements right it will be a bloody miracle!' He set off back down the stairway again and opened the big door. Bettis stood shivering on the sleeper bridge.

'You'd better come in here, before you shake yourself off the bridge into the water,' he said to Bettis. He came into the mill and began looking all around at the inside of the building.

'Thanks,' he said to Archie. 'It's nice to get out of the wind, I should have worn a top coat.'

'Most normal people would have done,' Archie agreed. 'What did you want to see me about that was so urgent?'

'Can we sit down here?' Bettis pointed to the bench.

'Of course you can,' Archie said. 'I'm afraid I can't offer you a drink, I only came over to finish a bit of woodwork.'
Bettis sat down and rested his foot on the bottom rail of the bench.

'First, I need to thank you for your help and your discretion yesterday. Then I must apologise for being so rude to you. When I started to come to, I thought it was you who had hit me.
In fact it wasn't until you told me to hold my handkerchief firmly on my head wound, that I noticed that you'd also been hit on the head.'

'How is your head now?' Archie asked.

'It's not too bad today thanks, I had a headache for most of yesterday. It just feels sore now. I had five stitches in it, look!' He bent forwards so that Archie could see. It looked a bit red and lumpy, but seemed to be clean enough.

'How about you, Mr. Leggitt, you had a bump as well, didn't you?'

Archie smiled,

'Yes, I had a bump, I've still got a lump, but it doesn't hurt until I forget and scratch it, or put my cap on! How did you get my phone number? We're ex directory, so it isn't in the book.'

Bettis smiled as he replied,

'Your friend, Peter Bailey kindly gave it to the young lady who was with me, but not without some hesitation. That was late on yesterday afternoon. She went back to the farm, to try to find out where I was. I couldn't let her know, she wasn't really supposed to be there. She saw the policeman coming up the lane and decided that she didn't want to become involved in anything. What have you said to them?'

'I haven't told the police anything at all,' Archie interrupted. 'That's mainly because I don't know anything, so that part was easy. I'm nobody's fool though, Mr. Bettis. So unless you're prepared to be honest with me, I can't see the point of continuing this discussion, or whatever it is. I know that the lady in your Range Rover wasn't your wife. I've seen your wife in her shop in Pudborough. Your Range Rover was pointing away from the farm, which tells me that she had dropped you off and turned around, ready for a quick getaway when you had accomplished whatever it was you were doing. I imagine that PC Pickering will also come to the same conclusion, if he hasn't already.

That said, although I'm sure it wasn't an ideal outcome for you, it may still have been better than getting caught doing something unlawful. Am I making any sense to you?'

Bettis looked down at the floor and nodded. He was obviously feeling neither comfortable or confident. He sat up straight and looked Archie directly in the eyes and said,

'Yes, Mr. Leggitt, you are making a great deal of sense. I must apologise for not appreciating your intelligence. I wouldn't ask, or even expect you to perjure yourself on my account. In fact I would understand if you chose to use this incident to exact revenge on me for my actions with regard to your friend, Mr. Skrobe and Don Palmer. I know that I was wrong in that and I have already as much as said so to the police. I don't know whether your friend has told you, but my partner, Jeff Davies has written to Mr. Skrobe. I understand that it is a conciliatory letter, expressing our regrets and attempting to rectify the damage to both his property and our reputation. I fear that when I tell you exactly what I was trying to do, but without success, yesterday morning, you will probably have an even lower opinion of me.'

Archie stroked his chin as he stood by the workbench. He looked at Bettis and said,

'Let me put it to you this way, I more or less knew that there was something 'fishy' about your presence at the farm. The lady lookout in your Range Rover was a dead give away for a start. When I heard the car horn, a few moments before Mr. Pickering arrived, I realised that it was probably a signal to warn you that someone was coming up the lane. Unfortunately, by then, you were in no condition to go jogging off to your lookout, so the signal was ineffectual. I have no doubt that had you even guessed that there might be someone else at the farm, you'd have been more cautious. Had you known it was a young man with a rifle you wouldn't have been in the garage at all, would you?'
Bettis gave Archie a look which told him that his assumption had been correct. Archie continued,

'If you wish to provide a truthful account of why you were there, you will earn a bit more of my respect, than if you attempt to construct another fairy tale.'
Bettis nodded,

'Thank you,' he said.
Archie sat down on the sawing horse, facing Bettis.

346

You are correct in your assumption that I will not perjure myself,' he told him. 'But for what it's worth, neither will I volunteer information to the police, out of sheer spite or, as you just put it, revenge. It's entirely up to you, Mr. Bettis, to do what you think you should do. There has already been too much deceit and destruction, if you choose to perpetuate it, then on your own head be it.'

'Thank you,' he replied. 'I'd just like you to tell me what you saw, when you arrived at the farm. I promise I won't lie to you about my motives, but I'd just like to know how you read the situation. Your arrival, as it turned out was most fortuitous, but how did you know to come to the farm?'

Archie gave a brief explanation,

'I was measuring the greenhouse, with Joe Skrobe. We were working out how many panes we would need to repair it. I saw your car parked in the lane, so I walked up to see what was happening. I had heard that Jeffery Davies was away, so I sent Joe to call the police, in case there had been a break in. Old Jason's car was parked outside the garage with the top down and the engine running and one garage door was open. It was opened right back as far as it would go, blocking the view to the path which goes round to the back of the house. At first I thought maybe someone was trying to steal the car and I wondered if perhaps you were checking for a prowler. When I reached the garage, I looked inside and saw a man lying on the floor, with blood coming from his head. As I bent to check how badly he was hurt, I felt a bump on the back of my head and must have passed out. I didn't know it was you until after I came to. I tried to rouse you, and asked you for your handkerchief, which you somewhat reluctantly gave me. I managed to get you into a half sitting position, to lessen the blood pressure to your head wound. By then, the car had been backed up to hold the garage doors closed. The engine was running and gradually filling the place with exhaust fumes, through the gap in the doors. The gear shift lever was in 'P" but I couldn't see whether the handbrake was on.

I managed to improvise a fishing rod from some old tomato canes and some lengths of baler twine. I used that to lasso the gear shift and pull it backwards into D, the drive position. When the car moved away, I had to run to stop it before it went into the lane. I came and checked on your condition and managed to sit you back upright. I don't like being hit on the head, so I then went to find out who had done it. Very quietly I went towards the back of the house, on the way I picked up the log which he had hit me with. I could hear heavy breathing in the back porch, the door was half open. I pulled myself up by the window sill at the side and had a look in. The culprit was sitting on one of the steps, changing out of old Jason's wellies into his trainers. I had the log he'd hit me with in my left hand, so I began panting like a dog and then nudged the door, just enough to make it move slightly. He heard me and cautiously came to investigate. He put his hand round to grip the edge of the open door and that's when I hit it as hard as I could, with the log. You know the rest because you had come to a bit more and followed me.'

Bettis had sat and listened to Archie's account.

'I really can't thank you enough,' he said to Archie. 'Whatever you decide to tell the police, I'm just thankful to be alive. If you hadn't managed to shift the car, we could both have been dead from carbon monoxide poisoning. I believe your presence saved my life, and also prevented me from committing a crime. I'll tell you the truth now. It was me who moved the car out of the garage, to get to a safe key. It was in a secret hiding place under a slab on the floor. I'd guess it was probably the sound of the car being started, which alerted that young man to the fact that someone was there. I was bending down to lift the slab, when he hit me. I went out like a light. I neither saw nor heard him. When I came to and saw you, I thought you were my attacker. I was still pretty dazed. I thought I'd blown it when the policeman said he'd seen my wife in the car. Thankfully you didn't contradict him.'

'So who was in your car?' Archie asked him.

348

'Her name is Patricia Walker, she's a private investigator, and she's working for Jeffery Davies. She can't afford to be found on the wrong side of the law, she could lose her license. He told me where the safe key was hidden, under the square slab in the garage floor. Jeff had said there was probably enough cash in the safe to keep us going until his father's will was read. With all the problems at the site, most of which I'll admit were of our own making, we're now almost bankrupt.'

He looked Archie straight in the eye and said,

'That's why I was there and that's the truth, Mr. Leggitt.'

Archie thought for a moment or two,

'I don't understand why you're telling me all this,' he said. 'Have you discussed it with your partner, Jeffery Davies, yet?'

'That's another problem, Mr. Leggitt. When he told me where the key was hidden, he also told me to leave it. He said he would get it, once the will had been read. Jeff is due back this morning. I suppose I'll have to tell him about it now. He's going to be pretty angry that I tried to get to the money, without waiting for him to return.'

'Yes,' Archie agreed, 'I suppose he will. He doesn't need any more problems just now, does he? So, did you get the key?'

Bettis shook his head,

'That's another problem,' he said. 'I looked under the slab, but the key had gone.'

Archie sat quietly for a few moments. He looked at Bettis who sat with his eyes closed and head bowed. He looked up as Archie began to speak,

'I won't be volunteering any information to the police, Mr. Bettis,' he said. 'Although you have now told me why you were at the farm, that is confidential information and I will keep it that way. All I will say to the police, if I'm asked, is what I saw. I will not be persuaded to speculate on why you might have been there,' Archie told him. 'How you choose to extricate yourself from your predicament is up to you. As far as I can see, you haven't actually committed any crime, other than perhaps trespass. You have betrayed the trust your business partner had put in you and you've got a bump on the head for your trouble. I just hope you have the courage to tell your partner the truth. It would be a good idea, in my opinion, to do the same with your wife. She will be sure to find out if you deliver a pack of lies to her. Women are very good at that sort of thing.'

'Yes, indeed, Mr. Leggitt,' said Bettis. 'I owe you a debt of gratitude. It will take time to rectify the problems which I have created, but I have learned a valuable lesson. Thank you for helping me yesterday and for listening to me today. I'll leave you to get on with your woodwork.'

They shook hands and he left. Archie returned to his guard rail on the milling floor.

'Measure twice, cut once,' he muttered to himself as he trudged up the last flight of stairs.

CHAPTER 51.

Bernard Cavendish, the young man who had been arrested at Ridge Farm, was charged with unlawful possession of a firearm, suspected theft of a firearm and ammunition, assault with a deadly weapon, common assault, two separate counts of grievous bodily harm, possession of a controlled substance and trespass, causing damage to property.

Not a bad start for a Wednesday morning!

DI Tony Church had spent a couple of hours trying to make some sense of this young man. Cavendish appeared to have been well educated, but the DI suspected he was still under the influence of whatever substance he had been using. He had been questioned about the rifle, but the answers he gave made no sense at all. Whilst alone in the holding cell he was heard to mumble, 'gas will kill me.' He had repeated this several times, but when asked, 'what sort of gas?' he just mumbled incoherently. DS Stuart had suggested that perhaps he had been sniffing butane from gas lighter refils. They had heard of this practiced by previous drug users. He had been completely reticent and had refused the offer of a solicitor to represent him.

Today, Thursday, he was in the waiting room of Chichelster Magistrates Court. He was handcuffed to another officer, PC Malcolm Foster, who was doing his best to ignore Cavendish's complaints.

'Bernard Sefton Cavendish,' the depositions clerk shouted down the hall.

'Come on, you're on stage now,' said the PC as he stood up. Cavendish followed sluggishly.

'Waste of time, if you ask me,' he said to Malcolm.
PC Foster half closed his eyes and shook his head.

'You'll have every opportunity to tell the magistrates what you think of 'em, but you have to go into the court.' He told the young man. 'Move yourself lad, they won't come out here for you, you're not important enough for that.'
The clerk held the door open and Cavendish was ushered in

'Please state your full name and address for the magistrates,' the clerk said to him.

'Cavendish,'

'Is that your full name?' the clerk asked again.

'You already know my full name,' he said to the clerk.
Edwin Sarkes, JP, chairman of the bench, addressed him.

'Mr. Cavendish, you will please provide the information which my clerk has requested. Should you refuse to do so, you will be held in contempt of this court and detained until your trial date can be set. Now, do you wish to co-operate with this court and answer the questions asked by my clerk? This is your final opportunity.'
Cavendish shrugged,

'I s'pose so,' he mumbled.

'Yes sir or no sir. Either answer will suffice,' the chairman said.
There was a pause, while the court waited to see his response.

'OK then, yes,' Cavendish said in a mocking tone, reluctantly adding, 'sir.'

'Thank you,' said the chairman.

'Please state your full name and address, for the court,' the clerk said to him.

'Bernard Cavendish,' he almost grunted.

'What is your address?' the clerk asked.

'Various,' said Cavendish.

'Are you saying that you have no fixed abode?' The chairman asked him.

'No fixed abode,' Cavendish repeated.

Another 'mini conference' with the other two magistrates followed. The chairman looked at DI Church and asked,

'May we try to proceed, please Mr. Church?'

DI Church read out the charge list. When he had finished, he looked up at the chairman of the bench.

'Is that all of them, Inspector?' he asked, a look of confused bewilderment on his face.

'Yes, sir,' he replied, 'that's all we know about, to date.'

The magistrates conferred briefly, the chairman addressed Cavendish once again.

'Mr. Cavendish, have you anything you wish to say in response to the charges which have been read out to you?'

'Load of rubbish,' Cavendish replied.

'Please show some respect for the court, or we will have you remanded in custody, pending medical evaluation.' The chairman of the bench told him, sternly. 'I will ask you once more. Have you anything to say in response to the charges, as read to you by Inspector Church? This is your last chance to respond to my question.'

'I didn't steal the rifle. It was lent to me by a friend.'

"Detective Inspector Church,' said the chairman. 'Can you explain the charge of, 'suspected theft', please?'

'Yes, sir,' Tony began. 'Mr. Cavendish is unable or unwilling to explain how the rifle came into his possession. He has insisted the rifle was lent to him by a friend, but has failed to provide us with any details. The absence of a valid firearms certificate is of great concern to us. The charge of theft of a firearm may be

dropped if Mr. Cavendish provides us with information which enables us to confirm the registered owner.'
The chairman consulted with his two colleagues. The lady magistrate on his left asked the DI.

'Inspector, if this young man happened to have a legal shotgun license, would the charge of unlawful possession be discounted?'
Tony Church addressed the bench as a whole and replied,

'Your worships, please understand that a rifle is a firearm, not a shotgun. There is a fundamental difference between the two. I will explain as briefly as I am able, what those differences are

A firearm has a rifled barrel, hence the nomenclature, 'rifle'. It has adjustable sights and professionally handled can be accurate up to half a mile. Even a small bore rifle can be lethal at distances up to a mile. That is why a firearms certificate will only be issued after stringent qualifying conditions are met by the applicant. Checks will be made to verify that the applicant does not have a criminal record. Character references of both the applicant and known associates will be checked, as will the security of the premises where the rifle will be kept.'
He paused and looked up at the chairman of the bench.

'Thank you Inspector Church, please continue,' he said.

'Thank you,' said the DI. 'A shotgun is a smooth bore sporting weapon, still lethal at very close range, but ineffective above a couple of hundred yards. A shotgun license may be obtained by a much simpler process. Character references will still be required by the magistrate who will countersign the application.'
The lady magistrate nodded her acceptance of the facts. She then asked,

'Inspector, are we to understand from your explanation, that it is therefore much more difficult to obtain a license for a rifle, than for a shotgun?'
The chairman of the bench conferred discretely with his female colleague.

354

'I'm sorry, I should have said certificate, not license,' she said to the DI. 'Thank you for your most concise explanation of the difference between the two firearms'

Malcolm Foster gripped his young charge's arm and whispered to him,

'Shut your mouth or you'll be held in contempt of court!'

'What was that, constable?' enquired the chairman.

'Nothing, sir,' the PC replied.

The DI successfully suppressed a giggle.

The chairman turned again to the DI.

'Thank you, Detective Inspector,' he said. Then addressing Cavendish, he asked,

'Would you care to explain yourself, Mr. Cavendish? Please tell us all, the name of this friend, who supposedly lent you a point two-two rifle.'

Cavendish shrugged but said nothing.

The chairman conferred with his two 'wingers' and then he said,

'Mr. Cavendish you have failed to respond to the charges which have been read to you and you have shown contempt for this court. You have refused the services of a solicitor and you have failed to answer the questions put to you. You will therefore be remanded in custody, pending medical reports. Do you understand what this means?'

Cavendish turned away from the bench as if to ignore the court.

'Remanded in police custody, pending reports,' said the chairman. 'Usual extensions apply. Take him away, please.'

PC Malcolm Foster smiled at the DI and re-attached the handcuffs. The clerk held the door open as they left and smiled at the PC as they passed him.

Back at the station, Cavendish was returned to a holding cell and offered a drink and a sandwich. He declined both, telling the custody officer to **** off and leave him alone!

DI Tony Church called Malcolm Foster to his office. DS Ian Stuart was already there.

'How did it go?' Ian asked.

'Bertram Mills', Tony said. 'I've asked Malcolm Foster to join us. He'll be here in a minute.'

There was a knock at the door,

'Come in Malcolm,' Tony called out.

'Thank you, sir,' the PC said as he entered. 'What a waste of time that was, wasn't it sir?'

Tony Church smiled,

'Ian just asked me, I just said, 'Bertram Mills'. It was a bit of a three ring circus. I think old George Cooper and Ed Sarkes felt like throttling their lady colleague and then clip young Cavendish's ear. What did Cavendish mumble after the honourable lady's remarks about my explanation?'

Malcolm laughed as he told Tony,

'She still hadn't grasped the difference, had she? Cavendish mumbled to me, 'is she effin' joking? Silly old bat!' I told him to shut up or he'd be held in contempt. Of course, old Sarkes heard me tell Cavendish to shut up and asked me what I'd said.'

'I thought it was something like that,' said the DI. 'She just couldn't get it right, could she? I was doing my best not to burst out laughing, if I'm honest, I was probably thinking the same as Cavendish!'

Ian laughed, 'what are we going to do with him now, Guv?' he asked. 'I think the 'wonderful weed' has probably addled his brain.'

'We'll have to get the doctor to take a look at him, he might respond better to him.' Tony said. 'Did he say anything noteworthy to you, Malcolm?'

'No sir, he just kept saying it was a load of rubbish. Why don't they just leave me alone?'

'What, so he can go round shooting things and battering people over the head?' Tony suggested. 'A perfectly reasonable way of looking at it, to him, I suppose. He's a danger to himself as much as to anyone else. The rifle he had was the same one which killed the woman whose skull we found, so we do need to

356

find out where it came from. The first step is to identify one or two of his friends, if he actually has any.'

'Perhaps old Doc. Bradley might be a good choice to chat with him,' Malcolm suggested. 'He's got a bit of psychiatric knowledge and he's a big enough bloke to keep Cavendish under control.'

'That's a good suggestion, Malcolm,' said the DI. 'We'll see if he's available. If anyone can get through to him Bradley will. Anyway, I just wanted to say, 'thanks' for keeping him under control. I was afraid he was going to begin another 'loony tunes rant' in the waiting room.'

'I think his mental state was alternating between Billy the Kid and Alice in Wonderland,' Malcolm Foster said. 'If that's all, sir, I'll get on with my reports. Do you want me to do anything else?'

'No thanks, Malcolm,' Tony replied. 'We'll see what else we can find out about him, if anything and then ask whether the doctor can get here today.'

PC Foster left the office and the two detectives continued with their work. Apart from Cavendish, they still had the two drivers awaiting crown court appearances and possibly another magistrates' court hearing to arrange for Bettis and Davies. The latter would also have to attend a Health and Safety board of enquiry and possibly an industrial tribunal.

CHAPTER 52.

Hilda arrived just after one. Hannah was still at her solicitor's, where she was arranging the legal separation order in advance of her divorce from Jeffery Davies.

'I had a letter from Jeffery's solicitor,' Hilda told them. 'The letter was most apologetic and said that Mr. Jeffery Davies had expressed remorse. The next sentence said that under the circumstances, he would not be pressing charges against Mr. Fielding, for assault! I gave the letter to Douglas and guess what he did?'

'Tore it up?' Elsie suggested.

'Better than that, Elsie,' Hilda replied. 'He read it to the court as a part of his statement. The magistrate glared at Jeffery and then said,

'How very arrogant, Mr. Davies, to attempt a half hearted apology only to immediately negate any vestige of sincerity, by expecting gratitude from your victim. You are a bully and have behaved like a common thug. Try to consider that Mr. Fielding's timely intervention probably saved you from committing an even more serious crime. I am minded to impose a custodial sentence, we will give it some thought.' He conferred with his colleagues and then asked, 'Have you anything else which you wish to add in your defense?'

Hilda went on to explain the rest of the court case.

'Jeffery has been ordered not to go within five hundred yards of my home. If he fails to comply he will face a prison sentence, so I don't think I'll have any more trouble with him.'

'That's good, Hilda,' Elsie responded. Hannah told us about the fine and costs. He's also got to do some community service, hasn't he?'

Hilda nodded and agreed,

'Isn't it strange, sometimes, the way that something good comes out of a bad experience?' Hilda said to them both. 'I've lived in that flat for about three years, but in all that time, I've probably only seen Douglas Fielding about a dozen times.'

'Is he the man who stopped Jeff Davies from attacking you?' Elsie asked.

Hilda blushed slightly as she replied,

'Yes, but it was only after we had completed our statements that we really had any sort of conversation. Before that it was just a polite, 'good morning' or 'how are you today?' He was very kind and considerate, when we were given the court times, he knocked on my door and asked me if I would like to go with him. It seemed the sensible thing to do, so I thanked him and said 'yes'. When I got back home from here on Tuesday evening, he heard me unlocking my door and called out to me. He said he expected I had had a busy and tiring day, and he asked if I would like to share a Chinese take-away meal with him. It sounded like a good idea, so I accepted his offer. I explained that I needed to have a quick freshen up and get my clothes put away, so he said,

'Yes, that's fine, Hilda, may I call you Hilda?'

I said yes, that would be fine, because that's my name. Doug asked me to tap on his door when I was ready. He has a lovely flat, slightly larger than mine. We chose the meal from their menu and Doug phoned it through. We had a drink and a good chat while we waited for the delivery. He had put plates to warm and we watched the news on the television whilst we enjoyed the meal.

I went back over to my flat at about half past eleven. It was one of the nicest evenings I've had since I've been in Lincoln.'

Archie and Elsie were smiling at her, Elsie remarked,

'He sounds a very nice man, Hilda. Is he older than you, or younger?'

Hilda suppressed a giggle as she told them,

'You won't believe this. Actually he's a whole month younger! Does that mean he could be my 'toy boy'? Ooh dear, what have I said?' She burst out laughing. 'Just wait 'til I tell Hannah.'

'You can tell her now,' Archie said. 'I think I just heard her car door bang.'

'That's started the ball rolling,' Hannah said as she came into the kitchen. 'Hello 'sis,' have you been here long? You look like the cat that got the cream, what's cooking?'

'She's found herself a 'toy boy' in Lincoln,' Elsie said with a smile.

'Oh, Hannah, you just wouldn't believe it,' Hilda began. 'Do you remember me telling you how my neighbour had dealt with Jeffery? Well, I hadn't realised what a lovely man I had as a neighbour. When I got back on Tuesday, he invited me to have a Chinese takeaway meal with him. I was a bit wary at first, I told him that I needed to unpack and freshen up. He said he understood and asked me to tap his door when I was ready and we could choose what we wanted from the menu. He phoned the order through and we had a drink and a chat while we waited for the meal to arrive. He asked me if we could go to the court together and I agreed. He took me in his car and then afterwards, we went for some lunch. I wanted to pay, because he had bought our Chinese meal, but he wouldn't let me. He said it was on Jeffery Davies. I took it that he meant it was paid for from our expenses, from the court case. He's asked me if we can go out for a proper meal one evening, when I'm back on my day duties. I said I would like that. He asked how you were. I'd told him a bit about you, he knows we're twins.'

360

'Wow!' Hannah said, 'so my sister has finally found herself a real live man! All I've done is spend an hour with a solicitor, trying to get shot of one!'

'What did the solicitor say, Hannah?' Hilda asked.

'I will get something called a 'Non Molestation Order', which means that he is not allowed to contact me in person, or by phone. He will need to write a letter each time he has anything to communicate with me. The solicitor advised me to wait until his father's will is read, before I reclaim my house. She is a very smart lady, Miss Jean Fullerton. She also made our separation official and stated the reason for the breakdown of the marriage as Jeffery's unreasonable behaviour. She said it would be a good idea to wait until I had regained possession of my house, before serving the divorce papers.'

'Did you get a restraining order, like the one I have in Lincoln? He's not allowed within five hundred yards of my flat. Hilda asked.

Hannah smiled at her sister,

'That would be a bit difficult at the moment, sis, wouldn't it?'

'I don't see why,' Hilda replied.

'But I do,' said Archie, grinning.

'Thanks, Archie,' Hannah said, 'just think about it, Hilda. I can't do that until I establish where I'll be living. If it's my house, I need to be there without him. I can't get an order restraining him from what is currently his home, can I? You're established at your permanent address in Lincoln, so it was straightforward for you.'

Hilda smiled,

'Sorry,' she said, 'Its a pity you can't get a 'containment' order, keeping him within five hundred yards of wherever he's living!'

Hannah grinned at Archie, and said,

'But he's living in my house, Hilda. The last thing I need is an order keeping him there! No, I'll do as Jean Fullerton advised and wait a week or so to see what Jason's will turns up. Jeffery might be moving into the farm house, which would solve the problem. I could then get a restraining order preventing him from coming back to my house. Has Archie told you about his bump on the head?'

'No, I'd only just got here when you came back. Let's have a look, Archie,' Hilda said as she went towards him.

'There's nothing much to see now, Hilda,' Archie told her. It was a bit sore for a while, but I got off light, compared to Mr. Bettis. He needed five stitches in his. All I got was a rub with a towel!'

Hilda examined Archie's head,

'What did you hit it on, Archie?' she asked.

Archie closed his eyes and shook his head.

'I don't know how to answer that,' he said. 'I suppose you could say that I hit it on a young hooligan who was holding a log, although even that's not quite correct.'

'You mean he hit you with a log? What sort of log?' Hilda asked.

'Might have been oak, it wasn't ash, but I didn't really take too much notice at the time.'

'I meant was it a long thin one or a short fat one!' said Hilda. Archie smiled at the two sisters,

'Well, if it was the same one I picked up from the ground outside the garage, it was a couple of feet long and about three inches in diameter. It was big enough to hurt, anyway, as he found out when I smacked his fingers with it.'

Elsie shrugged,

'That's Archie, I'm afraid. He can't just leave it to the police. He has to take action himself. I've told him to remember he's not a young man any more, but it makes no difference.'

Archie just sat and grinned, saying nothing.

'What did that Mr. Bettis want, Arch?' she asked him.

'Nothing much, Else,' he told her. 'He just wanted to thank me for helping him. He reckons we could have been gassed with

362

the exhaust from the car if I hadn't managed to shift it out of the way. I still think there was something fishy going on before I got there. Time will tell, I expect. Nothing stays secret for ever, does it?'

CHAPTER 53.

'What a week!' Tony Church said to his DS, Ian Stuart.

'It's not over 'til the fat lady sings,' Ian responded.

Their 'guest', Bernard Cavendish, had seemed to be a little more normal after his Thursday morning episode. Perhaps he was coming out of his drug induced brain fog.

'We'll try to interview him again later,' Tony said. Have we got the statements from Bettis and Archie Leggitt yet?'

'We've got the one from Bettis,' Ian told him, 'I think Bill Pickering is bringing Archie's in today or tomorrow.'

'We don't seem to be making much progress with JD's murder case.

The fingerprint on the bell push wasn't Cavendish's.'

'I didn't think it would be,' Ian said. 'He's not the type to use conventional methods to enter somebody's home. In fact I don't believe he's been inside the house at all. I'll bet it's not a local person, it'll be someone only known to Davies, maybe from outside the area.'

The DI nodded in agreement.

'I'll bet our first real lead will come from a pawnbroker or antique dealer and not necessarily one of our known fences. Let's hope our Worthing teams turn something up,' Tony suggested. 'We may need to expand our search for evidence to Brighton. There are a lot of devious characters with suitable retail outlets in Brighton. We've circulated the list of stolen items to our colleagues in the Brighton force. We can't spread ourselves too thinly or too far away.'

'My money's still on Worthing,' Ian ventured. 'The veneer of respectability can cover a multitude of nefarious operations. Our 'troops on the ground' have mentioned a casino. They had a problem there a few weeks back. One of the bar girls was caught giving drinks away to several young men. She was sacked, but I wouldn't mind guessing that there will be a repeat performance, sooner rather than later.'

'You think there's another bar girl under suspicion?' Tony asked.

'No, not exactly,' Ian began to explain his theory. 'What I meant was that there will probably be the same bunch of young 'chancers', trying to get a similar deal going with any new bar girls.'

'I think I'll ask Ken Foster and his sidekick to give it a once over.' Tony told Ian. 'I think a casino is probably one of the places where we might find the odd shady deal taking place. They are also a favourite haunt for professional criminals and drug dealers. Yes, I'll mention it to Ken, when he phones in.'

'It was Lesley who told me about the casino,' said Ian. 'She tells me that the secretary at the letting agency, a young lady named, 'Gloria', works in the bar there, a couple of evenings a week. Her boss, someone called 'Alec or Alex' is also the bar manager at the casino.'

'It might be worth Lesley befriending this young lady,' Tony suggested. 'She may provide some inside information about any 'iffy' looking customers. Maybe just pay a casual visit one evening when the young lady is on duty, but be careful not to ask too many questions. We don't want any of our troops to blow their cover by asking too many questions of people they've only just met.'

The telephone on Tony Church's desk buzzed, he picked it up and said, 'DI's office, Tony Church here.'

'I've got Shoreham 'nick' on the phone for you sir,' said the desk constable, PC Frank Burton.

'OK, I'll take the call, is that PC Burton?' Tony asked.

'Yes, sir' Frank replied, 'was there something else?'

'Who's your duty Sergeant today?' Tony asked.

'Mike Hodd, sir,' PC Burton replied. 'Did you want a word?'

'Not right now, thanks, tell him I'll catch him on my way out later,' Tony told him. 'You can hook me up to Shoreham now please Frank'

He heard the customary clicks and crackles and then a voice asked,

'Is that DI Church?'

'It most certainly is,' Tony replied, 'may I ask your name?'

'Yes, sir, Sergeant Cole,' said the voice. 'Duty Sergeant at the sub office, I've got one of your people here, DS Foster, can I put him on?'

'Yes, thank you Sergeant, please do,' Tony replied.

Ken Foster had waited while the DI was contacted.

'Ken, how's it going?' Tony asked, as the line cleared. 'What are you doing in Shoreham?'

'Hello Tony,' Ken Foster began. 'We're not actually in Shoreham. This is a sub office, staffed by HQ at Shoreham. It's at the Lancing end of Worthing and there has just been an explosion on a boat on the beach. It's almost opposite the golf course. In fact it was one of the golfers, who reported it. We heard the bang from right along the sea front and came to investigate. We were told to ****️ off, by the lads from the local force. We didn't want to break our cover, so we just watched from a safe distance. The fire brigade attended, but there were bits of boat all over the beach scattered around what was left of the hull. The cabin was destroyed and some quite big bits of decking could be seen in the surf and floating offshore.'

'Was the boat on the beach?' Tony asked.

'Yes, on the beach, they were working on the engine. It's what they call a 'day' boat. They use it to take fishing parties out in the channel.' Ken explained.

'Sounds to me it was a bloody good job they weren't out in the channel with half a dozen fishermen on board. That would have been carnage, Ken, wouldn't it?' Tony suggested. 'How is this anything to do with our enquiries though?'

'I'll get to that in a minute, let me just explain. The fire brigade reckoned it was a build up of gas in the bilge and a spark from the generator or one of the batteries, set it off. There are two casualties, one with third degree burns, he's gone to East Grinstead and another, a female, with cuts and bruises and a head wound. She's in a confused state, as you can imagine. She keeps on saying 'gas, I told him it was gas. I could smell it.' I overheard her telling the ambulance man what had happened, she said, 'He went to start the engine and there was a rumble, like thunder and then whole boat shook. There was an almighty 'BANG' and I was thrown up in the air.' Ken paused, when there was no response, he continued.

'I showed my warrant card to the medic who was with the ambulance and asked the injured lady if there was someone who should be notified, she said,

'Yes, but we don't know where he is. Our son is missing. We haven't seen him for almost three weeks. His name is, Bernard Cavendish, we think he's on drugs, so God knows where he's gone, or who he's with.'

I said I would do my best to help to find him for her and she thanked me. They put her in the ambulance and said she would be taken to the Sussex County, in Brighton. That's all I've got so far, but I thought I should let you know, Tony.'

Ken ended his brief report.

Tony blew out a breath between pursed lips.

'Thanks, Ken,' he said. 'Is your cover compromised as a result of this?'

'No, we're still good, Tony. I just remembered that your latest guest was also named, 'Cavendish', so I thought there was possibly a link. We'll go back to our original plan now.'
The DS continued,

'Lesley wants to tell me something, she's already buzzed Phil and he's told her I'll call her back. I'll update you if I get anything else. I'd better get going now.'

'Thanks, Ken,' said Tony. 'We're just going to try to interview him again. We'll feed him the information gradually, see where it takes us. Well done and good hunting!'
He put the phone back on its rest and relayed the information to Ian.

With the faintest of smiles, Ian remarked,

'It seems that 'gas' problems extend to the whole family. We'd better let our young guest know about the incident. If his mum and dad have been injured, he may decide to co-operate with us. We'll give it to him a bit at a time, just in case there's no connection, but it sounds pretty certain to me.'
The details were confirmed by the police and ambulance service a short while later. The two detectives felt that they were now ready to break the news to their young detainee. They were promised an update on his father's progress, later.
Young Cavendish was brought to the interview room, where Ian asked him if he would like something to drink.
The young man looked up and asked,

'What sort of drink? Yes, no, I mean, I don't know, you might have put something in it to make me talk.' He said, accusingly.

'Tea, coffee, milk or cola,' Ian informed him, ignoring his concerns about truth drugs!

'I'll have coffee then, white, two sugars....please.' The 'please' was added after a slight delay, almost as an afterthought. Ian smiled. This was the first intelligent answer Cavendish had provided since his arrest. Ian went to fetch the coffee, whilst

Tony sat with a silent and somewhat pensive, Bernard Cavendish. A couple of minutes later, Ian returned with three coffees, which he set down on the table.

'I think that one was yours,' he said to Cavendish, pointing at one of the plastic cups.

'What's this about?' Cavendish asked.

'We'd like to talk about your parents first,' Tony replied. Cavendish sat up, his eyes more alert than they had been since he was arrested.

'What about my parents? I don't live with them any more,' he said.

'They have a boat, don't they?' The DI continued. 'A fishing boat for taking anglers out for the day.'

'It's in the marina,' he volunteered, 'Brighton Marina.'

'I believe we may have some bad news for you, Bernard,' Tony said softly. This was the first time he had addressed him informally.
Cavendish appeared shocked, the colour drained from his face.

'Are they dead?' He asked anxiously.

'No, not dead, Bernard,' Tony told him as gently as he could. 'Your father has serious burns and has been taken to East Grinstead burns unit. Your mother has less serious injuries and is in the Royal County Hospital in Brighton.'

'What! How did it happen? They were fine, were they attacked? Has the house burned down?' Cavendish had his head in his hands. He began to reproach himself, his voice just a mumbled whisper. 'My fault again, I should have stayed with them. Who did it? Do the police know who set fire to the house?' Tony put a hand on Cavendish's shoulder as he explained.

'Listen, Bernard, it wasn't a house fire and we believe it was an accident. Their boat was on the beach at Lancing, we think it had some sort of generator trouble. Your father was trying to repair it when there was an explosion. The Fire investigator is still at the scene, but it seems there was an accumulation of gas in the bilge, where the inboard generator and batteries are sited.'

369

'You'll have to let me see my mother now,' Cavendish almost shouted. 'You can't keep me locked up, while my parents are both in hospital. Now you'll have to let me go. I want a solicitor, now……..Please.'

He finally remembered his manners, just in time, as far as Tony was concerned.

'Listen carefully, Bernard. We can't let you go, just like that,' he explained. 'I'll tell you what we can do, if you'll just be quiet while I explain.'

Cavendish nodded and the DI continued speaking to him.

'We can let your parents know where you are, but you cannot visit them at present. I can arrange for you to speak with your mother on the telephone. Before we go into that possibility, we need you to provide us with a few facts and truthful answers to our questions. In other words, if you help us, we will do our best to help you. Think about it Bernard, you're not stupid and you know it's the right thing to do. You can help yourself by co-operating or you can carry on being obstructive and accept the consequences.'

'How bad is my father?' He asked.

Tony explained that he really didn't have any of the finer details, only the basic information provided by the Shoreham police.

'I can telephone them again in an hour or so,' he said. 'They may have an update on your parent's condition and progress. It won't be any good trying yet, I only got this information within the last half an hour.'

Cavendish seemed different. Perhaps it was the shock of something happening to his parents, which had brought him back to some sort of reality. It may be that he now had something more important than his own situation to focus on. Something which he had suddenly realised, was more important to him than where he might get his next fix.

'Tell me what I need to do?' He asked, looking directly, first at Tony and then shifting his gaze to Ian. 'I know I've done it all wrong, but I haven't shot anyone. I just used the rifle for target practice, a bit of fun, that's all. It belongs to a friend of mine, like I told you. I shouldn't have hit that man with it, but I thought he was trying to steal the car or something else. I didn't know who he was. I was behind the house getting some logs to build a fire. I heard the car start up and came to see. He was a big man and he shouted at me, so I hit him.'

'You shot a fox on Monday, didn't you?' Ian said to him.

'But you're allowed to shoot foxes, aren't you?'

'Not with an unlicensed, borrowed firearm, on a public road, you're not,' Tony advised him. 'Let's say for instance that you had missed the fox and your bullet hit a pedestrian a mile further on. What then?'

'What do you mean, a mile away?' Cavendish queried. 'It wouldn't have travelled as far as that. Anyway, I didn't cause any danger to any people with it.'

'You put Mr. Bettis in hospital with the blunt end of it,' Tony reminded him, 'and what about the other man, the one you hit on the head with that log you had?'

'He shouldn't have been there either,' Cavendish said, defensively. 'I think he was just being nosey. He smashed my fingers anyway, so it's 'even stevens' now, isn't it?'

'You can try to over simplify this situation all you like, Bernard, but you are the only person who has broken the law. Just think, if you'd managed to gain entry to the farmhouse, you would now be a suspect in a murder enquiry.' Tony reasoned with him. 'Now let's offer another possible scenario, try to think about this. Suppose, let's just suppose that your mother or your father had been rendered unconscious by a thug brandishing a weapon. We won't say it's a rifle, but maybe a baseball bat or something. Someone else, a neighbour or maybe just a bystander, came to their assistance and also became a victim of the same assaillant. Where would your sympathies lie in that instance?' Cavendish appeared to be mulling it over.

'But that old man was a friend of the policeman, that's why he got away with assaulting me, wasn't it?

'That old man, as you rather unkindly refer to him, is a law abiding local citizen. He is an intelligent and courageous man, who has a sense of fair play which you seem anxious to deride. He would have been one of the first to have helped your mother or your father if they were attacked. He wouldn't have shrugged his shoulders and thought to himself, 'it's nothing to do with me, I'm not getting involved.' The prospect of becoming a casualty of his own selfless actions would not have deterred him. Believe me, Mr. Bernard Cavendish, when I tell you this.'

The DI leaned across the table, his face a few inches from the young man's.

'I have seen 'that old man', as you called him, Mr. Archie Leggitt, single handedly take on a younger man who was armed with a machine pistol. I witnessed him disarm the man and then keep him restrained until the police were able to handcuff him. There are policemen in this force, who would think twice before attempting to emulate his actions.'

Tony sat back in his chair. He studied Cavendish as he continued,

'I rather think that if your mother or father, were being attacked, you might welcome some interference by this particular, 'nosey old man', don't you think?'

Cavendish, his head bent down, sat looking at his hands which he rested on the table in front of him. He seemed to be reflecting on the DI's words as he spoke.

'Yes sir, I'm sure I would. I didn't mean to insult him, I'm sure he's a very good man. I'm sorry I hit him with that log and I'd like to apologise to him.'

'I believe you, Bernard. Now, are you willing to co-operate with us?' Tony asked.

'Yes, I'm sorry,' the young man said.

'Would you like to have a solicitor present whilst we conduct this interview?' Tony enquired of him.

'Do you think I should?' Cavendish asked.

'It is entirely your decision,' Tony advised him, 'but I think it may prove to be in your best interests. Did you have one in mind, or would you like us to provide one for you?'

Cavendish frowned,

'If you provide my solicitor, won't he be on your side, instead of mine?' he asked, puzzled.

Ian just smiled at him.

'It doesn't work like that, Mr. Cavendish. Whichever of us appoints your solicitor, he will work for you, not for the police. We just pay him! It's how our justice system works, so you have nothing to fear from whichever solicitor is representing you.'

Cavendish seemed pleased with this news,

'Thank you, Inspector,' he said. 'Yes, I'd like you to find a solicitor for me, please. My father would know who to appoint.'

CHAPTER 54.

Brian Pace carefully tipped the point two-five brass casing from Bill Pickering's envelope. Life for the forensics section had become exceedingly busy during the few days since JD had been shot. They still had more questions than answers, more loose ends than on a frayed woolly jumper!

The rifle which Bill Pickering had collected from the farm had three different sets of fingerprints on it. One set belonged to Cavendish. A thumbprint lifted from the front door jamb matched another set, but the third set was still unidentified. The test firing had proved conclusively that it was the same weapon which was used to kill the woman thirty years earlier. More recently, it had also killed the fox, which was found in Ridge Farm Lane on Monday evening.

The ammunition used to kill both the woman and the fox, did not match the half box of point two-two rounds, discovered in one of JD's kitchen cupboards. JD's fingerprints and DNA were on the suitcase of women's clothes, which had been left on the doorstep. There were also more fingerprints on the suitcase, which did not match any others on the database.

Brian was aware that he had initially failed to accurately measure the round which had killed JD. It was, in fact, not a point two-two, but a point two-five. He was mildly embarrassed, both for himself and for the officers who had searched the farm, that this detail had been overlooked by all, until noticed by Archie Leggitt!

'They say you're never too old to learn,' he said to himself as he began to examine the small brass casing.

There was a gentle tap on the glass door. Brian looked up to see the DI standing there.

'Come in, Guv,' he called out. 'I'll be with you in a few minutes. I'm just checking this latest find by our man in the field.'

'I suppose you mean, 'Mr. Archie Leggitt?' Tony enquired with eyebrows raised. 'Bill told me about it when he came in. He said he was told, 'not to move his bloody great feet,' or he would probably destroy some vital evidence.'

Brian laughed quietly,

'I can imagine him saying just that,' he said. 'Bill has a good friend in Mr. Leggitt and he's been more than useful to us over the past few years.'

'I've got to admit that, for an old boy, he's still as sharp as a pin,' Tony agreed. 'I once said to him that we could do with a few more young officers with his powers of observation.'

'From what Bill says, he's not afraid to get stuck in, when it comes to the physical end of the market either,' Brian confirmed.

Tony nodded,

'He made a mess of young Cavendish's fingers, that's for sure,' he said. 'He's a tough old boy, Brian. I wouldn't want to tangle with him and I think young Cavendish is having second thoughts on that front, as well.'

Brian closed an eye as he looked through the lens.

'There's half a decent thumbprint on this casing,' he said to Tony. 'Hold on a minute while I try to lift it.'

'Have you had any thoughts on this boat explosion?' Tony asked. 'I take it you've heard about it? It seems to have brought their son back to reality, from whatever dope induced fairyland he was living in before. The local CID are convinced it was an accident. They believe it was a spark from his generator, which ignited the butane gas which had built up in the bilges.'

'Could have been, I suppose,' Brian agreed. 'I always thought those day boats had outboard engines though. Where was the gas coming from?'

'Yes, most do have outboards, Brian,' said the DI. 'The spark wasn't from the engine. It was from a generator under the deck. They all use bottled gas, either propane or butane, for cooking and making tea and coffee. I just can't help wondering if it had been tampered with, you know, sabotaged by a rival or someone else with a grievance.'

Brian nodded. He was concentrating on the thumbprint, comparing it with those on the national database.

'All I was thinking was that it was a bloody good job it didn't blow up in the Marina,' he said. 'There would almost certainly have been more casualties, not to mention the damage to some of the other boats.'

Tony thought about the possible consequences.

'It could even have destroyed some of them,' he said.

'Destroyed some of what?' Brian asked.

'The other boats,.' Tony said.

Keeping a straight face, Brian answered,

'I said not to mention the other boats!'

Tony laughed,

'Alright, that's one to you! Are you having any luck with that print?'

'Got a match, but not from the database,' Brian said. 'The one on the bell push is by the same person. You know what that means?'

Tony smiled,

'Maybe we're getting somewhere at last,' he said. 'Whoever shot JD also rang the bell and handled the rifle we took from Cavendish. That means he's known to our young detainee.'

'Almost, but not quite conclusive, Tony,' Brian told him.

'What do you mean?'

'I mean it confirms that whoever pressed the door bell must have handled the rifle at some stage. The same person also loaded a weapon with that round, which probably killed Jason Davies. It doesn't prove that he fired it though, does it?

Brian looked up suddenly.

'Now we're cooking with gas,' he said, looking up. 'The same prints are on the kitchen door, cupboards and drawer handles.'

'I suppose that proves he was in the house,' Tony observed.

Brian nodded,

'You've heard of 'Bonus Print', haven't you?' he asked.

Tony nodded,

'You mean the photographic processing company? Yes.'

'Well this is an entirely different bonus print, Tony,' said the forensics officer. 'They also match the ones we collected from the lid of the kitchen bin, the handle of a broken knife and the backing from an elastoplast strip. He's even been thoughtful enough to leave us a blood sample, though it may be mixed with some from the deceased.'

Tony smiled,

'So as soon as we can identify him, we can charge him with murder.'

Brian nodded and continued,

'Incidentally, Doc. Gibb has said that JD's heart attack occurred at the same time he was shot, so he was either frightened to death or shot to death. Either way, it's a murder charge.'

Tony rubbed his chin,

'So now we have to find him and then prove that he fired the shot,' he said.

'There's just one other thing, which the 'Doc' told me,' Brian added. 'It was fired from a pistol, not a rifle. The bullet, as confirmed by Archie Leggitt's finding, was a point two-five, not a two-two. There was only a small amount of internal damage, which is indicative of a weapon with a lower muzzle velocity. He said that the same bullet fired from a long rifle would have pretty much turned the rest of his brain to mush.'

'So, we're looking for a person with a hand gun, not a rifle,' Tony observed. 'Now all we have to do is find him!'

'Yep, that's all, Tony,' Brian agreed, 'and he's not in here, so you'd better see if you can catch up with him somewhere else. We still have a bit to do here, filing the prints and other bits of material evidence. Try having another go at Cavendish, or if that still yields nothing, you could share this latest information with our two teams in Worthing. I think that's probably where you'll find our murderer and maybe his mentor.'

CHAPTER 55.

The 'Jempson twins' had gone to visit their father, to arrange the lunch at the Aftonia on Saturday. Archie had just returned from his walk with Jimbo. He called out to Elsie to let her know that he had returned.

'I'll put the kettle on, Else,' he said, 'do you want a cuppa?' Elsie came into the kitchen,

'No thanks, Arch,' she replied, 'but I really need to go into Pudborough to get another pair of shoes. You could do with a new shirt, we don't want to look like the 'poor relations' tomorrow, do we? Perhaps you'd better come with me.'

Now if there was one thing Archie really did not want to do, it was helping Elsie to choose a new pair of shoes!

'I don't mind coming with you, Else,' he told her, 'but I'm not following you round all the shoe shops. I know what it'll be, I've done it so many times before. We'll look at every pair of shoes that are your size, in every shoe shop in town. I'll stand there nodding approval each time you try a pair on, two hours later we go back to the first shop and you buy the pair you looked at first. All the way home you'll be asking me if I thought they were a good choice.'

'Are you coming with me or not?' she said in her stern voice.

'OK,' said Archie, 'I'll come with you, but while you choose your shoes, I'll have a look round in some of the other shops. I'll have my mobile phone with me, so you can call me when you've finished.'

'Well, you'd better go and tidy yourself up a bit then,' she said. 'You look like a cross between a tramp and a scarecrow!' Archie grinned,

'Tramp! Scarecrow! I'm wounded, Else. These are my new socks,' he said, pulling the leg of his trousers up to show her.' Elsie could do nothing but laugh,

'Go and change everything except your socks, then,' she said. An hour later they were in BHS looking at the shirts.

'This one'll do,' Archie said holding up a white shirt.

'It won't,' Elsie said. 'It's only a fifteen collar and it's a tailored fit.'

'What's it mean, 'tailored fit'?' he asked her.

'You need a seventeen collar, large plain shirt, Arch,' she told him. 'You haven't got a 'tailored' body or even a 'tailored' waist, so it won't fit you. It will be too tight and all the buttons will be straining against the button holes.'

Archie let Elsie pick his shirt, which was what she had wanted to do in the first place.

'Oh, look, they've got some ladies shoes over there,' Elsie exclaimed. 'Shall we go and have a look?'

Archie was in the check out queue, his new shirt under his arm. Selective deafness was an art form, with Archie. He paid for his shirt, dropped it into Elsie's bag and slipped quickly out into the street.

He stopped for awhile outside a second-hand shop to look at the assortment of items on display in their window. A selection of woodworking tools, some had been used to extinction, others were so ancient, that their original use could be the subject of a quiz question. Among them were some old agricultural bits and pieces. Archie saw a bale crook, a couple of hay knives and hanging on some mesh at the back of the display, a fine wooden hop scuppet. Its shaft and handle polished over many years of use, by the hands of the hop presser in the oast houses of Kent and Sussex.

'That would look nice on the wall of the milling floor,' he thought to himself. 'It could double up as a grain shovel and it would be an item of interest for the tourists.'

He ventured inside, to enquire the price of the item and maybe 'haggle' a bit, not for the actual sum, but more as a challenge. There was already a customer, or a potential customer, at the counter. He wore the uniform of a security officer at Gatwick Airport, the 'BAA' flashes on his shoulders, gave him a look of authority and respectability. Although strictly speaking, he had no such authority outside of his working environs. Archie hung back from the counter, to allow them to conduct their transaction in some privacy. The security man looked round at Archie briefly and then continued his discussion with the proprietor. Archie was listening, whilst appearing to be preoccupied with some other stock on display near to the door.

'I'd be taking a risk with it,' he heard the proprietor say.

'What risk?' the security man asked. 'Its solid silver, its hall marked, it belonged to my great grandmother. The scrap value would be more than you're offering and it's too good to scrap. A complete matching service like this would fetch more than a grand at auction.'

'You say it was your great grandma's, but have you got any provenance?'

'What do you want a bloody receipt from the shop where she bought it? It's about a hundred and fifty years old, man. It's lasted longer than the shop, and there's not a mark on it. It's in new condition, probably only been used a few times. Do you want it or not? I can't hang about all night waiting for you to make up your mind.'

'Can I help you, sir?' the proprietor called out to Archie, who pretended not to hear him at first.

'Good afternoon sir,' he called out again, 'can I help you?'

381

'Sorry,' said Archie, 'I was wonderin' how much you wanted for that old scuppet in the window?'

'What's a 'scuppet'? The proprietor asked. 'Point it out to me, so I know what you're talking about.

Archie walked over towards the counter, to be closer to the mesh where the scuppet was hanging. He looked at the items on the counter, which the security man was trying to sell.

'That's it, there,' he said pointing at the wooden tool.

'Oh, that old wooden shovel, what did you call it?'

'It's called a scuppet,' Archie told him.

'What's it for?'

'Ops!'

'What d'you mean, 'ops? What sort of, 'ops' are they?'

'Dried green 'ops,' Archie said, smiling. 'For the beer.'

Archie noticed the security man out of the corner of his eye. He was becoming impatient and was clearly having some difficulty keeping up with the monosyllabic conversation between Archie and the proprietor.

'Do you want to buy this lot or not?' he almost shouted at the shopkeeper.

'Excuse me a minute,' he said to Archie, as he went back to his counter.

'You didn't say how much,' Archie called over to him.

'Ten quid,' he said.

'Too much,' said Archie.

'Well how much will you give me for it?' He asked.

'Five quid,' Archie offered, 'take it or leave it!'

'I'll take it then,' the proprietor said.

Archie approached the counter and handed over four one pound coins and a handful of ten pence pieces. He dropped a couple of them and they fell into the silver jug on the tray, which the security man was trying to sell.

'Sorry,' Archie said, 'would you like me to get the scuppet down from where it's hangin'?'

The security man picked up the jug and tipped out the coins which Archie had dropped and handed them to the shopkeeper. He looked up to see Archie was about to begin untying the scuppet .

'No!' he almost shouted, 'you'll have the whole lot down, leave it please, I'll get it for you.'

Archie took it from him and looked it over, it was in fine condition.

'Can I have a receipt, please?' he asked politely.

'Right!' the security man shouted at Archie. 'I've had enough of you and your time wasting silly talk. Now clear off!'
The proprietor looked at Archie,

'I'm sorry, sir,' he said, picking up a triplicate notebook from a shelf behind him. He wrote the receipt with a biro and tore it from the book.

'Thank you sir,' he said as he handed it to Archie.
Archie checked that it had the details of the shop printed at the top of the page and then folded it and put it in his jacket pocket. He picked up the scuppet and opened the shop door to go.

'Thank you very much,' he said to the shopkeeper, smiling. 'It's been a pleasure doing business with you,' and he left. Outside the shop, he looked through the window again. Now that the scuppet ha been taken down, he had a clear view of the security man who was still at the counter. Archie took his phone from his pocket and checked to see whether Elsie had been trying to call him. She hadn't, yet! She was probably still trying on shoes. He dialled the number for Chichelster police station and asked to speak with either DI Church or DS Stuart.

'Who's calling, please?' the lady on the switchboard asked.

'Archie Leggitt,' he told her, 'and it's urgent. Just tell them who I am, they'll take the call.'

A minute later, he heard Ian Stuart's voice.

'Yes, Archie, what's the problem?'

'Hello Ian,' Archie replied, 'I think some of the stuff that was stolen from old 'Diddler's' is here in Pudborough. There's a bloke in the second hand shop I've just been in, trying to sell the proprietor a silver tea service on a galleried tray. I remember Bill saying something about a silver tea service being part of what was taken from the farm house.'

'Thanks, Archie, have you got the address of this shop now?' Archie pulled the receipt from his pocket and read the address from the tor of the page.

'Do you want the phone number as well, Ian?' He asked. Ian laughed,

'No thanks, Archie. I'll get on to the local force and ask them to deal with it urgently, but quietly, no sirens or blue lights. Can you see the shop from where you're standing?'

'I'm standing in the next doorway,' Archie told him.

'Can you keep an eye on things until they get there? Just in case he tries to slip away, I don't know if it'll be their CID or uniform, but I'll tell them you're keeping watch, so to hurry up!'

'Thanks Ian, you can tell them I'm the one outside, holding a big wooden shovel, if you like! I'll see you later,' Archie closed the call and waited in the next shop doorway. He could see if anyone came or went, in the reflection of the shop windows opposite.

His mobile beeped, he answered, it was Elsie.

'Can you meet me in the BHS cafeteria in about half an hour?' she asked. 'I've bumped into Joan, so we're going to look for shoes together.'

'You're kidding, Else,' he said. 'If you've met Joan it'll be at least an hour! I'll see you there at about four o'clock, OK?'

'Alright,' said Elsie, 'but no later, I want to get home before the girls get back. I've got some smoked haddock for our meal, I hope they like fish.'

'I don't think they're fussy,' Archie said. 'I'm sure it'll be fine. See you at four.'

He'd finished his call and was rolling himself a cigarette. He held the scuppet in the crook of his arm, as though it were a shotgun! He suddenly became aware of two men standing in front of him.

'Excuse me,' said one, 'are you Mr. Leggitt?'

'Yes,' Archie replied. 'Who wants to know?'

'Sorry,' he said, 'I'm DS Bingham and this is DC Cooke. We had a call from a DS Ian Stuart in Chichelster, I believe you know him. He thinks that some of the items stolen from Ridge Farm may be the subject of a transaction in this shop. Is that correct?'

'I can't positively identify the silverware, if that's what you mean,' Archie explained. 'I just remembered that a silver tea service, on a galleried tray were among the items listed as stolen from Ridge Farm, in Wigglesworth. It may be a bona fide sale, but the seller was becoming agitated when the proprietor was reluctant to buy the silver without some sort of provenance.'

'Thanks, Mr. Leggitt,' said DS Bingham. 'We'll go in gently and see what he has to say. He's a security officer at Gatwick, you say?'

'That's what his uniform says,' Archie confirmed. 'I think if I were trying to sell some dodgy gear, I'd be in mufti, not uniform. Perhaps he believes the uniform makes him appear more of an honest, upright citizen.'

The DC smiled and winked at Archie as they went into the shop. Archie stood in his doorway, holding his scuppet and smoking his cigarette as he watched the reflection in the shop window opposite. He was so engrossed in his observations that he was startled by a deep voice in his ear.

'Are you goin' to play that thing, or are you goin' to hit someone with it?' Bert Brooks asked him, a mischievous grin on his face.

'It's a scuppet,' Archie said, holding it up for inspection.

'I know what it is, Arch,' Bert said. 'Where did you find it?' Archie indicated with a nod of his head,

'I didn't find it, Bert, I bought it in that junk shop, next door,' he said. 'The police are in there now, there was a bloke trying to sell him some dodgy silverware.'

Bert went to the edge of the window, rubbed a hole in the dirt and peered in through the glass.

'It looks like the plain clothes police are arresting one of their colleagues in uniform,' he said to Archie. 'They've put handcuffs on him and the bigger one of the two is talking to the shopkeeper.'

'He's not a policeman,' Archie explained to Bert. 'He's one of them security guards at 'Gatport Airwick', he probably thinks the uniform makes him look trustworthy!'

'Doesn't seem to have worked, Arch, does it? Did he have any more?'

'Why? Did you want to buy some stolen silverware?' Archie asked his friend.

'Not silverware, you dope,' Bert answered, grinning, 'I meant scuppets.'

'Dunno,' Archie said. 'This one was in the window, so I went and asked how much. He wanted ten quid, but I got it for five.'

'Five quid?' Bert said, 'I'm goin' to ask him if he's got any more.' He went into the shop as the two detectives came out with the security man. One carried a large holdall, which presumably contained the silverware. Their suspect glanced at Archie as he passed him. Archie thought that he did not look a happy man. A couple of minutes later, Bert Brooks came out. He was carrying another scuppet. It was not in such good condition as Archie's and needed a bit of a repair and a good clean and polish.

'Twelve quid!' Bert told Archie in shocked tones. 'He wanted fifteen, but twelve was as low as he would go. He started telling me what they were used for. I s'pose you gave him that information?'

Archie laughed.

'I bet all the time he'd had 'em, he didn't know what they were. He probably thought they were just wooden shovels, I 'spect he just wanted to get rid of 'em. Once he found out from me what they were, he realised they had a value. As soon as you went in and asked if he had any more scuppets, he knew you would buy it, whatever it cost. What do you want it for, Bert?'

Bert smiled at Archie,

'I've got a job makin' a hop press to go in an old pub in Heathfield. It's a sort of educational talkin' point, I s'pose. I can probably charge the bloke twenty five or thirty quid for it. He'll put it on a wall display, along with a few other associated items. Don't worry, Arch, I'll get my money back and a bit more besides.'

Archie asked him,

'Did the shopkeeper say anything about the police going in and arresting that security bloke?'

'Yes, as a matter of fact, he did.' Bert told him. 'He said it was lucky for him that the sale was delayed and he hadn't bought the silverware. I told him that my friend had just bought a scuppet for only five pounds. I hoped he would say I could 'ave mine for the same price. All he said was that the delay you caused had saved him a lot more than five pounds. If he'd bought the silverware, instead of selling you the scuppet, he'd have been going to the police station as well!'

'I've got to go and meet Elsie, Bert,' Archie said. 'I might come up for a pint later, will you be there?'

'Yes, Arch, I shall be taking the vapours and a bit of light refreshment. Bring old Jimbo with you. I like that hairy little pal of yours.'

'See you later, mate,' Archie said as he wandered off to meet Elsie, with his scuppet held securely, blade downwards, at his side.

CHAPTER 56.

DI Tony Church studied the report from the fire investigation officer at Lancing. His findings had all but confirmed his initial thoughts that the explosion had been due to a large volume of leaked butane gas. Butane gas is heavier than air and in a vessel, it settles at the lowest point. It was known to have been the cause of several marine accidents and explosions, particularly where inboard engines were housed below the decks. There were however, some other factors involved in this particular incident. The cylinder of butane had been tampered with and the left handed thread on the pressure reducing diaphragm was damaged when it was attached to the cylinder valve.

A comprehensive search of the remains of the vessel had revealed several items in the rope locker. This was situated in the bow of the vessel which was about the only part of the hull which was relatively undamaged. Among these was a Verey pistol with flares and a carton of point two-five ammunition. These items were now on Tony's desk, awaiting forensic inspection by Brian Pace.

Ian Stuart knocked and entered,

'You asked to see me, Guv?' he said. 'I'm guessing it's about the silverware which Archie Leggitt spotted in the antique shop in Pudborough.'

'Yes, Ian, was the seller arrested?' Tony asked.

Ian grinned as he replied,

'To the victor, the spoils,' he said.

'What?' asked Tony with eyebrows raised.

'That was his name, 'Victor' and he was trying to sell 'the spoils' to that shopkeeper.'

'So they were identified as stolen from the Davies' house?' Tony asked.

'It took us a while to establish that fact,' Ian explained. 'He kept insisting that they were handed down through the family. He told us they had belonged to his great grandmother. Old 'JD' isn't around any more to identify the silverware, but when we checked, the inside of the jug and sugar basin, we found an excellent set of Cathy Simons' fingerprints. I bet she's glad she doesn't have to polish that lot any more. Cranham's prints were all over the outside of the jug, courtesy of our man Archie Leggitt's deliberate accident. He dropped a couple of his coins into it, and watched the seller pick it up to tip them out again.'

'No further questions, m'lud!' Tony responded with a smile. 'Who is he anyway? I don't suppose he's helped his job prospects by getting caught in uniform.'

'His name's Victor Cranham,' Ian read from the charge sheet. 'But it gets better as we go along, our Pudborough colleagues got lucky. They searched him before they brought him here. He had a gold watch in his pocket. It's inscribed, 'Gilbert Arnot Davies'. Even our Pudborough friends thought that was a strange name for a great grandmother! They've sent the evidence and the suspect to us. He's having a rest in the custody suite, so we'll have a chat with him presently.'

'I told you, Ian, they're smarter than they look in that part of Sussex. Shall we have a chat with him now, or see if our friend,

Mr. Cavendish is ready? His father's solicitor is with him now in room one.'

The DI looked enquiringly at Ian, who was staring at the Verey pistol on the desk.

'These were found on his father's boat,' he pointed at the box of ammunition on his desk. 'It's point two-five, but not the same make as his son had in the rifle.'

Ian looked at the box of ammunition. He turned it so that the percussion caps were visible and read, 'Herter 0.25'

'I traced the serial number on the rifle,' he told Tony. 'It was new in 1961 and was originally registered to a Charles Bowyer, with a Worthing address. He died back in 1984, but there's no record of his rifles before that date. The rifle he owned at the time of his death, a later model, is still held by the club He was a member of the Shoreham small bore rifle club. The club is still in existence but the membership secretary could not give me any more information. Apparently Mr. Andrew Bowyer was one of their best shots and helped to win several inter-club competitions. He died in a ski-ing accident in Canada in 1992. His wife, Delia, was several years his junior, they had one daughter, Sandra. The club secretary said she would now be in her mid to late twenties. He remembered her wedding to a local man a couple of years ago. He thought Delia had married again, but didn't know her married name.'

Tony frowned,

'So we hit a brick wall with that one, did we?' he asked.

Ian nodded,

'There's just one more detail,' he said. 'When I asked about the serial number of the rifle, he told me that they don't record serial numbers any longer. Bowyer changed his rifle every two or three years, always going for the best and the latest target model. He said that the only records of serial numbers nowadays would be on the purchase receipt and the sales ledger at the gun shop. The serial numbers of second hand rifles were not reliably recorded at all. Where the rifle we've got here now, ended up is anybody's guess and there's no way of knowing the date when he first changed it.'

The DI nodded, thought for a moment and then said,

'Let's have another crack at the Cavendish lad first. We can leave the other man to sweat for a while. He's probably got a lot on his mind. We'll give him time to think it over, before we go in.'

They went through to the interview room, where a custody PC waited in the corridor outside. It was 'Mercer of the Met', the tongue in cheek nickname bestowed on the PC by his colleagues.

'He's still got his solicitor with him, sir,' he said as the two detectives approached. 'They probably don't want to be disturbed.'

Ian smiled at him,

'You're probably right there, PC Mercer, but life's full of these little disappointments, isn't it?' Ian knocked loudly at the door and went in without waiting for an answer.

'Thank you, constable,' said Tony as he passed him. You can go back to the desk now. We'll call you when we're done.'

Mercer said, 'y yes sir, erm, thank you sir and shuffled off towards the front desk, where Sergeant Dean was waiting.

'Good afternoon, gentlemen,' Tony greeted them as he entered. 'I'm Detective Inspector Church and this is my sergeant, DS Stuart.' He held a hand out towards Cavendish's solicitor.

'Inspector,' said the solicitor, 'Julian Ford, of Anderton, Grimm and Partners, Worthing.' He shook hands with both detectives.

'I'd like to review the situation with your client, if you're ready,' Tony told him. 'Have you any objection to us re-starting the interview?'

'No, Inspector,' Ford replied, 'I think we're ready now. I have one question before we start the interview proper. Could you arrange for my client to be transferred to Worthing police, for future interviews and court appearances?'

391

'Absolutely not, I'm afraid,' Tony told him. 'Mr. Ford, you know as well as I do that all enquiries and any charges made, have to be in the area where the offences were committed. That is not just for our convenience, it is a matter of gathering evidence and taking statements from witnesses. It would be totally impractical to transport local witnesses to Worthing. More than that, the police in Worthing will not be familiar with the geography of this area, so would not necessarily ask the right questions. We must arrive at the truth and be able to accurately present the facts of the case to a judge and jury. Once the charges have been answered in a court, then your client may be moved closer to home, he may even be allowed bail, but that would depend largely on the outcome of his court appearance. Do you both understand?'

'I had already assumed that, Inspector,' Ford replied. 'I explained the situation to Mr. Cavendish, but you have clarified it admirably. I think he will now accept the answers which I gave him. Now, I suspect that you will want to set up your recorder for the interview. Before we begin, I wonder if my client and I might ask you for a drink?'

Ian stepped forward.

'Yes, certainly, Mr. Ford,' he said. 'Would you prefer tea or coffee, or maybe a cold drink? It's from the machine, I'm afraid but the quality is reasonable.'

They both asked for coffee, Ford's with no sugar. Cavendish's with two sugars.

'Shall I get us a cup at the same time, Guv?' he asked Tony. Tony nodded,

'Yes please, I'll have this set up by the time you return.' He took the cellophane wrapping from two new cassette tapes and wrote the time and date on each. He showed them to Ford who nodded his approval. They waited a few minutes for Ian to return with their drinks. Tony inserted the tapes into the machine and pressed the key to begin the recording. He stated the time and date and listed those present. He began the interview by asking,

'Mr. Cavendish, are you feeling better? I understand that you were somewhat confused and unwell the last time we spoke.'

'Yes thank you, Inspector, much better than I was. My hand is not so painful today. Have you any news of my Father's progress?'

'Yes, as a matter of fact, I have,' the DI told him. 'He's making good progress, but still in some pain from his burns. He has agreed to an interview by our Worthing colleagues tomorrow, so we may know more after that.
I'd like to begin by asking you to tell us how you got here and where you have been living in this area.'

'Trip gave me a lift from Worthing and I've been staying with him.'

'Do you know his proper name?'

'Terry Piper, his dad's got one of the fishing lodges at the old quarry.'

'So you've been staying with him at a fishing lodge?'

'Yes.'

'Did he loan you the rifle?'

'No.'

'Where did you obtain the rifle you were using?'

'I borrowed it from an acquaintance.'

'Will you please tell us the name of this acquaintance?'

'I don't know his proper name, he's called, 'Gas' that's all I know him by.

'Do you know how old he is or where he lives?'

'I think he's about twenty six or seven, I don't know where he lives, but I see him at the Wharf or the beach hut.'

'Do you mean he works in Shoreham docks?'

'No, he doesn't work anywhere. Oh, I see, no, not the dock wharf. It's the name of a pub along the beach road.'

'Tell me, Mr. Cavendish, why did he loan you the rifle? Did you tell him what you wanted it for? How much did he charge you for the loan of it, or what service did you have to provide as a payment in kind?'

'I lent him something in return. That's why I need to get his rifle back to him, so I can keep to the agreement. He can be a nasty bit of work if you cross him, the others will tell you that.'

'What others?'

'The others in our group, we go about together most of the time.

'Can you give me any names? I'm trying to help you, Mr. Cavendish. You are in a great deal of trouble, so please try to help yourself. Your friends are not here to help you.'

'I only know most of them by their nicknames. One or two I know their surnames, but that's all.'

'Do you have a nickname, Mr. Cavendish?'

'Yes, Inspector, I believe they call me, 'Boffin'. One of the others is Frank Ritsen, he's called, 'Fritz'. There is only one other whose name I know and that's 'Oxo', his surname is Bullock.'

Tony smiled and asked,

'Why do they call you, 'Boffin'?'

'It's because of my initials, BSC. 'Batchelor of Science', but I'm not as clever as that!'

His solicitor even managed a smile at this. He told him,

'I don't think we need any further proof of that, Mr. Cavendish. I'm sure the detectives will be happy to take your word for it.'

'Sorry,' said Cavendish, sheepishly.

The DI nodded to Cavendish and then asked him,

'Perhaps you could help us by giving the nicknames of the others in your group. We may be able to guess some of them.'

'Have you got a pencil and a sheet of paper?' Cavendish asked. 'I think if I write down the ones I remember, it might save me from missing anyone out.'

Ian provided the pencil and Julian Ford tore a sheet from his legal pad. They waited while the young man wrote several names on the sheet. When he had finished, he turned it around so that Tony Church could read it for himself.

'Thank you, Boffin,' he said, smiling. 'Now how would you propose to return his rifle to him?'
Cavendish's face brightened,

'Will you let me have it back? I can give it to him tonight, in the Wharf.' He asked.

'We could arrange for that to happen,' said Tony, 'but not without our supervision. We would need to ask your friend, 'Gas' a few questions. We'd also like to find out what you lent him, in exchange for the rifle. Are you happy to go through with this plan?'
The colour drained from Cavendish's face.

'No, no,' he said, in some anxiety. 'I could get killed if I did that. It would be suicide.'

'Tell me, please, Mr. Cavendish, does your father own a small bore pistol?'

'Yes, I believe he does,' He replied. 'What's that got to do with anything?'
Tony looked at his notepad, as though he was checking some details. In reality, he was looking at the visiting times for the Hospital. He looked up, straight into the eyes of Cavendish and said,

'I think it's time you stopped treating me like an idiot, don't you? Will you tell me the truth, or would you like me to explain it to your solicitor for you? I'd like an answer now. Please.'
Cavendish stammered,

'I'm sorry, yes, yes, I'm sorry. I'll tell you. Sorry Mr. Ford.'
He looked at the solicitor his parents had provided for him.
Julian Ford smiled at him,

'I think it would be in your best interests to minimise the amount of trouble you're in, don't you, Bernard?' He said.
'I rather think you will be treated more kindly if you co-operate with the police. It's not as though you've actually killed anybody, yet! You've certainly done enough to invite hostility from a couple of the local citizens and you were caught in possession of

an unlicensed firearm. Nothing I can say will mitigate these circumstances.'

Tony Church nodded his agreement with Ford.

'So, what's it going to be?' he asked Cavendish again. 'Our officers will make sure you don't come to any harm in the process of returning the rifle. You won't even be sure whether they are police officers, but they will know who you are.'

'Yes,' said Cavendish, 'I don't really have much choice, do I?'

'OK we'll set it up,' said Tony. 'We'll liaise with you, Mr. Ford and keep you in the loop. Mr. Cavendish will be detained following the transaction, along with anyone else involved, or anyone who decides to become involved.'

He turned to Cavendish again, saying,

'Your mother was very concerned for you, Bernard. I think you owe your parents an apology for the way you have behaved, but that is up to you and your conscience. We found the ammunition for the pistol you stole from your father's desk. It is the same size as the bullet which killed Mr. Jason Davies of Ridge Farm last week. Perhaps you should think about that whilst you wait. It might just wake you up enough to think about choosing a new set of friends.'

'Thank you, inspector Church,' Ford said to Tony. 'I think I'd like to take time for a chat with my client, if you've no objection.'

'That's fine,' the DI said. 'There will be an officer outside the door of this room. Will half an hour be enough time for you?'

'Yes, thank you,' Ford replied. 'That should be plenty, I'll let your officer know when we're finished and he can take my client back to the holding cell. Thank you for your courtesy.' He stood and shook hands with both Ian and Tony, as they left the room.

'This could be a bit tricky to organise,' Tony said to Ian, on their way back to the office. 'We can't have young Cavendish wandering into a pub, carrying a rifle! We'd get our knuckles well and truly rapped if we allowed that.'

Ian smiled,

'Like, 'High Noon at the Wharf pub', no it doesn't have the same ring to it as 'The OK Corral', does it?'

CHAPTER 57.

'The 'Holidaymakers' in their Worthing flat, had received an informal briefing from the DI regarding the interview with Cavendish. He had recommended that some enquiries begin in the Worthing and Brighton areas. As a result, Ken Foster and Phil Travis would carry out a 'recce' of the Wharf, pub. They would dress in workmen's clothes and stay for a while, listening out for any 'nicknames' on the list Tony Church had provided.
Lesley Stevens and Alan Bell would visit the casino. Lesley had discovered that Gorse occasionally used it both for the entertainment and also as a meeting place. They would observe the clientele and discreetly photograph any who appeared to be furtive or flamboyant.
Tony had advised them that some of the stolen property from JD's had turned up at a shop in Pudborough. He said that they should still keep an ear to the ground for any other pieces which may manifest themselves in the Worthing and Brighton areas.

'I think perhaps we'll have a quick word with Mr. Cranham,' Tony said.

'I think he's had time to cool off a bit,' Ian agreed. 'He hasn't asked for a solicitor, but I dare say he'll want one as soon as we begin the interview.'

Tony called the custody officer and asked him to bring Cranham to room two.

'Make sure you take him to room two,' he repeated. 'Room one is still occupied. Oh, and I suppose we'd better ask if he wants a cup of tea or coffee.'

The telephone on his desk buzzed. Tony answered it.

'DI's office, yes, thanks Mike, put him through please.'

DS Ken Foster spoke in hushed tones,

'I'll just give you a quick update, Guv. We've been and had a look at this pub, The Wharf. It's a proper dive, I can tell you. We're not really looking forward to our casual visit. There are a few scruffy individuals hanging about outside, possibly dealing drugs or planning something nefarious. We didn't go in, because we were not suitably dressed, just cruised slowly by. There were a few workmen who seemed to use the place as their local at lunchtime and early evening. They looked as though they were working on the sea defenses, there's a lot of shingle being moved in bloody great trucks with balloon tyres. There are ready-mix lorries all over the place and the beach is cluttered with shuttering ply and rusty steel rods. There are several beach huts just over the road from the pub. Some well maintained but a few are in various stages of disrepair. There's a car park at the end of the line of beach huts, that's where we are now. We've decided to give it a try this evening, but we'll park the car closer to the town and walk along the beach road. It's about half a mile, but if we park near to this pub, we'll probably find that the wheels have been pinched when we come out, it's that sort of area.'

Tony was chuckling to himself,

'Thanks, Ken,' he said, 'that was a fairly concise and mildly amusing update. Well done, so far, try to keep out of trouble tonight, just observe and record what you can. Have you seen Lesley since her visit to the office of the letting agency?'

'Yes,' Ken said, 'we saw her at tea time. They're going to visit the casino tonight. Lesley told us the young lady at the agency, her name's, 'Gloria', I think, works there on a Friday and Saturday evening. That's why Lesley and Alan decided to go tonight, hopefully to avoid bumping into her before they could 'suss' out the place. Anyhow, I think that's all for now, we'll get back to you tomorrow, Guv, to give you the latest.'

'Thanks, Ken,' Tony said. 'We're just going to have a chat with our 'stolen silverware salesman'. He's a security risk, sorry I meant security officer, at Gatwick Airport. We'll talk again tomorrow. Good luck tonight, give our regards to Lesley and Alan and be careful, that means all of you. We can't afford to cock this one up, we need to nail the sods and keep 'em nailed.' He put the phone back on the rest and turned to Ian,

'They're all fired up and ready to roll,' he told him. 'Let's see what we can extract from Mr. Cranham, to try to force the pace from this end.'

They collected the file and custody report from Mike Hodd at the desk, on their way to room two. PC Mercer was standing outside the door.

'Mr. Ford's gone, sir and Mr. Cavendish is back in his cell. He asked if he could have a word with you when you've got five minutes.' Mercer waited for a response from the DI.

'Yes, thank you Mercer, I'll see what I can do.' Tony said. Please go back to the desk with sergeant Hodd for now. I'll call you when we are finished.

'Thank you, sir,' said Mercer and walked away towards the front office.

The two detectives went into the room. Cranham was seated at the table, his head bowed.

'Good afternoon Mr. Cranham,' Tony said as they entered. I'm Detective Inspector Church and this is Detective Sergeant Stuart. We' like you to tell us what you know, but first we must formalise this interview.'

Ian Stuart set up the tapes and when they were ready Tony began.

'Please give your full name and address and your date of birth.'

Cranham gave his details and his date of birth as, 12th. May 1964. Tony thanked him and then spoke the usual details of the date and those present at the interview. He produced two photographs, which he laid on the table so that Cranham could see them clearly and then asked him,

'Mr. Cranham, do you recognise the items in these two photographs?'

'Yes,' he said, 'they were my wife's great grandmother's.'

'Why were you trying to sell them?'

Cranham looked up and said,

'My wife needs the money for Christmas.'

'Perhaps we should bring your wife here, to talk to us,' the DI suggested. 'She can probably tell us her great grandmother's full name and how she came to possess these items. Are there any other items that she wants to sell?' Tony glanced at the list of items taken from JD's home. 'From her great grandmother, I mean, will she be at home now? Perhaps you'd like to give us her address and phone number? Get this cleared up quickly and you could be on your way home'

The DI raised an eyebrow as he asked these questions.

Cranham looked about him, he was obviously uneasy about the questions he was being asked.

'I don't really want to involve her,' he said emphatically.

'But if what you say is true, it would seem that she wanted to involve you, Mr. Cranham,' Tony said. 'Otherwise it would have been your wife who was in the shop, trying to sell the stolen property.'

'No, you don't understand, it's not like that,' Cranham protested.

'It's exactly like that, Mr. Cranham,' said the DI. 'You are at present a suspect in a robbery. Unfortunately, the homeowner was found shot dead the morning after these items were taken. We are talking about somebody facing a murder charge. Now stop this charade and tell me how you acquired the silver tea service and the inscribed gold watch? Don't mention your wife's great grandmother or her inheritance. What is your wife's maiden name, Mr. Cranham?'

Victor Cranham was not quite as bright as the weather and today it was cold and raining.

'A murder charge!' He gasped. 'I might be a bit stupid, but I haven't killed anybody, not ever. What's my mother in law's maiden name got to do with it anyway?'

The DI shook his head as he replied,

'I don't suppose your mother in law has any legitimate connection with the items. I asked you to tell me your wife's maiden name, not your mother in law's. There may be no link to the previous owner of the property from either of them, but just for the record, we will check it out. Now, please tell me, what was your wife's maiden name, Mr. Cranham?'

'Bowyer,' he replied, abruptly.

'And her mother's maiden name?' Tony asked, equally bluntly.

'Bowyer, I s'pose,' Cranham replied, as though the answer was obvious.

'So she wasn't married?' Tony asked.

'Course she was,' said Cranham.

'So, what was her name before she married?' Tony tried another tack.

'Oh, I see what you mean,' Cranham replied, 'I don't know, you'd need to ask her.'

'Right,' said the DI, 'so now please tell me your wife's home telephone number, so that I can ask her to come and chat with us.'

'No,' Cranham said emphatically. 'I don't want her involved, I already told you. What's her mother's maiden name got to do with you, anyhow?'

The DI was beginning to tire of this stupidity. He turned to Ian and said,

'DS Stuart, would you mind?'

'No, inspector, I'll get right onto it. We'll have a couple of female officers bring her over.' Ian said.

He looked at Cranham's face as he was speaking. It had gone a very pale colour and his hands were shaking.

'Wait!' He called out to Ian as he was about to leave. 'Let me tell her, I'm allowed one phone call, aren't I?'

'Not for the purpose of warning someone that we are coming to arrest them, you're not.' Tony told him as Ian Stuart left the room. 'That constitutes the offence of obstructing the police in the execution of their duty. I'm afraid you'll be spending the night with us, Mr. Cranham, with or without your phone call. We really could manage without the pleasure of your company, but your reluctance to co-operate in this enquiry, leaves us with no other option.'

'I'll tell you the truth as soon as I've had a quick chat with my wife,' Cranham pleaded.

'Mr. Cranham,' said the DI. 'You don't seem to understand your situation. This surprises me, since by your uniform you are engaged in security services at Gatwick. Probably not for very much longer I suspect, once the news of your silverware sales technique gets out. However, let me explain something to you. You may appoint a solicitor, or we will provide one, at your request, but we don't do 'family group interviews' here. You and your wife will be interviewed separately and the answers you each give will be compared. Any discrepancies between the two accounts will be investigated until we are satisfied that we have the truth. That's the way it happens, always has, always will.'

The DI stood and crossed to the door, opened it and stood in the corridor. He held the door open and called out to the front desk.

'Constable Mercer, would you please escort Mr. Cranham back to his cell for an hour or two? Let me know when his wife is brought in please. Thank you.'

He stepped aside to allow Mercer to pass him and enter the room. 'I'll be in my office, please ask DS Stuart to come back when he has finished his telephone call.'

Tony was thinking of a way to expose the man who had lent Cavendish a rifle. It would necessitate opening some form of communication with the current owner, but any strangers who were watching Cavendish, would be regarded by the 'gang' as suspicious. This could result in losing Cavendish altogether, or risking a confrontation with their prisoner.

Ian Stuart returned to the office.

'No joy with Mrs. Cranham, she's not answering her phone and I would guess she's not there. I'll try to phone again later, I've left a message on the answering machine. We don't really need another guest tonight, do we? It might be a better idea to pick her up tomorrow.'

Tony agreed, saying,

'She'll probably phone us if she's worried about him. You left her a message, so we can't do any more to help if she's out.' He sat at his desk and indicated to Ian that he should take a seat.

'Cavendish,' he said. 'What are your thoughts Ian? How do we get this rifle business sorted? We can't have young Cavendish waltzing into the pub carrying a rifle. We need a plan which will work.'

They discussed a few possibilities and decided that the best and safest method, would be for Cavendish to contact this, 'Gas' character and tell him that the rifle was safe, but hidden. They would let him choose the hiding place among the dilapidated beach huts, whilst keeping him under discreet observation. On entering the pub, Cavendish would first check to see if his friend, 'Gas' was there. If he wasn't, he would leave a message telling him to phone a mobile number, when he would be told where his rifle was hidden. Once Cavendish had left his chosen hiding place, the weapon would be substituted for a dummy rifle of approximately the same weight. The mobile phone provided to Cavendish, would carry a small radio microphone, transmitting to a dedicated radio frequency. By this method, all calls would be monitored by detectives on the ground. Cavendish would believe that he was providing genuine information to his friend, which provided an invisible element of additional credibility. As an additional safety measure, the firing pin would be removed from the rifle, by the police armory. The location would be watched and a reception committee of officers would be concealed nearby.

'We'll need to convince Cavendish that the rifle will be left there,' Tony said. 'Otherwise he may be tempted to warn his friends that it's a trap.'

'I was thinking along those lines myself,' Ian suggested. 'We need to think this through thoroughly, before we mention any of it to Cavendish. We'll probably need to have a chat with his solicitor, as well.'

The telephone on Tony's desk buzzed.

'DI's office,' he answered. 'They what?' he said. He raised his eyebrows at Ian, but carried on listening. When he had finished, he replaced the phone in its cradle and said to Ian,

'That was Mike Hodd, on the desk. Worthing are saying it's our investigation, so it's not their problem. The message was to the effect that we'll have to deal with it from here. I think they're a bit 'miffed' by our CID working their patch. I don't know if that's come from the top, or somebody lower down who feels that we've trodden on their toes. Their duty Sergeant told Mike that Cranham was a good chap. He thinks that we've got the wrong man, and said that he would personally vouch for his honesty!'

'In which case,' said Ian, 'we'd better play our cards close to our chest on this job. Don't share too much information with our Worthing colleagues, until we've wrapped it up. It rather looks to me as though we may have a security problem. Either that, or a rather too trusting Sergeant with the wrong sort of friends.'
Tony nodded in agreement,

'Beware of leaks,' he said. 'Better warn our 'holidaymakers' as soon as we can. I'll try Ken Foster's mobile first, he can let the others know. I was a bit 'miffed' by something Bernice Tenham said. I didn't attach too much importance to it at the time, but do you remember? She said something about being glad she had brought the information to us, instead of the Worthing police.'

'I remember that, it's a bit worrying when the good citizens don't trust their local force. But first, let's have a word with young Cavendish,' Ian suggested. 'You never know, he may even come up with a plan of his own, which is more suitable than ours.'

Tony brightened,

'I think you may be right Ian, he'll have a better knowledge of how to deal with his 'cronies' than we would. We'll make it an 'informal' chat, completely off the record, no tape and no notes.'

CHAPTER 58.

The 'behind the scenes' brigade had been busy this week. Working with all resources available to them, they had managed the impossible, yet again. The late, Robert Bourner, whose skeletal remains had been found on Monday, now had a sister to bury him! They had located her through the electoral registers and, as promised, had put her in touch with his former friend, Peter Dennison. Although saddened to discover that her long lost brother was now dead, she had drawn some comfort from her meeting with Peter Dennison. Peter had kept his word to the detectives and would supply the burial casket free of charge.

The skull and a few other remains identified as the late, Mary Davies, nee Eldridge would also be laid to rest on the following Wednesday. Her husband's body could not be released for burial until the police and coroner's investigations were complete.

At the same time on Friday, that their son, Bernard was being interviewed at Chichelster, his parents were having a quiet chat with PC's Carol Hickson and Brian Taylor, at Mr. Cavendish's bedside in the East Grinstead Hospital. He had improved sufficiently to help them with their enquiries and his wife was anxious to get her son home again. The introductions over, Carol Hickson began to ask Mr. Cavendish about their son, Bernard.

'Mr. Cavendish,' she said, 'do you possess a point two-five hand gun?'

'Yes,' he answered. 'A Beretta 'Bobcat', I have a valid firearms certificate for it, I belong to the small bore shooting club in Brighton.'

'Where is the gun kept?' she asked him next.

He looked at his wife as he replied,

'I normally keep it in a locked steel safe at our home, but it has been missing since our son decided to leave home without telling us. I know now that I should have reported it, but I had hoped it would be returned in a short while. I didn't want to get my son into any more trouble. There was no ammunition with it. I keep that separately in a locked cabinet at home. Since the gun was taken, I have kept the ammunition on the boat, in a locker in the bow.'

Carol nodded her acceptance,

'I appreciate your honesty, Mr. Cavendish. I can tell you now that our officers found the ammunition in the course of their investigation to try to determine the cause of the fire. You will need to file a report about your missing firearm. I can't rule out the possibility of charges being brought, but we'll face that problem if and when it arises.'

'What I don't understand,' Cavendish said next, 'is why Bernard was caught in possession of a rifle? Has he exchanged the gun for a rifle? If so, then who has the hand gun now?'

'That, among a few other mysteries, is what we're trying to discover,' Carol replied. 'We've got a good lead from Bernard, who, I'm pleased to say, is now being more co-operative. With luck, we may be able to provide a full answer soon. Have you loaned your boat to anyone in the last few weeks?'

Cavendish looked thoughtful,

'The boat is usually kept at the Marina. It hasn't been out to sea for several weeks until Wednesday. Sometimes, Bernard likes to use it as a refuge, somewhere out of the house, to sit with his friends. He doesn't take it out, just sits in the saloon. He can make tea or coffee, all he has to do is take some fresh milk and whatever they want to eat. They can't afford to pay café prices. They get the food at a supermarket and cook it on the boat.'

Carol looked at her colleague, Brian Taylor and frowned.

'Mr. Cavendish,' she said, 'would the lads have changed your butane gas cylinder?'

'They may have done,' he said, 'why?'

Carol explained.

'Because the valve had been tampered with and the connector thread was damaged. Perhaps they hadn't realised it was a left hand thread, but it was quite badly damaged as though it had been hit with a hammer, or a heavy tool.'

Cavendish looked shocked and angry.

'Thank you, officer, for the information. It seems that I was almost killed by my son or his friends. I dread to think of the consequences if we had been at sea with four or five fishermen. We could all have been terribly injured, or even drowned, all through allowing my son to use the boat as a refuge. It won't be allowed in the future. We were lucky that we were on the beach and not out at sea.'

'Bernard will be charged with assault and unlawful possession of a firearm, Mr. Cavendish,' Carol explained. 'He may need a solicitor, we can appoint one if you don't wish to.'

'I have already contacted my solicitor, officer,' said Cavendish. 'I've allowed him the services of Mr. Ford. I want to make it clear that this is not to assist him in escaping punishment. I know that he is not good at expressing himself, the friends he has are a bad influence. He's so spaced out on cannabis, half the time, it's as though he's from a different planet.'

'Can you describe any of his friends, Mr. Cavendish?' Carol asked.

Cavendish was thoughtful for a few moments.

'I'm afraid my descriptions of the one or two I've seen him with, would be unprintable. The only one with a slightly respectable external veneer, is an even bigger villain than his father.'

'Who would that be?' Carol asked him.

'I'd better not say, officer,' he said. 'Knowing my luck and the way he thinks, it wouldn't just be a boat blowing up it would be my house, my wife and then me!'

Carol smiled,

'Have a think about it, Mr. Cavendish,' she said, taking a card from her pocket. 'If you want to tell us more, or feel you are being threatened, please call me on my mobile number, or in an emergency the Chichelster Station, that number there.' She pointed to the lower edge of her card. 'We'll leave you in peace now, I hope you continue to improve and thank you for your honesty.'

The two officers smiled and shook hands with the Cavendish's and left for the car park.

'We'd better call in before we head back,' Brian Taylor suggested. 'They might want to give us an update.'

Carol lifted the transceiver from its dash mounting and called in.

'Two niner to control. We're just leaving East Grinstead. Anything further for us? Over.'

She heard the operator's voice answer.

'Say again please.'

Carol tried again.

'Two niner, is that Hickson and Taylor, please?'

'Affirmative, anything for us?'

'Say again please. Intermittent reception.'

Carol repeated her message.

'One collection, address in Worthing. Bad reception. Please call base on your mobile, for details. Over.'

'Roger that, two niner out.'

Brian grinned,

'I s'pose Worthing's on our way back, but so is Ipswich if we go the pretty way,' he said.

Carol was trying to use her mobile and giggling at the same time.

'Shuttup, Brian,' she said. 'Mike Hodd's on the desk and he gets huffy if he thinks we're larking about.'
She managed to control her laughter as she got the details from Sergeant Hodd.

'Listen,' she said, 'Flat four,

'Probably an aero engine, most of the small ones are flat fours,' Brian told her, still grinning.
Carol tried her stern voice.

'Listen Brian, we're to collect a Mrs. Sandra Cranham, from flat four, Bethersden Court, Lancing Lane, Worthing. Do you know where that is?'

'I know where Worthing is,' Brian said, I think I know where Lancing Lane is, but I don't have the foggiest idea where the rest of it is. We'll have to ask a policeman!'
They continued on their way towards the coast.

'Do you want a sandwich or something?' Carol asked him. 'I can remember one of those tea wagons along here last time we came this way. Just after we left the A23, it might be on the other side of the road, I'm not sure.'

'On the old Shoreham Road, the A27?' Brian asked.
Carol nodded, 'yes, that was it, Old Shoreham Road. I remember now.'

'Us old 'Sussex' kids know a thing or two, don't we?' he said.

'We can find a cup of tea quicker than those 'met' boys,' Carol answered.

'Don't mention it to Mr. Mercer though, or he'll turn it into a competition.'
They both laughed.

'I suppose he'll either fit in or flit out, eventually,' Carol observed. 'He didn't make much of an impression on Tony Church, did he?'
Brian laughed, as he mimicked the DI.

'Thank you, Mercer, but I'll decide which officers are the most suitable for this operation, not you.'

'There,' Carol shouted. 'There, on the right, the tea van.'

411

'Oh, right,' Brian said as he indicated to cross the road. The lay by was quite long, so the pair of officers walked back several yards to the tea van.

'Two teas, please,' Carol said as the man raised his eyebrows to her. 'One with milk and sugar and the other with just milk please,' she added.

'Thank you,' said the owner of the unit, 'that'll be fifty pence, please.'

Carol paid him and said, 'thanks, have you been busy today?'

'No,' he replied, 'it's been very quiet since the accident this morning.'

'What accident was that?' Carol asked.

He leaned over his service counter and looked towards the back of his van. He saw Brian standing there and nodded to him.

'Bloke was pulling off the lay by to go up the road and some kid in a big 'Merc' took him out.' He said. 'He must've been doing more than seventy. We've had your lot here until about an hour ago. Tape measures, photographs, statements from all the customers, they even asked me what I saw. I told 'em, all I saw was what I can see now, the hedge and the fields in front of me.'

The serving hatch faced away from the road.

Carol laughed,

'Did they appreciate that?' she asked.

He grinned at her,

'They had to eventually,' he said, 'but not until one of 'em came and stood in here to check for himself. I didn't see anything of the accident, I heard the young bloke in the 'Merc' shouting that he'd be late for Gatwick. They closed the road for about twenty minutes, while they were taking measurements. That's what all the chalk marks are for. I'm surprised you hadn't heard about it.'

'We're not local,' Brian began to explain. 'We're Chichelster, we had to do an interview in East Grinstead, now we're on our way back. Were there any injuries?'

412

'It's a wonder nobody was killed,' he said. 'Bloke in the Rover was hurt, but he managed to hop into the ambulance. Fire brigade got him out, his foot was caught in the bent pedals and they had to cut the door off. They used a big hydraulic thing. There was a lot of petrol about so they couldn't risk a grinder because of the sparks.'

Both officers were listening intently, Brian asked,

'What about the chap in the Mercedes? Was he hurt?'

'I don't think he was hurt too bad, but his car was a write off. Apparently he bounced off the Rover and went into the ditch on the other side of the road. He'd clipped a tree on the way, so he must've been going like a bat out of hell. The police arrested him and took him off in a squad car. He said he was in a hurry to visit someone in hospital. He'd calmed down by then. He didn't seem so brave, sitting in the back of a police car with one of your very large officers sitting next to him. I think he got a bit 'lippy' otherwise they might have been a bit gentler with him. He'd been ranting at the driver of the Rover, who was still trapped in his car at the time. Apparently the 'Merc' was his father's, so I expect 'Daddy' will stop his pocket money for a while!'

'I expect we'll hear about it from our colleagues eventually,' Carol told him.

They had finished their tea and put the plastic cups into the bin.

'Thanks for the tea,' Carol called to him.

'And the traffic news update,' Brian added as they left.

'Keep a sharp lookout for airborne Merc's,' the proprietor called after them as he waved his hand.

CHAPTER 59.

Back in Worthing, on Friday afternoon, DS Stevens and Alan Bell had been taking a stroll. They had looked at the casino, which although open, appeared almost deserted. Perhaps it got busier in the evenings. They consulted their 'tourists' street map and headed for Courthope Street, the address of Gorse's office. They noted a few small estate agents premises and a pawn shop, opposite which was a double fronted office building. According to the brass plates on the door pillar, the office of, 'Gorse Associates,' was on the second floor. It was a fairly narrow street, leading down to the sea front. Double yellow lines prohibited parking on both sides. A number of pedestrians casually strolled across the road as they ambled between the various shops.

'We won't be visiting Mr. Gorse, Alan,' Lesley told him, 'not just yet, anyhow. We'll have a look in the shop windows for a while, see if he's busy. The other offices are all solicitors and insurance brokers. We'll just watch to see who comes and goes. We may be able to guess which ones are his clients.'

Whilst they watched the reflection of Gorse's office entrance in the pawn shop window, Alan noticed a police car coming down the road. It stopped outside the office building.

414

'I wonder what they're here for,' Lesley said. Two uniformed officers checked the brass plates on the doorframe and went in.

'I think perhaps I'll phone in and try to get an update,' she said, taking her mobile from her bag. She walked up the road a little further, in case they were being watched. Alan crossed the road and began looking at the photographs of some properties in the estate agents window. After a few minutes Lesley returned, she was smiling.

'What did you find out?' Alan asked her.

'Come on, we'll walk back towards the casino, I'll tell you on the way,' she said. They reached the sea front and crossed the road to watch the sea. Lesley leaned on the railings and began telling Alan what she had heard.

'It's all happening, Alan, whether we're here or not. Carol and Brian Taylor have been to interview young Cavendish's parents. The father is still in hospital in East Grinstead. Anyway, on their way back they stopped for a cup of tea at one of those roadside tea vans. The owner told them about an accident which happened there before lunch. Two cars were involved, a Rover which was leaving the lay by, was clobbered by a large Mercedes, travelling very fast towards East Grinstead. They believe the driver might have been Gorse's son, Lionel. He's been arrested and taken to Shoreham H.Q.'

'That's probably what the two uniforms were doing, telling his father about it,' Alan surmised.

'There's more,' Lesley told him. 'DI Church told me they've got a suspect for some of the stuff which was stolen from Ridge Farm. He's a security chap from Gatwick. His name's Cranham. He was trying to sell a silver tea service and an inscribed gold watch in Pudborough. He chose the wrong second hand shop. Old Archie Leggitt was in there and he heard enough to become a bit suspicious. He phoned it in and the Pudborough CID caught him in the act. He's at 'Chi' now. Carol and Brian have been asked to pick up his wife on their way back.'

Alan nodded that he understood.

'Is this bloke Cranham's wife involved, or didn't the DI say?'
Lesley smiled.

'He didn't say, but I expect they will want to question her about it. He said he'd given Carol Hickson my mobile number for back up, in case there was a problem.'

'Let's go and have a cup of coffee,' Alan suggested. 'There's a café over there,' he pointed across the road.

They crossed the road and went in. Alan ordered two coffees and Lesley took a window seat. They watched the traffic go along the sea front as they drank their coffees.

Lesley's phone began to ring.

'I expect that's Carol,' she said as she answered it.

It wasn't, it was DS Ken Foster.

'Where are you, Lesley?' He asked.

She told him and also mentioned the accident involving Gorse's son.

'We heard about it from the Shoreham boys,' Ken told her. 'They found a pistol in the car when they searched it at the police garage. Wait there, Lesley, we'll come and find you. We'll have a chat and decide what to do. We mustn't get in each other's way, but we all need to keep up to date with any new developments.'

Ten minutes later Ken and Phil appeared outside the café window. Alan beckoned them inside.

'Do you want tea or coffee?' he asked as he walked to the counter to order.

'Tea for me, please,' Ken said, 'and the same for Phil, thanks. They sat at the table and began to discuss their experiences to date.

'Wait for Alan,' Lesley said, 'otherwise you'll have to say it all twice.'

Two cups of 'builders' tea,' Alan announced as he put the cups on their table.

'Thanks Alan,' said Ken, 'now let's see what we know. Gorse's son has escaped from Shoreham. They left him sitting in a car on his own and whilst the 'plod' were discussing the

416

incident, he quietly slid off. He must have moved pretty quick, he'd cleared the yard before they could raise the alarm.'

'What were they doing, leaving him in a car, without being cuffed?' Alan asked Ken.

Ken Foster grinned,

'I think it's called 'complacency', Alan. We've all been guilty of it at times. I expect he'd been subdued and they thought he was tamed enough to trust. The bit I don't get is why they were so engrossed in their discussion that nobody noticed him getting out of the car.'

'Somebody will get a bollocking for it, I dare say,' Phil interjected. 'They'll be watching all possible contacts and hideouts now, that's a safe bet.'

Lesley suggested that the purpose of the police visit to Gorse's office may have been in connection with both his accident and his escape.

'I hope they don't believe that Gorse will deliver his son to them,' she said. 'Surely they can't be that green.'

Ken smiled,

'You'd be surprised, Lesley,' he said. 'We've got one or two like that ourselves. Mind you, we've also got one who would go to the other extreme. Mercer would have had him cuffed and shackled and padlocked to the nearest traffic sign.'

They all laughed,

'And then find that he'd lost the key to the padlock, so they'd have to take the traffic sign as well!' Phil said, still giggling at the thought.

'Right, enough of the hilarity for a moment,' Ken said. 'We've still got our job to do, so let's share a few ideas. Are you two going to the casino tonight?' he asked Lesley.

'That was the plan, Ken,' she said. 'We were just hanging on for a bit to see if Carol Hickson needed us. We'll go back to the flat and get cleaned up and changed. We need to look like a couple of holidaymakers, not a pair of vagrants. What are you two up to?'

'Surfin' the Wharf,' I suppose,' Ken told her. 'We've had a quick look from the outside, but we're not looking forward to our visit that much.'

Lesley's phone began to play 'Rondo', her selected ringtone. She said,

'It might be Carol, I'd better take it outside,' she got up and left them at the table. A minute or so later, she beckoned them to join her.

'Problem,' she told them. 'Sandra Cranham is not at home. She checked with a neighbour and was told that she may be at work. She works in the office at Barnards Garage. Carol phoned the garage and spoke with the accounts manager. He said that she hadn't come in today and hadn't phoned in, which was most unusual for Sandra. He told Carol that Sandra was a most reliable person and admitted that he was a bit concerned. I think perhaps Brian and I should meet up with her, see if we can help.'

Ken agreed,

'I think we need to feel assured of her safety, so call her back, Lesley and find out where she is,' he said. 'We'll get back to the less salubrious end of town and glean whatever information we can.' The two men walked back to the car park, leaving Lesley on her mobile, with Alan waiting for further instructions.

The four police officers met up at the end of Lancing Lane. Lesley and Alan left their car and got into the patrol car with their uniformed colleagues.

'It's a bit warmer in here,' Alan said as he got in the back seat next to Brian Taylor. Brian had left his driving seat, so that Lesley could converse with Carol

Brian smiled,

'We've done enough miles to warm the engine,' he said. I expect yours has been parked up most of the time.'

'Listen to Carol, please,' said Lesley. 'She'll tell you what we know so far.'

'Sorry,' Alan said, 'we're listening.'

Carol began to tell them what she had been able to find out.

418

'The neighbours didn't know very much at all, although one of them did tell me where Sandra worked,' she said. 'An elderly man in one of the bungalows opposite Bethersden Court, saw her this morning. He told me he was washing his car at about half past eight, when Mrs. Cranham came out and got into a car with two men. He said she seemed to be anxious, one of the men was pulling her by her elbow and she had her coat undone, even though it was cold and drizzling. The car was a silver Mercedes, it drove off at speed towards Brighton.'

'Have you called it in to the DI?' Lesley asked her.

'No, do you think we should?'

'I was just thinking, both her husband and Bernard Cavendish are being detained at 'Chi', Carol. If Sandra has been taken as a hostage to bargain with. I think DI Church should at least be kept informed.'

'You're right, Sarge,' Carol agreed. 'Should I use the phone, or the radio?'

'The mobile phone is probably more secure,' Alan suggested.

'And a bloody sight clearer than this radio,' said Brian. 'It needs a few coats of 'looking at' when we get back. It's got more crackling than a bag of pork scratchings.'

Carol pulled her phone from her bag and dialled the DI's mobile. He answered at once.

'Hello Carol, let me guess, she wasn't there, was she?' He said.

'No sir,' she replied, 'but how did you know?'

'DS Stuart just told me, He's psychic you know.'

Carol smiled, she heard Ian Stuart in the background,

'I'm not your sidekick!' He objected, laughing.

'I'll come clean, Carol,' the DI said. 'We'd already tried to collect her once, but then Shoreham found a few clues in the Mercedes. Besides the hand gun, they found Sandra's address on a scrap of paper in the glove box. But what clinched it was her mobile phone pushed between the rear seat and the backrest. It had some useful numbers on it and a couple of missed calls, one from her husband and the other from her boss.'

'Thank you, sir,' Carol said. 'We've got Lesley and Brian Taylor with us right now. What do you think our best course of action would be now?'

'It's a tricky one, Carol,' said the DI. 'We don't want to upset our colleagues at Shoreham, but from an ethical standpoint it's our murder enquiry, not theirs. I'd appreciate their help, but all they've managed so far is to lose one of our prime suspects. I'll have a word, probably more than a word, with their chief. In the meantime, since you've now got the company of two detectives, it might be a good opportunity to try a bit a bit of detecting. Have a chat with Lesley and tell her what I said.'

'Would you like to speak with her, sir?' Carol asked him.

'I'm sure you can work something out between you, Carol,' DI Church told her. 'I don't have any more information yet, so I'll leave it to the troops on the ground. Call me if you have any more problems. Good luck, Bye for now.' He closed his phone. Carol looked at Lesley, who had been sharing the mobile with her.

'So it's' 'goodnight from him and its goodnight from him'! Lesley said, laughing, as she mimicked the closing line from the television series, 'The Two Ronnies'.

'I think you and Alan might as well just go back to 'Chi' for now,' Lesley told them. 'We haven't got a photograph or a description of either Sandra Cranham, or even this Gorse character. Alan and I can go to her place of work, perhaps we'll get something from them. Failing that, we're as much in the dark as the DI. We've got a surveillance job for this evening, which is strictly undercover. Don't worry, Carol, I really don't think there is anything much we can do until we get more information. We'll just be wasting our time.'

Carol agreed, so they decided to head back to Chichelster and await further information.

They took the car back to the police garage and told John Griffiths, the fitter about the radio problem.

'It's worse than useless, John,' Brian told him. 'Perhaps you could check the tyres as well, there's a bit of a wobble at about fifty miles an hour. I don't think it's too serious because you can drive through it. It stops wobbling at about sixty five.'

'Might just be a wheel out of balance, Brian,' he said. 'I'll check it out anyway. The radio needs to be changed. You're the second one to complain about it this week.'

Brian thanked him and went into the station, where Carol was speaking with Sergeant Dean at the front desk. She turned as he entered,

'Brian,' she said. 'When we stopped for that cup of tea, do you remember what the tea man said about where the driver of the Mercedes was going?'

'Yes,' Brian answered, 'but it was a bit confusing. He's probably a more reliable witness because he didn't see anything, if you know what I mean, Sarge. He said the bloke shouted at the other driver, 'You've made me late for Gatwick' something like that, but definitely Gatwick. When he was telling the police, he said he was going to visit someone in hospital in East Grinstead.'

'That's what I remembered,' Carol agreed.

Sergeant 'Dixie' Dean smiled as he said,

'Sounds to me as though he was the only one who knew where he was going. But perhaps it's relevant, so we'd better tell the chief.'

CHAPTER 60.

On Saturday morning, Bill Pickering had been to Chichelster on his day off, to deliver some statements. He was on his way home when he noticed his car behaving oddly. It was obviously some sort of electrical fault. The engine was getting hotter and less powerful and there were two red warning lights glowing. He pulled over as close to the verge as he could get and switched off the engine.

'I bet it's either a belt broken or the bloody alternator,' he said to himself. He pulled the bonnet release and got out of the car. He opened the rear door and picked up his police overcoat from the back seat and put it on. Bill opened the bonnet and looked at the engine, his thoughts were immediately confirmed.

'Yep, busted belt, who needs electronic diagnostics,' he mumbled.

At least it was dry and daylight, he could probably stop someone and get either a lift or a tow. If he'd had the panda car he would have just radio'd in and they would have brought a replacement. But it wasn't his panda car. It was his wife's Ford Fiesta. He closed the bonnet and walked to the back of the car.

A lone motorcyclist appeared and slowed, then stopped.

'Is there something the matter, officer?' He asked.

Bill smiled at him,

'I appreciate you stopping sir,' Bill said. 'My alternator belt has broken, so I need either a tow or a lift to the garage. I expect there will be a car or van along presently, I'll ask them to help.' The motorcyclist wheeled his machine to the front of Bill's car and put it up on its stand. He took off his helmet and gloves and placed them on his pillion seat.

'I can help you, officer. It's your own car is it? Not one of the police vehicles?'
Bill nodded,

'It's my wife's car, actually,' he told him. 'I'm off duty. I just put the mac on because it was feeling a bit chilly. How can you help me?'
The motor cyclist explained,

'I'm the workshop foreman from Baldock's Service Station, just up the road. I'm a bit late for work because I had a dental appointment, but if we assume it to be just the belt, I'm sure we'll have one in stock. I'll send someone back to fit it, be about ten or fifteen minutes, that's all. You can call in and pay on your way through.'
Bill thanked him and said,

'Just when I begin to lose faith in the parable of the 'Good Samaritan', one appears on a motorbike! I'm most impressed by your timely arrival and your kind offer of help.' Bill once again released the bonnet catch and raised the bonnet to expose the engine compartment.

Look at that,' he said to his companion. 'Eleven hundred cc's of raw power, starved of energy by a broken belt. I expect you need the engine and chassis number, to be sure to get the correct belt?'

'I think the thirteen hundreds all use the same size belt,' the rider answered, 'but it won't do any harm to make sure. If you've got a pen and a slip of paper, I'll call out the numbers and you can write them down, OK?'
A few minutes later Bill's two wheeled 'boy scout' was on his way to his place of work. Bill sat in his car to await his return.

The garage was just out of sight around a bend in the road. Bill could see the greenhouses of the garden centre, which he remembered was next door to it, so it couldn't be far. He thought that if he'd kept going, he probably could have reached it. The only problem being that by then, the engine would have been too hot to work on. It didn't matter where he was, it would still take time to cool, so he might as well just sit and wait.

A few minutes later, he saw a green van approaching. It was indicating right to cross the road to where Bill had stopped. He watched as a dark green Range Rover began indicating behind the van. Surely he wasn't going to overtake! There was a lorry coming up behind Bill's car, there would be an accident if the Range Rover kept coming. At the last moment, there was a screech of brakes and it skidded to a halt behind the van, which had stopped to wait for the road to clear. Bill walked quickly towards the Range Rover and crossed his half of the road before the lorry reached him. It was Bettis' car, but it wasn't Bettis driving it. Bill opened the driver's door and said to the young man behind the wheel,

'I'm a police officer, switch your engine off and wait there.' The lorry went past, quite close to Bill, who had flattened himself against the car. As soon as the road was clear, he opened the driver's door again and switched off the ignition, removing the keys. The young man tried to grab Bill's hand, but missed.

'How do I know you're a policeman?' The man asked.

'Get out and come with me, stand over there, by the garage van, please sir,' Bill said. 'I'll show you my warrant card, before I phone my colleagues in Chichelster. They'll have a posh police car with blue lights and uniforms. Now, I need you to give me your name and address and show me your driving license and proof that you're insured to drive Mr. Bettis' Range Rover. If you can't do that, I will arrest you and make sure you get a ride in that nice shiny police car, the one I mentioned a few moments ago.' The young man tried to wriggle free of Bill's grip on his arm, but only succeeded in falling over onto the grass verge. The garage man was walking back towards him, with a drive belt and some spanners in his hand. It wasn't the same man who had stopped his motorbike.

'Can I do anything to help?' He asked Bill. 'I thought he was on a death wish or something. If he hadn't seen that lorry in time, I think he'd have taken us both out.'
Bill smiled as he replied,

'I believe you're correct there. Thanks for coming back to me. In the left hand pocket of this coat I'm wearing, there's a pair of handcuffs. If you wouldn't mind just reaching into the pocket and passing them to me, I'd be obliged. I can't let go of him for a bit, he's wriggling like an eel.'
The garage man approached and pulled the cuffs from Bill's pocket.

'Thank you,' Bill said as he took them from him and snapped one onto the man's right wrist. Bill turned him over and cuffed his other wrist.

'Now, stand up and behave yourself,' he told the man. Bill helped him to stand and then walked him back towards the rear of the fiesta, away from the garage man's vehicle. The mechanic had followed them back over the road and now stood next to Bill. He was glaring at the driver of the Range Rover. Bill handed him the Bettis' keys and said.

'I think we'd better move that or we'll be lined up for a bit of a 'smear up'. Would you mind shifting it over this side of the road, behind your van?'
The garage man took the keys from Bill and crossed the road to the Range Rover.
Bill quickly patted the man down and pulled a flick knife from his trouser pocket.

'Do you know it's an offence to even carry one of these?' He asked. There was no response.

'Now it's your turn to speak,' he told the driver.
Bill took a notebook from his pocket and uncapped his pen.

'Name?'

'Gorse.'

'Gorse what?'

'Gorse nothing,' he grunted.

'Address?'

'I'm not saying anything else,' Gorse said sullenly.

'Mr. Gorse, or whoever you are, you are under arrest on suspicion of taking a vehicle without the owner's consent, driving without insurance and carrying an offensive weapon. You are not obliged to say anything but you may harm your defense if you fail to mention, when questioned, something which you later rely on in court. Anything you do say may be used in evidence. Do you understand?'

No response.

The mechanic had moved the Range Rover and parked it half on the verge. He was now preparing to fit the new belt to the Fiesta. Bill took his phone from his pocket and dialled Chichelster police. It was answered by PC Eric Mercer. Bill recognised the voice.

'Hello Eric, it's Bill Pickering from Wigglesworth,' he said.

'Bill,' Mercer said brightly, 'what can I do for you this fine Saturday morning?'

'Do you know if the DI is in?' Bill asked.

'I saw him earlier, Bill. Let me see if I can put you through to his office. Don't hang up. If he's not there, I'll come back on.' Eric Mercer tried the line but there was no answer. Just then, DI Church came through the front office on his way out.

'DI Church,' Mercer called out to him. 'I've got Bill Pickering on the line, sir. He sounds as though it might be urgent.'

The DI crossed to the front desk and took the phone from the PC.

'Tony Church here, is that you Bill?' He asked.

'Good morning, Guv,' Bill began, 'I've got someone here who says his name is 'Gorse', can you send a car out for him? I've broken down in Kate's Fiesta. I'm just this side of Baldocks

426

Garage, on the Slindon Road. I've arrested him for 'TWOC' and an offensive weapon. He's driving Bettis' Range Rover.'

'Thank you, Bill,' the DI said. 'At least you've actually caught one. I'll get a car and a couple of uniforms out to you now. Shoreham put an appeal in the stop press of the Evening Argus last night and we've had sightings of him reported all over the place. According to reports from 'Joe public', at eight thirty last night he was in Haywards Heath, Eastbourne, Arundel and Hastings! The description in the paper was so vague it could have applied to half the male population under forty.'
Bill laughed,

'Well guv, if he was moving that fast, we'd never have caught him. I just broke down and waited for him to come to me!'
The DI replied,

'He wasn't moving fast enough, Bill, was he?'

'Well, he's guilty of stealing a car and carrying a flick knife, so he's 'nicked and cuffed', whether his name is 'Gorse' or not. Will you need Bettis' Range Rover for fingerprints?'
The DI thought for a moment.

'Good point, Bill,' he said. 'I don't suppose he's had it for very long, but you're right. We will need to check it out. Would you like to let Bettis know? You can tell him we'll drop it back to him when we're done. Tell him he can phone us if he has any problems with that. Do you mind?'

'No, I'll call him from home, when I get there. I haven't got his number on my mobile,' Bill explained.

'Thanks Bill, have you got the car fixed yet?' Tony Church asked.

'It's being fixed as we speak, Guv. One of the garage chaps stopped on his way to work and kindly sent a van out with a spare drive belt. Oh, it looks as though he's done it. He's just closing the bonnet and getting in to start it up.'

'OK, Bill, I'll get someone out to you in the next few minutes. We'll try not to hold you up for too long. Enjoy your week-end.'
He closed the call.

The garage man came up to Bill with the keys to his car and the keys to the Range Rover.

'All done, sir,' he said. 'I can see you've got your hands full just now, so don't worry about the bill. You can call in and settle up next time you're passing.'

Bill put his hand in his trouser pocket and pulled out three pound coins. He held them out to exchange them for the keys,

'Thank you very much,' he said. 'I'm sorry I haven't got much change with me, but perhaps you'll have a drink on me. Please thank your colleague, the one who stopped to help me earlier. I'm up and down this road several times a week, so I'll pop in and settle up next time I'm passing.'

'That's fine, sir,' he replied. 'You're from Wigglesworth, aren't you?

'That's quite correct,' Bill said. 'Do you know the village?'

'I know Archie Leggitt,' the man said, smiling. 'He did a wonderful job on that old watermill, didn't he? Next time you see him, tell him you've seen Trevor Williams. We've moved from Gandridge Farm Lane, we managed to buy a house in Slindon. I've written my phone number on this envelope, the address is on the front.'

'Thank you, Trevor Williams,' Bill said, as he shook his hand. 'I'll pass your greetings on to him, I know Archie very well as a matter of fact. Thank you very much for all your help.'

Trevor Williams got back in his van and drove away. He turned the vehicle round at the next junction and tooted his horn and waved as he passed Bill on his way back to Baldocks Garage.

About ten minutes later, a white police transit van pulled up behind Bill's car. There were three uniformed officers, the driver, an escort for their prisoner and another to ferry Bettis' car back to Chichelster. Bill's handcuffed suspect was beginning to feel the cold. He was hunched up and shivering as he was 'helped' into the vehicle. Bill heard him being given the usual warning of,

'Mind your head, sir,' as he was pushed in through the back door.

Bill handed the Range Rover keys to PC Frank Burton.

'Make sure you keep your gloves on, Frank,' he told him. Try not to smudge too much of the evidence.'

PC Burton laughed.

'I don't want to spoil your day, Bill,' he said, 'but your capture is not who he says he is. I had him in a couple of weeks ago on a public order offence. I think you'll find his real name is, Terry Piper. His dad came and bailed him. He owns the fishing lodges up at the old gravel pit at the back of your village.'

Bill smiled at him and said,

'Dad will need to come and bail him out again, won't he?'

Frank Burton shrugged,

'Most of these kids are from well to do families, Bill. They have no respect for anybody or anything. Every bit of trouble they get themselves into, either Mum or Dad rescue 'em.

If they were our kids, they'd get a dry slap and told to behave or take the consequences.'

The escort officer, Peter Hayles came back from his transit vehicle to give Bill his handcuffs back.

'Thanks, Bill,' he said. 'He's gone all quiet now, says his name's not Gorse and the flick knife isn't his either. I told him it was quite believable, since the bloody Range Rover wasn't his either. I explained that ownership of the knife was not the issue, the offence was, 'being in possession' of it. He went all quiet at that, so we'll waste a bit more time on him back at the nick.'

Bill put the cuffs back in his coat pocket, got in his car and drove home.

Bettis was most civil when Bill phoned him. He thanked him for saving his car and was most grateful when he was told that the police would deliver it to him after it had been checked for prints.

429

CHAPTER 61.

Sandra Cranham was a very unhappy woman. She awoke in darkness, her hands and feet bound with strong tape. Her hands were taped behind her back. A piece of foul smelling adhesive tape kept her mouth closed and was wound round her head, keeping her hair stuck to the back of her neck. She was half sitting, half lying on a damp wooden floor.
As her eyes became accustomed to the darkness, she realised that she was in a shed of some sort. How long had she been here? Why would those men have taken her from her home? They said she was needed by her husband, who was in trouble. She had wanted to telephone work, to let them know she would be late, but they would not let her. It was too urgent, they'd said. She had managed to grab her mobile phone, but she must have dropped it, probably in the car. They kept asking 'where's Vic? They'd said it was Vic who needed her, so they must have known where he was. Tell us now or it will get worse.' The older one had said. She didn't know where he was. He hadn't come home last night. His supervisor had phoned to ask why he wasn't at work. The older man had told her to calm down and everything would be alright. She remembered him making her drink something, to

help her to calm down. That's what he'd told her, but now she realised she'd been drugged. That was all she could recall as she sat now in this cold, damp and dark shed. Her head hurt, she needed a drink, water, anything to get this taste out of her mouth. Sandra listened, she could hear the sea. There was a gap at the top of the double doors. It was dark outside. She wondered what time it was. Her wrist watch was under the tape binding her hands. It was digging into her wrist and becoming painful. She tried to loosen the tape by wriggling her hands, but it only made the watch dig into her skin more deeply. The two men seemed to know all about her, but she didn't recognise them. She thought she had seen the car before, or one like it. Her stepfather had one. Yes, it had been a Mercedes like his, same colour and everything. Sandra listened again. She heard distant noise from a road, the wind and the smell of the sea. She realised that it wasn't just a shed, it was a beach hut. That meant that she was at Ferring. There were beach huts at Ferring, but there would be no traffic, especially at this time of year.

But wait! A car engine, perhaps they were coming back for her. She heard unfamiliar voices and heard the car doors slam shut. There was a beachside car park at Ferring, she remembered. She heard footsteps on the shingle outside. Yes, they were coming back for her. The shingle crunching footsteps receded into the distance. Sandra caught a few words of their conversation. They were going fishing.

She tried to make a noise to attract their attention, but it was ineffectual and by then they would be too far away to hear. She saw through the gap at the doors that it was beginning to get light. It must be around half past seven in the morning. Her limbs ached and she was cold, so very cold. She had been crying, not loudly, but quietly sobbing. It made it more difficult to breathe. She had wet herself, it must have happened whilst she was knocked out. Sandra thought to herself that she must stay awake, to listen for anyone coming her way. She needed something to make a noise with. As it gradually became light outside, she began to make out

431

a few shapes inside the hut. An old wooden framed deck chair was leaned against the wall, by the door. Perhaps she could shuffle over on her bottom and somehow pull it over. It might land on her legs, which would hurt and deaden the sound. No, that was not a good idea. She needed something to continue making a noise, not just a single 'bang'. Half way up one of the upright timbers, someone had knocked in a nail, probably to hang something on. It was quite a large nail. Its rusty head protruded a couple of inches from the wood. If only she could manage to stand up, perhaps she could use it to loosen the tape which bound her wrists.

Sandra leaned against the wall behind her and began pushing herself upright. It hurt to move after being restrained for so long. She had almost made it, but suddenly her calf muscles began contracting in the most excruciating cramp attack. She fell back to the floor and tried to stretch her legs out in front of her. After a few minutes, the cramp subsided and she tried again. Her back hurt as it scraped against the rough wood of the hut wall behind her, but she was determined and eventually she was standing. She took a few moments to get her breathing regulated and then began to work her way towards the nail. She could manage a kind of twisting shuffle, her ankle bones were sore from rubbing against each other. She didn't dare try to jump, if she fell in the middle of the floor, she was not sure she would be able to get up again. Eventually her efforts were rewarded and she leaned on the wall next to the nail. Sandra moved her hands up behind her until she could feel the nail begin to hook into the tape. Her shoulders ached and her back was so painful, but she began to work at loosening the tape. At one point she felt it begin to tear, but it broke free of the nail and was still holding her wrists tightly. She tried again and felt the tape tear again. How many layers of tape had they wound around her wrists? Perhaps now there were two less than before, so she continued to work at it. The tape was definitely loosening. She could move her wrists apart a little now. One final attempt and her hands were free.

She massaged her hands and wrists and then began to unwind the tape from her face. It was pulling her hair out as she pulled it from the back of her head. Finally she had it completely unwound. It was good to be able to breath normally again. The horrid taste was still in her mouth. Sandra sat on the floor and removed the tape from her ankles. She stood and walked back and forth to try to revive the circulation and loosen her stiff and aching joints and muscles.

Now she could think better. She examined the doors of the beach hut. There were a couple of hasp and staple fixings, padlocked on the outside, no doubt. Sandra pushed on the doors where they closed. There was no 'give' at all. The light was improving now. She cast her eye around the interior of the hut. A wooden tool box was on a small bench at the opposite end from the doors. She opened the lid to see if there was anything she could use to escape. Wait! There was a name burned into the lid. 'Poker work', she thought it was called. Sandra tilted the box to get more light from the gap above the doors.

'L. C. GORSE' it said in capital letters. Her stepfather's initials! It was his hut!

Her immediate thought was that it had something to do with him. But no, he wouldn't do anything as brutal as this, would he? The answer was still 'no', but her step brother? Yes! Lionel would. He was half crazy on drugs most of the time and he had some very dubious and sometimes dangerous friends. Probably it was a couple of them who had kidnapped her. Maybe it had actually been Leon's car. Lionel could have borrowed it for the purpose, or even stolen it from his father. She knew he had stolen things before, to buy his drugs. But why kidnap her? What had Victor done? Vic knew that Lionel was nothing but trouble, she had warned him so many times. Surely he wouldn't have risked everything on one of Lionel's crazy schemes.

Sandra continued investigating the contents of the tool box. The tools were old, some of them rusty, but still useable and better than nothing. She found a small hammer, a pair of pliers and a couple of large screwdrivers. She could make a noise with the hammer. That was fine if somebody came along, but what if those two men who brought her here came back? She didn't want to warn them that she was free of her bonds. She tried the screwdriver in the gap between the two doors, but it wasn't strong enough to lever them apart. She leaned on the bench and looked around the hut. Her eyes had grown used to the gloom and there was enough light now to see quite well. Sandra looked under the bench a circular spot of light, shone through a knot hole in one of the boards of the back wall. She knelt down on the floor and hit the board as hard as she could with the hammer. It sprang away from the upright timber, but not enough to come loose. She pried it against the upright with the larger of the two screwdrivers. There was a sharp 'crack' and the board splintered. She hit it again with the hammer, once twice again, it was gradually breaking up. There was now a gap of a couple of feet long and a four inch board width. She held her head close to the floor and looked through the gap. Sandra could see the car park through it. There was one car, a big estate, probably the one which the fishermen had arrived in.

She needed to make the hole bigger, to be able to escape. She would be able to see if anyone else came to the car park now. Sandra sat on the floor and used her feet to kick away another three boards. The ends splintered, leaving a jagged hole, just big enough for her to climb through. She felt warmer through her exertions, although her clothes were cold and damp. It was a cold morning and beginning to drizzle in the light breeze. Her greatest fear was that those men would return before she had secured her freedom. Sandra thought about what she should do. She decided that her best bet would not be to run up to the main road, but to find the fishermen, down on the beach and ask them to help her. She kept hold of the hammer and crawled carefully through the hole she had made. If she was attacked again she would try to use the hammer to defend herself. Sandra walked cautiously around the hut. The men were on the beach down towards the waters edge. The incoming tide had covered the sand and was just lapping the pebbles. They had their rods set up in stands made from metal tubing. They saw her coming down the beach and began walking towards her. She was shivering with both the cold and she suspected delayed shock. One of the fishermen took off his waterproof coat and put it round her shoulders.

'I think you'd better sit down, love,' he told her. 'You look as though you'll fall down if you don't. Whatever's happened to you?'
Sandra sat on the pebbles,

'I'm sorry,' she began to say, but her voice had all but died on her.
The other fisherman came towards her with a flask top of hot sweet coffee.

'Here, drink this, you look as though you've been in an accident,' he said. 'Tell us what happened, I'll phone for an ambulance.' He pulled his mobile from his pocket.
Sandra nodded and took a sip of the hot coffee.

'And the police, please,' she said in a hoarse whisper. 'I've been abducted and locked in that beach hut,' she pointed up the beach. As she turned around to look at the fisherman, the world began to spin and she passed out.

Her head was aching the lights were too bright. She was in bed, but not her bed.

'Hello, dear,' it was a female voice, 'are you awake now?'
Sandra put her hand to her eyes and tried to see who was talking to her. She felt gentle hands on her shoulders, pulling her forwards.

'Would you like to try to sip some water, you've been through a terrible ordeal my dear. When you feel up to it perhaps you'll tell the policeman what happened. There's no hurry, you're safe now. Would you like a cup of tea?'
Sandra was vaguely aware of a dark uniform sitting in a metal chair next to her bed.

She nodded and took a sip of water. It was wonderful!

'Don't drink it too quickly,' the nurse told her. 'Just take small sips, or you'll feel sick. When you're ready for it, I'll bring you a nice cup of tea. Don't try to wake up too quickly, you've had a shock and you need to give yourself time.'

Sandra looked to her right and saw the policeman clearly for the first time. He smiled at her and said,

'Good afternoon Mrs. Cranham, we'll talk when you're ready. As the nurse just told you, there is no need to hurry, Take all the time you need. I can wait as long as it takes. I'm pleased to see that you are recovering your complexion. You were very, very pale when they brought you in.'

Sandra tried to sit up a bit more. She still hurt all over and her head was aching. She looked at the nurse,

'Do you think I could have an aspirin please? I've got a really bad headache.'

The nurse smiled and told her,

'Somebody has made you drink a cocktail of alcohol and drugs, Sandra. As far as we are able to tell, the drugs used were a combination of valium and anti-histamine. Probably ground up tablets mixed with a little hot water and poured into an alcohol based liqueur. If you took an aspirin now, it would either make you ill, or could send you back into a semi comatose state. Your best option would be to have a cup of milky tea and then have a sleep. That's the best way to get the drugs out of your system.'

Sandra looked at her and then at the policeman.

'I'm sorry,' she said to him. 'I don't think I can concentrate enough to be helpful just yet. I don't know where my husband is, I think he may be in danger from the men who kidnapped me.'

'He's quite safe, Mrs. Cranham,' said PC Brian Taylor. 'He's at Chichelster police station. Just to put your mind at rest, for now, we've caught the men who abducted you. They are behind bars at Worthing police station and likely to remain there until we formalise the charges against them. So you just relax and we'll have a chat when you feel a bit better. I'll go and get a cup of tea and then I'll come back and sit with you.'

Sandra thought he was a very kind man.

'Thank you very much,' she heard herself say as she drifted off to sleep again.

The nurse returned with her milky tea and saw that Sandra had gone to sleep. She smiled at Brian Taylor.

'You look as though you could use a cup of tea, officer,' she said as she handed him the saucer. 'I hope you take sugar.'

Brian took the tea from her,

'Thank you,' he said. 'She looks as though she's been through a lot in the last twenty four hours. A sleep will do her more good than anything, won't it?'

'I know it's none of my business, so don't feel obliged to reply, but is her husband in a lot of trouble?'

Brian just looked up at the nurse.

'I can't really answer that, as I'm sure you are aware. Perhaps he's been a bit stupid, but I can't go into details. I can tell you that whoever abducted his wife is in twenty times as much trouble. She doesn't need to be worrying about it now though. We'll do all we can to help her overcome her ordeal. We just have to wait until she feels well enough to talk to us.'

'You look as though you're feeling the strain, PC Taylor. Why don't you go and have a rest in the coffee shop? I can send for you if she wakes up before you come back.'

'Thanks,' Brian said as he handed her the cup and saucer. 'Perhaps I'll do that. I suppose I'd better give my boss an update. He may have some more information by now. You will be sure to let me know when she wakes up, won't you?'

'I promise,' the nurse smiled at him, scout's honour!'

CHAPTER 62.

DS Ken Foster had heard about the abduction of Cranham's wife from the chief 'Super' at Worthing. Because she was linked to their current case, the Superintendant arranged for the Chichelster force to continue with their enquiries.

DI Tony Church had sent one of his officers to wait by Mrs. Cranham's bedside at the hospital. He was to remain with her until she had recovered sufficiently to be able to provide some details of her ordeal. Circumstances permitting, he was to try to obtain a statement from her, but not if it would be likely to cause her any further distress.

The two men who had abducted her were identified as George Warder, known to his friends as 'Keys' and James (Jack) Bull whose nickname was 'Target'. Both were acquaintances of Gorse's son 'Lionel'. The police had confirmed that it had been Leonard Gorse's car which was used in the abduction. Lionel Gorse had reclaimed his father's car after Sandra had been locked in the beach hut by Warder and Bull. They told police that young Gorse had feared that his step sister might recognise his voice. Leonard (Leon) Gorse had married Sandra's mother, Delia Bowyer, a year or so after the sudden death of his former wife. She had been found in her car, which appeared to have been

438

driven into Shoreham dock. Police had regarded the death as suspicious at first. The car was found to be well maintained and without any obvious defects. The coroner found no injuries on her body, other than those which would be expected as a result of the incident. Her friends were questioned as to her apparent state of mind, but all said that she seemed normal and quite contented. Following these extensive enquiries, and the lack of tangible evidence to suggest foul play, the coroner's court returned an 'open verdict' and further enquiries were suspended.

Following young Lionel Gorse's escape from the police at Shoreham, his photograph had been circulated throughout the forces of the southern counties. There had been many reports of sightings, but none confirmed. He seemed to have evaporated! However it seemed likely that he would eventually make contact with his father, for financial support, if nothing else.

The DI and DS Ian Stuart were interviewing Bernard Cavendish again.

'We believe you might know this man,' DI Church said as he showed him Gorse's photograph.

When he saw it his eyes opened wide with surprise.

'That's him, yes!' he exclaimed, 'that's 'Gas', the one who lent me the rifle. Now perhaps you'll believe me.'

'I think I've got it now,' Ian said, looking at the DI. 'Liquid Petroleum Gas or L.P.G. equals Lionel Peregrine Gorse'

Tony Church raised his eyebrows.

'Lionel Peregrine Gorse,' Ian said. Then there's 'Keys' Warder, 'Target' Bull and 'Trip' Terry Richard Piper.'

'Right,' Tony said as he grinned at Ian. He looked at Cavendish and asked, 'what were the other nicknames you mentioned, Bernard?'

Cavendish seemed reluctant to divulge any more names. Tony thought he was possibly afraid of reprisals.

'Don't worry, Bernard,' he said, 'we'll capture them all, whether we know their proper names or not. We suspect that young Gorse was intending to use some sort of coercion on your parents. It's our opinion that he had decided that you were a security risk. He believed that your parents knew where you were hiding. We think it was his intention to take advantage of their vulnerability to frighten them into disclosing your whereabouts. He was on his way to East Grinstead when he was involved in a car accident and arrested, so he never made contact with your father. We will be able to confirm all of this when we question him.'

The DI didn't mention the fact that Gorse had escaped, following his arrest. He decided that the full information at this stage, may have been counter productive and negated the prospect of further information from Cavendish.

'The only other one I know for sure,' Cavendish began, 'is 'Snort', that's Simon Norton, but I don't know where he lives.'

'How about, 'Medal', have you heard that name?' Ian asked.

'I've heard the name, but I don't know who he is,' Cavendish told him. 'I expect it's probably someone who has meddled with 'Gas' in the past.'

Ian looked smugly at the DI and placed his forefinger alongside his nose.

Tony gave his colleague a quizzical look.

'V.C. perhaps?' Ian said. 'Victor Cranham'.

'It's a good guess,' Tony said as he smiled at Cavendish. 'What do you think, Bernard?'

'What's 'VC' anyway?' Cavendish asked them.

'In our world it's 'Victoria Cross', a medal. It's the highest military award for bravery. The inscription on it reads, 'For Valour,' but there are very few live recipients. It is an unfortunate fact that most are awarded posthumously,' Tony said.

'I've never heard of it,' Cavendish said. 'What do you mean when you say in my world'? Cavendish asked. What do you think 'VC' is 'in my world? Just because I don't know about medals, why couldn't it be because somebody meddles with someone?'

'You possibly think VC is the infection you get before VD.' Ian suggested.

Cavendish scowled at the two detectives.

'I'm not saying anything else now,' he grunted. 'You're just taking the piss. OK, so you're smart and clever and maybe I'm not, but I'm not going to be your joke for the day.'

Tony smiled at him and said,

'Thank you Bernard, we'll come back when we've got a bit more information to share with you. We're close to a decision on which offences we should charge you with. Of course, if you had been more co-operative at your initial court hearing, you would probably be out on bail by now. As soon as you stated your address as, 'no fixed abode,' you precluded the chance of being released on police bail.'

The two detectives left the interview room. PC Derek Simms had been waiting outside for them.

'Thanks, Derek,' Ian said to him. 'You can put him back now please. We'll have a chat with our security risk! Sorry I meant to say, 'security guard', next. Give us a buzz when he's ready and we'll come back. You've got time to get yourself a 'cuppa' first. Say, about twenty minutes or so.'

'Thanks, Sarge,' Derek said, smiling. 'I'll let you know when he's in the interview room. At least it's getting a bit warmer in there now, it was bloody freezing first thing.'

Back in Tony's office there was a relayed note from the Shoreham police.

For the attention of DI Church.

Tony,

The Beretta 'Bobcat' hand gun, which was recovered from the crashed Mercedes, had been fired recently. There were seven rounds of ammunition left in the magazine. They were ACP point two fives. The weapon and the ammunition will be delivered to Chichelster this afternoon. Please be advised that Shoreham forensics have not checked these items, but tell me that all prints and DNA are intact and as found. The weapon and ammunition has been handled remotely since it was discovered, using only gloves and forceps.

441

Regards,
Geoff Fordham.
D.C.I. Sussex C.C.

Tony passed the paper to Ian.

'Well, Tony,' Ian said, 'The ammunition matches the casing that Archie Leggitt found at the farm, doesn't it? So I reckon that puts young Gorse in the frame for JD's murder. How say you, Guv?'

'Well, I'd say he'll need a bloody good alibi and an even better solicitor, if he's going to try to wriggle out of this lot,' Tony replied. 'We've got to collar him first though. Our teams in Worthing are doing all they can. I think probably he'll try to contact his father sooner or later. Ken and Phil are watching his office and his house. He lives in one of those big houses on Woodland Rise, back of the golf course. I think Phil is watching his office and Ken watches the house. I expect we'll find him sooner or later.'

'Have we got any taps on his phones?' Ian asked.

'Only the house phone,' Tony replied. 'We couldn't get authorisation for his office, because of the nature of his business.'

'Has anyone checked the tapes?' Ian asked, 'I mean recently. Tony looked up,

'I think the 'Comms Office' checked them yesterday,' he said. 'We could try checking his phone bills for details of the past month's calls, I suppose. It won't help us to find his son, but it may provide us with a list of people he has contacted. I'll ask the Super to obtain copies from B.T. if he can.'

The telephone on the desk buzzed. Tony answered it, it was Ken Foster.

'Morning Guv,' he said, 'I think I just missed young Gorse. I'm parked up the road a little way from the house. There's a five series black BMW and a silver Volvo estate in the driveway. 'His and Hers', I suppose. As I was watching from the car, a motor

442

cyclist just went into the driveway. I got out of the car to check and he must have become suspicious of me, because he tore off again. It's a trials bike, a two stroke. He was wearing a silver coloured helmet and dark goggles. It may not have been him, but from the way he took off when he saw me, I'd say it probably was. Phil's watching the office, so I'll phone and tell him what I think. Sorry it's not a 'capture' but I think we can mark it down as a confirmed sighting.'

'Thanks Ken,' the DI responded. 'It looks as though he's trying to find his dad or his step mum. I'd take that to mean he's running out of options, so keep at it. Call me if you get anything else.'

'Will do, Guv,' Ken answered, 'I'll hang up and get on to Phil. Bye for now.'

Tony Church looked across at Ian and said,

'I think it would be a good idea to give Archie Leggitt a quick call, to thank him for his help. Would you mind doing that please?'

Ian nodded,

'Yes, he put us on the right track with that point two-five casing, as well, didn't he?' Ian picked the phone from its cradle and dialled Archie's number. Elsie answered.

'Good morning Mrs. Leggitt,' Ian began, 'is young Archie about? It's Ian Stuart at Chichelster.'

'Good morning Mr. Stuart,' Elsie said. 'He's in the back garden. I'll call him for you.'

A few seconds later, Archie picked up the phone.

Good morning, Ian,' he said, 'what can I do for you this fine morning?'

'Hello Archie, how are you?' Ian asked first.

'I'm fine thanks,' Archie replied, 'but that's not why you phoned, is it?'

Ian replied,

'No, Archie, there's not much gets past you, is there? Tony Church asked me to phone to thank you for your information

443

about the silver salesman in Pudborough's 'emporium'. We've got him in custody and he's helping us with our enquiries.'

'Do you think he killed old Jason Davies?' Archie asked.

'No, Archie, but he's linked to whoever did,' Ian said. 'Did you read the stop press in the Argus last night?'

'You mean the bit about this 'Gorse' bloke?' Archie asked. 'Do you think it's him, the one who escaped from the police after he was arrested?'

'Well, he's certainly our prime suspect at the moment,' Ian told him. 'We're watching his father pretty closely as well. He's a private investigator in Worthing. By all accounts, he's as crooked as they come, but he's clever enough that he hasn't been caught out so far. The hand gun used to kill old 'JD' was found in his car, the Mercedes which his son was using when he crashed.' Archie had wondered how a Gatwick security man could have been so reckless as to become involved in a crime like this.

'Is the other young lad, the one who we caught at the farm, something to do with it as well, Ian? I keep thinking how stupid it would be for a security guard to risk a good job like that, to try to sell stolen goods for someone else.' He said.

'You're not wrong,' Ian confirmed. 'The security guard's wife was kidnapped by the same group. We managed to rescue her this morning and we're waiting until she's recovered enough to tell us exactly what happened to her. This young Gorse lad is a danger to himself as well as anyone else who tries to stop him. His father's Mercedes was wrecked, but 'Daddy's' got another car, a big BMW so he doesn't seem bothered.'
Archie told Ian,

'We're all going for lunch at the Aftonia hotel in Worthing, later today. Bob Jempson and the two girls have invited Elsie and me, as a 'thank you' for helping them.'

'Have a good day Archie and give Elsie our best wishes,' Ian said. 'I'm sure you'll enjoy the food, it looks like a very good hotel. It was featured in the paper a few weeks ago, with some excellent reports from customers. The weather forecast is dry but cloudy, so you might fancy a stroll along the front afterwards, to walk off your lunch. Thanks again Archie, we'll bring you more news when we have any.'

'Thanks, Ian,' Archie said, 'I'll let you get on, have a good week-end. Bye for now.'

'Goodbye Archie,' said Ian and closed the call.

Tony Church looked at him,

'You know, if I heard you giving that much information to any other member of the public, I'd be worried, but I know he's safe and a good friend to have. He's always been the soul of discretion.'

'Yes, he's an asset to us and to the rural community,' Ian agreed. 'I do sometimes worry that he puts himself in danger, but it's often been his quick reaction that's saved the day.'

Tony's desk phone buzzed, he picked up,

'Me again, Guv,' Ken Foster said. 'It looks as though Gorse senior and his wife are off somewhere. I take it it's his wife, though she appears to be a lot younger than him, early fifties, I should think. They've both got in the big BMW, I'll try to follow at a discreet distance. I think I'll Phone Lesley and ask her to help out. He won't recognise her car. It's too late to get Phil, he's not mobile anyway. Got to go, or I'll lose him, they're just pulling out now.'

DS Lesley Stevens and DC Alan Bell were sitting in their car in one of the sea front car parks. The radio chirped up with Ken's 'basso profundo' voice.

'Lesley? Ken here, I'm tracking Gorse senior and his missus. They've just left the house in a big black BMW index, golf, nine one five two, lima, uniform, foxtrot. He's heading towards the sea front on Pericles Avenue. Can you get ready to tail him?'

'Affirmative, Ken,' Lesley responded. 'DC Alan Bell is driving. Tell us which direction he takes at the sea front and we'll try to connect with you.'

'He's indicating right, right, Lesley.' Ken said. 'Are you able to follow? I'll stay with him until you can confirm.'

445

Alan saw the big 'BM' as it swept across the road. It continued at a steady pace as he gradually caught up with it. Alan could see Ken's hire car behind him.

'We're in place and following,' Lesley called to Ken. 'We'll keep a safe distance, but he's not in any hurry.'

Gorse indicated right and turned off the sea front again. There was a fair bit of traffic coming in the opposite direction, so Alan had to wait for a gap. He turned into the road Gorse had taken, but there was no sign of him.

'We've lost him, Ken' said a disappointed Lesley. 'He could have gone almost anywhere from here. I don't think he knew he was being followed.'

They tried a few side roads, but without success. As Lesley had observed, he could have gone anywhere. Ken's mobile phone played an oriental melody, either 'Japanese or Korean'. It was Phil Travis.

'Gorse just turned up on a motorbike, Ken,' he said. 'He's gone into the office building, what do you want to do?'

'I'm on my way, Phil,' Ken Foster replied. 'See if you can pull the plug lead off the top of the spark plug. Be quick about it, don't let him see you, he might have got another hand gun.'

Before Phil had a chance to do anything, young Gorse came out of the building. He looked at Phil who stood, hands in pockets watching the reflection in the shop window opposite. Gorse had not taken off his helmet, so Phil could not be certain it was actually him. Before he could pull his phone out of his pocket to tell Ken, the biker had gone. Phil could still hear the noisy two stroke machine as Ken's car appeared in the road. Phil got in and explained what he had seen.

'I'm pretty sure it was him, Ken,' he said. 'He seemed to be in a bit of a panic, he wasn't gone for long enough for me to do anything.'

'We're not having much luck, Phil,' he said. 'We've just been given the slip by his old man and step-mum. I think the best thing we can do is have a break to gather our thoughts. We really ought to get something to eat as well. It's almost lunch time now. I'll call Lesley and Alan, maybe they'd like to join us.'

CHAPTER 63.

'What time are we thinking of going out?' Archie asked the girls.

Hannah thought for a moment before replying.

'How long will it take us to get there from Dad's? He's booked the table for one, I think.'

Quick as a flash Archie responded,

'That won't be any good. There's five of us. Four of us won't even get a seat!'

They laughed,

'Very sharp this morning, aren't we Archie,' Elsie said. 'Now can we please have a sensible answer?'

'Well, it's about twenty five minutes or so to Bob's and another twenty minutes to the hotel.'

'So if we leave at about mid day, we'll have plenty of time to get there and park the cars,' Hannah said. 'We'll have to take two cars. It'll be too much of a squash to get us all in one.'

I'll follow you two,' Archie announced. 'We'll all get there at the same time then. I expect there's a car park at the hotel, probably round the back. We'll find it when we get there.'

They were about to leave, at a few minutes before twelve, when the telephone rang. Elsie answered it.

'Hello, is that Mrs. Leggitt?' said a female voice.

'Yes, Elsie Leggitt here, who is asking?'

'I'm sorry, Mrs. Leggitt, its Cathy, Cathy Simons. I used to work for old Mr. Davies, at Ridge Farm.'

Elsie was slightly puzzled,

'Yes, Cathy, I remember you,' she said. 'I was friendly with your old 'mum'. We were sorry to hear about old Mr. Davies. It was a dreadful thing to do, to shoot a poor defenseless old man. What can I do for you, Cathy?'

Cathy sounded a little more confident now,

To tell you the truth, Mrs. Leggitt, it was your husband I needed to talk with. You'll probably think I'm being silly, but old Mr. Davies left me a sort of letter. The policeman found it when they came to investigate his death on the Monday morning.'

'Why would I think you were being silly?' Elsie asked her. Cathy hesitated again, 'well there's something strange about it. I mean the way it's been written. It's almost as though there's some sort of hidden code in it. I didn't notice it at first, but every time I look at it now, I'm convinced there's another hidden meaning in it somewhere.'

'Just a minute, Cathy,' Elsie said. 'I'll get Archie and you can explain it to him. I'm sure he'll help, was it a strange letter?'

'No, No, Mrs. Leggitt, it's a lovely letter, I shall treasure it until the day I die. I never realised that old Mr. Davies thought so highly of me.'

'Here's Archie now,' Elsie said, handing him the telephone. 'It's Cathy Simons,' she told him, 'she used to work for old Jason.'

'Hello Cathy,' Archie greeted her, 'Elsie says you've got a letter from old Jason and you think there may be something odd about it. Is that right?'

Cathy stammered a little,

'Well, it's not quite what I said, Mr. Leggitt,' she tried to explain. I think the letter is most sincere, in fact one of the loveliest letters I've ever had. I keep reading it and I think there's a hidden meaning in the wording. Oh, it's no good. I can't seem to explain what I mean. I expect you all think I'm making it up.'

'I don't think anything of the sort,' Archie reassured her. 'From what you've just said, it seems to me that the only way to explain what you're thinking about it, is to let me have a look at it. I'll understand if it's too private, I wouldn't mention it to anyone without your say so.'

Yes, yes please, Mr. Leggitt,' Cathy said, 'when can I bring it to you?'

'There's a temporary problem today, Cathy,' he began to explain. 'You see we have guests at present and we're all out to lunch in Worthing in a short while. In fact you only just caught us, another five minutes and we'd have left.'

'Oh, I'm sorry,' said Cathy, 'I don't want to disturb you, Mr. Leggitt. I mentioned it to Mr. Skrobe, you know, next to where the young Mr. Jeffery is building that hotel place. He said that you'd probably have a look at it and you were the best person to ask. I did think about taking it to the police, but then I'd feel stupid if it was nothing and anyway they'd probably want to keep it. I don't want to lose it, as I just said to Mrs. Leggitt, it's very precious to me. I know he wasn't a very popular man, but he always treated me very well. I can only speak as I find, can't I?' Archie smiled to himself,

'Yes, Cathy,' he agreed, 'that's the best way to be. Sometimes we can be too quick to judge people. Why not phone me again tomorrow, Sunday, we'll arrange a time that's convenient to both of us.'

Thank you Mr. Leggitt,' she said. 'I'll phone you tomorrow, late morning, about eleven, is that OK?'

'Yes, that'll be fine, Cathy. You can call me, 'Archie', everyone else does. We'll arrange something tomorrow, I've got to go now, or we'll be late. Bye Cathy.'

'Bye, Mr. Leggitt and thank you very much,' she put the phone down.

Elsie smiled as she looked at Archie,

'Do you think there's anything in it, Arch?' she asked.

'I'll let you know tomorrow,' he replied. 'Now come on everybody, let's go and enjoy our lunch in Worthing.'

Bob Jempson was waiting for them in the entrance hall at the nursing home. He was looking well and had on a smart jacket and a new pair of black trousers.

'Will I need a coat?' he asked Hilda as she went up to greet him.

'I think you'd better bring one, Dad, even if you don't wear it just now. It might be a bit cooler when we come out of the hotel. It always seems cooler on the coast than it does here.'
He went back to his room and returned with a coat over his arm. Archie and Elsie remained in the car and watched as the two young women got him seated comfortably.

'You can see the nursing training coming out there,' Elsie remarked. 'They think the world of their old Dad, don't they?'
Archie smiled and nodded.
The 'Aftonia' hotel was right on the sea front, the road next to it had a sign pointing left to, 'Aftonia Car Park' underneath it said 'Patrons Only'. They turned into the road in 'convoy' and found the car park on their left. There were plenty of spaces, so the girls drove into one close to the hotel's rear entrance. Archie parked at the end of the same row. Elsie got out and began walking towards the others, leaving Archie to lock up and follow. He had just got out and closed his door, when a big black BMW pulled into the next space. The passenger, a woman in her fifties, opened her door rather too quickly and it hit Archie's back.

'Oh,' she said, 'I'm so sorry. It's such a heavy door. I didn't mean to bump you. Are you alright?'
Archie turned to look at her and said,

'Yes, I'm fine thank you, no harm done,' he locked his door and went to join the others as they entered the hotel.
They followed the signs to the restaurant, where they were met by the head waiter.

'Have you a reservation?' he asked.

Archie was giggling to himself behind Elsie's back.

'Do we look like 'red indians' he muttered.

'Be quiet Arch,' Elsie told him, 'don't you dare show us up.'

'Yes,' Bob told him, 'the name's Jempson. I requested a window table, so that we could enjoy the view.'

The waiter checked his list,

'Yes sir,' he said, 'a window table for five persons, is that correct?'

'Yes, that's right,' Bob said.

'Would you like to walk this way please?' He said, as he set off across the room.

Archie was still giggling.

'Now what?' Elsie asked, crossly.

He leaned towards her and said,

'If I walked that way the whole village would be talking about me! Even you'd be wonderin' Else. I'd wear me trousers out from the inside!'

'Shut up Archie,' she said grinning at him.

'What's he doing, Elsie?' Hannah asked.

'He's being his usual stupid self, Hannah,' Elsie told her. 'I'll tell you when we've got our seats.'

'Can I take your coat, sir?' The waiter asked Bob.

'Thank you,' Bob said, and handed it to him. They sat at their table. It was a very nice restaurant. Everything still had that new smell and feel to it. Their view over the channel was superb. There were a few sailing dinghies out, and some larger ships on the horizon. The hazy sun was warm, through the big picture windows. They sat chatting for a few minutes and the waiter brought the menus for them to study. Archie decided on his choice in about two minutes and began to look around him. The woman who had bumped him with her door was with an older man. They were at the table to Archie's right. From the odd snippets of conversation he overheard, he gathered that they were married. Her name was Delia and his was, Leon. They were also studying their menus and discussing their choices.

'Have you decided, Archie?' Hilda asked him.

'I think I'll go for the fillet steak, please,' he said. 'I'd like mine medium rare, if you don't mind.'

'What about a starter?' Elsie asked him.

Archie shook his head,

'No thanks, but you all have one if you want to. I'll be happy to wait. I usually find the starter too filling and then don't enjoy the main course as much.'

Archie listened to the conversation and was a little relieved when he heard that nobody else wanted a starter. Hilda raised a finger to summon the waiter. She held the wine list and asked,

'Please tell me, what is the 'house' red?'

The waiter looked at his list and replied,

'It's an Australian Merlot, madam. It is a very popular choice. Would you like to try it? I can bring you a sample.'

'No need for that, thank you,' Hilda told him. 'I'd like a bottle of that and two of the Chardonnay please.'

'Thank you, madam,' said the waiter. 'Are you ready to order your meals?'

Hilda consulted the menu and placed the orders for everybody. She gave precise instructions with regard to how the steaks should be cooked and which vegetables she had selected.

'Very good, Madam,' the waiter bowed. 'I'll bring your drinks straight away. The food will be twenty minutes or so. Everything is freshly cooked to order, most people don't mind waiting.'

Archie, never one to miss an opportunity, smiled at the waiter and said,

'I thought you were doing the waiting.'

He grinned at Archie,

'Yes sir, I will wait on your table, if you wouldn't mind waiting at your table.'

Bob was laughing, as the waiter patted Archie's shoulder and said,

'Can I get you anything else? A jug of water, perhaps?'

'Oh, yes, please,' Hannah said. 'Thank you.'

The drinks arrived and Bob and Hilda tasted both the wines and gave their approval. The waiter went away again and they began to chat amiably. The hotel was first class, they were all impressed with the both the décor and the quality of the service. The house red was quite pleasant, Archie would have preferred a pint of Harvey's bitter, but decided to keep that thought to himself for now.

Their food arrived about half an hour later. They continued their conversation as they enjoyed their meal. It all looked excellent, well presented without being pretentious like some of the so called 'elite' gourmet establishments. Archie's steak was cooked just the way he liked it and the red wine complimented the flavours to perfection. The couple sitting to his right seemed to be in serious discussion. The man raised his voice a little now and then, but softened it when he realised that he was attracting the attention of some of the other diners. Archie caught the odd word or phrase from their conversation. Not because he was intent on eavesdropping, but more because of the occasional increase in the volume. Once he thought he heard the woman say, 'Lionel', which rang a distant bell in Archie's mind. Where had he heard that name? It must have been very recently. He put it to the back of his mind, whilst he joined in the groups chatter about what Hannah's intentions were with regard to her job. It seemed that she was seriously considering a return to the Chichelster hospital, where she did her training. She was insistent that she would not be returning to Belgium, neither did she wish to return to the hospital in Lincoln, where Hilda worked.

'It's too far away from Dad, for a start,' she said. 'It's not fair to you, Hilda, to keep imposing on you in your little flat. The other thing I'm not too keen on is the Lincolnshire weather!'

The others laughed, when Bob said,

'That's a good one, Hannah. 'I'm afraid I can't take the job, because the weather's not good enough.' I don't suppose many employers have heard that given as a reason to decline their offer of employment.'

Hannah was also laughing at herself.

'I'm only telling the truth, Dad,' she said. 'That's the way I feel about it, I've only got my comfort in mind.'

'There were several adverts in the jobs section of last night's Argus,' Elsie said. 'There are vacancies at Chi as well as East Grinstead and the Royal Sussex at Brighton. We've still got it haven't we Arch?'

Archie nodded, a little vaguely,

'Yes Else,' he said, 'I haven't thrown it out yet.'

That was it, the Argus, in the stop press. That's where he'd seen it. It was the bit about the young man who had been arrested and then escaped from Shoreham police. Ian had told him he was wanted in connection with old Jason's murder. What was his other name? Something quite short, he seemed to recall.

Archie's mind was sifting through the information he had stored.

'Are you alright, Archie?' Hannah asked him. 'You look a bit uncomfortable.'

Archie sat upright,

'Sorry, everybody,' he said, 'I was miles away, thinking about something else. Probably I was concentrating a bit too hard, trying to remember something, but I'm fine thanks Hannah. It was a lovely meal, lovely company and a splendid location.'

'What were you thinking about, Arch?' Elsie asked.

'I was trying to remember something,' he said, 'that's all. It doesn't matter now. It'll probably come to me eventually.'

'Well, what were you trying to remember?' Elsie asked.

Archie just looked at her and grinned. Bob and the girls looked at Archie enquiringly.

'D'you know,' he began, 'I sometimes wish I had a tape recorder with me, to capture this sort of conversation.'

'What do you mean?' Hilda asked him.

Archie smiled at her and explained,

'Hannah asked if I was OK and I told her I was trying to remember something. In the next second, Elsie asked me what I was trying to remember! If I could tell her that much, I wouldn't still be trying to remember it, would I?'

Hannah was laughing,

'I know what you mean Archie,' she agreed. 'It's like when you've lost something and someone asks, 'where did you put it?' If you knew that, it wouldn't be lost!'

While Hannah was speaking, the waiter came to clear the next table. Archie heard him ask, 'Was the veal to your satisfaction, Mrs. Gorse?'

'That's it!' Archie thought, 'Gorse.' He didn't hear her reply. Archie seemed to come awake with a sudden sense of urgency. He mustn't let the others notice, but knew he had to act quickly. When he returned his attention to his own group, he realised that Elsie was recounting their shopping trip on Thursday. He heard her say,

'Yes, I suppose it was a bit of a silly question, but you're just as bad, Archie Leggitt. When we got back from shopping on Thursday, I took my handbag and let myself in, while you got the shopping from the car.' She looked up at old Bob, who was enjoying the banter. 'Then, when we'd put the shopping away I said to you that I couldn't find my door key.'

Archie was giggling self consciously as he recalled the occasion.

'Yes Else,' he admitted, 'and then I asked whether you had it when you came in?'

Everyone was laughing, even the two people at the next table were grinning. They'd probably caught the gist of the conversation, or at least the last bit.

Archie dared not say precisely what he had remembered. Discretion was essential, but he must let Ian Stuart know what he had accidentally discovered. The parents of the suspect in the murder case, were sitting relaxed at the next table.

'I hope you'll excuse me,' he said. 'I'll be back in a few minutes, but I need to find the Gents toilet.'

'I saw one on the way in, Arch,' Bob told him. 'There's one just inside the back door on the left. So it'll be on your right as you go out.'

'Thanks Bob,' Archie said as he got up from his chair. He folded his napkin and left it by his empty plate. He noted the toilet, just inside the door to the rear car park. Archie nipped outside to the footpath from the car park. He could see the BMW parked next to his. There didn't seem to be anyone else around, apart from an elderly couple. The man was getting a folding wheelchair from the luggage boot, whilst the lady, presumably his wife, stood by the car, supported by a younger woman.. Archie pulled his mobile phone from his pocket and selected Ian Stuart's mobile number from his list of contacts. It was answered on the third ring.

'Stuart here, can I help you?' Ian said, in an official voice.

'Ian, its Archie Leggitt. I don't like to disturb your Saturday, but your escapologist's parents are dining at the next table to us, in the Aftonia hotel in Worthing.'

'Archie, thank you very much,' he said. 'Is there any sign of the son, Lionel?'

'Not yet, but I overheard them talking about him as though they were expecting to see him. His parent's car is a big BMW and it's parked next to ours in the car park behind the hotel.'

'Archie, thank you very much for the update, I must act on this immediately,' Ian Stuart said. 'One of our teams in Worthing had followed him from his house, but he got away from them in the traffic on the sea front. I'll phone Ken Foster and tell him where they are. Oh, and just one thing, if you should happen to see any of our chaps, don't acknowledge them, they are working under cover. Sorry, must go, no time to lose on this one.' The call ended abruptly.

Archie began to assure Ian that he understood, but realised that he was talking to nobody. The line was dead. He closed his phone and replaced it in his pocket. When he returned to his group at their table, Hilda was reading aloud from the dessert menu. The others had chosen theirs, Elsie wanted the apple pie with ice cream, Hannah and Hilda both chose the banoffee pie and Bob opted for the cheeseboard.

'I think that'll do me please,' Archie said. 'I prefer cheese to sticky stuff, especially after that lovely succulent steak.'

At the end of their meal they decided on a gentle stroll along the sea front, before the drive home. Bob summoned the Maitre D and asked for the account which was brought in a hard backed leather folder. Bob noted the details and nodded his approval. He placed the money in the folder, along with a generous tip and handed it to him, saying,

'An excellent meal and first class service, thank you very much.'

The Maitre D thanked him and said that the waiter would bring their coats to them as they left. Archie noticed that the couple at the next table had ordered more coffee.

When they got to the car park, Archie noticed a car with two occupants, parked almost opposite the entrance. He guessed this was probably the undercover policemen whom Ian had mentioned. Before they got into their cars, Archie and Elsie both thanked Bob for a lovely outing. The girls would take him back to the nursing home and follow on to Wigglesworth a little later.

CHAPTER 64.

Sandra Cranham was awake and feeling much better. PC Brian Taylor sat by her bed and waited for her to drink her tea. She thanked him for waiting and asked about her husband.

'Has he done something really stupid? Will he go to prison?' Brian was conscious of the fear in her eyes and didn't want to say something which may cause her to regress.

'All I can tell you at the present time is that he's helping us with our enquiries into the attempted sale of some stolen items,' he said. 'We realised that something had happened to you when we couldn't contact you, Sandra. You don't mind me calling you 'Sandra', do you?'

'No, of course not,' she said. 'I'm sorry I couldn't tell you much when I first woke up. I'll tell you everything I can remember now, though. One thing I do know is that beach hut belonged to my stepfather, Leon Gorse. That makes me think that his wayward junkie son had something to do with my abduction. I'm almost sure it was my stepfather's car they took me away in.'

'I'm Brian,' he said, 'Brian Taylor. We've got the two men who abducted you, but they are not co-operating with us, as yet.

They are saying that they were told exactly what to do by someone called, 'Gas'. Do you know someone by that name?' Sandra's eyes showed fear again.

'Yes,' she said, 'that's him, Lionel Gorse, he's pure evil. I'm thinking he probably arranged for his friends to take me as a hostage to make my husband, Victor, do something. His full name's Lionel Peregrine Gorse, so his initials are LPG. That's why they call him 'Gas Gorse'. Have you got him in custody?' Brian looked at her and he could see the fear in her eyes.

'Not yet, Sandra,' he told her, 'but soon, very soon. He managed to escape from Shoreham police after he crashed the Mercedes, but we're confident we'll get him soon. We found your mobile phone in Gorse's Mercedes. We also found a hand gun. When we catch up with him he'll find he's in more trouble than he can handle. Have you any thoughts on where he might try to hide out?'
Sandra sat quietly thinking.

'My head's still aching a bit, but I'll try to work out what he might do,' she said. 'The thing is, most of the time he's as high as a kite on some drug or other. I almost disowned my mother when she married Len Gorse. His name is Leonard, by the way, not 'Leon'. Anyway, my mother can't stand Lionel.
He shows no respect to her, or anybody else, come to that. I know she hates the way he always refers to her as 'Dolly Delila'. Her name is Delia and he should call her that. Sorry, that's not what you asked me, is it? My first thought is that he'll go to 'daddy' for some more money and a hidey hole. I just hope he doesn't let him use the boat.'

'Boat?' PC Taylor asked. 'What boat would that be, Sandra?'

'It was my late father's boat. When he died it became my mother's but since she married Gorse, they both own it jointly.'

'Is it a big boat?' Brian asked her. 'Where do they keep it?'
Sandra looked directly at him, her eyes wide open,

'It is quite big, I don't know the dimensions, but it's got a big cabin with beds and a proper kitchen. It's at the Brighton Marina.

I don't know the berth number, but it's quite close to the town end. It's got a name, 'Saxon Bowyer', that was my dad's name, Bowyer.'

'Would you mind if I let my colleagues know about it?' Brian asked her. 'They could watch the boat, in case he tries to get on it.'

'Yes, alright,' Sandra agreed, 'if he's reckless enough to have me abducted and tortured, what else might he be capable of?' Brian thought for a moment, wondering whether he should say anything at all to that question.

'Reckless and stupid,' he told her.

'Do you think he would go as far as killing someone?' Sandra asked. 'Would he be capable of that?'

'I'm not really supposed to give out this sort of information,' he said. 'You've been very honest with me, Sandra, so I feel I should be the same with you. This is strictly confidential, so I'm relying on your discretion, but I can tell you that Lionel is at present one of the main suspects for the murder of a man in Wigglesworth. That's why it's most important that we catch him quickly. He's dangerous and he may be armed, we don't know. That is another reason we need to ensure your safety. Unless we can arrest and hold him before you are discharged, you will have police protection until he is behind bars.'

Sandra was not just concerned for her own safety, but also for her husband's.

'You'd better go outside to use your phone, but go now, please,' she said. 'We've got to help your colleagues to stop him. My mother won't do what's right. She's been brainwashed by Len Gorse. I think he's probably a bit of a crook, but he's clever enough not to get caught. Go now, Brian. Phone your boss, quickly. Lionel may already be at the boat, if that's his plan.'

Brian nodded and smiled at her as he went out to reception to phone the desk at Chichelster police station.

Mike Hodd answered the telephone,

'Hello Sarge,' Brian said. 'Can you get a message to either Ken Foster or Lesley Stevens? It's urgent, I'm with Mrs. Cranham, she's still in hospital, but she's just told me she thinks she might know where young Gorse may be hiding.'

He explained the details to Mike Hodd and told him that DI Church ought to be informed of these developments.

'Yes Brian,' said Sergeant Hodd. 'Chief Purvis is here, I'll tell him, so that he can keep Brighton police up to speed. Our teams may need their assistance. Just a minute Brian, I'll give you Ken and Lesley's mobile numbers, you can call 'em direct. Tell 'em that I've given the details to Ron Purvis and Tony Church.'

Mike Hodd consulted the list on his desk. 'Have you got a pencil?' he asked.

'Ready and waiting, Sarge,' he confirmed.

He wrote the numbers in his pocket book, thanked Mike Hodd and telephoned Ken Foster. Brian explained what he had learned from Sandra Cranham.

'Mike Hodd's going to tell the DI and get Chief Purvis to let Brighton know what's happening.' Brian told him, 'You'll probably need some uniform help if you manage to catch him. The only problem I can see is the uniforms won't know who you are, so you'll need to identify yourselves pretty quick or you could find they've arrested you for civil disturbance.'

'Well done, Brian,' Ken said, laughing. 'Don't worry about that, we'll make sure they know who we are. Old Archie Leggitt found Gorse senior for us, after he gave us the slip. I'll tell Lesley what you've found out, she's just over the road, in case he went left when he came out of the car park. She can take over my 'obbo' and I'll get along to the marina. You say, 'Saxon Bowman', is the name of the boat?'

'Nearly right,' Brian said, 'Saxon Bowyer.' Bowyer was Sandra's father's name.'

'Right, gotcha,' Ken said. 'Give me your mobile number Brian, if you're in Brighton already, we may need your help.'

462

Brian told him the number and asked, 'you'll let me know what's happening, won't you?'

'Yes, we'll keep you informed Brian, and thanks for that.' Ken told him. 'We'll get moving now. You go back and keep watch over Mrs. Cranham, just in case he decides to try something silly again with her. Keep your phone switched on, just in case we need you.'

Brian Taylor went back into the hospital to sit with his charge,

'Did you manage to find someone to tell?' She asked him. 'I just thought it's Saturday, isn't it? I seem to have lost track of time since I was taken on Thursday morning.'

'That's not uncommon, Sandra,' Brian reassured her. 'You've been traumatised by your ordeal. The basic human instinct is survival, which thankfully you've succeeded in accomplishing. Everything else is of secondary importance. Don't worry about it being Saturday, the police are there twenty-four seven.'

'When will I be able to see my husband?' Sandra asked him. 'I want to find out exactly what he's done to land himself in so much trouble.'

Brian frowned,

'It may be a day or two yet, I'm afraid. Although the police operate twenty-four seven, I'm afraid the courts don't. He'll probably get a bail hearing on Monday and with a bit of luck he'll be allowed home. I think he may have blown his job, that's the down side.'

Sandra began to look tearful again,

'Vic had a good steady job at Gatwick, if he's lost it because of Lionel I don't know how we'll manage. I still don't understand what hold he could have had over Vic. My husband is a big man. He's obviously been threatened with something, but I won't find out until I can talk with him.'

Brian smiled at her. She was obviously an intelligent woman and had shown remarkable courage.

'Just try not to guess too much,' he said. 'I know it must be difficult for you, but you'll be more able to help him if you're

rested and recovered from your ordeal before you see him. If you want to have a sleep, Sandra, don't think about me being here. I'm just making sure that nobody can get at you.'
Sandra nodded he acceptance,

'I think perhaps that would be a good idea,' she agreed. 'I still feel very tired, you will wake me if anything happens, won't you?'

CHAPTER 65.

Tony Church was asleep in his armchair. He'd had his lunch and been to the pub with Ian Stuart, for a couple of beers. His mobile beeped and for a second or two he was confused by the sound. If he had been out of the house, he would have reacted instantly. He pulled it from his pocket and answered it. It was Chief Inspector Purvis.

'Ron Purvis here,' he began. 'Sorry to disturb you on your day off Tony, but I need to bring you up to speed on this Gorse thing.'

He told Tony everything he had found out and also that he had alerted the Brighton Chief to the possible dangers when Gorse was captured.

'Another thing which I've just found out about is that you've got PC Taylor on Saturday overtime, sitting in a hospital watching a female patient. Why, Tony? Is she dangerous?'

Tony had been expecting this reaction.

'No Ron, but she's in danger. She was abducted assaulted and left bound and gagged in a locked beach hut. She was unconscious when we got to her. Her husband is in the cells at Chichelster, on a receiving and handling charge. Another of our 'customers' is Bernard Cavendish, whose father's boat was blown up on Worthing beach last week. He had borrowed a rifle from Gorse and was in fear of his life because he was unable to return it. This whole sequence of events, plus the cold blooded murder of old Jason Davies, is the work of the Gorse family. Until they are both safely under lock and key, I'm not prepared to put anyone else's life at risk. So, Brian Taylor or another officer will remain with Mrs. Cranham until I feel that she is safe. I hope you don't have a problem with that Ron but if you do, please take it up with the Super.'

'No, Tony, don't go there,' the Chief said. 'If that's what we need to do to ensure her safety, that's good enough for me. The sooner we catch this evil piece of garbage, the happier I will be.

'There's no point in my going over to Brighton,' Tony explained. 'It's not our patch for a start and the two teams I've put in place know what they're up against. I'm happy that the local police have been informed, but I'm just hoping they don't go in too soon or too heavy and spook him before we can grab him.'

'I know it can be difficult working outside our own box,' said Ron Purvis. 'Just keep me informed, please Tony. If you need any help, just give me a call, I'm here at home, you've got my number, haven't you?'

'Yes, but I'll try not to disturb you, Ron.'

'OK understood and good luck'. He rang off.

CHAPTER 66.

DS Ken Foster explained the situation to Lesley and Alan. They would wait for the Gorse's to leave the hotel car park and follow them. Ken phoned Phil on his mobile and told him to get down to the sea front at the end of his road, where he would pick him up on his way to Brighton Marina. Within about ten minutes of Ken driving away, Lesley saw the big black BMW pulling out of the car park. To her surprise, he turned left, away from the sea front. Alan used the car park to do a quick turn round and followed Gorse's car. Taking care not to get too close, he followed it through several junctions until it turned right onto the A27. Through the top end of Portslade, Gorse forked right onto the Old Shoreham Road, and then right again onto Station Road. When they reached the sea front again he turned left towards Brighton. Lesley was on her mobile telling Ken what was happening. He had picked up Phil Travis and was almost at the Marina, when Lesley told him that they were now heading towards Brighton on the A259, the coast road.

Ken found a parking spot, just before the Marina. As they pulled into the space, Phil said,

'There's a couple of uniform PC's coming along the Marina, Ken. They don't look as though they're looking for any boats, so it's probably just a routine foot patrol.'

Ken had already seen them,

'I'm going to ask them a question, Phil,' he said. 'Wait in the car for me, I'll be right back.'

The two officers seemed to be chatting and just strolled casually towards Ken. He stood and made to check his watch, looking around as though he was meeting someone. As the two policemen drew near to him, he stood in front of them and showed his warrant card.

Could I have a word please, Gentlemen?' he asked. 'Over there by the maroon Vauxhall please, make it look as though you're checking the tax disc, if you don't mind.'

They followed Ken back to the car, where Phil sat waiting in the passenger seat.

'Have you been notified of our operation?' Ken asked the two officers.

'Yes,' said the older one, 'we don't know much in the way of details though. Who is it we're supposed to be looking for?'

Ken smiled at him,

'This is my colleague, Phil Travis,' he told them. 'We will probably be glad of your help presently, but we don't want to chance spooking him. There are a lot of people about, so we have to consider public safety. Our suspect may be armed, we don't know. All we do know is that he's dangerous and desperate. We'd really appreciate it if you could make yourselves invisible, just until we manage to corner him. Can you manage to do that?'

The older of the two nodded his acceptance.

'Yes, OK, we'll just wait over by the information stand, next to the office. Have you got radios?'

'No,' Ken replied, 'just mobile phones, but you'll be able to see us from the kiosk. We're looking for a particular boat, it's called, 'Saxon Bowyer', do you know which one it is?'

The two officers looked at each other.

468

'It's the fourth one past that flagpole,' said the younger of the two officers. 'There are a couple of people on board now, looks as though they're getting ready to go out. Mind you, with the way the wind is picking up, I'm glad I'm not going with them.'
Ken raised his eyebrows in alarm,

'What do these people look like?' he asked.
The alarm showed on Ken's face, so that the older officer realised that something was very wrong.

The young bloke is wearing a white baseball cap, back to front and there's a dark haired woman. She's a bit older than him. I'd say she was in her forties. He was giving the orders and she was trying to do as she was told, but it was obvious to me that she didn't know much about boats.'

'Did she seem to be afraid of him?' Ken asked.

'Now you come to mention it,' the officer said, 'I think perhaps she was, a bit.'

'Did she see you as you walked past the boat?' Ken asked him.

'No, I don't think so,' he said. 'The youngster did, he put his head down and went down into the cabin. She followed him and I heard him shout, 'I mean now, do it now Elizabeth,' then she came back out to the open cockpit and took a mobile phone from her coat pocket.'
Ken nodded to him,

'Thanks very much,' he said. 'I've got another colleague on her way, so we'll try to contain this situation without anyone getting hurt. The fourth one past the flagpole, you say?'
The officers both nodded.

'You'd better leave us now, in case he's watching.' Ken said. 'Although he won't see us here from down on the water, the concrete quay will shield us from view.'
The two uniforms walked slowly across to where the information kiosk was situated. Ken saw the older one begin talking on his radio. Ken pulled his mobile from his jacket and dialled Chichelster front desk.

Mike Hodd answered and Ken began speaking in an urgent tone.

'Mike, Ken Foster here, can you tell me the first names of Cavendish's parents, it's urgent.'

'You're in luck, Ken,' he said. 'Carol's report is right here, father is, Gordon George Cavendish and the mother, wait a minute, ah, yes, Elizabeth Ann Cavendish. Is there anything else I can do for you?'

'No thanks, Mike,' Ken said. 'You just found the right piece of our jig saw puzzle. I'll get back to you later.' He closed his phone and turned to Phil.

'It's looking like more than a coincidence, Phil,' he said. 'When young Gorse pranged his father's Merc, he was on his way to East Grinstead, to visit Cavendish's parents in hospital. I'll have a little side bet with you that he's taken Mrs. Cavendish as a hostage, thinking it will guarantee his own safety.'
Phil Travis grinned,

'I know better than to take a bet with you, Ken,' he told him. 'All I'll say is that if we can contain him and get a result, I'll buy you a pint anyway.'

'Two pints,' Ken said, grinning at him. 'Guinness, not that old 'Euro fizz' stuff that you lads drink, OK?'
Phil nodded his acceptance.
The big black BMW slowly turned into the car park, and drove into the owners' section. There was an automated security system which lifted the barrier as Gorse senior put his card into the slot. He retrieved his pass card and drove past the two policemen and parked facing the railings.
Ken was about to ask, 'where's Lesley got to,' when he spotted Alan, parking a few spaces behind him. Lesley got out first and came up to meet them.

'Wait for Alan to join us,' Ken said, 'then I won't need to say everything twice. You took your time getting here, Lesley was there a problem?'
Lesley looked down and shook her head,

'Let's just say he did everything we didn't expect him to do. Instead of coming back to the sea front, he drove up to the A27 then forked right on the Old Shoreham Road, before hitting the sea front again at Portslade.'

'Here's Alan, now,' Ken said, 'gather round, children, I'll tell you the story so far!'

Ken gave them all the information which he had gained from the two uniformed officers, who were still in view by the kiosk. As he spoke, Alan interrupted to say,

'Gorse has just taken a holdall from the boot of the car. Don't all look at him, he might see us and get suspicious. She's staying in the car by the looks of it He's going into the office now.'

'We need to move quickly,' Ken said. 'Lesley, you and Alan look like a young couple. I want you to stroll along the quay and have a look at the boat. If there's anyone in sight, try to have a quick chat. Admire the boat. Ask if they're going out in it, you know the sort of thing. See if there are any signs that the woman doesn't want to be there. I'd bet Gorse has got a change of clothes for his son in the holdall. Don't just stop at his boat, let him think you're looking at all the boats, as though you're admiring them. Keep an eye open for him to arrive. Don't get in his way. He's probably as devious and dangerous as his son. Right, off you go, before he comes out of the office.'

The young 'couple' strolled slowly along the quay, admiring the boats as they went.

'Look at this one, Lesley,' Alan said as they got to Gorse's boat. 'Now that really is a lovely boat, look at her lines.'

'Yes,' said Lesley, 'look, there's someone on board, it looks as though they're getting ready to go out.' Lionel Gorse came out of the cabin, followed by the woman.

'Did you want something?' He shouted up to them.

'No,' Lesley replied. 'We were just admiring your lovely boat. My boyfriend thinks she's got beautiful lines.'

The woman turned her head to look at them both.

471

'You look as though you're getting ready to go out in her,' Lesley said to her.

'No, we're just having a tidy up, aren't we?' She said to the young man. 'I think it would be a bit too windy to be out in the channel today.'

The young man looked up at Alan.

'Have you got a boat here?' he asked.

Alan smiled,

'No, but I'd love to have one,' he said. 'How expensive are the mooring fees here?'

The man shrugged,

'I don't know, it's my father's boat, here he comes now, you could ask him.' He paused and then added, 'perhaps not, he looks as though he's in a bad mood.'

The young 'couple stepped back as Gorse approached.

'What do you want?' he asked abruptly.

Alan replied in an equally abrupt manner,

'We don't want anything. We were admiring the boats whilst we had a stroll. I stopped here because I thought this boat was very nice. That's all.'

Gorse scowled,

'Well you've had a look now, so clear off and look at some of the others.'

Lesley and Alan moved slowly along to the next boat.

Gorse tossed the holdall down to his son, who was till standing in the open cockpit. The zip fastener was broken and a couple of items fell from it onto the deck.

'I told you it was broken,' young Gorse shouted to his father, who was now beginning to glow with anger.

'All the money you've had off me, you could have bought a new holdall every week. But no! You'd rather buy drugs and go robbing people. It's cost me a fortune to protect my good name and what do you care?' He shouted. 'I'm coming down now, and you'd better behave yourself, or it'll be the very last time you get any help from me.'

Lesley and Alan sauntered away a few paces, to stand and look at the next boat. Gorse senior could still be heard, even though he was in the cabin. Alan began pointing at the boat next to where they stood, as though he had lost interest in Gorse's. He said in an undertone to Lesley,

'I'm just doing this in case he happens to be looking at us. I'm pretty sure he thinks we're just a couple enjoying a stroll, but I can still hear them talking, so we'll hang on for a bit, shall we?' Lesley agreed and began to join in the charade, pointing at other boats and reading their names. They could still hear Gorse, who continued to shout at his son.

'You're a bloody waste of space, Lionel. You don't think about anybody but yourself, in fact you don't think, full bloody stop. Why did you lend her son my rifle? What's she doing here, anyway?'

'It's your fault really,' Lionel shouted back. 'You wanted me to collect ten grand from Davies and I didn't have anything to threaten him with. I couldn't go in there with a bloody great rifle, could I?'

'So you traded my rifle for Cavendish's hand gun, is that it?' Elizabeth Cavendish began to cry,

'He made me come here, Mr. Gorse,' she said between sobs. 'He's got a knife and he said if I didn't do as I was told, he'd make sure my husband never left the hospital.'

'Go and wait in my car with my wife, Mrs. Cavendish. I'll phone and tell her you are coming. She will meet you at the entrance to the owner's car park. Don't worry. Nothing will happen to either you or your husband.'

Alan and Lesley moved on a couple of moorings and began looking at another boat.

Mrs. Cavendish nervously climbed from the boat and began to walk back along the quay. She glanced round a couple of times and saw Gorse watching her. Gorse's wife walked towards her and put an arm round her shoulders to support her. They walked together, back past the two policemen and got into the BMW.

Gorse returned to the boat's cabin.

Alan heard what he took to be a cry of pain, from the son.

'That's just a start,' Gorse shouted. 'There's more to come, you can try to fight back if you think you're big enough, but you prefer to threaten old men and women, don't you?

There was no response that Alan or Lesley could hear.

'You arranged to have your step-sister kidnapped and assaulted. Then left her unconscious in my beach hut, for two fishermen to find and rescue. All because you wanted to hurt her husband who, unbeknown to you, you bloody imbecile, had got himself arrested while trying to sell your stolen goods. He's lost his job and got himself a criminal record, because and God alone knows why, he's afraid of what you might do. Then you think you can get at young Cavendish through his parents. You've left a trail of destruction a mile wide, and still think you've got away with it, don't you?

This time they heard the son shout back at his father.

'You got away with it for years, why shouldn't I?'

'You want me to answer that?' His father bellowed back at him. 'I'll tell you why, because I'm not stupid like you. I didn't think I was the bloody 'Godfather' in the Mafia. I didn't get greedy or careless. I kept myself to myself. I didn't involve any outsiders. I didn't get high on drugs then crash my father's car. Nor did I get myself arrested and think I was clever to escape from the police. Have you got any more questions?'

'No.' Lionel shouted. 'I could have dropped you in the shit several times, how about family loyalties?'

There were the sounds of a scuffle, followed by a loud 'thump'.

'Did you really think you could attack me with a knife in this small space? You make me sick. Now get up off the floor and sit there,' Gorse shouted. 'I want to ask you some questions.'

'You've broken my wrist, I think.' Lionel whined.

'I should have broken your neck, probably years ago,' said his father.

Lesley could see Ken and Phil standing at the end of the Marina. Ken held up his mobile and pointed at it with his other hand. Lesley shook her head, no, not yet. She placed her finger on her lips and then pulled her ear. Basic sign language usually worked. Ken pointed at his chest and then at Lesley. He made his fingers simulate walking. Lesley shook her head again and Ken held up his hands in defeat.

Gorse had begun to thump something solid, possibly a part of the cabin. He raised his voice and shouted the words individually for greater emphasis.

'Why - did - you - shoot - old - Davies?'

'He wouldn't give me the money, the ten grand.'

'Did you get it after you'd shot him?'

'No, course not, he was dead then, wasn't he? I taught him a lesson though, didn't I?'

'I bloody give up!' Gorse shouted so loudly that Lesley jumped.

'I'm surprised Ken didn't hear that,' she said to Alan. 'I'm sure he would have done if it wasn't for this wind.'

'What? What do you mean?' They heard Lionel ask his father. The silence was deafening!

'You taught a dead man a lesson, did you? Well how do you top that? I suppose you'll be in the cemetery next, threatening a few headstones!'

'You shot his wife,' young Gorse shouted back. 'What's the difference?'

'That was years ago, it's all forgotten now. Anyway, I did that so your mother wouldn't leave me. I've given you everything, is this how you repay me? By bringing it all up again? If you hadn't shot Davies it would have stayed buried, just like Mary Eldridge.'

'You probably had something to do with mum's accident as well. I wouldn't be surprised. You're the clever one, but what have I got to do now, to get out of this mess?' Lionel asked.

'You are a mess,' Gorse shouted at him. 'Get into the shower and get yourself cleaned up. There's a change of clothes in the holdall. Go on, Move! For God's sake, wake up!'

Lesley and Alan had heard enough. They began strolling casually back towards Ken and Phil.

'We might need a bit of local muscle, Ken.' Lesley told him. 'We'll take them both in. They're in it up to their necks.'
Ken noticed that the two uniformed officers were still standing by the kiosk. He turned to Phil and said,

'Phil, we've got to play this about right. Gorse's wife is sitting in his car, probably watching everything. We need those two to move so that she can't see them. We don't want them to come and stand with us. That would break our cover. Go over there, walk around behind the kiosk and ask them to please move away a bit. The other side of the road would do, just so Gorse's wife can't see them. We can call them over when we're ready. Just ask them to try not to be too conspicuous.'

'Will we go onto the boat and just grab them?' Lesley asked. Ken Foster's face was a picture of horror!

'No,' he said, emphatically. They both looked at him in surprise.

'Lesley,' he began, 'let me explain the law as it applies to this situation. Their boat is moored in a tidal basin, which affords it more than just protection from the ravages of the open sea. It is protected by Maritime Law. We cannot board the vessel without the owner's permission, or we would be committing an act of piracy. The only force which can legally do that is H.M. Customs. They have the right to board any vessel in British Territorial Waters. We will have to wait until the Gorses leave the boat, before we can detain them. We need to be absolutely correct on this. The last thing we want is for them to escape justice on a technicality.'

476

Lesley and Alan were surprised to learn this, but it had shown them that their proposal to grab the pair from their boat would have been fraught with problems.

'So what do we do?' Lesley asked, as Phil Travis returned to join them..

Ken thought for a few moments and then said.

'We can't afford any mistakes,' he told them all. 'I've phoned our 'Paddy Wagon', we can't rely on Worthing for co-operation. They are parked at Shoreham, waiting for instructions. I've told them to get over here and park somewhere back along the sea front. I don't want them to get too close until we've detained our suspects. Now Lesley, I think it best if you and Alan walk along the quay as you did before. Make it look as though you're still checking out the boats. You'll probably find one or two which are for sale. You could examine those a bit more closely. The main thing is to get yourselves the other side of Gorse's mooring. Keep your eyes open and as soon as he and his son leave the boat, you can close up behind them and prevent their retreat. When I see them both leave the vessel, I'll phone for the 'Paddy Wagon'. It shouldn't take too long to get here. If we need any extra help, our two colleagues across the road will oblige.'

'Yes, they said they'd contacted their Sergeant and explained the situation to him,' Phil said. 'He told them to wait until we'd got the two suspects in custody.'

'We'll toddle off for another look at our boats,' Lesley said.

'Isn't that the Cavendish woman, walking out of the car park?' Alan asked.

Ken looked to where he was nodding his head.

'Yes, you're right,' Ken said. 'Go on, you two, if they come off the boat now, we're stuffed. They could turn around and go straight back on board.'

Mrs. Cavendish walked past where Ken and Phil were standing. She was speaking on her mobile phone as she walked towards the taxi rank.

Phil looked towards the owner's car park and saw the BMW reversing from its parking place by the railings.

'Something's on the move, Ken,' he said. 'His wife's just reversing out of her space.'

They looked towards the moorings and saw the young Gorse's head appear above the quay.

'Don't do anything yet, we want both of 'em. If we go for him, his father will get by us and escape. He's using his son as a decoy.'

Ken held up his hand to halt Alan, who had begun to approach the vessel's mooring.

'Get in and start the car, Phil,' Ken said. 'If he gets in the BM, drive in front of it so she has to stop. Try to look apologetic and if she remains stationary, get out and say you're sorry, it was your fault. Say anything to cause a slight delay, so that her husband can get off the boat.'

Lionel Gorse sauntered along the quay towards the BMW. He held the holdall slung over his left shoulder, with two fingers of his left hand through the handles. Gorse's wife stopped the car level with the quay. As Lionel got to the car, he needed to change hands to open the passenger door. As he brought the holdall down from his shoulder, his father left the boat and began running along the quay towards them.

'Go. Go. Go!' Ken shouted. At the same time as he waved urgently at the two uniformed men on the other side of the road. Phil drove their hire car towards the front of the big BMW, which began to move forwards in anticipation of Gorse reaching it. There was a loud crunch! Phil had driven into the front of Gorse's car. Gorse senior reached the car and went for the rear door handle as Alan Bell, in hot pursuit, rugby tackled him. Both men went down, Gorse's head hit the rear door of the car as he went. His wife was trying to use the sheer weight and power of her car to push Phil's vehicle out of her way. The rear tyres were smoking as they spun on the damp asphalt. Phil held his car hard against the big German machine. Gorse aimed a kick at Alan

Bell's head, causing him to momentarily lose his grip on his legs. Ken Foster ran to Alan's aid and placed his size eleven shoe onto the side of Gorse's face, as he lay on the ground.

'Leonard Chater Gorse, you are under arrest on suspicion of aiding the escape of a fugitive, attempting to pervert the course of justice and the murder of Mary Davies. You do not have to say anything, but it may ......stop trying to fight us, or I will stand on your face with both feet…...harm your defense if you fail to mention, when questioned something which you later rely on in court. Do you understand?

Lesley had handcuffed him now, so Ken took his foot off Gorse's face and repeated, very slowly, Do - you - under - stand?'

'Yes, yes, I understand,' Gorse said as he was helped to his feet.

One of the uniformed officers had arrived just in time to avoid Phil's car being destroyed. He had opened the BMW driver's door and snatched the keys from the ignition switch. His colleague had to run around Phil's smoking hire car to grab Lionel Gorse from the front passenger seat. As he pulled him from the car, Lionel thrust his hand through the broken part of the holdall's zip fastener and pulled out a small hand gun. Before he could turn to use it, Phil opened his driver's door with great force and knocked the gun from Lionel's grasp. It clattered across the ground and came to a stop under the size eleven boot of the driver of the Chichelster force's 'Paddy Wagon'. Everything had happened so fast that none of the officers had noticed its arrival.

'Do you want this shiny metal toy for fingerprints, or shall I pick it up?' PC Mercer asked, grinning.

Ken Foster had heard some of the station banter related to Eric Mercer.

'Well, how would you play it in the 'Met', Eric? He joked.

Eric smiled. This was a signal that he had been accepted by his 'country yokel' colleagues.

'Bag it and tag it, Sarge,' he replied.

'Carry on, Mr. Mercer,' Ken said, as he grinned at him.

Ken picked up the holdall and looked inside. It contained a very nice Carriage clock, some items of jewelry, several coins and a wad of banknotes.

'I think you'd better, 'bag and tag' this, as well, please Eric,' he said, passing him the holdall. 'It'll all come in handy for evidence.'

Lionel Gorse was handcuffed and charged with the murder of Jason Davies, unlawful possession of a firearm with intent to endanger life, theft and criminal damage. Other charges would follow in connection with the abduction of Sandra Cranham and the dangerous driving incident.

He was quickly searched and placed in the front cage of the police van, along with his father.

Lesley walked around the rear of Gorse's car and formally arrested Delia. She was helped from her sumptuously upholstered luxury seat, handcuffed, searched and charged. She was led from her car and placed into the separate wire caged area at the back of the police van. Lesley was respectful and took care not to cause her any injury, although the lady seemed more concerned about damage to her new suede jacket. A small crowd of onlookers had gathered to watch the show.

Alan Bell had a nasty cut above his left eye, from Gorse's shoe. They would add 'resisting arrest and assaulting a police officer,' to his already rapidly expanding charge sheet.

Ken Foster thanked the two uniformed Brighton officers for their help and took details of their identity for the report. They agreed to provide their statements, which would be forwarded by the Brighton city force. He phoned Chichelster and asked Mike Hodd to notify Tony Church and Chief Inspector Purvis.

'The 'Paddy Wagon' is on its way in,' he told him. Three persons detained, two male, one female. We'll need the police recovery vehicle to Brighton Marina to recover one five series black BMW and one sadly, badly, damaged hire car. We'll wait here for the recovery vehicle. Lesley is taking Alan Bell to casualty, with a cut eye, from a hostile boot, so you'd better send another car for us. We'll need to clear our digs and I don't think there'll be room in Lesley's car for us all.'

'You got 'em both then, Ken?' Mike Hodd asked. 'Is young Alan going to be alright?'

'Affirmative to both questions, thanks Mike,' Ken answered. 'We won't need crowd control, they're losing interest already. I did see a couple with cameras, so they might make a couple of bob out of the Argus. It'll be too late for tonight's news though. Just let the others know it's 'mission accomplished,' for today. Thanks Mike, see you later.' He closed his phone.

Tony Church's peaceful Saturday was not very peaceful! At four pm his phone rang again. Sergeant Mike Hodd apologised for interrupting his week-end for the second time. He listened while Mike told him that The Gorses were on their way in from Brighton Marina. Father and son had both been arrested on charges of murder. Gorse's wife had also been arrested on other charges. They would need to be processed tonight and it may involve the need for a special hearing at the magistrates' court.

'There's no way we're going to agree to bail,' Tony told him. 'I'll have to come in and sort it out, does Chief Purvis know?' Mike Hodd told him, 'yes' and said that he was also on his way in.

'The only magistrate who will be available tonight, is old Edwin Sarkes,' Tony told him. 'I'll wait until I get there and decide whether to call him tonight or wait until the morning. I'll hear what the Gorse's have to say first. They'll probably want to make a meal of it, but they won't be going home anytime soon.

CHAPTER 67.

Sunday morning was cold, dull and drizzly. The Leggitts and their two guests were enjoying a cooked breakfast.

'What time are you leaving for Lincoln?' Hannah asked her sister. 'Will you be here for lunch?'

Hilda smiled at them all and said,

'No, but thank you Elsie, I think I should go back later this morning. I've got work tomorrow and I'd like to spend a few hours with Doug this evening.'

'I've got to meet this man of yours, Hilda.' Hannah replied, 'Your 'knight in shining armour' hasn't got a twin brother, has he?'

'No, I don't think so,' said Hilda, smiling. 'He's just a very intelligent and protective man. He didn't show any fear when he dealt with Jeffery. He's got that aura about him which sort of commands respect. I know you'll like him, when you do eventually meet.'

Elsie was smiling to herself,

'Well, Hilda,' she said, 'if he's the right man for you, I'm sure we'll all be very happy for you.'

'Would you mind if I stayed for a few more days?' Hannah asked Elsie. 'I'd like to wait until I know what's happening with old Jason's will. If Jeffery gets the farm house, I can get my solicitor to make him give me mine back again. I could get an eviction order, but apart from the antagonism that would cause, it would also be more expensive.'

Archie looked at her and said,

'Hannah, I'm sure I speak for both of us when I say this. You are welcome to stay for as long as you need to. You've already told us you don't want to go back to Belgium, so the sensible thing would be to do what you've just suggested. I'm sure the General Hospital would be pleased to have you back, and you'd be closer to your dad if he needed you.'

Hannah smiled,

'I almost knew you would say something like that,' she said. 'Thank you both, very much. I expect old Jason's will to be read within the next week. Do you know if the police have released his body for burial yet?'

'I don't think they have, Hannah,' Archie said. 'They'll probably want to catch his killer, to complete their enquiries. I'm hoping they've caught him by now..'

Hilda finished her breakfast and Elsie poured her another cup of tea.

Hilda looked up at her and said,

'Thank you Elsie. That was a lovely breakfast. I won't need anything else until this evening. I won't call in on Dad, I'll go straight back home when I leave here.' She turned to Archie and asked, 'Is there a garage open before I get to the A23, Archie?' She asked.

He thought for a few seconds,

'Yes, there's one in Pudborough. He's open seven days a week, or there's a big one, both sides of the road, just before you get to Billingshurst. Have you got enough to get you there?'

'Yes, thanks Archie. I've got just under half a tank. It may be enough to get me home, but I don't like to chance it these days.'

Hilda finished her tea and stood up,

'I'll go and get my things and get moving now,' she said. 'Thank you two for everything,' she gave Archie and Elsie a hug. 'Take care, Hannah, I hope it all works out for you. Give me a call on Monday. You've got my home number, haven't you?' Hannah smiled at them all,

'Yes, sister dear, I've got your home number and your mobile number and your car registration number. I've got the number of your flat, the number of the hospital where you work and the extension number for the ward station. Fear not, one way or another, I will phone you on Monday.'

By now, they were all laughing, including Hilda. She was still giggling as she came back down the stairs with her suitcase. Archie carried it out to her car and put it in the boot. They stood and waved her off, as she drove away up Slindon Road.

Back in the house, they cleared away the breakfast things and Archie took Jimbo for his walk.

On his way back from the mill, he saw Bill Pickering in his car. Archie waved to him and he pulled over and stopped.

'Good morning young Arch,' he said as he lowered the driver's window.

'The Gorses were captured in Brighton yesterday,' he told him. 'Tony Church has had to go in this morning to try to sort something out. They'll be our guests for a while. He's opposing bail, except possibly for the woman. I don't know what's happening about her, Gorse's wife, but they reckon she was as bad as her step-son and husband.'

'I 'spect we'll find out sooner or later Bill, don't you?' Archie said. Do you know when old Jason's funeral will be?'

Bill shrugged,

'Not yet Arch,' he said. 'They'll all have to wait until the body is released for burial or cremation. Now they've caught the suspected perpetrators it might speed things up a bit.'

'OK Bill,' Archie agreed, 'I'd better get back. Young Cathy Simons is coming to see me later. She believes there's some sort

of hidden message in the letter old 'Diddler' left for her. It may be nothing, but she seems keen to let someone else take a look.'
Bill frowned, saying,

'That poor woman must have really felt his death, Arch. When you think about it, she probably knew the old sod better than anyone, including his son. Let me know what you think, after you've seen her. It would be nice if there was something decent and good to inject into this sad business.'
Archie nodded,

'I promise you'll be the second to know,' he said, touching the side of his nose with a forefinger.

'Take care, Arch, give Elsie our love,' Bill said as he drove away.
Archie arrived back home to find that Elsie and Hannah were busy stripping the beds and changing the bed linen.

'Is that you, Arch?' Elsie called down the stairs.

'Is that you, Else?' He called up to her.
Elsie came half way down the stairs,

'If you were any sharper, you'd cut yourself,' she said. 'Cathy Simons phoned, she'll be here in a few minutes, with her letter. You'd better put the kettle on, Hannah and I could do with a cup of tea, as well.'

'You want tea? I was thinking coffee,' Archie said.

'Yes, alright, Arch, we'll all have coffee please,' she said.
He changed Jimbo's drinking water, re-filled the kettle and switched it on. As he was taking off his jacket, there was a tap on the glass of the back door. He opened it to see Cathy standing there. She held the letter in her hand.

'I hope you don't mind, Mr. Leggitt,' she said as she held the letter out for him to take. 'It's very kind of you to take the time to help me. I'll show you some of what I was telling you, when you've read it through.'

'Yes, I'll do that Cathy, but first, come in and let me take your coat,' he said. 'I'm just making coffee for Elsie and Hannah, would you like one, or would you prefer tea?'

'If you're sure I'm not imposing on you,' she said, timidly. Archie assured her that she was most welcome and he was only too pleased to try to help.

'As a matter of fact, Cathy,' he told her quietly, 'I'll admit that I'm a bit intrigued. Let's make this coffee first. Hannah is here, staying with us for a few days. Do you remember her and Hilda, the 'Jempson' twins?'

'Yes, oh yes, of course I do,' Cathy said. 'I haven't seen Hannah since she married Jeffery. I know they're not together any more. Mr. Davies still thought very highly of Hannah, he knew what Jeffery was like. I once overheard him telling Jeffery that he didn't deserve Hannah and do you know what Jeffery said in reply?'

'No, what did he say, Cathy?' Archie asked as he poured the coffee into the cups.

Cathy lifted her head and spoke quietly, lest Hanna should hear her.

'He said that Hannah was just a means to an end. That it was just so that he could live away from his father. He only wanted his father for his money, but Hannah had her own house, you see.'

'She still owns the house, Cathy,' Archie told her. 'It was what they call a 'pre-nuptial' agreement that the house would always remain in her name. I think her father, Bob Jempson, had weighed him up quite early in their relationship. He knew young Jeffery was a greedy man and his daughters were everything to Bob, still are, come to that'

Archie showed Cathy into the lounge and called up the stairs to Elsie and Hannah,

'Coffee's made, Cathy's here, we're just going to have a look at the letter.'

He carried the tray in and placed it on the low table,

'Help yourself to milk and sugar Cathy,' he told her. 'Make yourself at home, don't mind old Jimbo, he's very fond of all our visitors.'

486

Cathy smiled as she rubbed the dog's head.

'I like dogs,' she said. 'Perhaps I should get one to keep me company, now I'm on my own.'

Archie nodded his agreement. Elsie and Hannah came down the stairs with armfuls of bedding.

'Hello Cathy,' Elsie called as she passed the lounge doorway. 'I've got one of your old friends here with me.'

Hannah came into the lounge and greeted Cathy warmly.

'Oh, Cathy, it must have been a terrible shock for you.' She said, as she joined her on the sofa. 'To find poor old Jason the way you did. I expect you're still having nightmares about it.'

Cathy was on the point of becoming tearful. Archie looked up and saw that Hannah had her arm around Cathy's shoulders.

'I'm sorry,' Cathy mumbled. 'Give me a moment, I'll be alright.' She began to regain her composure. 'Thank you, Hannah, yes it was absolutely awful. I know he wasn't a popular man in the village, but he always treated me very well. I don't think he was inherently bad, maybe just a bit insensitive.'

Elsie came in and took her usual armchair.

'If you sit in my chair, Hannah,' Archie said. 'Cathy and I can have the settee and look at her letter.'

Hannah moved to Archie's chair and Archie, complete with pencil and a pad and went to sit next to Cathy. They chatted amiably for a few minutes and then Archie said,

'Let's see what we can discover about this letter, Cathy.'

She took it from the envelope and passed it to him.

'Yes, thank you, Mr. Leggitt.'

Archie smiled at her,

'Please call me 'Archie',' he said. 'We're all friends here, so there's no need for formalities. Would you like me to read your letter out loud first, or would that be too painful to you?'

'Yes, read it out loud, it's not too personal and as you said, we're all friends.' Cathy said. 'I'd appreciate any comments from you two ladies as well. I just hope you'll all excuse me if I get a little upset when I hear it again. I don't know why, but when it's read by a man, I can almost imagine old Jason saying it to me.'

'If it's going to upset you, I won't read it aloud,' Archie said to her.

'No, no, please do, it just seems to affect me that way,' Cathy explained. 'I really would like you all to hear it. It may help you to understand him a little better as well.'

Archie opened the letter and quickly glanced through it before he began to read from the page.

Dear Cathy,

Today has been a day of reflection for me. I had a drive out this morning, it was Armistice Day. I saw people gathered around the war memorials of Several villages. I stopped for some lunch at a pub in Tarring, where I met a delightful young couple who shared my table. They were most courteous and I enjoyed their company for An hour or so. I began to think that perhaps if I had been a more considerate man, I would not have led such a lonely life. It is true that I have never wanted For the material things, but there is no substitute for friendship. You have been a good friend to me and have kept house and cooked for me for a great many years. Such loyalty should not go unrewarded. I know that I have not always shown my appreciation, but I have made arrangements with my solicitor to Ensure that you are not forgotten.

You may have noticed that I have not been a well man just lately and I fear it may signal a recurrence of my heart trouble. I do not wish to distress you, but just to thank you for your eternal Kindness.

I have had two sets of visitors this Evening. The first was from my sister, Bernice and her husband. They provided me with some information which lifted a great burden from me. For Years I blamed myself for the loss of my late wife, Mary. IN that I was not as kind to her as I should have been. I Learned this evening that another person was guilty of ending her life, not me.

My second visitor Of the evening was my son, Jeffery, who was accompanied by a female companion. Maybe it was her presence which influenced him, but he was unusually pleasant, which was Good. Perhaps he has finally come to realise that he can accomplish more by treating people with respect, than by bullying or threatening them. I do hope So.

With my sincere and heartfelt thanks,

Jason Davies.'

When he had finished reading, it wasn't just Cathy with a tear in her eye. Both Elsie and Hannah were also using tissues. Even 'big old softie' Archie, found it hard to suppress a tear.

'That is a truly lovely letter,' Hannah said, as she moved to hold Cathy again.

Archie continued to study the letter,

'I think Cathy's right,' he suddenly said. 'There are capitals where there shouldn't be capitals. Take the pencil Cathy and write down the letters as I call them out.'

He started from the top and called out,

'S, A, F, E, K, E, Y, N, L, O, G, S, have you done that?'

'Yes,' Cathy said as she handed the sheet back to him.

Archie checked it against the letter and inserted a capital I between the Y and the N.

'Safe Key In Logs' he read out. 'Does that mean something to you, Cathy?' he asked.

Cathy looked puzzled as she responded.

'I know he has a safe in the cellar,' she said, 'but why has he told me and nobody else? Why has he decided to hide the message, instead of just putting it in the letter in so many words? I'm sorry, but I just don't understand this, any of it.'

'I think I do,' Archie said.

They all looked at him.

'It's you, Cathy for the simple reason that he knew he could trust you. He didn't trust anyone else, they'd all let him down at various times, but you hadn't.'

'I suppose I should tell Jeffery,' she said.

All three of them said,

'No!'

Archie looked her in the eye,

'If Jason had wanted Jeffery to know, he would have written a letter to him, not to you,' he told her. 'What you should do is tell PC Pickering about it. Do you still have a key to the farm house, Cathy?'

Cathy nodded,

'Yes, the police told me to keep a key. They took Jason's keys with them. The forensics officer, Sergeant Pace, told me that it is still officially a crime scene, until the investigation is closed.'

'Would you like me to phone Mr. Pickering and ask him what we should do?' Archie asked her.

'Yes please,' Cathy said. 'Perhaps you would come with me, if I'm allowed to go into the house. Do you think PC Pickering would mind?'

'I don't suppose so, but let's ask him, shall we?' Archie said as he went out to the hall telephone. He dialled Bill's number and heard Kate's voice answer.

'He's out in the garden, Archie,' she told him. 'Hang on. I'll call him for you.'

'Am I really the second person to know, Arch?' Bill said, when Archie told him about the hidden message.

'Not quite,' Archie said, 'but you're only the fourth, so that's not too bad, is it? What do you think she should do?'
Bill thought for a moment before replying.

'I think I'd better phone Tony Church and see what he thinks. I know he's in the office today, processing the Gorse's case. If he says we can go into the house, then I'll come with you. That way if anyone else comes along and asks why we're there, I can put 'em straight, without giving anything away. I'll call you back in a few minutes, Arch.'
Archie went back into the lounge and told Cathy what Bill had said. He turned to Hannah and said,

'I know you're the absolute soul of discretion, Hannah, but please don't mention this to anyone. Not even to your Dad. There may be a confidential issue involved, which is Cathy's business and hers alone.'

'I understand Archie,' she said. 'My lips are sealed, it's Cathy's business and nobody will hear anything from me. I'm here for Cathy if she wants my support, whatever comes out of the mystery.'

'Thank you, Hannah,' Cathy said, 'and thank you both, Elsie and Archie. I knew there was something odd about the way he had written the letter. But I'll feel better about it once I've seen what he wanted me to find in his safe.'
Bill phoned whilst they were talking, Archie answered it and when he had finished he went into the lounge and told the ladies,

'Bill says he'll meet us up at the house in about a quarter of an hour. He said not to go inside until he's with us. It is still a crime scene, but it won't be for much longer. DI Church says his body will be released for burial in the next couple of days. He also has to notify Davies' solicitors. Apparently, they are also the only named executors of his estate. They will advise all creditors and anyone likely to benefit from his estate, giving seven days notice of the reading of the will.'

491

'Shall we go in my old car?' Cathy asked Archie. 'I can bring you back here afterwards.'

'Yes, OK,' Archie said. 'That will save asking Hannah to move hers, so that I can get ours from the garage.'

'Why don't you stay and have some lunch with us, afterwards?' Elsie asked her. 'There's plenty to go round, I'd expected Hilda to be here for lunch, but she decided to go back this morning.'

Cathy looked surprised, but happy.

'If you're sure it's not too much trouble,' she said to Elsie. 'You're very kind, thank you. I'd like that very much. I do get a little fed up with my own company and cooking just for myself is not the same'

'Good,' Elsie said with satisfaction. 'You'd better go now, or Mr. Pickering will be waiting.'

Archie led the way out of the back door and waited by the passenger door of Cathy's Ford Escort.

A few minutes later they were driving up Ridge Farm Lane. Bill's own car was parked in the driveway. He got out as he saw them arrive. He came up to Cathy and shook her hand,

'Hello Cathy,' Bill said. 'I expect it feels strange to you, to be here as a result of a hidden message.'

'Yes, Mr. Pickering,' she replied. 'I'm not really comfortable with it, to be honest. I would have thought Mr. Davies would have told his son, or his sister, what he wanted them to do.'

Bill smiled,

'I expect the old boy knew exactly what he was doing. He knew that he could trust you to do the right thing, Cathy. That's why he left you the message. May I see the letter?'

Cathy handed Bill the envelope and watched as he read it. When he had finished reading, he handed it back to her, saying,

'Cathy, that's a lovely letter. Better than any reference he could have provided, if you had been looking for another job.'

Cathy took her letter back from Bill,

'Why do you think he hid the message in the words of the letter, Mr. Pickering?' She asked.

Bill looked at her.

'When you received it, the envelope was sealed and addressed to you, correct?'

'Yes,' she said.

Bill smiled at her as he answered her question.

'I would say that he had a fair idea that someone else might want access to his safe, perhaps young Jeffery. Even if you had read the letter out loud to someone, the message would not have been obvious. If the message had been any more direct, anyone could go to the log store and then, assuming they knew where the safe was, go and empty it!'

'That's what I was thinking,' Archie said. 'Shall we see what we can find in the logs? Would you like to lead the way, Cathy?'

'Don't you want to check the house, first?' She asked Bill.

'No, I don't think we need to do that, Cathy,' he said. 'If we don't find the safe key, it might mean that someone else has beaten us to it. I'd have to report that, wouldn't I? Don't forget, it's taken a week to notice the hidden message.'

The trio walked around the back of the house, past the back porch where Archie had smacked the young lad's fingers against the door.

'The log store is this way,' Cathy said.

'Yes, I came down here to collect the rifle that Cavendish boy was using,' Bill told her. They reached the lean-to log shelter and began looking at the logs.

'Would he have just laid the keys on any old log?' Archie said, thinking aloud. 'I bet he's hung 'em on a nail or something.' They began looking at the sides of the shelter and then towards the back, where a length of black plastic soil pipe was secured to the wall.

'What's that bit of soil pipe for?' Archie asked, as he put his hand into the open end of it.

'Safe key, and, hold on a minute, yes, I think its a rifle!'

493

'Don't touch it Arch,' Bill said urgently. 'I'll go and get some gloves from my car.'

Cathy just stood holding the key ring which Archie had passed to her.

'I didn't think he still had the rifle,' she said to Archie. 'Jeffery wanted to borrow it a couple of months ago and Mr. Davies told him he hadn't got it any more.'

Archie grinned at her,

'Cathy, your Mr. Davies was a wise old boy. What you've just told me is further proof that he didn't trust Jeffery. He had no intention of lending him the rifle, so he took it out of the gun cabinet and hid it. Jeffery saw it was missing from its usual place, so he believed Jason, when he said he hadn't got it any more. Do you see it now?'

'Yes, its beginning to make a bit more sense to me now,' she said. 'I hope there are no nasty surprises in the safe, that's all.'

Bill returned wearing his plastic gloves and removed the rifle from its hiding place.

'This is a beauty,' he said to Archie. 'Look, Martini action and all nicely oiled to keep it from going rusty. The stock is like new. We should get a few decent prints from it. I'll put it in the car for now, I'll hand it in tomorrow morning.'

'Will you both come down to the cellar with me, please?' Cathy asked. 'There's bound to be spiders down there and maybe even mice.'

Archie laughed,

'Yes, we'll come with you, Cathy, don't you worry. You're safe enough with my big policeman friend here. He'll soon arrest any spiders we find!'

Cathy showed them the cellar hatch. The light switch was at the top of the bare wooden stairs. Bill went down first, followed by Cathy and then Archie. The safe, an old Chubb model, stood on a concrete plinth against one wall.

Bill inserted the large brass key and turned it, the lock released with a loud, 'clunk'. Bill pulled on the brass handle and the heavy steel door swung open. Inside they found a cash box, probably one of the smaller keys on the same ring, would open it. Next to the box there was a sealed envelope and an old letter. A substantial bundle of bank notes, in a clear plastic bag was tucked at the back of the safe, behind the cash box.

Bill passed the envelope and the letter to Cathy. She studied the small envelope containing the letter first.

'This came on Saturday,' she told Bill. 'Mr. Davies seemed rather agitated by it. He was out in the log store when I got here and when he came in he was out of breath and feeling rather poorly. Bill took the envelope and looked at the front of it. It was beginning to yellow with age, the postmark was 'Brighton and Hove' it was dated 22nd Sept. 1966!

Bill pulled the note out of it and read,

10th Nov.

£10K BY MONDAY 12TH.
SECOND CASE AND KEY TO DEPOSIT BOX.
I WILL CALL AT 12.00 L.G.

'This looks remarkably like a threat to me,' Bill said as he showed the note to Cathy and Archie. 'What's in the other envelope, Cathy?'

She read the message on the front,

'It says here, 'Recording of telephone call to Len Gorse.
11th. Nov. 9.35pm.
Please pass this and the warning note to
West Sussex Police.'

Cathy handed the still sealed envelope to Bill. He carefully opened it and looked inside.

'It's a mini cassette from his answering machine,' he told them. 'I'd better let Tony Church know about this now. It might help with his interviews with the Gorse family. Excuse me but I'll need to go upstairs to get a signal on my phone.'

495

Cathy looked at Archie and said,

'I'm so glad I came to you with the letter. I kept on thinking about it. I knew there was something odd about the words, but I don't think I would have worked it out myself. I just hope it will do some good.'

'It certainly won't do poor old Jason any harm now, Cathy,' Archie told her. 'It looks to me as if it might help the police to convict the Gorses. What does it say on the plastic bag? There's something written on a sheet of paper inside it.'

Cathy turned it towards the light and read through the clear plastic,

Cathy,

If you are reading this note, it means that I have passed on. I'm sorry to have caused you any distress in the course of my departure from this life. Just one more thing I ask of you. Should you require any help or advice in carrying out my wishes, please confide **only** in persons whom you know you can trust and specifically **NOT** my son Jeffery.

This money was originally intended for an entirely different purpose, namely to pay a blackmailer. A turn of events has removed the need to consider that purpose. The enclosed 'surplus funds' may now be put to a better use.

First, I would like you to take £3,000 from the bag and donate it to the Village Hall Fund.

Next, please pay my outstanding accounts at Ned's Garage, the Village Stores and Ingram's Ironmongers.

The rest may be shared between other village facilities, the old watermill, the youth club and the football and cricket teams. Please use any balance as you see fit, but make sure you keep enough to cover your out of pocket expenses.

I will leave it to your discretion to do whatever you deem to be appropriate. I know that you will make the right choices.

Take care of yourself, my dear,
Jason Davies.'

Note: This is NOT for use by my son, Jeffery. His inheritance
will be more than enough for his needs.

She turned and looked at Archie. Her face had drained of colour.

'Oh, Archie, I don't know what to do,' she said.

Archie looked her in the eye and told her,

'Wait for a minute, Bill will be back soon, he'll probably help
you to do it right. He's a good man, Cathy. He's been a friend to
me and a friend to the village, ever since he came here.'

They heard Bill's footsteps coming back down the stairs.

'Sorry folks,' he said, 'I've got to go. The DI wants to listen
to this tape before he interviews the Gorses.'

'Just a minute, Bill,' said Archie, 'have a look at this and give
Cathy your opinion.' He passed the plastic bag of money to Bill.
He read the message and then looked at Cathy.

'Well Cathy, its Sunday so you can't do very much about it
today. I suggest you take it with you and we'll get our heads
together tomorrow, how about that?'

'Yes, thank you, Mr. Pickering,' she said. 'What shall I do
about the cash box?'

'Have you looked in it yet?' Bill asked her.

'No, not yet,' she answered.

'Take it all with you, lock the safe and keep hold of the keys,'
Bill advised. 'I wouldn't mention this to anyone yet, Cathy. There
will be somebody who will either want to criticise your decision,
or want to suggest some sort of impropriety. Probably young
Jeffery Davies, for one! Look, I've got to go now, make sure you
lock everything up securely and I'll get in touch with Archie
tomorrow morning.'

They both nodded and thanked Bill for his help. Cathy took the
money, the cash box and her letter up the stairs, while Archie
locked the safe and followed her. They closed up and then left

together through the front door. Cathy double checked that it was locked and then drove them both back to Slindon Road.

'I know Mr. Pickering said not to tell anyone,' Cathy said. 'But surely we can tell Elsie and Hannah, can't we?'
Archie laughed,

'Yes Cathy, I don't think we're in any danger from those two. What Bill meant was don't let it become public knowledge until you know where all the money is going.'
Cathy smiled,

'Oh good, I don't want any of it for, what did it say, 'outside expenses' wasn't it?'

'Out of pocket expenses,' Archie corrected her. 'It means that if you have to buy petrol or postage stamps and stationery, then you shouldn't have to pay for them yourself. That's what it means.
People usually decide on a nominal amount, say, five or ten pounds. Don't overlook the fact that you may need to attend the will reading in Worthing. I'd say probably you need to keep about fifty pounds back to cover that sort of thing. If you don't need it, you can always donate it to a charity after everything is settled.'

'Thanks Archie,' she said. 'Mr. Skrobe said I'd find you very helpful and he was right. I didn't expect to be invited to lunch! I must say that my day is turning out to be much more enjoyable than I had envisaged.'

CHAPTER 68.

It was almost lunchtime when Bill arrived at Chichelster police station. DI Tony Church had delayed interviewing the Gorses until he had listened to Jason Davies' recording of the telephone call.

'Thank you Bill,' he said as he accepted the threatening note and the tape cassette. 'I appreciate you giving up your time on your day off.'

'I expect you can guess where my involvement came from,' he said to Tony. 'My friend, Archie Leggitt, saw me this morning and mentioned a letter with a hidden message contained in it. That got my curiosity going and when he said it was the letter Jason Davies had left for Cathy Simons, I decided to take a look at it. Sure enough there was a hidden message, disguised within the main text of the letter, so I offered to meet them at the farm.' Tony smiled,

'It all sounds a bit, 'Hercule Poirot', but we'll try to keep an open mind until after we've heard the tape. This note looks threatening enough. I can understand how relieved he must have felt after his sister told him what she had learned about Gorse. Ian's waiting for me, so I'd better get moving, or we'll still be here at midnight.'

He shook hands with Bill and took the tape to the player in his office. Ian Stuart was waiting for him. Tony showed Ian the note, as he fitted the tape into the player and switched it on. There was the usual crackle at the beginning and then they heard Davies' voice.

'This is Jason Davies, the time is a little after eight pm on Sunday the eleventh of November. My sister, Bernice, called this evening and gave me some important information relating to the death of my wife, Mary. For many years I believed that I had accidentally shot my wife, whilst indulging in target practice in my barn. In my desperation, and feeling sick with worry, I was persuaded by Len Gorse, whom I had thought of as a friend, to hide her body and invent a story to cover her disappearance. He helped me to bury her in the field and later provided information to the police to endorse my report of her as a missing person. When it was revealed that the skeletal remains found at my son's hotel building site, were possibly those of my late wife, I began receiving blackmail demands from Gorse.

Tonight, when my sister visited me, I learned from her that Leonard Gorse was actually responsible for shooting her. Mary had been fooled by him into believing that he wanted her to run away and begin a new life with him.
I had initially employed him as a private investigator, since I had my suspicions that Mary was seeing someone. I little knew at the time, that the person she was seeing was Leonard Gorse himself. Bernice explained to me that she had gleaned the information from one of Mary's former close friends, a lady named, 'Olive Duxon,' whose daughter worked at the same bank as my sister. It appears that Mary had confided in her that she was intending to leave me and begin a new life with her lover, a man she referred to as, 'Leon'.
This is my confession.

Now, I am about to telephone Mr. Leonard Gorse, to tell him that I will not pay him any more money and that I am going to expose him as a murderer, a cheat and a blackmailer. Please wait until the connection is made, I will attempt to record the whole conversation on this tape.'

There followed a series of clicks and tone pings as Jason Davies dialled Gorse's home number. The ring tone stopped after four rings and the tape then reverted to the spoken word.

'Gorse here, can I help you?'
'Good evening, 'Leon'. Is your wife there?'
'Who is this? What do you want with my wife?'
'I wanted to ask her to meet me at Haywards Heath Station!'
'That isn't funny, Davies. Have you got the money?'
'I've got more than that, dear 'Leon.' I know that you shot Mary. There won't be any more money for you, only justice.
'There had better be money, Davies. My son will collect it for me. You won't be so brave with him.
'I'm not afraid of your son, 'Leon'. You're both blackmailing scum and when I tell the police, you'll both be in prison for a long time.'
'But you won't be telling the police, my son will see to that. How did you find out I had killed her? How long have you known about our meeting at Haywards Heath?'
'I have my sources, 'Leon' they're more reliable than you.'
'Stop calling me 'Leon' that's what Mary called me, so you wouldn't know it was me who she was seeing.'
'You took money from me on the pretext of investigating her affair. All that time, you were deceiving us both. Then when it got too hot for you, you killed her and tried to put the blame on me.'
'You can't prove that. You were stupid and gullible then and you're stupid and gullible now. The car I brought her back here in was torched, so they won't find anything in that. The police are too slow. All they want to do is close these cases. They're not interested in justice. Their world is only concerned with clear up rates. You won't find any evidence and neither will the police. The bullets could have come from your rifle, just as easy as mine.

Anyway, you helped me to bury her body, so you broke the law as well.'

'*I'll own up to that, but it doesn't make me a murderer, like you, 'Leon'. You'll pay the ultimate price, even though it's thirty years ago.*'

'Stop calling me, 'Leon' and tell me how you found out the truth. I'll bet it was that 'Duxon' woman. She was the only one who knew about us. I can silence her before the police have a chance to interview her. I could arrange for that to happen tonight, with no involvement by me, whatsoever.'

'*It doesn't matter what you do 'Leon,' the police will know the truth now. I've had thirty years to think about this, but it has never seemed so clear as it does now..*

'You're annoying me now, Davies. Remember how clever I can be. I had an affair with Mary for over a year and then you paid me to find out about it! I bet that makes you feel stupid. I had to kill her to save myself. You thought she'd died in your barn. That shows how stupid you are. I shot her in some woods at Haywards Heath and brought her back to your barn in my old Volvo, the same evening. I even remembered to place her book in her lap. You were so distraught, you couldn't think straight. You made it easy for me. If they hadn't found her body, we'd both still be in the clear. I had to get rid of her. I was very fond of Mary, but she was going to tell my wife about us. I couldn't risk that. It would have bankrupted me. It was Jean's money that set me up. Mary had been dead for three days when you found her in the barn. You think you're so clever, but you're not clever enough! You didn't even notice how cold she felt.'

'*I've had plenty of time to think about things you've done. Your wife, Jean, died in mysterious circumstances, 'Leon'. About the same time as your friend, Rex Biker's little car business went under. Either you killed her or you paid someone to do it for you. I can get the enquiry re-opened on that. They'll probably get a result this time.*

502

'I have friends who will do what I tell them, in exchange for favours. I don't have to pay them. You don't have any friends, do you, Davies?'

'Smart answers won't save you now, Gorse. Your son will be unlucky in his attempt to collect money. He might as well save himself the trouble of driving out here.'

'He's coming anyway. He'll collect the money. You got both the suitcases, didn't you?'

'Yes and now I have the evidence to deal with you, Gorse. You'll be too late for Mrs. Duxon, but there are others who will testify against you. Some of them have been clients of yours.'

'What do you mean, 'clients'? Which clients will testify from thirty years ago? Don't make me laugh.'

'Not just thirty years ago, Gorse. I'm talking about your late wife, Jean. Tied to her steering wheel with PVA tape and sent to a watery grave whilst she was in a diabetic coma. How much did that cost you Gorse? Thirty grand? more? Then there was another client who approached you with a view to arranging a contract on her husband. You even charged her a deposit on that deal.'

(Gorse's tone changed to one of alarm here.)

'What? How do you know about that? Who told you? Not Rex Biker himself? He's in Lewes for money laundering. How did you find him?'

'You can ask him yourself soon, you might even find you're cell mates. You're not so smart, Gorse. I didn't know about Rex Biker for sure, but his garage business closed a short while after Jean was found in the water. I guessed he was something to do with it. I thought about the PVA tape, he would have known about that, being a fisherman. It had to be something which would have dissolved in water, leaving no trace. I just knew something wasn't right. Would you like me to have a chat with your current wife now?'

'You're a bastard, Davies, but I still want my money. You won't be able to tell the police anything. My son will see to that.'

*'There are other people who will testify. Do your worst
Gorse. You won't get another penny from me and that's a
promise. You can spend the next few days thinking about what
you've lost. Reflect on some of your mistakes, there are plenty to
choose from. You still won't get anything more from me. My
legacy to you is justice, that's all. I hope you get to enjoy it.
Goodnight, 'Leon', sweet dreams.*
Clunk! Gorse slammed his phone down.

Jason's calm voice continued giving the names of the other
people who would testify and the actual name of the bogus client,
which his sister Bernice had provided to him. Finally he said,
    I think that is all, thank you for listening.
The tape ended.

The two detectives just sat and looked at each other for a few
minutes.
    'What did you think of that?' Tony asked Ian Stuart.
Ian looked thoughtful as he replied.
    'I'll tell you some of the things I'm thinking, apart from the
fact that the Gorses are both murderers. I'm thinking 'cover up'
by the police who investigated his wife's death, for a start. I'm
still convinced that there's at least one 'bent' copper at Worthing.
Why would he offer to vouch for Cranham's honesty, unless he
was getting something in return?'
Tony was nodding in agreement.
    'I'd never have thought of PVA used as a binding, would
you?' He asked.
    'No, but it makes sense to me now.' Ian said. 'I wonder how
quickly it dissolves in cold water. Old Jason's obviously been
doing a lot of thinking. It was a stroke of genius putting the bait
there for Gorse. He's even given us the name of his 'hired help'
and we know where to find him, don't we?'
Tony agreed,

'Perhaps we should have a chat with Mr. Biker before we interview Gorse. By the way, his son's prints were all over the house and on the hand gun and the blood Brian Pace found in the kitchen bin is a direct DNA match to young Lionel Gorse.'
Ian gave a smile of satisfaction,

'We've got him bang to rights, for robbery and murder. What we really need is a bit more evidence on his father.' Ian observed. 'Perhaps now that we've got Gorse in custody, perhaps Bernice Tenham will persuade her friend to help us. I know we've got Biker and I expect we can extract some info from him. We could offer an incentive if he co-operates with us.'
Tony was writing a few notes on his pad. He looked up and said,

'We'll see what we can get from the Duxons, as well. It's a fair bet they'll have told other people about it at the time Mary disappeared. Let's make a few enquiries and a couple of phone calls, before we interview them. We'll do the son first, he'll be one of our main witnesses against his father, I'll bet. He's more interested in self preservation than getting his dad off the hook.'
Ian laughed quietly,

'I think you've got him sussed out pretty accurately Guv,' he said. 'He's all bravado until he gets caught. Then he's like a frightened rat. He'll say anything he thinks might help him to escape the consequences of his actions. Should we get some search warrants under way, for Gorse's home and office?'
Tony thought for a moment,

'Yes Ian,' he said. 'We'll need one for the boat, as well, I think. We'll need to liaise with Shoreham and Worthing for the actual searches. They can do the boat, but I'm going to request that they leave his home and office to us. We know what we're looking for, they don't.'
He phoned Ron Purvis, the Chief Inspector, and asked him to arrange the warrants.

'OK Tony,' he had said, 'we'll have them within a couple of hours. I'll let you know when they're here and you can collect them when you're ready.'

CHAPTER 69.

As the two detectives approached the interview room, the solicitor and PC Mercer were conversing in the corridor.

'I'm afraid that your 'customer' has decided that he doesn't require my services,' said the lawyer. 'I was about to try to locate you, but your constable informed me that you were probably on your way, so I decided to await your arrival.'

The DI thanked him saying,

'As you realise, we cannot force him to have legal representation, so his decision has to be respected. Thank you for attending, he may change his mind when it comes to the court appearance. Please tell the desk sergeant and I'm sorry for the inconvenience it has caused you.'

PC Mercer told Tony that he had not been in the room when Gorse had made his decision, but added that their suspect appeared to be in a fit state of mind.

As they entered the interview room, Lionel Gorse sat, stone faced at the table. He looked up as they entered and began to stand up.

'Good afternoon Mr. Gorse,' Tony Church began.

'There's no need to stand, please sit down. Now, before we begin, I understand that you have declined the services of the solicitor we provided for you, is that correct?'

'Yes,' he replied emphatically. 'I don't need a solicitor to tell me to plead guilty. I can do that myself, without a legal bill to pay.'

'There would not be a legal bill,' the DI explained. 'If that is all you were concerned about, I can ask him to return.'

'No,' said the young Gorse, 'I just want to tell it without being interrupted by a solicitor. He may have made me say something I didn't want to, or even stopped me from giving a proper account.'
Tony nodded his acceptance of his reasoning.

'Very well, Mr. Gorse, but if you change your mind, just tell us and we will re-appoint some legal representation for you.'

'OK thank you,' the young man replied.

Ian Stuart removed the wrappings from two new cassette tapes and inserted them in the machine. He explained to Gorse,

'When we begin the interview I will start the recording. One tape will be kept by the police. The other cassette will be given to you. In the event that you later decide you require a solicitor, you will have an accurate copy of the interview. Do you understand?'
Gorse nodded,

'Yes, thank you,' he said. 'But I don't see me changing my mind. Can we start now?'
Ian started the machine and waited for the blank tape leaders to pass through the recording head.

'We're ready now,' he told the DI.
Tony nodded to Ian and he switched the machine to 'record'.
The DI announced to the tape machine,

'Chichelster Central Police station, Saturday November 17th at seventeen-forty hours. Interview with Mr. Lionel Gorse. Persons present. DI Church, DS Stuart and Mr. Lionel Gorse. For the record, Mr. Gorse has declined the services of a solicitor.'
Tony looked up at Gorse and said,

'Now, Mr. Gorse, for the tape, will you please state your full name and address and confirm that you do not wish to be represented by a member of the legal profession.'
Gorse obliged, in a polite and clear manner, though his voice seemed a little shaky.

'Thank you,' said Tony. 'Please will you now explain the circumstances of your visit to Ridge Farm on Sunday last, the eleventh of November?.'
Gorse sat upright, he looked nervous but in a steadier voice he said,

'To collect ten thousand pounds, which my father told me Davies owed him.'

'At what time did you arrive at Davies' home?'

'It must have been late, probably midnight or just after. He was still awake, the downstairs lights were on.'
Tony nodded and continued,

'How did you gain access to the house?'
Gorse smiled as he said,

'I rang the door bell and he let me in. He didn't know who I was at first, but he said, 'You'd better come in here, it's too cold to hold a discussion on the doorstep.' I followed him into his front room and he sat down in an armchair.'

'So what happened next?' Tony asked.

'I told him who I was and said that my dad had sent me to collect the money. Old Davies just smiled, sarcastic like and said, 'Well, there won't be any more money for you young man, nor for your father.' It was weird, as though he was ridiculing me. Then he said he'd made a discovery which would see my dad sent to prison. He said he now had proof that my dad had killed his wife, before I was born. He said my dad had a lot to answer for and now he'll have to pay the price.'

'So, what did you do next, Lionel?' The DI asked him.
Lionel hung his head and said quietly,

'I was out of my head on 'coke'. I know that's no excuse, but I knew I could make him give me the money. I was holding the gun I'd borrowed from 'Boff' Cavendish, but he didn't seem to care. I thought he'd be frightened and give me the money.'

'Where did your friend Cavendish get the rifle he was using when he was arrested?' Tony asked him.

'It's my dad's. I took it and lent it to 'Boff' in exchange for borrowing his pistol. I couldn't walk about with a rifle, could I? Someone would have reported it, before I even got to the farm, wouldn't they?'

The DI nodded,

'You're probably quite correct in that assumption,' he said. What was Mr. Davies doing, while all this threatening was going on?'

Lionel Gorse looked up at Tony.

'He was still just sitting in his chair grinning at me. He told me that I'd get nothing from him, whatever I threatened to do . Then he said he'd make sure the police had all the information they needed to put my father away for a very long time. I thought, 'No you won't!' and I shot him in the head. He shouldn't have kept goadin' me. I'd warned him enough and he knew I meant it when I threatened him with the pistol.'

Tony Church was staggered to think that this young man had actually admitted to murder, in a police interview.

'How did that help?' He asked.

'It stopped him from giving the police any information, for a start. At least he won't be able to get my father into trouble, now he's dead, will he?'

'I wouldn't count on that, Lionel,' said the DI. 'You didn't get any money though, did you?'

Lionel Gorse looked puzzled. He asked,

'What do you mean? You wouldn't count on it. How can he tell you anything now?'

'Perhaps he'd already told the police, before you got there,' Tony suggested.

'I don't see how,' said Lionel. 'He said he would make sure, not that he had already told them.'

Tony smiled and looked at Ian Stuart.

'Why did you steal the silverware and the other items?' Ian asked.

'I just thought I might as well have something for my trouble,' Gorse answered. 'I mean it was obvious I wasn't going to get any money. I had a good look for the ten grand, but I couldn't find it. So I took what I could and got out. I got the shotgun, but I cut my hand when the knife broke in the door of the gun cabinet. I had plenty of time to look around, he was dead by then and it wasn't as though he'd have any visitors at that time of the morning.'

'What time would it have been when you cut your hand?' Ian asked him.

'I don't know, probably about one o'clock, maybe a bit later. It was after I'd put the stuff in the holdall. I found some plasters in his bathroom cabinet, so I stuck one over the cut. Then I took the holdall with the stuff in it and went out through the back door.'

Tony looked up from his note pad and asked Gorse,

'When did the zip fastener break on your holdall?'

'How do you know about that?' Gorse asked.

'We already know quite a lot about your visit to Ridge Farm,' he told him. 'My guess is that you broke the zip while you were trying to get the silver tray into it. Is that correct?'

Gorse nodded,

'I think it probably was, yes. It was too big to close the zip and I lost my temper with it. It tore the end off the zipper.'

'Yes, we found it on the kitchen floor,' Tony told him. 'Does your father know what you did at Jason Davies' home?'

'I think I told him all of it,' Lionel replied. 'I might have left out a few details, but he knew I'd killed him. He just said it was a good job I'd got there before Davies could phone the police with his new information.'

Tony looked up at Gorse and said,

510

'So your father knew that Davies had got some new information?'

'Yes, obviously, that's why he was glad I'd shot him. He knew he was safe after I told him that.

'I think we'll take a short break for a cup of coffee. Is that OK with you, Lionel?'

He nodded and said,

'Yes, fine, thank you. I'd prefer tea please, with milk and two sugars.' He paused to glance at the recording equipment, before continuing. 'I expect you'll want to know about Cavendish and the gun?'

Tony smiled and replied,

'Indeed we will, Lionel, we have a long list of questions for you. We'll need answers from you regarding Victor Cranham's involvement and the kidnapping and assault on your step sister. Whilst the tape is stopped, we cannot discuss any details of the case.' The room returned to silence as he said,

'Interview suspended for refreshments at eighteen hundred hours.' He then stopped the machine.

Ian got to his feet and left the interview room to collect their drinks.

Lionel Gorse sat quietly for a few minutes and then said,

'I know you said we can't discuss the case, but can we talk about something else? I don't like just sitting quietly with all this hanging over me.'

'What would you like to talk about, Lionel?' Tony asked him. The young Gorse shrugged his shoulders. 'Anything,' he said, 'I just can't stand the silence.'

'Do you have a good relationship with your stepmother?' Tony asked him.

'No, not really,' he said. 'She's OK while she's getting her own way, but she can be a nasty cow when it goes wrong. I don't trust her. She tries to control me, the way she does my father. She thinks I'm stupid, but I know she was sleeping with dad while my mum was still alive. She'd lost her husband and my mother had felt sorry for her. Delia was bloody spiteful to my mum, couldn't care less about her. I wondered afterwards, whether my mother's death really was an accident or if they somehow had a hand in it. I wouldn't put it past her. She's got no consideration for anyone except herself. Even Sandra, her own daughter, hasn't got a good word to say about her.'

'How about your father,' Tony asked, 'do you get on well with him?'

'Sometimes,' he said, thoughtfully. 'I'm never sure whether he likes me or resents me. He has helped me now and then, but mostly he's telling me I'm useless. He gets paranoid about his business dealings. I think he's worried that someone will find out what he's doing or how much money he's taking. His business is not exactly about being honest, is it?'
Tony smiled,

'I expect it's difficult to be an open minded private investigator, Lionel,' Tony said. There's sometimes only a very thin line between confidentiality and criminal deceit. His clients need to believe they can trust him, but if trust is compromised, there's no telling how the clients may react.'
Lionel nodded in agreement.
Ian returned with their drinks. He passed Lionel his tea, put their two coffees on the table and sat down.
Lionel remained head down and silent for a few seconds. He suddenly looked up at the DI and said,

'I used to think my dad was the greatest, Inspector Church,' he paused and then continued. 'Then when I was in my early teens, I started to notice certain things he said and did were not so honest or open. He cheated people. Some were my friends' parents, so I started losing friends. He had people who did what he wanted, but then he dropped them in the muck when it suited him. He always seemed to get away with everything but some of his friends went to prison because of what they'd done for him. He began getting me to do his dirty work. At first, he covered for me, but then he began to say I'd done it all the wrong way, not how he'd told me. He called me stupid and unreliable, said I was worthless. That's when I started to rebel against him. I started by trying drugs and met a new group of 'friends'. Now I realise that they're all just as treacherous as my father. At least now I'll be away from him. I'll get help with my drug habit in prison, try to get clean. I'm sorry I shot old Mr. Davies. He was another of my father's mistakes. Now I've shot him so that my father can get away with whatever he did to him. Old Mr. Davies won't be able to defend himself now, will he?'

The room was quiet. Tony watched as Lionel Gorse sipped his tea, his hands wrapped around the mug. Tony noticed that he had begun to weep.

'I'm sorry,' he said, wiping his eyes and sitting up straight in his chair. 'Thank you for the tea. Do you want to finish the interview now?'

'Give yourself a few minutes to recover your composure, Lionel,' Tony said. 'We'll continue whenever you are ready.'

Tony Church looked at Ian and asked,

'Shall we tell him now?'

Lionel looked up sharply,

'Tell me what?' He asked.

Ian smiled at him and said,

'Before I continue, I must advise you that you won't be allowed any direct or even indirect contact with your father until after we have interviewed him. We have not re-started the tapes, so this is strictly off the record, you understand?'

Lionel Gorse nodded his agreement as Ian continued to explain.

'Mr. Davies recorded a telephone call with your father, earlier on Sunday evening. He also provided us with a lot more information, including names of witnesses. We have checked their reliability and I can tell you that your father will not be returning to his business. I hope that this will make you feel better able to continue your co-operation with us. We appreciate your honesty, Lionel. You have taken responsibility for your actions, without prejudice and you have expressed remorse. I would, however strongly advise you to take advantage of free legal representation at your court hearing tomorrow.

'Thank you,' said the young Gorse. 'I will take your advice on that. I don't think I need any help with this interview though. I just want to tell you the truth and get it over with.'

The interview was resumed and Lionel Gorse explained that he had told Victor Cranham to try to dispose of the stolen items via either pawn shops or antique dealers.

'I didn't know he'd been arrested in Pudborough,' Gorse said. 'I just thought he'd sold the stuff and pocketed the money. I got some of my acquaintances to grab Sandra, to make him give it back. I didn't want her to be hurt, just kept out of the way until Vic showed up with the money. They were supposed to stay with her in my father's beach hut, not lock her in and clear off.'

'Where are the other items which you stole from Davies?' Tony asked him.

'All in my room, at home,' he replied. 'There's some 'coke' in there as well, but it's hidden under my bedside cabinet. A bit of floorboard lifts up, you'll find it there. I may as well get everything cleared up while I'm here,' he said. 'The gun in the 'Merc' belongs to Cavendish, the other one, the one in the holdall is my Dad's. There's ammo for it in the kitchen cupboard at home.'

It was after seven when the interview was concluded. The DI had advised him that there would be a list of charges for him to face. Besides the murder of Jason Davies, he would also be facing charges of theft, conspiracy to kidnap, possession of an illegal firearm with intent to endanger life, possession of a controlled substance and dangerous driving.

Quite a collection of serious offences for a young man to face at his first court appearance!

He had agreed to have a solicitor to represent him at his hearing. To avoid any possibility of collusion or intimidation from his father, Tony had him transferred to the care of the Arundel police, until the hearing. It was turning out to be a very long day.

Back in the office, the two detectives had a chat about the ongoing cases. They decided that Leonard Chater Gorse could stew in his cell until the morning. His wife had been interviewed by DS Lesley Stevens and DS Stan Williams. This interview had taken place at the same time as Lionel Gorse's, but had been concluded an hour or so earlier. Delia Gorse had been charged with aiding and abetting the escape of Lionel Gorse, conspiring to pervert the course of justice, obstructing the police in the execution of their duty. She was further charged with dangerous driving and criminal damage. She was detained in Chichelster's police cells overnight but was first escorted to her home, to retrieve her small dog. The animal would be cared for at the kennel which she normally used, pending the outcome of her court hearing tomorrow.

Tony Church had hinted that provided no further offences came to light, the police would not, in her case, oppose bail, but that would be the magistrates' decision.

Whilst the interviews were taking place, officers of Worthing CID were conducting a thorough search of Gorse's boat. They had found another firearm, a point three-eight revolver and ammunition. There was also a substantial amount of cash and a quantity of uncut cocaine, enough to charge him with intent to supply.

Rex Biker would be interviewed by DS Poole, as soon as it could be arranged with the Shoreham police.

DI Church had requested that his officers be assigned to search Gorse's home and his vehicles. This was agreed by the senior officers at Worthing and the search would commence tomorrow morning. In the meantime, the house was secured and as a precaution against Gorse's devious methods, a couple of uniformed officers would guard against the possibility of intruders.

CHAPTER 70.

The special Magistrate's Court session had been arranged for mid-day today, Sunday. Edwin Sarkes JP had contacted his two 'winger' magistrates, who had accepted that the Sunday sitting was necessary. He had asked the DI to try to keep it as short as possible.

DI Tony Church and DS Ian Stuart were at their desks before eight thirty am. The court documents for Cavendish and Cranham had been presented to the clerk to the justices on Friday. The time allowed for Cranham's detention, had almost expired, so it was a case of either releasing him or going to a magistrate for an extension. The police would not oppose bail for these two, but there would be stringent conditions imposed.

Delia Gorse's charge sheet had also been prepared, so once the court had set bail conditions, she could possibly be released. She would not be permitted to enter their home, until the search was completed and would need to report daily to the Worthing police.

Leonard Gorse and his son, Lionel, both faced more serious charges. Police would oppose bail in these cases, which would be tried at Crown Court in due course.

'Has Gorse's solicitor arrived yet?' Tony asked Sergeant Dean, on the front desk.

'He's just come through reception, Tony,' he said. 'He's left his bag here and gone into the gents. Did you want to see him before he has another chat with his client?'

516

'Not especially, Dixie,' Tony replied. 'When he comes back, ask him if he's ready to continue, would you? Can we use room one again this morning?'

Dixie Dean laughed quietly,

'I was hoping you'd say that,' he said. 'I put the heating on in there about an hour ago, in anticipation of 'sir's' request.'

Tony thanked him and put the phone back on its rest.

'I think we're going to have to play this by ear, Ian,' Tony said. 'I'll use the recording as an incentive to get a reaction, if we need to. I'll ask Dixie to send someone to escort them to the interview.' He picked up the phone and called the desk sergeant again.

'I'm as ready as I'll ever be,' Ian said. 'Might as well get it over with, I've got a feeling it could be a bit prickly.'

Tony took a quick look at his notes and picked up the mini cassette and player. His phone buzzed. It was PC Malcolm Foster on the front desk.

'Good morning sir,' he said cheerfully. 'Mr. Gorse and his lawyer are in the interview room waiting for you. I think you'll enjoy this bit, his lawyer is Mr. David Bush.'

Tony smiled.

'Thanks Malcolm, we'll try not to start a heath fire, gorse bushes are like tinder just now.' He turned to Ian and said, 'that was young Malcolm Foster. Gorse's lawyer's name is Bush!'

Ian laughed and said,

'Shall we venture into the prickly shrubbery?'

David Bush stood as they entered the room, his hand outstretched towards Tony.

'Good morning, Inspector Church,' he said. 'I'm David Bush, of Bush, Clements Partnership, Worthing.'

Tony shook his hand,

'Detective Sergeant Stuart,' Tony said as he introduced Ian, who also shook Bush's hand.

'Would either of you like a drink, before we begin?' he asked.

'No thank you,' Gorse replied, 'I'd prefer to start now. I'm a busy man and I'd like to get this misunderstanding cleared up quickly.'

Tony sat whilst Ian set up the recorder with two new tapes. He began with the usual statement of time and date and listed those present.

'Exactly what is my client charged with, Inspector?' Bush asked.

Referring to his notes, Tony replied,

'There are several charges, Mr. Bush, and there will be others which will be brought, following our further investigations. Shall we take them in chronological order?'

Bush nodded.

'Right,' Tony began, 'I'll begin with the oldest offence, which is that Mr. Gorse murdered Mrs. Mary Davies on or about the tenth of August nineteen sixty five. The second charge, also in chronological order is that following this offence, Mr. Gorse was complicit in the unlawful burial of her remains. Those are the two initial offences, but your client is also charged with blackmail and extortion against the late Mr. Jason Davies over an extended period. Have you got that?' He asked Bush, who was furiously writing on his legal pad.

'Just a moment, please,' he replied. He then looked up and said to Tony,

'I presume you have sufficient evidence to support these charges, Inspector?'

Tony nodded and replied,

'I think we can just about manage that, Mr. Bush. Are you ready to continue with the balance of the charges against your client?'

'There are more?' he asked incredulously. 'Very well, let's hear them.'

Tony continued,

'Mr. Gorse will also be charged with, incitement to commit a felony, conspiring with others to pervert the course of justice, aiding and abetting a fugitive, namely his son, Lionel Gorse and lastly, for the time being, resisting arrest.'

There was a pause to allow Bush to complete his notes.

'Inspector,' he said, 'what do you mean by your last comment, 'for the time being'? Is there another charge or charges pending?'

'That may depend on what we find when we begin our full search of Mr. Gorse's home and business premises, Mr. Bush.' Tony said. 'I'm ruling nothing out at this stage. The serious nature of the charges to date, demand that our investigation shall be extremely thorough and the evidence we present will need to be both accurate and irrefutable.'

Gorse had been very quiet up to this point. He now leaned forward towards Tony and said,

'I'm sure that most of these charges will prove to be unsubstantiated, any witness evidence you have will probably be classified as, 'hearsay'. Our lines of work are very similar, Inspector Church, we're both professional investigators, albeit with different motives. Mine is to ensure the results I achieve are satisfactory to my clients, who will then pay me appropriately. Your rewards are the same, whether you are successful in your endeavours or not.'

Bush looked at his client and said,

'I would strongly advise you not to pass such comments, Mr. Gorse. It would be better for you to remain silent than to risk compromising your position by saying something which you may later wish to retract. Don't forget that this interview is taped, and the content can be used as evidence in a court of law.'

Tony nodded at Bush,

'Thank you, now has your client anything to say in his defence of the first charge?'

'I strongly deny any knowledge of this offence,' Gorse said in a defiant tone. 'What evidence do you think you have to connect me to the death of this woman, thirty years ago?'

Bush smiled and raised his eyebrows enquiringly at the DI.

519

'Firstly, the two bullets recovered from the skull of the deceased were fired from a rifle belonging to you, Mr. Gorse,' Tony informed him.

'Nonsense,' Gorse said, 'they could have come from any rifle. One bullet looks exactly the same as any other.'

Bush turned to his client and said,

'I'm afraid you are not correct in that assumption Mr. Gorse. Each rifle has its own individual rifling marks. It could be described as the rifle's 'fingerprint' for identification purposes.'

'There's still no proof that I was holding it, when those bullets were fired.' Gorse insisted.

'Were you in the habit of lending your rifle to other people?' Tony asked.

'No, but someone could have taken it without me knowing,' Gorse countered.

'Was it kept in a secure metal cabinet, approved by the police only four months earlier?' Tony asked, as he checked his notes.

'I can't remember the circumstances, it was thirty years ago. I wouldn't just lend it to anyone. Perhaps it was another member of the rifle club.' Gorse added.

'Mr. Gorse,' Tony said as he looked him in the eye. 'You'll by now have realised that I am not speculating, as you seem to be. I am stating what I know to be facts. You are attempting to cast doubt on these facts, by offering a selection of alternative scenarios and claiming loss of memory of this crime. Let me try to restore your memory of the events immediately prior to you murdering Mary Davies, by shooting her in the back of her head.' The DI referred to his notes before continuing.

'I can tell you that the Rifle Club met on the eighth of August that year. I can also tell you that you were at the club that evening, with your rifle. There are a number of older members who remember you being there on that date. The club records also show that you purchased a box of ammunition that evening. In accordance with the law, your signature appears in the register against that purchase. I am now going to ask you another question, to which I already know the answer. You would do well to bear this in mind when you give your answer, only the truth now, please. Where did you shoot Mary Davies?'

Gorse tried to stand up, but was pulled back into his seat by Bush.

'I told you already,' he bellowed, 'I didn't shoot her, Davies shot her!'

Tony smiled,

'So when did you lend your rifle to Jason Davies?' He asked.

Gorse was silent for a moment and then said,

'I didn't, but he could have taken it.'

'From a locked gun cabinet in Worthing?' Tony asked.

'Or from my car,' Gorse suggested.

'Are you now admitting that you carried a firearm in your unlocked car? That's another serious offence, Mr. Gorse,' The DI told him. 'Presumably it was loaded, which constitutes yet another offence.

Bush placed his hand on Gorse's arm and said,

'As your legal representative, I'm advising you not to continue with this dialogue. It is purely hypothetical and is serving no useful purpose. I think it would less damaging to your case to just answer the questions which you are asked.'

Gorse grunted and sat tight lipped, as Tony continued.

'We know that you did carry your loaded firearm in your car on at least one occasion. Which if nothing else had occurred would render you liable for prosecution for possession of a loaded firearm in a public place. The fact that you used it to shoot Mrs. Mary Davies and then re-loaded it to shoot her a second time is the reason you now face a murder charge.'

Gorse laughed,

'Where's your evidence?' he sneered. 'All you've got is what somebody else has told you. They're all liars, I deny everything. Now let's see what you've got in the way of real evidence.'

'Do you recall a telephone conversation you had with Jason Davies, on the eleventh of November?' The DI asked.

'I didn't have a telephone conversation with Davies,' Gorse said, defiantly. 'Who says that I did?'

Tony smiled as he said,

'I'm now going to ask you to listen to a recording of that telephone conversation. Please listen without interrupting until the tape ends.'

Bush held up a hand to Tony,

'Would this be admissible as evidence, Inspector?' He asked.

'We shall see in due course,' Tony replied. 'Just listen to the tape first, please. You can raise any points you wish to, after you have heard the recording.'

He produced the mini cassette player and attached it to a more suitable amplifier and speaker unit. Ian switched it on and they heard Davies give his introduction.

'He's just play acting!' Gorse said as he stood up. 'This is nothing more than a farce!'

Ian stopped the tape.

'I have asked you to listen without interrupting,' Tony said in a stern voice. 'If you are not prepared to comply, I will ask for you to be returned to your cell, whilst it is played to your lawyer.'

Bush turned to Gorse and said,

'If you want me to defend you in any or all of the charges leveled against you, it is important that I am aware of all of the evidence, whether documented or not. This recording may or may not be admissible as evidence in any trial, but I cannot act in your best interests if I am unaware of its content. The inspector has asked that we hear the tape, now I am asking you to please listen, without comment, until the recording is stopped.'

'Alright, but under the strongest possible protest,' Gorse said, somewhat grudgingly. 'I refute anything said in the conversation. The tape could have been made at any time and it has no relevance to my case.'

'So you are aware that you had a conversation with Jason Davies on November the eleventh?' Tony asked, as he raised his eyebrows to Bush. 'Please re-start the tape, DS Stuart,' he said.

They heard the full conversation, but Ian stopped the tape as Gorse cut off the call, before Davies' final summary.

'Now, Mr. Gorse,' said the DI. 'Did you recognise your voice on that recording?'

'No, it wasn't me,' Gorse said.

'You didn't go to Haywards Heath on the ninth or tenth of August that year? Is that what you want us to believe?' Tony asked.

'No.' Gorse said.

Tony looked at Bush as he asked,

'Was that, 'no, you didn't go to Haywards Heath,' or 'no it's not what you want us to believe'?'

'Just a simple, 'no', to everything on the tape,' he said. 'He should have said he was recording the call, before I spoke, anyway, shouldn't he? So it can't be used as evidence without something material, can it?'

'We could add, 'demanding money with menaces', as a result of the tape.' Tony said. 'The tape would be admissible as evidence for that charge. After all, you did send your son to collect money and he did shoot Jason Davies, didn't he?'

'You've still got to prove that,' Gorse said.

'Actually, we haven't,' Tony informed him. 'Unlike you, Mr. Gorse, your son was both helpful and co-operative when we interviewed him. He has admitted that he killed Jason Davies, whilst trying to collect money on your behalf.'

'He's out of his head on drugs, half the time,' Gorse said. 'You can't believe a word he says. He'll probably deny it all tomorrow.'

'Whether he does or not,' Tony replied, 'he seems to endorse the information we have just heard from the telephone recording.'

Bush held up his hand again as he addressed the DI.

'May I have a few moments alone with my client, please?' He asked, 'without the tape recorder running.'

Tony nodded and spoke for the tape,

'Interview suspended at,' he looked at the clock. 'Ten fourteen a.m.'

Ian hit the pause button and together they went to the door to leave the room.

'Get those tapes!' Ian heard Gorse say to Bush.

'No!' Bush said urgently. 'Don't touch anything unless you want to be charged with destroying evidence.'

Ian returned to the interview room.

'Mr. Bush,' he said. 'You may have a few moments alone with your client, but it will be in the comfort of a cell, I'm afraid. Thank you for preserving the evidence, your client appears to lack your integrity, so we are not prepared to allow any more latitude.'

PC Malcolm Foster appeared in the doorway, behind Ian.

'If you'll please follow me, gentlemen,' he said. 'I'll escort you back to your cell, Mr. Gorse.'

Gorse and his solicitor obediently went with Malcolm Foster. Ian and Tony returned to their seats in the interview room.

'Can you believe the audacity of the man?' Ian said as they resumed their seats in the interview room.

Tony laughed,

'It's a good job his lawyer is an honourable man,' he agreed. 'In fact, I'm forming quite a liking for him. Gorse will have to face the fact that he's incriminating himself almost every time he opens his mouth. I expect that'll be the gist of what Bush tells him in the course of their little chat.' He looked at Ian and asked him, 'Do you mind hanging on here for a few minutes? I just want to nip to the office, to see if there are any messages for me from our search teams.'

'No, I'm fine with that,' Ian replied. 'Some feedback from Biker would come in very handy just now, wouldn't it?'

Tony left the room, as he passed the front desk Sergeant Dean waved to him.

'I've got Brian Pace on the line. Do you want to take it out here?' He asked.

Tony walked over to the desk and took the phone from Dixie Dean.

'Hello Brian, what have you got for us?' He asked. He listened as DS Pace told him they had found a large square of canvas in Gorse's garage.

'It looks as though he uses it for hedge trimmings and the like,' Brian explained. 'There are several spots and splatters of what could be old dried blood on it. Maybe it's nothing, just cuts and scratches from whoever was doing the pruning, but I'll bring it in. There's always the chance that it was used to wrap or cover a body. We'll DNA test it anyway, it could prove to be a useful bit of material evidence.'

'Yes,' Tony acknowledged. 'Canvas is the material and any blood could be evidence, so 'material evidence' is a most apt description. If it turns out to link Gorse to the murder of Mary Davies, it will be highly appreciated. Thanks Brian, let me know of any developments. I'll chat with you later. Bye for now.'

The DI continued to his office where he found a recorded message on his answering machine. Rex Biker had been interviewed by DS Bob Poole in Lewes prison. He denied any involvement in the murder of Jean Gorse. He knew that she was a diabetic and had witnessed her collapse on several previous occasions. He said that usually she revived quite quickly after either an insulin injection or by consuming something sweet. She had twice been involved in motoring accidents as a result of her condition. He confirmed that Gorse had asked him to provide a quantity of the PVA mesh, which he obtained for him from his local tackle shop. Biker was reluctant to implicate anyone else in Gorse's crimes. Bob Poole described Biker as co-operative, but got the impression that he felt no particular loyalty to Gorse. He had not seemed surprised to hear that the circumstances of Jean Gorse's death were being re-examined. Nor at Bob Poole's hint that maybe Gorse had contrived to arrange the demise of his late wife. He'd said that he would put nothing past him. Biker maintained that he was not aware of any other person's

525

involvement in her death, but hinted that Delia Bowyer had been very secretive about it, when the police had questioned them. He said he had believed Gorse had some sort of a hold over some of the Worthing officers. He knew that Gorse had on several occasions, succeeded in manipulating various people into doing his dirty work for many years. He told Bob Poole that Gorse had threatened to expose him over a car insurance scam, which was why he agreed to help him to clean some unexplained cash receipts. He later discovered that Gorse had obtained the money by deception, but by then it had become Biker's problem. He accepted that he was guilty of the offence and knew that if he tried to involve Gorse, there would be even worse retribution to face from him. Biker said that he would not wish to give evidence against Gorse for that reason. Tony again thought of the possibility of a corrupt officer in the ranks at Worthing. He would need some outside help to investigate this.

Tony returned to the interview room, where Ian Stuart was sitting with Gorse and his solicitor. They were ready to resume their interview.

Once they were seated, Ian re-started the tape machine as Tony spoke for the recording.

'Interview with Mr. Leonard Chater Gorse resumed at ten forty-two am. Those present, as before.

Bush was the first to speak.

'Gentlemen,' he began, 'I have conferred with my client and he has accepted that some of the details of the telephone recording are correct. Because of the time which has elapsed since the death of Mrs. Mary Davies, he has no clear recollection of the details surrounding the accident.'

Tony looked directly at Bush,

'Mr. Bush, let me make this quite clear to you and your client. It was thirty years ago, so some details may be lost in the mists of time, but it was not an accident. It was murder. Furthermore, it was a particularly cold blooded murder, planned in advance, in a most elaborate way. He had deceived Mary Davies into believing that he cared enough for her, to risk losing everything just to be with her, when in fact he was in fear of his wife discovering his affair and leaving him. The pre-nuptial agreement, which Jean Gorse had insisted on, would have seen her take her wealth with her. This would have left your client close to bankruptcy, so for insurance against that possibility, he blamed the totally innocent, yet admittedly gullible, Jason Davies. I make the point here, that your client's memory is still clear enough, after thirty years, to attempt to extort a further blackmail payment from Jason Davies, using his own son as an instrument in the felony. Has your client any comment to make on this, my summary of events?'

Gorse sat shaking his head,

'I'm admitting nothing,' he said defiantly. 'The burden of proof is yours. You have to prove I'm guilty and that telephone call recording won't be admissible as evidence.'

Bush frowned as he said to Gorse,

'I wouldn't count on that, the last words of a man, shot by your son, will probably carry quite a lot of weight with any jury.'

'I think you'd better make up your mind whose side you're on,' Gorse snarled at his lawyer.

'And I think you'd better find some manners or find another lawyer, Mr. Gorse,' said Bush. 'I'm acting in your best interests, but I will not fabricate facts to suit your predicament, neither will my replacement, whoever he may be. Let me lay it on the line for you. This is what is known as a 'cold' case, meaning that it has never been closed. I have known of such cases coming to prosecution fifty or sixty years after the event. The time which has elapsed does not make murder any less of a crime. We have just discussed this in our private meeting, where, albeit with some reluctance, you acceded to this fact. You are facing a jail sentence which may last for more years than you have left to live. I am prepared to act in your defense and do my best to minimise your sentence. More than that I cannot promise. Now you must decide whether you wish me to continue to defend you, or elect to engage the services of another legal representative.'

That did the trick!

Gorse sat with his head down for several minutes. The others just sat quietly watching, waiting to see what he would do next.

'I could have moved to Spain last year,' he said. 'I only stayed here because of my son, but now he's turned against me. I've lost everything because of him. Davies should have told me he was recording the phone call. He phoned me, I didn't phone him. I think it could be classed as 'entrapment' the way he's done it and I thought that was against the law.'

Tony Church glanced at Gorse's solicitor as he remarked,

'Murder is against the law, Mr. Gorse. Blackmail is against the law. Demanding money with menaces is against the law, as is possession of a firearm without a certificate and inciting a person to commit a criminal act. Aiding and abetting a fugitive, resisting arrest and assault against a police officer, are the latest in what you must surely agree is quite a list of offences. Circumstances play a big part in any evidence, Mr. Gorse. Your son murdered Mr. Davies, whilst attempting to extort your blackmail payment. I believe that this will add considerable weight to the content of this recording of his last conversation with you.'

Bush nodded in agreement, he said,

'Mr. Gorse, have you decided who you wish to represent you?'

'Yes,' Gorse replied. 'I'd like you to continue to work for me on this case, Mr. Bush. I'll take your advice and hope the court will believe me when I tell them that I did not want Lionel to shoot Mr. Davies. The hand gun he used was not mine and I didn't know he was armed. That was his decision and his alone.'

Bush looked up at the DI and asked,

'May we take a few minutes to prepare, before we attend the hearing?'

'Yes, that's fine with me,' Tony told him. 'I will advise you that Lionel will be attending the same court, but your client will not be permitted any contact with him. Do you understand that?'

Bush nodded,

'Yes, Inspector, there will be no problems from this quarter, he said. 'It would not be helpful to either of them to engage in any verbal or physical altercation at this stage. What will happen with regard to my client's wife, or is that confidential?'

Tony smiled,

'Mrs. Gorse has her own charges to answer,' he told Bush. 'She has her own legal representative to defend her. Depending on the magistrate's ruling, she will possibly be allowed bail, but there would almost certainly be conditions attached to the order.'

The four of them sat quietly for a few moments. Tony was the first to speak.

'Interview terminated at eleven-ten.' Tony stated as Ian switched off the machine. He extracted the tapes, wrote on the label, the time and date and persons present. He passed both tapes to Tony, who signed them and then passed them across to Bush.

'I'd like you both to append your signatures to these, if you would be so kind,' he said to Bush.

Gorse signed them and pushed them across to Bush for his signature. Tony took them from Bush and checked their signatures. He handed one to Bush and said,

'This is your client's copy, which I advise you to listen to after the hearing. If you have any questions, please contact me and I will do my best to answer them. Before we go to the court building, I'd like to thank you both for your tolerance and good manners in what is obviously a traumatic experience for you, Mr. Gorse. Your transport is arranged, you will be taken from your cell at around a quarter to twelve. We can discuss the outcome later, when all the other cases have been heard.

They all shook hands and then Gorse was escorted back to his cell. Bush thanked the two detectives and left via the front office.

The court hearing had gone as planned. The extensions for questioning the Gorses were approved and Mrs. Delia Gorse was released on police bail. The search of their home had revealed a quantity of drugs, most of which were in Lionel's bedroom, along with what appeared to be the balance of the items stolen from Davies' home. There were another two unlicensed guns, a Heckler and Koch nine mm. pistol and a Webley point three-eight revolver. The documents found in Gorse's home office provided further proof of extortion and blackmail on Jason Davies and two other persons. There were also details of Biker's involvement in the death of Gorse's late wife, Jean in 1993. At the Coroner's inquest the jurors were directed to return an open verdict. This case would now be re-opened.

Back in their office at around one-thirty pm, the DI discussed his proposals with DS Stuart.

'The Gorses will be heard again on Tuesday, Ian,' he said. 'In my opinion they should be remanded in custody until their trial. That should give us ample time to put the case together. Delia Gorse has been instructed not to discuss the case with the media, or she will be arrested and detained under the prejudice laws. Her solicitor understands this and has given assurance on her behalf.' Ian was listening and making notes, he asked,

'I suppose we can release JD's body for burial now, can't we?'

'Good point, Ian,' said the DI. 'I'll tell young Jeffery now.' Tony checked his list and found Jeffery Davies' number.

'Good afternoon Mr. Davies,' he began. 'DI Church here, I'm sorry to disturb your Sunday afternoon, but I have some news for you.'

'Oh, good afternoon, Inspector,' Jeffery Davies replied, 'what sort of news would that be?'

'Well, firstly, we are now in a position to release your father's body to an undertaker. That can wait until the morning, of course, but the other good news is that we believe we have recovered the items stolen from your father's home on the eleventh or twelfth of this month.' Tony consulted the list of items recovered and read from it. When he had finished reading, Jeffery asked him to repeat the details of the coins which were found at Gorse's home.

'I think you said, 'forty six gold sovereigns' Inspector,' he said. 'I do know for certain that there were sixty-seven sovereigns. They were originally collected by my Great Grandfather and passed to Grandfather when he died in 1934. My Grandfather left them to Dad in his will. There was one for each year of Great Grandfather's life from the year he was born, 1850, until the last year they were minted, which was 1917. Did your men find any of my grandfather's medals?'

'If they did, they're not on this list, Mr. Davies,' Tony said. 'I'll have to make some more enquiries and get back to you when I find some answers.'

'Thank you, inspector,' Jeffery said, 'and thank you for letting me know about Dad. I'll get on to the undertaker in the morning and I'll need to tell Dad's solicitor I suppose, so he can get the insurance sorted out. What do I need to do about the death certificate?'

Tony thought for a moment before replying.

'I'll have a word with the coroner about that, Mr. Davies,' he said. 'In this instance I'm sure we will have already dealt with that aspect. I'll make sure you have a couple of originals, one for the undertaker and one for the Registrar. I would suggest you obtain several copies from the Registrar. You'll need them for the bank, the insurance company and your father's solicitor. It may be that your Aunt Bernice will need one, perhaps you will ask her.

'Thank you, Inspector Church,' said Jeffery Davies. 'Any help at this stage is more than welcome. I'm sure you'll get to the bottom of the problem with the missing coins, so I'll wait until you contact me on that score. I'll call in to the station in the morning. Thanks and goodbye for now.'

Tony looked at Ian Stuart,

'I don't know if you caught the gist of that, but it looks as though there are still twenty-one sovereigns missing,' he told him.

'We'll need to press young Lionel for some more information then, won't we?' Ian said. 'That can wait until tomorrow, he's safely back at Arundel for now.'

Tony smiled,

'I think that's about all for now, have you got any questions?'

Ian smiled,

'Only one, Tony,' he said. 'Have we got time for a pint on the way home?'

Tony laughed,

'You'd better believe it, pal,' he replied. 'Come on, let's enjoy what's left of our Sunday off!'

CHAPTER 71.

Monday the nineteenth of November began with a violent thunderstorm. As it got light, it was apparent that it had been raining for most of the night. Many of the low lying fields were flooded and debris and leaves littered many of the roads. Archie switched on the radio to hear the news. Sussex Radio reported that a special Magistrate's court had been held yesterday to deal with suspects involved in the recent murder of Mr. Jason Davies, who was shot and killed in his home at Wigglesworth. Most of the items stolen during the incident had been recovered by the police, but Detective Inspector Church, of the Chichelster Force, said that enquiries were still ongoing. The Worthing police had been involved in the eventual apprehension of several suspects and Inspector Church said that he was relying on their continued co-operation to bring the matter to a conclusion.

The storm of last night had left several acres of farmland flooded and there had been reports of some trees having been blown down. All major routes were unaffected, but care should be taken when negotiating some of the minor roads.

The weather was expected to improve as the day progressed and there would be no frost this evening.

Archie switched off the radio and said to Jimbo,

'It looks as though we're going to get a bit damp this morning, old boy.'

The dog looked knowingly at Archie. It was as though he completely understood what Archie had said. He went to the kitchen door and sat, looking round at his master. Archie put his mac and boots on and picked up Jimbo's lead.

'Come on then,' he said as he opened the back door. 'Let's get out and sample the elements, we'll go and have a look at the mill pond, see if it's flooding.'

Together they walked down the footpath to the mill, where Jimbo bounded along in the wet grass, in front of Archie.

The pond was a little higher than usual, but the weir was clear of any obstructions, so Archie turned and began his walk back. He noticed Martin Bettis' Range Rover parked by the mill and saw the man get out and begin walking towards him.

'Good morning, Mr. Leggitt,' he called out as Jimbo bounded towards him, tail wagging and looking very friendly.

'Look out!' Archie called to Bettis, 'he's soaking wet.'
Bettis laughed as he stopped to rub the dog's head.

'Hello boy,' he said as he continued walking towards Archie, Jimbo following at his heels.

'Good morning,' Archie said as he approached. 'What brings you to Wigglesworth mill at this early hour?'
Bettis smiled and said,

'I needed to see you, Mr. Leggitt, for some advice on the best way to overcome a problem. Can we have a chat? Perhaps in the mill would be best, I don't want to disturb your household.'

'I didn't bring the key with me,' Archie explained. 'We can sit in your car if you like, Jimbo won't mind being outside.

'He can sit in the back,' Bettis said. 'There's an old blanket on the back seat and I'll open a few windows so it doesn't get too steamed up.'

Jimbo was quite happy to lie in the back whilst the two men got in the front. Bettis opened the windows about a third of the way down and began to explain to Archie.

'Jeffery Davies asked me to come along, he's not allowed to contact Hannah, as you probably know. He's going to collect the death certificates for his father this morning, so he's going to be busy for most of the day. He'll need to make arrangements with the undertaker and then see his father's solicitor. What he's asked me to do is get a message to Hannah, unofficially at this stage, to let her know that she will get her house back very shortly. It's in her name and there was something of a pre-nuptial agreement, to cover her assets, if the marriage failed. Jeff wants me, through you, Mr. Leggitt, to send his apologies to Hannah and her sister, Hilda. He's been told unofficially that he will inherit his father's farmhouse, so he will be moving in as soon as he can, once the will has been read.'

'You said there was a problem of some sort,' Archie reminded him. 'What you've just told me sounds more like a solution to a problem.'

Bettis smiled,

'Yes, of course,' he said. 'The problem is this. We will be resuming work on the hotel site, probably next week. What we would like is to begin with a clean sheet as far as your friend, Mr. Skrobe is concerned. We have already told him that we wish to rectify the problems which we created for him and we want to offer him some compensation for the inconvenience he has endured. My wife, Elaine was so embarrassed by the way we tried to trample on anyone who stood in our way, she was going to leave me if I didn't change my ways. I know that Jeff and I were to blame for just about everything, including the accident involving the young moped rider. Now we both want to do whatever we can to put things right. We almost went bankrupt over this and we have learned our lesson the hard way. We tried to cut corners and got too greedy. Please believe me when I tell you that we are humiliated by our selfish actions and both wish to do all we can to apologise and compensate the people who have suffered because of our actions. You probably know that Jeff has now completed his community service as far as the courts are concerned, but he wishes to continue to perform some of those duties. He realises now that there is more satisfaction in helping people than there was in antagonising them.'

'So you want me to deliver his message to Hannah and then try to persuade my friend, Joe Skrobe to accept the offer with regard to the damage to his property. Is that about the size of it?' Archie asked.

Bettis nodded, he looked Archie in the eye as he said,

'I didn't know you, or even know of you, until you found me unconscious in the garage at Ridge Farm. You're a good man, Mr. Leggitt, better than me, by far. You've shown me that you earn respect by caring about people and helping them, not by misusing the power which wealth can bring. However wealthy a person may be, they will be judged by the way they treat people. Jeffery and I have had several discussions on this subject. I've told Jeffery how you saved me from a great deal of embarrassment that day and I was most grateful for your discretion. Jeffery was almost sent to prison because he thought that his power over his estranged wife, allowed him to abuse anyone who stood in his way. It was a good job that Hilda had a neighbour who thought about things the same way that you do. He wasn't a wealthy man either, but he had principles and he wouldn't tolerate bullying, especially against a woman. I think that's when Jeff began to realise that unless he changed his outlook, he would be doomed to fail in everything he tried to do.'

Archie had begun to understand this man a little better. He was still a little puzzled as to why he had asked for his help, but he could see that both men had created a barrier by their previous selfish actions.

'Just one thing, Mr. Bettis,' Archie said. 'Have I got your assurance that this is not just another ploy to enable you both to resume your project without regard for others, as you did before?' Bettis looked him in the eye and said,

'You have my word, Mr. Leggitt. I can promise you that we will not repeat our previous mistakes. Jeff has seen the folly of his ways and is trying hard to make amends. He has found himself a new lady, her name is Patricia Walker and she is a private investigator. She is a very intelligent lady and has convinced Jeff that he has to change if he wants to keep her. He has said that he would very much like to meet you but he understands that you do not hold him in very high esteem. It is also a bit difficult for him because he doesn't want to cause Hannah any more distress. He has acknowledged that he treated her badly and the way is open for her to divorce him, if that's what she wants. He admits adultery with Tricia so her petition would not be contested.'

Jimbo was becoming restless and nudged Archie's head with his nose.

'I think he's trying to tell you something,' Bettis said, grinning at the dog.

'Yes,' Archie replied, 'he wants his breakfast, I expect. Tell me what you and Mr. Davies are proposing to do to help the lorry driver. I understand that he will shortly lose his driving license, or haven't you given that matter any thought?'

Bettis smiled as he replied,

'That's one thing to which I can give a positive response. Jeffery has been paying him since the accident and has offered him a yard job when we re-commence work at the site. You can confirm that with the driver himself.'

'I'll take you at your word, Mr. Bettis,' Archie said as he reached for the door handle. 'I'll do my best to help you with your situation, but I can't control the way others may think about you and your previous actions. You'll need to demonstrate your change of heart, not just make a statement about it. Time is on your side and time heals most wounds. Just make sure you keep that in mind.'

Archie turned towards Bettis and offered his hand, which Bettis grasped firmly.

'I will do just that, Mr. Leggitt and thank you for taking the time to listen to me. Although we don't really know each other, I recognised from our first meeting, that you were a fair minded man. I won't let you down and neither will Jeffery Davies.'

'I hope you don't,' Archie said as he got out of the Range Rover. 'Come on Jimbo, let's get some breakfast.'

One man and his dog walked home through the footpath. Jimbo bounced along in front, Archie, wrapped in thought, felt somehow a little lighter.

CHAPTER 72.

Arundel police waited for a few minutes until the Chichelster custody Sergeant had taken Lionel Gorse to the interview room. Sergeant Mike Hodd returned to the front office and signed the transfer sheet.

'Thanks very much lads,' he said, smiling. 'You'll possibly have him back for another night's bed and breakfast.'
The officer smiled back,

'He wasn't any trouble Sarge,' he said. 'In fact he was one of the best mannered young men we've had in our 'hotel' for quite some while. I expect your 'Mr. Church' will get to work on him soon.'

'He's already in there with him now,' Mike Hodd explained. 'He'll arrange for his safe return when he's got what he needs from him. Why don't you park your van and go for a cuppa? The canteen's open, you know where it is, don't you?'
The driver nodded,

'Thanks Sarge,' he said, as he got into the van and drove round to the car park at the rear.
Mike Hodd walked back to his position behind the desk as Ian Stuart passed through the office on his way back to room one.

The tapes were prepared and inserted into the machine, DI Tony Church advised the young Gorse of the procedure and asked him,

'Are you ready to begin, Lionel?'

'Yes Inspector,' he replied.

Tony started the tape and waited for the leader to pass through the recording head. He stated the names of those present and the time and date.

'Now,' he said to Lionel Gorse, 'for the tape, please state your full name and address.'

Gorse obliged.

'Lionel,' the DI began, 'we have some more questions for you. What did you do with the rest of the gold sovereigns? We know that there are twenty one missing and some war medals with ribbons attached.'

Gorse leaned forwards and held his head in his hands.

'Vic took them,' he said. 'He was going to give them to his wife's aunt Davina, to get them valued. I expect he can get them back from her, if you ask him.'

'Do you know his aunt Davina's name and address?' Tony asked.

Gorse nodded,

'I know her name, Davina Cox,' he said. 'I don't know her address though, but Sandra will know it. She was her late father's sister. She lives in Worthing, but I don't know which part.'

Ian looked at the DI and asked,

'Shall I get the Cranhams in and ask them?'

'Yes please DS Stuart,' Tony replied. He turned to young Gorse and said,

'If you had told us this at your first interview, it would have saved us a lot of wasted time. Is there anything else we need to know, before we suspend this interview?'

'I know the coins and medals will be safe, Inspector,' he said. Her husband is a policeman.'

'Interview suspended at ten fifteen,' Tony said as he stopped the tapes.

He turned to Gorse and explained,

'You will be returned to your cell for the time being, Mr. Gorse. We will ask you to help us again when we have established the facts regarding the coins and medals.'

Gorse was escorted back to a cell by the duty officer and the two detectives returned to their office.

Ian picked up the telephone and requested the Worthing police to bring the Cranhams in for further questioning. Whilst they waited for a response, Tony re-examined the statements in the Victor Cranham enquiry. He suddenly sat bolt upright!

'Got it!' he exclaimed. 'Ian, we'd better get over to Worthing right now, we don't have time to wait for them.'

Ian looked startled,

'What is it, Guv?' he asked.

'Cox!' The DI shouted. 'That's what it is, Ian, Cox. Remember that Sergeant at Worthing, who vouched for Cranham's character? That's his name, Robert Cox. By asking Worthing to pick up the Cranhams, if he's on duty, we've warned him we're on to him. We need to get to him before he can dispose of the coins and medals. It will cause a bit of a stink, but I'll get the 'super' to clear it with HQ. You go and organise a fast car, I'll see you out front in a few minutes. See if you can grab a couple of uniform boys to come with us.' He picked up the file and raced upstairs to the Superintendent's office. Glover's secretary was somewhat flustered, but when she saw that Tony was determined to see him, she said,

'I think it'll be OK if you just knock and go in, Mr. Church. Superintendent Glover is always approachable in an emergency.'

The 'Super' was at his desk. He looked up as Tony entered.

'This looks urgent, Tony,' he said. 'You'd better tell me about it as quickly as you can.'

Tony explained the situation as briefly and concisely as he could.

'Yes, go for it Tony,' Glover said. 'I'll clear it with HQ. The Worthing brigade won't like it, coming from us, but I just hope the infection hasn't spread to any other officers.'

'Thank you, sir,' Tony said, 'We'll keep you posted.' He left the office and raced out to find Ian at the wheel of the Volvo estate.

'It's all approved, Ian, let's go,' he said. He looked over his shoulder and saw PC's John Levett and Malcolm Foster in the rear seat.

'Thank you chaps,' he said, nodding to them. 'Has DS Stuart explained what it's all about?'

'We got the gist of it sir,' Malcolm said. 'We're just here as enforcement, if we're needed. I take it we'll be in order to restrain a Sergeant from another force, if we have to, that is?'
Tony grinned at them,

'You'll be in more trouble from me if you don't,' he told them, adding, 'if you have to, that is. But make sure you mean it, won't you?'

'You'd better believe it sir,' they replied in unison.
The group arrived at the Worthing station to find Chief Inspector Harris, from the Shoreham HQ. He introduced himself and explained.

'Sergeant Cox is waiting in the interview room for a federation representative. We have been told that he made an urgent telephone call to the Cranham's number, immediately following your request for Worthing to pick them up. Fortunately your call was taken by another officer and they were apprehended as they attempted to leave in their car.'
Tony nodded and asked,

'So now what happens, sir? Do we still get to question the Cranhams, or is it all taken out of our hands by HQ?'
Chief Inspector Harris smiled,

'It's still your case, DI Church,' he said. 'You are free to question the suspects in connection with the missing coins and medals. In the event that Sergeant Cox is implicated in the matter, in any way, he will be dealt with by HQ and the Chief Constable. If it helps for you to know, he has refused us permission to check his locker. We are, as we speak, obtaining a search warrant for his home, which we currently have under surveillance. That's as much as I can say until you have interviewed Cox. I'm sure you understand our situation. You did well to alert us as quickly as you did, DI Church. We need to establish a few more facts before we proceed, everything must be done by the book, or it could be an escape route for his legal team.'

'Yes sir,' Tony agreed. 'If you don't have any objection, perhaps we can begin our interviews with Mr. Cranham. Is there another room which we can use, with recording apparatus, we've brought some tapes with us?' He held up the briefcase which contained the tapes and the relevant files.

CI Harris answered,

'I'm sure Inspector Broome will accommodate you as far as that is concerned. Here he is now, I'll introduce you and you can arrange something to suit you both.'

Ian went out to the car and spoke with the two constables.

'I think you'd better go and find a cup of tea, lads. It looks as though we'll be tied up here for an hour or so.'

'Is it OK if we have a quick stroll along the front, before we go to the canteen?' Malcolm Foster asked.

Ian grinned at him as he replied,

'Yes I should think so, try not to drip any ice cream down your uniform and make sure you're back here in about half an hour, in case we need you.'

'Thanks, Sarge,' they both said as PC Levett locked the car. He handed the keys to the DS and the two PC's walked towards the exit at the rear of the parking area.

As Ian returned to the front office, he saw the DI returning from one of the other areas. He was chatting with a uniformed Inspector, whom Ian took to be Broome.

'Ian,' the DI called out to him, 'Inspector Broome has found us an interview room and the Cranhams have just arrived at the back door.'

Tony decided to interview Sandra Cranham first and asked for a female officer to be present. It soon became apparent that she knew nothing of her husband's dealings with her Aunt Davina.

'I have very little to do with my aunt,' she said. 'She has tried to interfere in our marriage too many times. My Dad fell out with her a long time before he was killed. She is a nasty, mean and overbearing woman. She hasn't a good word to say about anybody. I've told Victor not to have anything to do with her. She's always been trouble, with a capital 'Tee'. When she heard that I'd been abducted, all she said was, 'I expect she deserved it, she should learn to do as she's told.' She meant that I should do whatever Vic says, even if I know he's wrong.'

After a very short interview, Tony thanked her and told he that she would be allowed home as soon as the police had finished their search for the stolen items.

Victor Cranham was not co-operative. He was in fear of reprisals from Robert Cox and his wife, Davina. Eventually he admitted that he had handed over twenty-one coins and four medals to Davina Cox, which she had told him she had given to her husband for the purposes of obtaining a valuation.

Tony and Ian packed up their equipment and returned to the front office. CI Harris called them over to where he was engaged in conversation with another officer. He signalled for them to wait a few minutes and then approached the two detectives.

'This has all become extremely complicated,' he told them. 'Internal affairs and the IPCC have been called in. I'll tell you as much as I can, but the truth is that I am not privy to the finer details. Cox's wife has been brought in, she has been arrested for obstructing the police. She tried to prevent them entering their home, even though they showed her the search warrant. The search team discovered a quantity of stolen goods, including the medals belonging to Gilbert Davies. Robert Cox attempted to delay opening his locker, on the pretext of having mislaid his keys. A helpful colleague found them for him and that became his point of no return.'

'Did he have the coins in his locker?' Tony asked incredulously. 'That would be incredibly foolish of him.'
CI Harris nodded,

'He did, Inspector Church,' he said. 'He's a very silly man. It seems that his wife has been the driving force which has fuelled his greed and recklessness. His locker also contained a large quantity of cigarettes, all duty free packs of 200 and several other high value items, some still in their BAA security bags.'
Tony shook his head,

'The problem is,' Tony said, 'this will also have a negative effect on many of his colleagues. Some will feel that they have let him down, whilst others may now be worried that they may also become implicated. What a bloody mess!'
CI Harris agreed, he explained,

'Obviously you'll be able to return the stolen items to their rightful owner eventually, but we'll need them as evidence for a few weeks. Have you completed your interviews Inspector Church?'

'I think we're about done,' Tony replied. 'Cranham is the villain. His wife is not even slightly involved in his nefarious dealings. I believe that marriage is destined for the scrap heap. His was yet another instance of greed causing the destruction of a career. He was a security officer at Gatwick, you know.'
CI Harris looked down at the floor and said,

'Whatever the outcome of this business, Cox has nobody to blame but himself. You and your men have done a great job, Inspector Church. You have nothing to reproach yourselves for. I'll make a point of mentioning you in my reports and hopefully I will pay you a visit on your home turf in the near future. I'm sure that under different circumstances we would enjoy a chat and some light refreshments. Thank you for your efficiency and give my regards to your 'Super'. He's a great guy, I've known him for more than thirty years.' He turned to Ian and said,

'Good to meet you DS Stuart, keep up the good work. I wish you both a safe journey home. I'll be in touch very shortly, as soon as I have some more information.'
They shook hands and the two detectives left via the canteen, where they found their PC's had just finished their third cup of tea and needed to use the facilities before driving back to Chichelster.

'I think we've earned a pub lunch,' said Tony as they got back to the office. 'We'll get the court paperwork done this afternoon. There's nothing more for us to do with Sergeant Cox. That's out of our hands now, but we need to get the Gorse cases to crown court as soon as possible. I still believe he had a hand in his first wife's demise, but we can investigate that element later.'
Ian agreed,

'I've got a feeling that we'll find someone else with information on that one,' he said. 'There must have been somebody who saw Gorse go onto the dock that night. I wonder why nobody heard or saw the car go into the dock, unless they were paid or threatened not to hear anything.'
Tony smiled as he said,

'That thought had crossed my mind, Ian. We know what a devious and manipulative sod he can be. We'll give it some more time after we've buttoned this lot up. I'm going to ask the 'Super' what he thinks we should do about Cranham and Cavendish. He may think they should go to Crown Court as well.'
Ian nodded in agreement.

'Let's go and find some lunch,' he said, 'while they've still got some of today's specials on the board.'

CHAPTER 73.

There were two letters for Hannah on Wednesday morning. Archie left them on the kitchen table as he went out with Jimbo. He had thought about what Martin Bettis had said and decided to wait until Jason's will was read, before saying anything to Hanna. He would have a word with Joe in the next couple of days. Joe had already told him that he had received an apology from Jeffery Davies. Archie thought it would probably be accepted by Joe. He was not a bitter man and would see no point in perpetuating any animosity.

The weather had improved considerably and the pair returned from their walk much drier than they had on Monday. As Archie entered the kitchen, he sensed a buzz of excitement. Elsie and Hannah sat at the table, both were wearing smug smiles.

'Feed Jimbo and then come and sit down, Arch,' Elsie commanded. 'Hannah has something to tell you.'

He did as he was asked and poured himself a cup of tea.

'What are you two cooking up?' He asked.

Hannah held up two letters,

'Some long awaited good news,' she announced. 'I've got a letter from Jason's solicitors. It says that the will is to be read on Thursday and I am advised to attend the reading as it would be to my advantage. It's at Barker and Pelham's in Worthing at 11 am.

I'm a bit concerned that Jeffery might be there to cause problems.'

'I'll explain something to you presently, Hannah,' Archie said. 'I had a chance meeting with his business partner on Monday and I can promise you that there will be no problems at the solicitors.'

'You crafty old devil,' Elsie said. 'Why didn't you tell us about it on Monday?'

'I'll explain that later, when Hannah has finished giving us her news,' he said. 'Go on, Hannah, what other good news do you have/'

She smiled at them both and said,

'My sister is getting engaged to her neighbour, Doug Fielding. She's coming down with him at the week-end to introduce him to Dad and she wants to know if she can bring him here to meet you two. She suggests going to the local pub for lunch, if that's alright with you both.'

'Oh well,' Archie said, 'that is good news. Please congratulate her from us both.' He looked at Elsie and said,

'Right, now I'll tell you what I learned from Martin Bettis on Monday. Jeffery Davies appears to have learned his lesson. He is continuing with his community service on a voluntary basis, even though he has discharged his obligation. Apparently he has found more satisfaction in doing something for the community than he did in using them for his own ends. Bettis also told me that he has written an apology to Hilda, he asked me to assure you that he will be moving into the farmhouse as soon as possible, so that you can have your house back. He is hoping that Cathy Simons will agree to continue with her old job, and keep the house clean for him. He has a new lady friend, Patricia Walker, who has told him that she will not tolerate any bullying of either her or anyone else. Jeffery Davies has written to Joe Skrobe, asking for a chance to put right the damage he caused to his property. Martin Bettis also told me that he is taking care of the financial needs of the young man who was injured in the accident with the lorry.

The Lorry driver has been kept on full pay and Davies has promised him a yard job when he resumes work at the hotel site, probably next week. They have the revised plans approved and they can start with the rectification work to shore up the perimeter. Their original client has re-commissioned them to complete the project, so they should come out of it without too much of a loss.'

Both women had listened without interruption until he had finished.

'Are you sure he was speaking about the same, 'Jeffery Davies'?' Elsie asked him.

Hannah laughed,

'I must confess that it sounds like somebody else, Archie,' she said. 'But perhaps we should give him the benefit of the doubt. At least I feel a bit better about going to the solicitors on Thursday.'

'It's the hearings today for the murders of Jason and Mary Davies,' Archie told them. 'That young lad who was walking about with the rifle, got a 2 year suspended sentence at the Magistrates Court. He would have gone to prison but Bettis dropped the 'Actual Bodily Harm' charge and saved him from that. Gorse's wife is up before the Magistrates today, but it looks as though she'll get away with a suspended sentence as well.'

'Who gave you all this information, Bill?' Elsie asked.

Archie smiled and nodded,

'Yes, Else,' he said. 'He's my 'inside' man on these subjects. He reckons that the Gatwick security guard and the corrupt policeman at Worthing will both be going down. He says that the case could drag on a bit, it's being investigated by their Internal Investigations people. Bill will probably know a bit more by tomorrow afternoon.'

Hannah had been listening intently and said,

'Perhaps I'll know a bit more by then, as well. I still can't understand why I've been asked to attend the will reading. I know I always got on well with old Jason, but I can't imagine being a beneficiary in his will. He didn't seem to be nearly as bad as he was painted. He always took my side whenever Jeff and I were at loggerheads.'

Archie smiled,

'I think you're probably right there, Hannah,' he agreed. 'Young Cathy Simons felt the same way about him, so he can't have been all bad. I wonder if she will be at the solicitors tomorrow, as well.

Elsie began cooking the breakfast. She was obviously thinking about everything she had heard.

'Cathy already said that he'd asked her to give that money to the Village Hall fund,' she observed. 'It makes you wonder how much the old boy was worth, doesn't it?'

CHAPTER 74.

Hannah left for Worthing at around ten o'clock on Thursday morning. She wanted to leave plenty of time to find somewhere to park. Elsie went into the garden, where Archie was raking up leaves.

'Would it be nice to find a small gift for Hilda, to mark their engagement, Arch?' She suggested.
He stopped raking and put the lawn rake back in the shed.

'Yes, Else,' he said. 'I think that would be a nice gesture. Put the kettle on, I'll come in for a cuppa and we'll have a think about what we could get for her.'

'It's for 'them', Arch,' she said. 'Not just for Hilda, it should be something for both of them, really. I'll put the kettle on anyway, tea or coffee?'

'Coffee, please,' he said, 'and a couple of chocolate digestives, I think. I'll follow you in. I just want to squirt a drop of oil into this padlock.' He went into the garage, by the side door.

'I was thinking perhaps we should get them something for their home,' Elsie said, as she looked through a mail order catalogue.

'Yes,' Archie said, 'but not from that book.'

Elsie looked up and frowned at him,

'I know, not to buy from mail order books, Arch,' she said. 'I was just using it to get a few ideas, that was all. It's no good buying them bed linen, if we don't know what size bed they'll have.'

'What about towels?' Archie suggested. 'We've got a rough idea what size faces they've got!' He grinned as Elsie shook her head.

'I suppose they are always useful, aren't they?' She agreed.

'Yes, Else, especially when you're all wet!'

'Oh shuttup! If you can't be serious, don't say anything at all,' she scolded.

'Sorry 'mum', I was only stating the obvious,' he countered, grinning.

Elsie closed the catalogue and put it away.

'I could go through to Chi and get some in Roseby's,' Elsie said, thinking aloud. 'If I go now, will you be here, in case Hannah gets back before me?'

Archie looked up at her and said,

'Why don't you go tomorrow? Hannah might want to come with you, there's no great hurry.'

Elsie thought for a moment,

'I suppose you're right, Arch,' she said. 'Perhaps Hannah would like to get them something as well. She might have a few ideas of what they would like. I wonder how the will reading is going. Do you think he might have left something for her?'

'I don't know, Else,' Archie replied. 'I suppose there must be a reason why the solicitor wanted her to attend the reading. We'll have to wait until she gets back. I know you can't bear to be kept guessing, but that's all we can do so try to think about something else instead. What's for dinner tonight?'

Elsie smiled,

'I thought that would be your idea of thinking about something else,' she said. 'It had to be food related, didn't it?

There's some pork chops in the fridge or we could use the rest of that ham in a ham and mushroom omelette.'

'Yes, with a few chips and a tin of garden peas,' Archie said quickly. 'We'll have the chops tomorrow.'

'Yes sir,' Elsie mocked, 'and what would sir like for pudding?'
Archie laughed,

'Dunno yet, Miss,' he teased, 'I'll have to study the menu!'

Hannah arrived back at around half past two. Archie was in the front garden, tidying the flower troughs under the window. He could see that she was happy. She had a couple of carrier bags with her, from fashion shops in Worthing.

'Hello Archie,' she called as she locked her car on the garage apron. Is Elsie in?'
Archie smiled.

'You look like the cat that got the cream, Hannah,' he said to her. 'I take it that all went well? No problems from Jeffery?'
She walked over to where he stood and said quietly,

'None at all, Archie, he behaved like a perfect gentleman. Old Jason was more than generous in his will. I had no idea that he was such a wealthy man. There will be quite lot which will go in death duty, but there's still plenty after that. Why don't you come in and I can tell you both all about it. I hope Elsie won't mind, but I've bought her a little gift.' She held up one of the bags.

'I'll need to wash my hands before I do anything else,' Archie told her. 'Hold the information until we've got a cup of tea.'
He followed Hannah in through the kitchen door.

'Elsie!' Hannah called out as she entered. 'We're both here, Archie's just washing his hands and then I can tell you all about it.'
Elsie came into the kitchen and began making a pot of tea.
Hannah put her bags down by the wall and made a fuss of Jimbo, who was obviously delighted to see her.

Archie dried his hands and began pouring the tea. Hannah picked up one of her bags and handed it to Elsie.

'I hope you don't mind, Elsie,' she said, 'but I saw this and thought it was just made for you.'
Elsie looked into the bag. She looked up at Hannah and said,

'Oh, Hannah, you really shouldn't do this,' Elsie pulled it from the bag and held up a navy blue Melton car coat. 'It's lovely Hannah,' she said. 'You shouldn't be spending your money on expensive things for me.' She slipped off her cardigan and put it on.

'Give us a twirl, Else,' Archie said. 'It's really smart and it looks like a perfect fit.'
Elsie went over to Hannah and gave her a hug.

'Thank you very much, Hannah,' she said. 'It really is lovely and so warm. I absolutely love it.' She put her hands in the pockets and then took them out and turned up the collar. She went out into the hall to look at herself in the mirror. Her face was beaming with pleasure as she returned to the kitchen. 'It's just the right colour, it will go with almost anything. I'll take it off now and go and hang it up later,' she told them. 'Now, Hannah, tell us all about your morning.' Elsie sat at the table with them as Hannah began to explain.

'I was a little bit early,' she said, 'Cathy Simons was in the car park, she told me that her old car was becoming unreliable, so she always made sure she had time to allow for a breakdown! I asked her if she was in the AA or the RAC, she said she was a member of the AA but thought she ought to belong to them both, just to be on the safe side! We laughed at that, she's a lovely person and so natural. She sends her love to you both. Anyway, there were so many people there, some I didn't know at all and some I had heard of, but never met. The reading was in what the solicitor called, the 'Conference Room'. There were thermos jugs of coffee for anyone who wanted it and bottled water as an alternative. Cathy was asked to go into the office first, on her own, Mr. Barker explained that it was in connection with an insurance policy. She came out after about ten minutes. She looked as though she had been crying. She sat next to me and I asked if she was alright. She said, 'I'll tell you afterwards,' and squeezed my hand.' Hannah paused and took a couple of sips of her tea, before continuing.

'Mr. Barker read a bit about Jason and his father, Gilbert and then went into the main body of the will. Before he gave any details, he explained about the forty per cent inheritance tax, or as we know it, Death Duty. He said that there were some exemptions, but these were mainly charities and trust funds.' Hannah pulled a piece of paper from her handbag and glanced at it.

'I'm sorry,' she explained, 'I'm doing this from memory, so I might miss a bit out and have to come back to it later. Right, the first and main beneficiary is Jeffery. He has the farm house and four hundred thousand pounds.'
Archie and Elsie let out a great expulsion of air.

'Say that again, Hannah,' Archie said. 'That's almost half a million!'
Hannah looked down at her piece of paper.

'Yes, that's right,' she said. 'It would have been closer to a million, but the death duty on the house and farm had to come out of it. Jeffery smiled at me and whispered, 'I'm sorry for the way I treated you, Hannah, but at least you will have your home back now.' I just nodded my appreciation, I didn't know what else I could do.' She took another sip of her tea. Archie looked into her cup and said,

'Why don't you finish that and I'll pour you a fresh one?'

'You can pour me another one as well, please Arch,' Elsie said, handing him her cup.
Hanna resumed her account of the will reading.

'I've never been to anything like this before,' she told them. 'The next beneficiary was Jason's younger sister, Bernice. She seemed a very nice lady and seemed to know Cathy, fairly well.

Bernice was left the land which is currently rented to a local farmer, on condition that if she wishes to dispose of it, he must be offered it first at a reduced price. His rent must remain the same for the next three years. Bernice also inherited two hundred thousand pounds and there was a further fifty thousand pounds in a trust fund for their son Barry. The fund is not accessible until he reaches the age of twenty-five.'

'That's sensible, Hannah,' said Archie. 'It's less likely to be wasted then and if the boy goes to university, it will pay his fees.' Hannah nodded,

'Yes, Arch,' she said, 'several comments of approval followed that condition, including Bernice. Cathy was left his car and twenty five thousand pounds and he left me the same amount, twenty-five thousand. We sat together just looking at each other, I didn't know what to do and then Jeffery, of all people began clapping us, Cathy and me. It was a bit embarrassing really.' Archie began clapping as well. Hannah had seemed lost in thought, but this brought her back to reality.

'I wouldn't mind being embarrassed to the tune of twenty-five thousand pounds, Hannah,' he said, grinning.
Elsie came around the table and put her hand on Hannah's shoulder.

'I expect those people realised that you had both earned Jason's respect, Hannah,' she said. 'That's why they applauded his decision. Are you OK to continue, or was that all of it?' Hannah smiled,

'I'm OK thanks, and there's still some more, but I may not get it in the correct order. He left his collection of sovereigns to Jeffery and his father's war medals to the Royal Sussex Regiment's museum at Eastbourne. There were also some old photographs to go with them. He left funds for the Parish Council to use for the supply of a new bus shelter by the War Memorial, in memory of his late wife. The inscription must state that she was 'killed by another's hand' and her name is to be written as, 'Mary (Eldridge) Davies. There were several other causes which benefitted from his fortune, but I don't suppose I'll remember them all. Oh, and he wants the village to produce a small booklet, outlining its history and the items of interest to tourists. He specifically mentioned the church, the old farm cottages with the flint knapped walls, in Ledham Lane and your watermill, Archie. That's it, I think. Oh no, I almost forgot! He left two thousand pounds to the village youth club and the same to the W.I. There were some others, but I can't remember who or what they were. Apparently it will all be detailed in the paper at the week-end, under, 'Wills of the Week.'

'Did you find out when the funeral will be?' Archie asked her.

'Oh, yes, sorry everyone,' Hannah said. 'It's on Monday at Wigglesworth Church at eleven am. Jeffery requested no flowers, but donations to the British Heart Foundation, could be made via the undertaker. Oh, and I almost forgot, the wake will be at the Old Bell in Forge Lane, everybody is welcome.'

'I bet old Arthur will be rubbing his hands,' Archie said. 'The pub will be bursting at the seams. Marjorie will be busy preparing the food. She always lays on a good spread for such occasions.

Cathy and I had a coffee and a sandwich after we left the reading. She told me what the insurance business was all about. Old Jason had asked her to witness a document for him, after she had been working for him for about a year. She knew it was something to do with an insurance company, but that was all. It turns out that it was a fifteen year endowment assurance for Cathy. He'd kept it quiet all those years. The solicitor told her to think of it as a pension or a loyalty bonus. Jason had paid it right up to when it matures in January next year. All she has to do is notify the Insurance Company and collect the money. It was for ten thousand pounds, but the solicitor told her it was a 'with profits' policy, so it could pay out closer to fifteen thousand.' Elsie was quietly amazed,

'He really thought a great deal of Cathy, didn't he Hannah?' She observed. 'I think she probably knew him better than anyone, including his son.'

557

'Yes,' Hannah replied, 'and she really misses him, you know. I think she'd just got so used to his ways, he had almost become more of a friend than an employer.'

The two detectives had also had a busy day on Thursday. They had spent several hours at the Magistrates' Court, where their efforts spent gathering and collating evidence were eventually rewarded.

Leonard Gorse was charged with the murder of Mary Davies, on or about the 10th September 1966. The tape recording of Jason Davies' conversation with him was accepted as evidence. He was further charged with a string of other offences, including, demanding money with menaces, illegal possession of a firearm, incitement to commit criminal damage and aiding and abetting a fugitive.

The Magistrates conferred briefly before committing him for trial at Crown Court. He was remanded in custody at Lewes Prison, to await his trial.

His son, Lionel was also remanded in custody at Lewes. He was charged with the Murder of Mr. Jason Davies, to which he pleaded guilty. Other charges brought against him were, robbery with violence, illegal possession of a firearm, incitement to commit a criminal act, namely the kidnap and false imprisonment of Sandra Cranham.

The two accomplices in the kidnap, James Bull and George Warder were sentenced by the Magistrates to six months imprisonment, to be followed by 100 hours community service.

Cavendish was charged with illegal possession of a firearm, behaving in a manner likely to cause a breach of the peace and possession of a controlled substance.

He was sentenced to 6 months imprisonment, suspended for 2 years. He was released into the custody of his parents.

Delia Gorse was sentenced to 3 months, suspended for 1 year, for obstructing the police and resisting arrest.

'That was a good result, all round,' Ian said as they got back to the office.

Tony Church smiled and said,

'Yes, not bad Ian, but I'd hoped those two who kidnapped Sandra Cranham would have got a longer sentence each. There was also an element of assault involved. I got the impression that she was a little frightened when she gave her evidence.'

'I thought the same,' Ian agreed. 'We've got a bit more digging to do with that particular crowd. Once the Worthing force has put their house in order, we could give them the details. They're in a better position to watch them than we are.'

Tony looked at his watch,

'I expect the will reading is over by now, it will be interesting to see just how well off old Jason was, won't it?' he asked. 'We'll have a quick cup of coffee and then begin on a summary of events at the Court, for the press and the media.'

'I saw a couple of reporters in the gallery,' Ian told him. 'There may have been more, but I recognised the girl from the 'Argus' and the young man from TV South. I think the main thing to do is to emphasise the Gorses' crimes. We could put out a request for further information regarding the death of his late wife, Jean Gorse.'

'Do you think that will do any good at this late stage?' Tony asked.

Ian thought for a few moments and then replied,

'I was just thinking that if Gorse had managed to frighten someone else into keeping quiet. They might now feel it would be safe to tell what they know. He can't come after them if he's locked up in Lewes Prison, can he?'

'Good point, Ian,' said Tony. 'We'll make that a separate paragraph, so that it stands out from the Court reports.'

'And the same appeal for the TV?' Ian asked.

Tony nodded his agreement,

'Absolutely, we may just get lucky with a response, but we won't hold our breath. At least it was only a few years ago, not like Mary Davies.'

CHAPTER 75.

Hannah and Elsie went to Chichelster on Friday and bought a few gifts for Hilda and Bob. Hannah thought that they would probably move to a larger flat or a house, so they decided the best plan would be to buy neutral items like towels or cushions. Elsie found some nice Egyptian cotton towel sets in Roseby's. Hannah bought a rather nice table lamp with a decorated ceramic base.

The week-end passed pleasantly enough, Hilda and her fiance phoned Hannah and asked her to meet them on Saturday at her father's retirement home. They were staying at small pub on the outskirts of Arundel, so took Bob there for lunch. Doug Fielding impressed Bob with his good manners and intelligent conversation. Hannah was equally pleased with her sister's choice of man and told her so!

They arranged to go to Wigglesworth on Sunday and Hannah phoned Archie to ask him to book a table for five at the Old Bell for Sunday lunch. Hannah returned at around five o'clock on Saturday afternoon.

'Are you going to Jason's funeral on Monday?' Elsie asked her.

'Yes, of course,' Hannah replied. 'I thought we could all go in my car and then you and Archie could have a drink if you wanted to.'

'Don't you want to have a drink afterwards? Archie asked her.

'No,' Hannah told him, 'I don't like to drink in the daytime. It makes me sleepy.'

They spent the evening chatting about Doug and where Hannah thought they might find a slightly larger place to live. Their speculation was to no avail as they discovered the next morning.

Hilda and Doug arrived at around ten-thirty and after a chat over a cup of coffee, Hilda suggested that Archie might like to show Doug the watermill.

'Fantastic!' Doug exclaimed, 'is it far? Will we need the car?' Archie chuckled,

'No, Doug,' he said, 'it's just over the road. We'd better take our jackets. It's not all that warm out, is it?'

Doug smiled,

'I don't really know, Archie,' he said. 'I've only been outside very briefly, just from the pub door to the car and then from the car into your nice warm kitchen. My jacket's in the car, so I'll grab it on the way out.'

It was the best thing the two men could have done. As an engineer, Doug was not just interested in the mill, he was positively ecstatic about it.

'I really didn't expect a treat like this,' he told Archie. 'It just amazes me that something as old and complex as this can still be restored to full use after standing idle for so many years. You've really impressed me, I can tell you. Old Bob said you were a bit of a 'one off'. He's got a very high opinion of you, Archie and so have the girls. Hilda kept talking about you and Elsie when she came back from her stay with you last time.'

They're a bit special in their own way,' Archie told him. 'It was tragic when their mum died in that fire. The whole village was worried for them, but old Bob managed to work things out. They both turned out alright. Both dedicated nurses and both of them level headed and self confident.'

They locked up and walked slowly back to the house.

'What time did we book lunch for? Doug asked.

'I think we just said, 'about half past twelve,' Archie replied. The three girls were chatting away in the lounge as Archie and Doug returned through the back door.

'Guess where we're going to live? Hilda said as the two men went in.

Doug smiled, he hadn't told Archie, but he knew their decision would be a popular one.

'Chichelster,' Archie guessed.

'You're on the right track, but, no,' Hilda said. 'Try again.'

'There's a track at Goodwood,' Archie said.

'Wrong again!' Hilda giggled.

'Pompey,' he said.

'Next west,' Doug called out.

'Really?' Archie said, 'You're going to move to Southampton?'

Hilda and her sister were laughing loudly.

'They were good guesses, Archie,' Hannah said. Doug has been offered a teaching post at the university and Hilda is waiting to hear whether her application for a sister's post at Southampton General is successful.'

Archie and Elsie were happy to hear their news.

'That means we'll be closer to Dad and Hanna and we can still come to see you both, a bit more frequently. Hilda said, giving Doug's hand a squeeze.

'Let's get some lunch and a drink to celebrate your engagement at the University and the one to Hilda as well,' said Archie as he passed Elsie her new car coat.

CHAPTER 76.

Monday 26th. November was a good day for a funeral. The dark clouds threatened heavy rain and the light winds meant that once it started, it was unlikely to stop. There were a lot of people at the church, to remember old 'Diddler'. It seemed that the article in the local paper, revealing how much his estate was worth had promoted a great deal of interest. Some said that he had helped more people in his death than he had throughout his life, but those few who had become closer to him, refuted this. The police were represented by Bill Pickering and the two detectives from the Chichelster force. Tony was chatting to Bill Pickering and Archie, as they waited to go in.

'The sad part about his life,' said Tony Church, 'is that he spent a great many years feeling guilty for something he had not done. I suppose it was a comfort in his final hours, to know that Gorse was his wife's murderer. If he's looking down on us now, he'll know that at least his name has been cleared of any suspicion.'

'What do you think Gorse will get, Tony?' Bill asked. 'Do you think he'll be able to wriggle out of it?'

'Not a chance, Bill,' Tony replied. 'That recorded phone call made a great impression on the magistrates and we've now got witnesses from Haywards Heath, who can testify that he was there.'

'Yes, and don't forget the tarpaulin sheet with her blood on it,' Ian interrupted. 'He can't refute that and it was found in his garage.'

'If they tot up all the charges,' Tony ventured, 'he'll be in prison until he dies.'

Archie smiled as he approached the detectives,

'What was that appeal for witnesses about?' He asked. 'Do you think he killed his late wife? I thought that was an accident.'

'We are trying to keep an open mind about it, Archie,' said Ian. 'The coroner recorded an open verdict at the time, but that was because there seemed to be no evidence to the contrary. We now believe it's possible that Gorse had something to do with it. Old Jason's recorded phone conversation put us on to it. We had a call from the security guard who was on gate duty the night she died. He reckons he's got some sort of proof, but he's been threatened that if he says anything his house will burn down.'

'Gorse threatened him with that?' Archie asked.

Tony leaned towards him and whispered,

'Not Gorse, he's too smart for that, but someone else. You'll be able to read about it eventually, but for the moment it has to be left on the back burner. The suspect is under investigation on another matter, as is his accomplice, Victor Cranham. I didn't tell you this, so don't mention it to anyone else.'

'That's the security bloke I saw in the shop in Pudborough, tryin' to sell that silver, isn't it?' Archie said. 'So he had an accomplice, did he?'

Tony smiled,

'It looks as though we're going into the church now, Arch,' he observed. 'At least we won't get wet before the service.'

The Rev. Hobson conducted the service, he paid tribute to the way Jason had supported the local societies and the Heart Foundation in his will. He told the congregation,

'Jason Davies has paid the maintenance costs of the upkeep of the churchyard for the past ten years. This has been a private arrangement, for which he has asked for no acknowledgement or thanks. He has also left a legacy to ensure that these costs are borne by his estate for the next ten years. His quiet generosity has been noticed by only a few local people, but over the years, he has provided help and financial support to many good causes It is fitting, therefore that he should wish to be interred here, in the heart of the village which he came to accept as his own.'
The vicar then said that his son, Jeffery would like to say a few words.

'I would like to thank everyone for attending today,' he began. 'I have not always seen eye to eye with my father, but I am thankful that I was able to make my peace with him before he was so cruelly murdered. I thank Rev'd. Hobson for his kind words and testimony and I promise that I will do my best to live up to my father's name. I have been foolish and selfish. I have hurt a number of people who did nothing to deserve my anger or spite. Most of this was the result of my greed for wealth and power. In my pursuit of these two I lost my self respect as well as the respect of others. I now wish to make amends and I promise, before you all, that I will use my father's legacy to me, to conduct my business interests with honesty and integrity. I will continue to perform the community service which was imposed upon me, even though my obligation is now discharged. I have met so many of you, ordinary decent people, in the course of my punishment, that I feel, in some way, a sense of acceptance back into the village community. I hope you will all join us later for refreshments at The Old Bell, to drink a toast to Dad and to the future well being of our village. Thank you one and all.'

The service continued with the committal and burial in the churchyard. As the vicar gave his blessing the first few spots of rain began to fall. Some who had umbrellas tried to share them with more people than could get shelter from them. By the time most had returned to their cars, the grass was rapidly becoming a muddy swamp. Shiny black shoes were spattered with mud, overcoats flapped outside hastily closed car doors. The entire congregation developed an urgent sense of self preservation at all costs. A funereal 'car rally' tore into the car park at the Old Bell. The rain was by now a continuous torrent. People, reluctant to leave the comfort of their cars, sat in them until all the windows were steamed up. Their soggy overcoat bottoms soaking up the water which ran off the doors. The undertakers' cars arrived. Jeffery with Jason's sister, Bernice and her family, were shepherded into the pub under large golf umbrellas. Rev. Hobson arrived in his old Morris Minor, the fabric roof leaking like a sieve. He stepped out into a large puddle, which was deep enough to cover his shoes. As he put up his umbrella, it caught in the closing door of the old car and turned inside out.

'Bugger!' said the vicar. 'Bugger, Bugger and Damn.' Unaware that everyone was still sitting in their steamed up cars, he shouted it again, 'Bugger the bloody weather!'

A muffled cheer went up from the collection of steamed up and overcrowded vehicles. Everyone got out into the rain and gave Rev. Hobson a round of applause as they hurried behind him into the public bar.
Jeffery Davies and Jason's sister and her family were at the bar,

'We thought nobody else was coming,' Arthur Hoskins, the landlord said. 'I was thinking, all this food and nobody to eat it, a car park full of cars and four people in the pub!'
A red faced Rev. Hobson stood at the bar and asked for a moment's hush. The former congregation waited to hear what he had to say.

'To all of my parishioners and visitors who were sheltering from the rain in their cars, I wish to apologise for my most ungodly language,' he said.
There was a roar of laughter from the crowd and a puzzled look from the Tenhams and Jeffery Davies.
Archie broke the spell by announcing in his best 'Sussex',

'You're only human, 'Rev.' you just gave us all something to laugh about. We all felt pretty much the same about the 'bloody' weather, so have a drink and relax, we won't tell your 'guvnor'.

Most had heard what he had said as he got out of his car, but a few were asking, 'what did he say?'
Nobody answered, the moment was gone and the company was there to celebrate Jason Davies' life.
Bill Pickering, now off duty, was acting as a waiter, bringing plates of food and drinks to the customers who were seated at the tables, unable to even see the bar, let alone get to it.
The two detectives had left the gathering and were on their way back to Chichelster, to continue their investigations into the other 'forgotten' suspicious death.
On their way back, Ian asked Tony Church whether he knew the identity of the other person threatening Beckett, the gate keeper at Shoreham docks. He guessed it would not have been Gorse, he was too smart to become directly involved.
'No names have been mentioned yet, Ian,' Tony Church told him, 'but I will tell you what our Mr. Beckett told me.
He said, "I'm not afraid of Gorse, now he's safely 'banged up', but that wouldn't stop that bloody copper and his crooked cronies. They're bloody 'fireproof, aren't they?"
'Gotcha!' Ian replied with a wink.